'I haven't had sex for months,' Alison giggled as the vodka began to take effect. 'I haven't even laid *eyes* on a dick, let alone my hands.'

'Neither have I,' Christina said, forcing a smile as she again recalled Doogan's solid penis in her grip.

'Met anyone you fancy at the college?'

'No, no. They're too old for me.'

'The teachers might be too old but what about the students?'

'The students?'

'They're – what – seventeen, eighteen?'

'Yes, they are, but . . .'

'We're in our early twenties, so they're not *that* much younger than us. Some of the girls I've seen look at least twenty. What are the fellas like?'

'Alison, I've not looked at them in that way. They're my students.'

'I know, but one of them must have caught your eye. Imagine having an affair with a student. God, that's the sort of thing you read about in the papers.'

'Yes, well . . . No one's going to read about *me* in the papers.'

RAY GORDON

School of Corruption

NEW ENGLISH LIBRARY
Hodder & Stoughton

First published in Great Britain in 2002 by Hodder and Stoughton
A division of Hodder Headline

The right of Ray Gordon to be identified as the Author
of the Work has been asserted by him in accordance
with the Copyright, Designs and Patents Act 1988.

A New English Library paperback

9

A CIP catalogue record for this title
is available from the British Library

ISBN 978 0 340 82161 9

Typeset in Plantin by Hewer Text Ltd, Edinburgh
Printed and bound in the UK by
CPI Mackays, Chatham ME5 8TD

Hodder and Stoughton
A division of Hodder Headline
338 Euston Road
London NW1 3BH

School of Corruption

'Good morning,' she said, her mouth dry, her voice croaky. 'I'm Christina Shaw, your new English teacher.'

'Are you sure?' a lad called from the back of the class.

'I'm positive,' she chuckled amid a roar of laughter.

'And who might you be?'

I

Spadger Heath Sixth Form College huddled behind an engineering works amid acres of tower blocks and run-down terraced houses. The nineteen-fifties building, with its cracked windows and peeling paint wasn't what Christina had envisaged, but this was her first job after qualifying as an English teacher and she was determined to make the best of it. A year or two at Spadger Heath and she'd move on, perhaps secure a post at a private school. But now she had her first day to get through.

Standing behind her desk at the front of the class, Christina gazed at the sea of expectant faces. Although she'd excelled herself during her training, nothing could have prepared her for her first day at Spadger Heath. Recalling the advice she'd been given, she leaned on her desk, clutching its sides to steady her trembling hands as her lecturer's words came to mind. *You must remain calm. At least be seen to be strong even if you're falling apart inside. Don't let them get to you. There will be pupils who dislike you, and pupils you despise. Come across as friendly, but with an air of authority.*

'Good morning,' she said, her mouth dry, her voice croaky. 'I'm Christina Shaw, your new English teacher.'

'Are you sure?' a lad called from the back of the class.

'I'm positive,' she chuckled amid a roar of laughter. 'And who might you be?'

'I might be anyone,' he replied.

'His name's David Brown,' a petite blonde called.

'Obviously it's going to take me a while to get to know your names,' Christina said, sitting at her desk as her trembling legs sagged beneath her. 'I'd like you to take some paper and write your names down. Place them on your desks so that I can see them from here and I'll do my best to get to know you all before the day's out.'

So far so good, Christina thought, glancing at her watch. It was going to be a long day, but she felt positive, if a bit panicky. Watching the teenagers scribbling at their desks, she was looking forward to the evening. Her flatmate, Alison, had suggested that they find a local pub and celebrate Christina's first day at Spadger Heath College. Alison had come to London to find work and had bumped into Christina at a letting agency. The girls had got on well and had decided to share the only property the agency had within their price range. It was a small two-bedroom flat above a Chinese takeaway, but it had been recently decorated and was clean.

'OK.' Christina smiled, glancing at the sheets of paper propped up on her pupils' desks. 'Let's start with you, Carole,' she said, gazing at a dark-haired girl at the front of the class. 'Tell me a little about yourself.'

'I'm seventeen, I hate school, and I want to be a model,' the girl replied morosely.

'She's a lesbian,' a boy guffawed.

'Fuck off, Smith,' the girl returned.

'Er . . . You want to be a model?' Christina cut in, trying to show an interest.

'Me dad wants me to work in the box factory with me mum,' she sighed. 'But I want to get out of this dump and be a model. I know I can do it.'

'I'm sure you can. OK, Jerry, tell me about yourself,' Christina said, smiling at the boy next to Carole.

'Ain't nothin' to tell,' he murmured.

'Oh, come on. What are your interests?'

'Ain't got none.'

'All right, we'll come back to you in a minute. Brian, you're next.'

'I want to be a pimp,' the boy told Christina. 'It's good money, a good life.'

'It's also illegal, Brian.'

'Everything he does is illegal,' Carole giggled.

'Yeah, but I've got money. You work for me, and you'll have money.'

'Yeah, go on, Caz,' David Brown laughed from the back of the class. 'Work for Brian as a prostitute. You might as well, seeing as you're a whore anyway.'

'That'll do, David,' Christina broke in.

'She *is* a whore,' he persisted. 'Everyone's fucked her.'

'Shut your fucking mouth, Brown,' Carole yelled.

'I'll bet Jones hasn't fucked her,' a ginger-haired lad chortled. 'He prefers blokes' arseholes.'

'Let's move on,' Christina said firmly, thinking it best to ignore the expletives for a while.

'Have you got a fella, Mrs?' Brown asked.

'Er . . . no, not at the moment,' she replied. 'So, who's next? John Whiting. Tell me about yourself.'

'I'm into Trance music, I work in a pub . . .'

'You work in a pub?' Christina breathed surprisedly, her blue eyes narrowing as she frowned.

'Yeah, the Steampacket – down by the station.'

'And 'e don't give us no free drinks,' someone complained.

'I'm going to the dentist,' Brown announced, leaving his desk and walking to the door.

'Do you have an appointment . . .' Christina began as he left the classroom and closed the door.

'He's going to meet Delainy,' a girl called out.

'Who's Delainy?'

'Keep your mouth shut, Burrows,' a boy hissed.

'It might be best if you write about yourselves,' Christina said, glancing at her watch again. 'Take your time, and write as much as you can about your likes and dislikes, your interests and aspirations.'

'Our what?' someone asked.

'Your dreams, your ambitions. Leave your papers on my desk before you go to break.'

Christina made it through to the first break and flopped into an old armchair in the empty staffroom. She'd not yet exerted her authority over the students, she reflected. The foul language, the lewd comments . . . It was best to allow the teenagers some leeway. Her plan was to mould them over time. After all, she was the newcomer and she would have to be accepted by her students before she could begin to lay down the law. Mentally exhausted, she focused her thoughts on the evening. The prospect of going out for a drink with Alison would get her through the day.

'Carter,' a man in his mid-forties said, walking into the room and sitting next to Christina. 'Geography.'

'Pleased to meet you.' Christina smiled, shaking his hand. 'Er . . . Christina Shaw, English.'

'Yes, I know. So, how's it going?'

'Not too bad. I'm trying to get to know the students before I . . .'

'You'll never get to know the little bastards,' he

laughed, sitting down beside her. 'You don't *want* to get
to know them.'

'They *are* people,' Christina said. 'No matter what sort
of upbringing they've had, they are people who deserve a
chance to—'

'How old are you?'

'Twenty-four.'

'Fresh out of training, keen, eager . . . I know the type.
They're little shits, Christina. No-hopers, losers, scum.'

'I'll form my own opinion once I get to know them a
little better,' she replied, surprised by his attitude.

'I'm sure you will. That's Rogers,' he said as a tall, thin
man wandered into the staffroom. 'Science.'

'Oh, right.'

'He's a psychological mess. The little shits broke him
down.'

'Why does he stay?'

'What else can he do? There's no other work around
here.'

'He could go to another school.'

'He'd never get a job at another school. He's a ruined
man. If you want my advice, get out of here now. I'm not
being sexist, but a young woman like you doesn't stand a
chance in hell in a dump like this.'

'I'm determined to give it my best,' Christina said.
'These kids deserve—'

'Kids?' he laughed. 'They became adults years ago.
They're streetwise, and you'll never change them. I can
tell you that at least one girl in your class is on the game,
another makes blue movies, a group of lads . . .'

'If I could get to know them, understand them . . .'

'Understand pond life? Get out of here while you can.'

Returning to the classroom, Christina gazed at the

words scrawled on the blackboard. 'Do you suck cock and swallow spunk?' she read, shaking her head as she grabbed the rubber. Cleaning the board, she knew that they were going to do their best to grind her down, but she wasn't going to allow that to happen. Turning, she looked at the sheets of paper on her desk. *They have hopes and dreams*, she mused, reading one girl's neat hand-writing. *I want to get out of this area and make something of myself*.

Hearing a noise coming from the stockroom, Christina listened at the door. Someone was in there, she knew as she turned the handle and inched the door open. A tall, good-looking lad was going through some papers, searching the shelves for something. Wishing she'd taken the headmaster's advice and kept the stockroom locked, she found that she couldn't recall the lad's name.

'What are you doing?' she asked, entering the room.

'Nothing,' he answered, grinning. 'What are *you* doing?'

'You shouldn't be in here. What's your name?'

'Doogan, Barry Doogan.'

'OK, Barry, I think you'd better put those papers down and leave.'

'You're not bad-looking,' he said, stroking her long blonde hair. 'Fancy coming out for a drink sometime?'

'Barry, please put those papers . . .'

'You've got a good body on you. Nice curves, nice tits.'

'That's enough, Barry,' she said firmly, backing off towards the door as she realized that she could be in danger.

'What's the matter? I'll bet you like a bit of rough. Do you think I'm a bit of rough?'

'Do you want me to get the headmaster? Unless you leave here now—'

'You asked us to tell you about ourselves. Now you tell me about yourself.'

'I will, once you leave the stockroom.'

'Don't tell me what to do, Mrs,' he said, walking past her and closing the door. 'Experienced, are you? The young tarts don't know what they're doing, but I'll bet you know exactly what to do.'

Backing against the wall as he reached out and squeezed the firm mounds of her breasts through her blouse, Christina tried to push him away. He was strong, his large hands clutching her wrists as he pushed his crotch hard against her lower stomach, sandwiching her between his obvious erection and the wall. Cold fear gripping her, unable to speak, she tried to kick out but couldn't move.

'I like you,' he said, his face close to hers. 'I'll bet you're a good fuck. I'll tell you what I'll do. I run things around here, ask anyone. You keep me happy, and I'll make sure that—'

'Get off me!' she finally screamed.

'I like a fighter,' he laughed, releasing her.

'I'll report this to—'

'You do that, and I'll make your life a misery. You said you hadn't got a bloke, a man friend. You must miss a length of cock. I'll bet you're gagging for it. Think about it, Mrs. I run things around here, remember that.'

As Doogan left the room, Christina slid down the wall and sat on the floor. Her heart racing, her hands trembling, she'd not expected anything like this. The expletives, the lewd comments . . . She could have dealt with that. But not . . . Finally hauling herself up and wiping her tear-stained cheeks, she left the stockroom and grabbed her bag from the locked drawer of her desk.

Taking the papers from her desk, she stuffed them into her bag, walked briskly along the corridor and fled the building. She'd failed, she knew as made her way through the narrow streets to her flat. Perhaps Carter had been right. They were little shits, bastards, scum.

Home at last, Christina wished that Alison was there. She was out job-hunting, had three interviews to attend and probably wouldn't be back until late afternoon. Filling the kettle for coffee, her breathing slowing as she calmed down, she took a mug from the cupboard. She couldn't go back to the college, she knew. She'd find another job, ask Alison what was on offer locally – if anything. As a last resort, she could go back to her parents' house in Hertfordshire.

Her father had wanted her to join the family firm of accountants, but Christina had set her heart on teaching. He'd said that she wouldn't last five minutes in London, which had fired her determination to make a go of it. He was right, she reflected. Not even managing to get through the morning, she had failed miserably. Pouring her coffee, she sat at the kitchen table and hung her head.

Recalling the young man's words, she sighed. *You must miss a length of cock. I'll bet you're gagging for it.* Her one and only boyfriend worked for her father. He was an up-and-coming accountant from a good family, the sort of man her father would have liked Christina to marry. Life could have been easy, she mused. Working for her father, a company car, good money . . . . Had she agreed to marry Charles, she'd have lived the good life. Holidays abroad, money . . . .

'Fuck Charles,' she breathed, surprised by her choice of words. With good looks and a brilliant future ahead of him, Charles would make a fine husband for someone.

But not for Christina. He was haughty, staid. Never doing anything on the spur of the moment, his idea of fun was a picnic down by the river. Christina would have enjoyed the picnics, but Charles had always invited his friends along. They'd talk shop and drink too much wine and Christina would have to drive them home.

Christina recalled their lovemaking. The act was cold, wooden, performed in silence. Charles would breathe deeply, grunt and pump his sperm into her vagina before rolling off her naked body and going to sleep. Did she miss a length of cock, as Barry had crudely put it? Finishing her coffee, she pushed all thoughts of Charles out of her mind and pulled the papers from her bag. Some of the pupils' work was appalling: the spelling was atrocious and the grammar non-existent.

'I'm sixteen and pregnant,' she read. There was no name on the paper. 'I don't know who the father is.' Taking another paper, she sighed. 'I want to learn to play the piano but we haven't got any money.' Placing the papers on the table, Christina wandered though the hall into the lounge and gazed out of the window at the busy street. A scruffy man was sitting on the pavement opposite, drinking white cider from a bottle. *No-hopers, losers, scum.*

'What are you doing here?' Alison asked as she breezed into the room and tossed her long black hair over her shoulder.

'I . . . I have a free period,' Christina said, smiling.

'Guess what? I've got a job,' the other girl trilled.

'Oh, that *is* good news. Tell me about it.'

'Assistant to the receptionist at a local doctor's surgery. The receptionist is leaving in a couple of months and, hopefully, I'll take her place.'

'I'm pleased for you, Alison,' Christina said warmly.

'So, how's *your* day been so far? Are you all right? You're not your usual bubbly self.'

'I've had a hard morning,' Christina confessed. 'The students are difficult, to say the least.'

'But you expected that.'

'I didn't expect the girls to tell the boys to fuck off.'

'This is London, Christina, a run-down part of London. You must have realized that . . .'

'One boy got me in the stockroom. Boy? What am I saying? He's a six-foot young adult. He pushed himself against me, squeezed my breasts and . . .'

'God. What did you do?'

'What *could* I do?'

'Go to the headmaster.'

'And have that yob make my life a misery? I walked out.'

'What? You can't do that.'

'I've done it.'

'Go back, Christina. For God's sake, are you going to allow one boy to destroy your career?'

'I don't know.'

'Go back. You know what'll happen if you don't.'

'I'll get the sack.'

'Yes, but worse than that. You father will laugh at you.'

Alison was right, she knew. If she walked out on her first day, her father would laugh at her and she'd never get another teaching job. Congratulating Alison on her job, she grabbed her bag and walked back to the college. No, she wasn't going to allow one boy to destroy her career. Boy? That was a joke. They were all adults. Taking a deep breath, Christina walked through the gates, half expecting the headmaster to be waiting for her. Funnily enough, no one had missed her, and she walked into the classroom with her head held high.

'OK,' she shouted above the bedlam. 'Settle down, please.' Glancing at the blackboard, she found herself gazing at a colour picture of an erect penis rising above a huge scrotum. 'The erect penis,' she said loudly. A hush fell over the room as dozens of eyes gazed at her expectantly. 'I don't know who drew this, but it's not bad. Presumably, these white squiggles represent the sperm issuing from the . . . Can anyone tell me the correct name for this part?' she asked, pointing to the neatly coloured purple glans.

'That's the knob,' a boy laughed.

'I said the *correct* name. Come on, surely someone knows?'

'Purple-headed warrior,' another boy called out.

'It's the glans,' she enlightened them, writing the word on the board. 'The plural, anyone?'

'Glanses?' a girl suggested.

'Glandes,' Christina corrected her, writing the word on the board. 'As you're all so interested in the penis, I wonder whether anyone can tell me where the seminal fluid is produced in the body? I'm not talking about the sperm, but the liquid containing the sperm.'

'Bollocks,' a lad chuckled.

'No, Jackson, you're wrong.'

'He ain't,' another boy called. 'Spunk comes from your bollocks.'

'Sperm is produced in the testicles. The whitish liquid is produced in the prostate gland. It seems that the boys know nothing about their own bodies,' she smiled.

'We know about girls' cunts,' someone yelled out, laughing coarsely.

'Do you? Do you really, Davis?'

'I never said it,' he complained.

'Yes, you did. OK, let's see just how much you know about girls. Where and what is the hymen?'

'Well . . . It's, er . . .'

'I know,' a lad said eagerly, raising his hand.

'I'm asking Davis. All right, here's another one for you, Davis. In the female, what is the prepuce?'

'I . . . I dunno,' he murmured.

'For someone who professes to know all about the female pudenda, you appear to know nothing at all.'

'Yes, I do,' he retorted. 'Just because I don't know your fancy words . . .'

'All right, I'll keep it simple. You've heard of the cervix?'

'Yeah, I have,' he replied triumphantly. 'It's where birds get cancer.'

'That's right, Davis, well done. So, where is the cervix?'

'Well, in tits. Cervix cancer in breasts and that.'

'The cervix, Davis, is located at the far end of the vaginal canal. I suggest that you read up on female anatomy before going out with girls. Right, let's move on. I noticed some books on punctuation in the stockroom,' she said, moving to the door. 'I'll pass them round and we'll begin with the basics.'

In the stockroom, Christina felt rather pleased with herself as she sorted through the pile of books. She'd certainly shot Davis down in flames, and very much doubted that he'd give her any more trouble. Barry Doogan had kept quiet, she reflected, making a mental note to thank Alison for her support and encouragement. Once she'd asserted her authority, shown that she was in charge, she was sure that the students would settle down and she could get somewhere.

'Oh, you can pass these round,' she said as Barry walked into the stockroom.

'You made Davis look like a prat,' he whispered angrily, his dark eyes staring hard at her.

'If Davis looked like a prat, then it was his own doing,' she responded.

'I've already told you, Mrs. *I* run things around here.'

'No, Barry, you don't. You might run things out of school but, in class, I—'

'Think you're clever with your big words, don't you?'

'Big words?'

'This pudenda thing or whatever it is. Round here, cocks are cocks and cunts are cunts, OK?'

'Do you know where the word "cunt" originates?' she asked.

'No, and I don't care. But I do know that you've got a cunt. And I'd like to see it.'

'Get back to your desk,' Christina hissed through gritted teeth.

'Would you like this shoved up your cunt?' Barry sniggered, unzipping his trousers and pulling his flaccid penis out. 'You make prats out of my mates, and I'll shove this down your throat.'

'Put that pathetic thing away,' she murmured.

'OK, teacher, let's go back to class. I'll show you who how I can fuck things up for you.'

As he left the room, Christina grabbed the pile of books and tried to compose herself. She knew that she mustn't appear ruffled, she mustn't allow them to get to her. Barry Doogan was trouble, she reflected. The ring-leader, he was going to have to be tamed before she could make any progress with the others. He certainly had a big penis, she found herself thinking as she returned to the classroom and dumped the books on Carole's desk. Even flaccid, the thing was huge. Asking Carole to pass the books round, she did her best not to catch Barry's gaze. Cleaning the blackboard, her breathing slowing, she finally turned and faced the class.

'OK,' she said. 'Open the books at the section headed "commas", please. You'll see from the first example how, when used incorrectly, commas completely change the meaning of the sentence. John was sick, and tired of working.'

'Aren't we all,' Barry laughed.

'Now look at the second sentence. John was sick and tired of working. You'll notice that the comma in the first sentence—'

'This is kids' stuff,' a pretty auburn-haired girl complained. 'We did this in junior school.'

'Er . . . Janice,' Christina said, reading the girl's name. 'I'm trying to establish how much you've learned. I realize that this will be kids' stuff to some of you, but please bear with me.'

'I'd rather go back to talking about cunts,' Barry chortled, the class roaring with laughter as he lit a cigarette.

'Please don't smoke in the classroom,' Christina snapped.

'Tight, hot, wet cunts oozing with spunk.'

'I shall go to the headmaster and have you removed from my class,' she said, leaving the room and slamming the door shut.

Making her way to the headmaster's study, Christina knew that Barry Doogan had to be dealt with if she was going to make any progress. *Don't let them get to you. There will be pupils who dislike you, and pupils you despise.* Again recalling her lecturer's words, she was determined not to be beaten by one student.

'Ah, Miss Shaw,' the headmaster murmured as she knocked and entered. 'I was about to send for you.'

'Oh?' she said, closing the door.

'I've had a complaint. Barry Doogan came to see me earlier.'

'A complaint? But I've come to see you about *him*, Mr Wright. He's been—'

'This is a serious matter, Miss Shaw. Please, sit down.'

'Barry Doogan is . . .' she began, sitting opposite the balding man.

'Miss Shaw, I realize that this is your first day at Spadger Heath and that things can't be easy for you. Doogan said that you grabbed him in the stockroom.'

'*I* grabbed *him*?' she gasped.

'His crotch, Miss Shaw.'

'But he—'

'Whether you grabbed him or not isn't the issue. The point is that a complaint has been made against a member of my staff.'

'So the fact that he pulled his penis out in the stockroom is neither here nor there?'

'I know Doogan of old, Miss Shaw. I know his tricks. And I don't believe for one minute that you did anything of the sort. But do be aware that complaints of this nature can be very dangerous, very damaging to the college.'

'So what do you suggest I do the next time he shows me his penis?'

'Never get yourself into a situation where you are alone with a student. I would have thought that was obvious.'

'He was going through papers in the stockroom during break.'

'Why wasn't the stockroom locked, Miss Shaw?'

'Well, I . . .'

'You'd better get back to your class.'

Leaving the study, Christina couldn't believe the man's attitude. Doogan had pressed himself against her, pulled his penis out, and had then made a complaint about her? Returning to her class, she felt anger welling from the pit of her stomach as Doogan folded his arms, reclining in his chair and grinning triumphantly. This was war, she thought, doing her best not to show her rage. Ordering the class to read up on the use of commas, she called Doogan to the front of the class. Slouching, he mooched up to her desk and grinned.

'I want a word with you,' she said, walking into the stockroom.

'Yeah?' he chuckled, following her and closing the door. 'Old man Wright give you a bollocking, then?'

'You seem to think that you're some kind of bigwig,' she said, looking him up and down. 'You're a silly little schoolboy, Doogan.'

'You want to watch your mouth, Mrs,' he murmured, unzipping his trousers and taking his penis out. 'As I said, I'll shove this down your throat.'

'Look at it,' she laughed, gazing at his flaccid penis. 'Is that it? Is that the best you can do?'

'I've never had any complaints.'

'This is supposed to shock me, is it? You pull your cock out and think that I'll faint?'

'As I said, you watch your mouth or I'll—'

'Shove it down my throat? I doubt that it would reach the back of my mouth, let alone—'

'Don't push your luck, teacher,' he hissed, thrusting his hand up her skirt and clutching the swell of her panties.

Christina knew that she'd pushed her luck too far as he yanked her panties to one side and massaged the swell of her fleshy pussy lips. This was tantamount to rape, but no one would believe her story. The headmaster would probably sack her if she ran to him crying rape. After all, he had the reputation of the college to think about. *Some reputation*, she reflected, Doogan's crude words about her wet cunt battering her racked mind. She knew that she had to put a stop to Doogan or leave her job. Pushing him away, she forced a laugh as she again looked down at his flaccid penis.

'So this is your manhood?' she asked sarcastically, taking his fleshy shaft in her hand. 'Come on, then. Stiffen up and show me how big a man you really are.'

'What are you doing?' he asked, confusion reflected in his dark eyes as she ran her hand up and down his inflating shaft.

'You mean to say that a girl's never done this to you?' she asked, laughing softly. 'The big man, Barry Doogan, is a virgin?'

'No, no, I meant . . .'

'Come on, Barry, get it out of your system,' she breathed, wanking his solid cock faster. 'Come on, shoot your sperm.'

Breathing deeply, his legs sagging, Doogan gasped as his sperm shot from his throbbing knob. Christina moved to one wide, aiming his spunk away from her skirt as the white liquid splattered over the tiled floor.

She felt her stomach somersault as she wanked his solid shaft, gazing at the sheer size of his erection as she brought out his spunk and drained his full balls. The creamy liquid running down her hand, her clitoris swelling as she thought of his rock-hard shaft thrusting deep into the tight sheath of her vagina, she finally let go of his penis and wiped her hand on the side of a cardboard box.

'I hope that will shut you up for a while,' she said, leaving the young man shuddering in the aftermath of his orgasm as she returned to her class. Sitting at her desk, her gaze darting between her students as they stared at her, she wished that she'd never taken Doogan into the stockroom. It had been a grave mistake, she knew. She was sure that he wouldn't go running to the headmaster, but he would probably be back for another hand job. If word got out . . . She tried not to think of the consequences as she watched him returning to his desk, a huge grin on his face.

The rest of the day passed pretty much without incident, and Christina was pleased to get home. Keeping her guilty secret from Alison, she cooked a stir-fry for dinner and they broke open a bottle of red wine. Alison was full of life, chatting about her new job, but Christina was quiet and withdrawn. Doogan would probably tell his friends about what had happened in the stockroom. Christina could only hope that they wouldn't believe him, thinking that he was mouthing off to look big in front of his mates.

'You didn't tell me what you did about that lad in the stockroom,' Alison said as she washed up the dinner plates.

'Barry Doogan,' Christina murmured. 'I . . . I put him straight. Told him that there'd be trouble unless he behaved himself.'

'Good for you. Shall we find a local pub, then?'

'Yes,' Christina replied abstractedly.

'There's one down the road. I saw it today when I was job-hunting. It's The Steampacket, by the station. They have live music and—'

'Let's find somewhere quiet,' Christina broke in. 'Somewhere to sit quietly and chat.'

'Whatever. There's a pub round the corner at the end of the road. The Hen and Chicken or something. It looked quiet enough when I passed it earlier.'

'That'll do,' Christina said and smiled. 'It's been a long day, a noisy day. I need to sit quietly and relax.'

'Right, I'll get changed and then we'll go.'

Christina wandered into the lounge as Alison went to her room to change. Riddled with guilt as she pictured Doogan's rock-hard penis in her hand, his sperm shooting from his throbbing knob and splattering the tiled floor, she wondered what day two at Spadger Heath College would bring. Doogan would want his cock appeased again, she was sure. *Come across as friendly, but with an air of authority*, she mused, recalling again her lecturer's words. *Intimate, but with an air of authority?* she speculated.

'Ready?' Alison asked, appearing in the lounge doorway wearing a white blouse and red miniskirt.

'Ready,' Christina answered cheerfully, taking her bag from the sofa.

'I've been looking forward to this all day,' the dark-haired girl said as they left the flat and walked down the busy road. 'I've got a job and you got through your first day. Now we can relax and down a few vodkas.'

Entering the pub, Christina glanced at the half-dozen customers dotted around the bar. Much to her relief, none of her students were there. The pub was traditional – no music, no entertainment. Not the sort of place where youngsters would gather. Thinking that the pub would become her regular haunt, Christina ordered the drinks and sat on a bar stool. Alison began chatting about London, hoping she'd meet a young man and fall in love. That was the last thing Christina wanted. Away from her parents, she was looking forward to her freedom, doing what she wanted when she wanted without having to answer to anyone.

'I haven't had sex for months,' Alison giggled as the vodka began to take effect. 'I haven't even laid *eyes* on a dick, let alone my hands.'

'Neither have I,' Christina said, forcing a smile as she again recalled Doogan's solid penis in her grip.

'Met anyone you fancy at the college?'

'No, no. They're too old for me.'

'The teachers might be too old but what about the students?'

'The students?'

'They're – what – seventeen, eighteen?'

'Yes, they are, but . . .'

'We're in our early twenties, so they're not *that* much younger than us. Some of the girls I've seen look at least twenty. What are the fellas like?'

'Alison, I've not looked at them in that way. They're my students.'

'I know, but one of them must have caught your eye. Imagine having an affair with a student. God, that's the sort of thing you read about in the papers.'

'Yes, well . . . No one's going to read about *me* in the papers.'

'Oh, I forgot to tell you. A man called for you. Charles.'

'Oh, God. I'll bet my father gave him the number. What did he want?'

'He wants you to call him.'

'Did he say what about?'

'Nope. Who is he?'

'My ex-boyfriend. I'll ring him later.'

'He sounded very posh.'

'He *is* very posh. That's the trouble with him, among other things.'

'He wouldn't fit in around here, then?'

'No way. Let's have another drink.'

'My turn.' Alison smiled, opening her bag. 'Same again?'

'Please.'

Wandering over to a table, Christina sat down and gazed out of the window. Charles wouldn't fit in at all, she thought. He'd be horrified if he knew that Christina was sitting in a smoke-filled pub, knocking back vodka. And if he discovered that she'd wanked a student to orgasm in the stockroom . . . But Charles was no longer part of her life. At least, he wasn't supposed to be.

'Here's to day two at your job,' Alison beamed, placing Christina's drink on the table and sitting down. 'Cheers.'

'Cheers.' Christina grinned back at her flatmate and raised her glass.

'And let's hope that Doogan or whatever his name is leaves you alone now that you've put him in his place.'

'Yes, let's hope.'

2

Christina had taken a shower and had had her breakfast by seven-thirty. Wandering around the flat, feeling a little panicky, she tried to plan her day. Now that Doogan was under control, she might be able to assess the students and discover the extent of their education. *If* Doogan was under control. Wondering whether to divide the students into groups, dependent on their ability, she looked up as Alison peered round the lounge door.

'Morning, Alison,' she greeted her flatmate. 'You're bright and early.'

'I don't start work until next week but I don't want to slip into the habit of getting up late,' the other girl said. 'You've finished in the bathroom?'

'Yes, it's all yours.'

'A coffee wouldn't go amiss.'

'All right. You take a shower and I'll make you a cup of coffee.'

Alison was OK, Christina thought happily as she filled the kettle. Despite initial concerns, the flat-share was working out extremely well. Pouring the coffee, Christina glanced at the kitchen clock. She didn't have to leave for another hour and so she decided to ring her mother. She should have phoned the previous evening but by the time she'd got home it had been too late. Praying that her mother wouldn't talk about Charles, she grabbed the wall phone and punched in the number. The woman was pleased to hear from her, asking why she'd not rung before and how her first day had been.

'I couldn't ring last night,' Christina said apologetically. 'But my first day went very well.'

'What are the children like?' she asked.

'Children?' Christina laughed. 'Mother, they're young adults.'

'Of course, it's a sixth-form college, isn't it? Will you be coming home at the weekend?'

'If I can. I'll have to see how things go.'

'Have you phoned Charles yet?'

'No, no, I haven't,' Christina sighed, raising her eyebrows as Alison wandered into the kitchen naked.

'You should have called him, Christina.'

'Yes, I . . . Why, mother? Why should I have called Charles?'

'Because he'd like to know how you're getting on. He must miss you terribly.'

'We've split up, mother. We're no longer . . .'

'It's such a shame, Christina. Your father was hoping that you'd—'

'Look, I have to go,' Christina said, gazing at the firm mounds of Alison's breasts, her sex crack clearly visible through her sparse pubic curls. 'I'll call you this evening.'

'All right, dear. Do call Charles.'

'Yes, yes – I will.'

Hanging up, Christina tried to avert her gaze as Alison sipped her coffee. The girl seemed oblivious to her own nakedness, wandering around the kitchen displaying everything she had. She was extremely attractive, Christina observed, eyeing the violin curves of Alison's young body. She'd never seen another girl naked before, and began to realize what a sheltered life she'd led. Trying not to look as if she was staring, she eyed Alison's long black hair cascading over her shoulders, the brown teats of her young breasts pointing to the ceiling . . . Gazing out of the window, Christina dragged her thoughts away from the girl's beauty and remarked on the hot weather as the sun shone in a clear blue sky.

'I don't know what I'm going to do today,' Alison said. 'It's a shame we haven't got a garden. I could have sunbathed, got myself a nice tan.'

'You've already got a tan,' Christina murmured, turning and staring at the girl's naked body again.

'I went to Cyprus a few months ago. The trouble is, the tan's wearing off.'

'Aren't you going to put something on?' Christina asked, her gaze riveted on the girl's elongated nipples rising alluringly from the dark discs of her areolae.

'Oh, sorry . . . I'm used to wandering around like this. If it's a problem—'

'No, no – I don't mind.'

'There was a garden at my last flat. It was completely private, no one overlooking the patio or the lawn. I spent most of my time in a bikini – or naked.'

'It would be nice to have a garden,' Christina said, finishing her coffee. 'That's one thing I miss about my parents' house. Still, you never know. We might move on to better things once we've got some money coming in.'

'God knows what sort of rent they'd want for a flat with a garden,' Alison sighed. 'Right, I'm going to get dressed. I might go for a walk later, get to know the area.'

'I'll leave you to get on,' Christina said, glancing at the

other girl's full sex lips. 'I know it's rather early, but I think I'll go to the college. I'll see you this evening.'

'OK. I hope you have a good day.'

'Fingers crossed.'

'Don't let that Doogan lad get to you.'

'No, I won't. I'll see you later.'

Grabbing her bag, Christina left the flat and walked the short distance to the college. What plans had Doogan in mind? she wondered, musing on what the day might bring. Bringing out his sperm had certainly quietened him down, but it was hardly the way for a teacher to behave. Doogan would want more, she knew as she passed through the gates of the college. He'd try to get her into the stockroom, haul his solid penis out and . . . She dared not take her involvement with the lad any further. Wanking him had been a grave mistake, so she intended to put the incident behind her and move on.

Dumping her bag on her desk, she looked around the deserted classroom. She could be happy at Spadger Heath, she reflected. If only she could settle in and establish herself, gain a little respect from the students, she'd enjoy the work. Smiling, she realized that the day would come when she'd look back on her time at Spadger Heath College and laugh. The months passed so quickly, she mused. Before she knew it, she'd have been at the college for a year, two years . . . Things were going to work out well, she concluded. The flat was all right for the time being, she got on well with Alison . . .

'You're an early bird,' Carter chuckled as he appeared in the doorway. 'You must be keen.'

'I am,' Christina replied. 'My first day went well, and I'm looking forward to the challenges today brings.'

'Challenges?' he snorted. 'That's one way to put it. Any trouble from Brown or Doogan yet?'

'Brown disappeared yesterday morning and Doogan . . . well, he's OK.'

'Doogan's OK?' Caster laughed disbelievingly. 'If he hasn't started on you yet . . . Christ, he must have taken a shine to you.'

'We get on,' she said softly.

'You must have a magic touch.'

'A magic touch,' she echoed, recalling her hand running up and down the solid shaft of Doogan's penis. 'Maybe I have.'

'You'll have to let me in on your secret. Well, I'd best prepare for the arrival of the scum. See you at break.'

A magic touch? she mused, recalling again wanking Doogan's huge cock to orgasm, his sperm running over her hand, splattering on the floor. *If Carter knew*, she reflected fearfully, imagining her name splashed across the front pages of the Sunday tabloids. But no one would ever discover her sordid secret, she thought. Even if Doogan took it upon himself to spread the dirty word, no one would believe him. His friends would laugh at him if he said that the teacher had wanked him. They'd think that he was trying to show off.

Walking into the stockroom, Christina sorted through the books, trying to bring some semblance of order to the mess. The stockroom was a shambles, with boxes full of old newspapers and other rubbish lining the shelves. Reckoning that the previous teacher had had no interest in the job, she placed the books into neat piles and began to stack the boxes of rubbish on the floor.

'Ah, Little Miss Hand Job,' Brown chortled, leaning in the doorway.

'Good morning, David.' Christina smiled back, dreading to think what he meant.

'I hear you're pretty good with your hands,' he said, walking into the room.

'With my hands?' she murmured, realizing that Doogan had opened his mouth. 'What *are* you talking about?'

'Baz Doogan. You tossed him off in here.'

'I did *what*?' she gasped, forcing a laugh. 'He's been dreaming.'

'That's what he reckons.'

'He's having you on, David. Would you mind taking those boxes out, please?'

'He told me that you—'

'David, I don't know what Barry has been telling you. And I don't think I want to know.'

'Oh, come on. Give me a quicky, like you did . . .'

'I'm sorry, David, but I have no idea what you're talking about. I suggest you go back to Barry and ask him—'

'He told me what you did to him. Baz doesn't lie.'

'I'm not saying that he's lying. He's joking, David, winding you up.'

'Ah, Miss Shaw,' the headmaster said gruffly. 'Brown, what are you up to? What are you doing in here?'

'Taking these out,' the youth mumbled, grabbing the boxes from the floor and leaving the room.

'Miss Shaw, there have been some changes to the timetable. There's a copy for you.'

'Oh, thank you,' she said, smiling and taking the papers.

'How are you getting on?'

'Fine, fine. I'm just sorting out . . .'

'As I said yesterday, don't put yourself in a position where you're alone with a male student.'

'No, I was—'

'And keep this room locked when you're not around.'

Wandering into the classroom as the man left, Christina sighed. He was hardly the sort of headmaster one could approach, she reflected. Carter would have made a better head than Mr Wright. At least his timely entrance had saved her from Brown's sexual demands. Wondering what Doogan had said as Brown walked towards her, she knew that she was going to have to nip this in the bud. First Doogan, then Brown, then . . . This was going to have to stop, and stop now.

'I want what you gave Baz,' Brown said.

'David, I've already told you that I . . .'

'OK, if that's the way you want it. Don't expect things to be quiet in class today.'

'Oh, I see,' she laughed. '*Now* I get the picture.'

'Good. In that case . . .'

'You're a virgin, too?'

'*What?*' he breathed, his dark eyes frowning. 'I'm not a bloody—'

'Look, we'll talk about this later. The others will be here at any minute.'

'Talk about what?'

'Your virginity, David.'

'No, you don't understand.'

'I understand only too well. We'll have a chat during break.'

As the students began filing into the room, Brown mooched towards his desk and sat down. Christina knew that she had one hell of a problem on her hands. She should never have appeased Doogan's lusting penis, but she couldn't turn the clock back. What was done was done.

Strangely, Brown didn't disrupt the lesson as he'd threatened. Christina put it down to his confusion. He was probably waiting for the outcome of their forthcoming chat during break before carrying out his threat to disrupt the class. What Christina was going to say to him, she had no idea. Doogan was a fool, she reflected. To open his mouth like . . . One thing was for sure. He'd ruined his chances of any further sexual contact with her. Would she have appeased his cock again had he not blabbed to Brown? Christina dreaded to think.

Barry Doogan didn't turn up for class, which Christina thought was probably a blessing. The morning going fairly well with only a few minor disruptions and she thought that she might be winning. Carole had taken an interest in the lesson, much to Christina's surprise, and Davis hadn't dared to comment on penises or vaginas. As the students left the classroom for break, Christina kept her eye on Brown. He was hovering by his desk, obviously waiting until the others had gone before making a move.

'So,' he said, walking up to Christina's desk. 'What's this chat about?'

'I would have thought that you'd have a girlfriend,' Christina said.

'I've had a few,' he responded.

'So why do you want me?'

'I don't want you. What I said was that I want you to give me what you gave Baz.'

'Barry and I had a long chat. He was worried about girls and . . . I don't know what he told you, David.'

'He said that you'd tossed him off.'

'He's winding you up, like I said. We talked about relationships. He has a problem, which I'm not prepared to tell you about.'

'Baz has got a problem?' he echoed, puzzlement mirrored in his wide eyes.

'What's *your* problem, David?'

'I haven't got any problems.'

'Then why do you want me to masturbate you?'

'I . . . well, because . . . Why the hell do you think?'

'I really don't know. Unless you want me to teach you, that is.'

'Look, don't mess me about. You wanked Baz. He told me in secret.'

'In confidence.'

'What?'

'Go on, David.'

'I want the same. If you don't, then I'll tell everyone what Baz told me.'

Biting her lip, Christina wasn't sure what to do. She'd already made the mistake of wanking Barry to orgasm. To appease David's cock by bringing out his sperm wasn't going to help the situation. If anything, wanking another student would only make matters worse. Or would it? Gazing into the lad's dark eyes as she pondered on her next move, she felt her stomach somersault, her clitoris inflate. He *was* good-looking, she mused, realizing that she was setting out on a dangerous road as she glanced down at the crotch of his tight trousers. Recalling Doogan's words about a bit of rough and missing a length of cock, she realized that her arousal was soaring.

Having spent too long with Charles, she felt that she needed to catch up, to make up for lost time. This was an ideal opportunity, she reflected, her blue-eyed gaze fixed on David's bulging crotch. Not only could she gain a little sexual experience, but she'd be able to control the ringleaders. Once Brown and Doogan were beholden to her, she'd have no trouble controlling the rest of the class. But was this the right way to exert her authority over the ringleaders? There was no *other* way, she knew as she walked slowly towards the stockroom with David in tow. It was this, or walk out on her job.

Shit, she thought, her conscience nagging her as David followed her into the stockroom and closed the door behind him. Turning to face David, she wished that she'd dumped Charles long ago and gone out with several men. Having endured sex with Charles, she was still as inexperienced as a virgin. Charles and his fumbling and grunting had taught her nothing. *A bit of rough?* she mused, feeling a wetness between the full lips of her vagina. She'd never really had a proper length of cock. Was that what she wanted now? Was this to control the ringleaders, or satisfy her craving for sex?

'Well,' David breathed, grinning as he unzipped his trousers and hauled his erect penis out.

'Yes,' Christina murmured abstractedly, gazing at the lad's purple knob as he fully retracted his foreskin.

'Want to suck it?'

Suck it? She'd never taken a penis into her wet mouth. Sex with Charles had consisted of the missionary position, vaginal penetration, humping and grunting and sperming. Dropping to her knees, she gazed longingly at the youth's glistening purple glans, the small sperm-slit. As he eased his full balls out through his zip, she gazed at his veined shaft. He was so big, she thought. Charles's prick was nothing in comparison – she couldn't believe the sheer girth of David's huge organ.

Moving her head forward, Christina parted her succulent lips. This was wrong, she knew as she took the ripe plum of his twitching cock into her hot mouth and licked his sperm-slit. Savouring the salty taste of his swollen glans, she closed her eyes and breathed deeply through her nose. This was wrong, word would get out, there'd be trouble . . . Trouble or not, she had succumbed to her latent desires. She sucked and mouthed on the huge glans, taking the solid shaft in her small hand and beginning her wanking motions as David gasped in the grip of his male pleasure.

She needed sex as much as any other woman, she knew as she waited in anticipation for his sperm to gush and fill her mouth. After three years with Charles, her one and only boyfriend . . . Did Alison suck men's cocks? she found herself wondering as she wanked David's rock-hard shaft faster in her desperation to taste his sperm. Her thoughts drifted, lurched. She couldn't stay on at Spadger Heath now, she reflected. Wanking Barry and now sucking David . . . She'd have no authority over the students now that she'd behaved no better than a common whore. And they'd have no respect for her.

'God,' David breathed, his cock twitching as he pumped out his creamy sperm and filled his teacher's mouth. Christina savoured the warm liquid, running her tongue over his throbbing glans as her mouth filled and overflowed. Finally swallowing her prize, she wanked his cock shaft faster, draining his heaving balls as he towered above her. On and on his flow of semen gushed, flooding her tongue, filling her cheeks as she did her best to drink from his fountainhead.

'You're good,' the lad gasped as his flow finally stemmed.

'Thank you,' Christina murmured, slipping his sali-vated glans out of her mouth and lapping up the last of the sperm oozing from his slit.

'You've obviously sucked a few cocks in your time.'

'Quite a few,' she said, wondering why she was lying. What was she trying to prove?

'You're the sort of teacher we need,' he laughed.

'Are you going to be the sort of student I need?' She smiled, rising to her feet. 'Or are you going to disrupt the lessons and—'

'Not me,' he said, zipping his trousers. 'I like you, and I reckon we'll get on well.'

'I certainly hope so, David. If we work together rather than against each other, I'm sure we can make our days pleasant.'

'You've made *my* day,' he laughed.

'And I'll make your day again, if you deserve it. Mess me about, and you'll not find yourself in the stockroom with me again.'

'I wouldn't mess you about. Baz Doogan . . . Did you . . .'

'That's my business, David. And what *we* did is *our* business. I don't want you telling the others about it, do you understand?'

'Of course.'

'One word about this to anyone, and you can forget any future . . . As I said, you won't find yourself in here with me again. Right, I have things to do. You've got geography after break, haven't you?'

'Yes.'

'OK, off you go.'

As he left, Christina licked her sperm-glossed lips, her stomach somersaulting as her expectant clitoris swelled and her juices of desire flowed into the tight crotch of her cotton panties. Confusion swamping her mind as she made her way to the staffroom, she tried to come to terms with her guilt. Was it guilt or triumph? she wondered. She'd tamed the ringleaders, and yet . . . She didn't know what to think. She'd brought off two students in as many days. What the hell would day three bring? Trying to clear her mind of images of David's purple knob pumping sperm into her mouth, she sat in the armchair next to Carter.

'All right?' he asked, smiling.

'Yes, fine,' Christina replied.

'Still no problems?'

'No, not really. One or two disruptions but, apart from that, things are great.'

'I don't know how you do it,' he sighed. 'You carry on for three months, and you'll hold the record.'

'The record?'

'As form teacher. The one before you lasted just short of three months. Of course, you have a long way to go yet.'

'Yes, yes, I have,' she murmured abstractedly, the taste of sperm lingering on her tongue.

Three months? she wondered. How many cocks would she have sucked and wanked by the time she held the record? This was so far removed from her parents' house and her life in a leafy country village. She'd visited London several times but had never seen the run-down areas, let alone been part of the community. It was a different world, she reflected. Only sixty miles by car, but it seemed like a thousand miles away from the world she'd grown up in.

Carter mumbled something about a geography lesson and the 'little shits' as he left the room. He had the wrong attitude, Christina thought as she poured herself a cup of coffee. But did she have the right one? she mused, returning to her armchair. More than an English teacher, she knew that, to an extent, she had to become part of the class, one of the students. They weren't interested in geography. What did they care which city was the capital of America? What did they care about punctuation or grammar? One of them worked in a pub during the evenings. Was he really bothered about geography or English? But Christina hoped that she could at least try to give them some sort of start in life. Perhaps she could open their eyes to . . . Hadn't Brown and Doogan opened *her* eyes? She had as much to learn as the students, if not more.

'No class, Miss Shaw?' the head murmured as he entered the staffroom.

'I have a free period,' she replied. 'I'm going to take a look around the college.'

'You seem to be settling in quite well.'

'Yes, I am. I'm enjoying the challenge.'

'Let's hope you continue to do so.'

'Thank you.'

Heading for her classroom, Christina felt positive. The situation with Doogan and Brown wasn't ideal, but at least she had some sort of control over them. She also had some sort of sex life, which pleased her. Wanking and sucking the boys brought her pleasure, she had to admit. Noticing a young girl sitting at the back of the room, Christina closed the door and walked over to her. It was Bryony Philips, an attractive blonde who'd kept herself to herself during lessons. Her head hung low, she hadn't appeared to notice Christina.

'Are you all right?' Christina asked the girl

'Oh, I didn't see you come in,' Bryony said, looking up in surprise and giving a slight smile. 'Yes, I'm OK. Just feeling a little down, that's all.'

'Anything I can do to help?'

'Well, I . . . Actually, you might be able to help me.'

'Go on,' Christina said, pulling out a chair and sitting down opposite the girl.

'I was hoping you'd come back. I've been waiting for you.'

'Oh?'

'I feel that I might be able to talk to you. It's my . . . my breasts.'

'Your breasts?' Christina echoed, involuntarily looking down at the girl's partially open blouse. 'What's wrong with your breasts?'

'They're very small,' the girl confessed.

'I wouldn't worry about that.' Christina smiled. 'You're young. They've plenty of time to develop.'

'Yes, but . . . I'll show you what I mean,' Bryony said, unbuttoning her blouse.

'Bryony, there's no need to . . .'

'I have to show you,' the girl persisted. 'I can't ask my mum about it. You're the only one I can turn to.'

'It's one thing talking your problems over with me, but quite another to show me your breasts. I don't need to see them, Bryony.'

'I only want your opinion, Miss. As I said, I can't ask my mum because . . . well, I just can't.'

'All right, you'd better come into the stockroom,' Christina suggested, getting up. 'Just in case someone walks in and gets the wrong idea.'

As Bryony followed her to the stockroom, Christina felt pleased that the girl had been able to come to her with her problems. But she also wondered why she wanted to expose her young breasts. This was all part of the job, Christina thought, closing the door. Bryony had been unable to go to her mother for help and advice and had turned to her teacher. There was obviously some trust developing, she thought happily. Watching the girl open her blouse and lift the silk cups of her bra away from the petite mounds of her breasts, Christina was almost mesmerized as she gazed at the brown teats of Bryony's elongated nipples.

'There's nothing wrong with you,' she said, smiling reassuringly.

'But they're so small,' Bryony sighed.

'I had the same problem . . . Not problem. "Concern" would be a better word. When I was your age I used to wonder why my breasts were so small.'

'Touch them,' the girl said, moving closer to Christina. 'They don't feel right, somehow.'

'Bryony, I . . .' Christina stammered, realizing that she'd been gripped by an overwhelming sudden desire to reach out, feel the girl's small breasts and stroke the brown protrusions of her sensitive nipples.

'Squeeze them and tell me if you think they're all right.'

Reaching out, Christina tentatively squeezed the girl's left breast. The petite mound was firm, the skin unblemished and smooth in youth. Her fingertips brushing against the girl's milk teat, she felt her stomach somersault. Was Bryony leading her on? she wondered, circling the darkening disc of her areola with her fingertip. Was this a dare? Or was the girl genuinely concerned about her small breasts? Brown or Doogan might have put her up to this, Christina reflected, squeezing and kneading both breasts.

'There's nothing wrong with you,' Christina finally said, lowering her hands.

'If you say so,' the girl sighed.

'I *do* say so,' Christina said softly, her gaze transfixed on her student's ripening nipples. 'Bryony, has anyone said anything about me?'

'Said anything?' Bryony echoed, cupping the mounds of her breasts in her bra and buttoning her blouse. 'Said what?'

'Brown or Doogan . . . Have they said anything?'

'No, nothing. Miss, would you look at my . . . you know, down there?'

'Bryony, I think this has gone far enough,' Christina said firmly, aware of an unfamiliar yearning to gaze at the girl's young pussy. 'You'd better go to your next class.'

'It's just that I . . .'

'Just that you what? Look, there's nothing wrong with you.'

'You're the only one I can talk to, Miss.'

'Talking is one thing, but showing me your—'

'You won't help me, then?'

'All right,' Christina conceded, realizing that this really was going too far. 'Show me what the problem is.'

As Bryony lifted her skirt up over her stomach and tugged her panties down her firm thighs, Christina was sure that the girl was leading her on. The boys had put her up to this, she knew as she gazed in awe at the fleshy cushions of her student's hairless pussy lips. Her pink inner labia protruding invitingly from her tightly closed sex crack, she parted her feet and lifted her skirt higher. Unsure what to do, Christina couldn't drag her stare away from the perfectly formed lips of Bryony's young pussy. Her heart racing, her breathing quickening, she stepped back and turned her head away.

'That's enough,' she said. 'I know what you're up to and . . .'

'Up to?' the girl breathed, cocking her head to one side. 'What do you mean?'

'Bryony, schoolgirls don't show their breasts to their teachers. Or pull their knickers down in front of them.'

'But, Miss . . .'

'But nothing. Go to your next lesson, please.'

'I have a small lump just inside me. I thought . . .'

'A lump? Are you sure?'

'Yes, Miss.'

'Then, you must go to your doctor.'

'I can't. He . . . he's a strange man. Whenever I go to see him, he examines me down there. No matter what's wrong with me, he . . .'

'You should report him, Bryony.'

'What's the point? No one would believe me. I was hoping you'd feel me and . . . Please, Miss. I can't ask my mother.'

'All right,' Christina sighed, reckoning that the girl was genuinely worried. 'This is unethical, to say the least, but I'll . . . Just quickly, all right?'

'All right.'

Kneeling, Christina parted the hairless lips of Bryony's vulva and slipped her finger into the tight, wet sheath of her student's teenage pussy. She could feel nothing out of the ordinary as she massaged the hot walls of the girl's pussy. Pushing her finger into her tight sex shaft, she gazed at her clitoris emerging from beneath pinken hood. This was another mistake, she knew as Bryony began to breathe deeply, heavily. Unethical, dangerous . . . But Christina's main concern was her own rising arousal, the unfamiliar thoughts surfacing from the murky depths of her mind as she massaged the young girl's inner flesh.

Slipping a second finger into Bryony's tightening vaginal sheath, Christina began to tremble. Her mind thronging with uncharacteristic thoughts as the girl parted her feet further, she knew that she was teetering on the edge of committing a lesbian act. Examining the girl was one thing, but massaging deep inside her pussy, gazing at her ripening clitoris, imagining sucking and tonguing her there . . . *God, no*, she thought, licking her succulent lips. Taking a deep breath, Christina slipped her wet fingers out of the girl's snug quim and stood up before she went too far.

'There doesn't seem to be anything wrong,' she said softly, aware of the girl's juices of arousal running down her sticky fingers.

'I hope you're right,' Bryony mumbled.

'Sort your clothes out and go to your next class.'

'Yes, Miss.'

Watching the girl leave, Christina raised her hand and gazed at the girl-juice glistening on her fingers. Had the boys put Bryony up to this? If Christina had been set up . . . Sure that the girl was honest, she left the stockroom and wiped her hand on a tissue. The experience had unnerved her, she knew as she pictured the young girl's hairless vaginal lips and recalled the inner heat of her young body. 'God,' she breathed, realizing suddenly that Bryony had shaved. Holding her hand to her mouth, she was sure that Bryony had been conning her. Displaying her young breasts, dropping her panties and exposing the shaved lips of her vagina . . . Why had the girl shaved her vulval flesh?

Despite feeling that she'd been taken for a ride, Christina had to admit that she'd enjoyed the experience. In a way, she was hoping that the girl would come to her again, allow her to finger her tight pussy and . . . Shaking her head, Christina tried to push all thoughts of the girl's beautiful young body from her mind. It was bad enough that she'd wanked Doogan and sucked Brown, let alone fingered a young student's pussy. Eyeing Alison's naked body that morning had roused *something* within the dark depths of her mind, but she wasn't sure exactly what latent desires lurked deep within her subconscious.

Her thoughts focusing on lesbianism, she bit her lip as she recalled a girlfriend she'd had at school. She'd been blonde, young and extremely attractive. Christina had fallen for her, had a crush on her, but nothing had come of it other than one stolen kiss. She recalled locking her lips to her friend's mouth, tasting her saliva, breathing in the scent of her hair. But that was normal, she tried to convince herself. It wasn't unheard of for young schoolgirls to become close, intimate, during their growing.

'Sorry, Miss,' Bryony said as she entered the classroom. 'I thought I'd better explain.'

'Explain what?'

'There's nothing wrong with me,' she confessed, hanging her head.

'I realized that, Bryony. So what's this all about?'

'I . . . I like you,' the girl admitted.

'Bryony, I know what it's like to be your age. Your feelings are confused, you—'

'I'm not confused. I know what I feel, what I think.'

'Yes, but you can't . . .'

'Did you like what you did to me?'

'I . . . Bryony, whether I liked it or not . . . Look, I

examined you because I thought there was something wrong with you. There was no other reason.'

'Oh, right.'

'Have you been out with boys yet?'

'No, I haven't.'

'You'll sort your feelings out once you've got a boyfriend. In the meantime, try not to think about . . . well, you know.'

Watching Bryony walk away, Christina knew exactly how the girl felt. What worried her was that she was beginning to feel the same. Sighing, she tried again to push all thoughts of the girl's young body from her mind. This was ridiculous, she reflected. Doogan, Brown – and now Bryony. Living with her parents in a country house, Christina had never mixed much with teenagers before, and she thought briefly that the attraction was innocent enough. But she was kidding herself, she knew. The excitement, the danger . . . The feel of Doogan's solid cock in her hand, his sperm running over her hand . . . Brown's knob in her mouth, pumping sperm over her tongue . . .

'Shit,' Christina breathed, banging her fist on her desk. Unsure of her feelings as she again pictured Alison's naked body, imagined Bryony standing naked before her, she knew that she had to pull herself together. Her first two days at Spadger Heath had been a total disaster. If she were found out, she'd be in real trouble. But she had only been trying to fit in with the students, to get them to accept her and . . . 'That's not the way to do it,' she sighed, walking to the window and looking out across the car park to the engineering works. Cursing her stupidity, she decided to put an end to the ridiculous games she'd started. Doogan and Brown were just going to have to accept her without the wanking and sucking. Bryony would just have to . . .

'Miss,' Bryony said softly as she approached from behind.

'What is it now?' Christina snapped. 'I'm sorry, I didn't mean to be angry. What is it?'

'Would you mind if I came to your flat this evening?'

'My . . . Yes, Bryony, I *would* mind. I'm your teacher, for God's sake.'

'I know where you live.'

'How?'

'I followed you home.'

'Christ, this is getting out of hand. Go away, Bryony. Please go away and leave me alone.'

Somehow managing to get through the rest of the day, Christina knew that she couldn't stay on at Spadger Heath. She'd made a complete mess of her first two days, and realized now that she had no choice but to leave her job. She'd meant well, she reflected. Trying to get on with the students, trying to . . . Grabbing her bag after the class had left, she avoided Bryony and headed home. Perhaps she'd be able to talk to Alison, she mused. Get her flatmate's advice and . . . and what? 'What's done is done,' she breathed as she neared the flat. 'I've fucked up big time.'

3

Reading the note that Alison had left, Christina felt despondent. Her flatmate had gone to visit her parents and wouldn't be back until late, at least midnight. Although she didn't feel like eating, Christina did her best to force down a tin of soup and two slices of bread. She'd been looking forward to the evening, talking her problems over with Alison. Now she had nothing but an empty flat and several boring hours ahead of her.

Switching the TV on, she flicked through the channels and turned it off. She slipped a CD into the hi-fi and mooched around the room before flopping onto the sofa. Normally, she'd have busied herself with something, but her mind was brimming with thoughts of the stockroom. Unconsciously slipping her hand between her thighs as she pictured Bryony's naked pussy lips, she massaged the swell of her moist panties. Her hand slipping in around the edge of the flimsy undergarment, she parted her thighs wider and toyed with the petals of her wet inner lips. Breathing deeply as she pulled and twisted her inner labia, she again pictured Bryony's hairless sex slit.

Telling herself that her thoughts about the girl were uncharacteristic, Christina knew that she wasn't a latent lesbian. It had been a long time since she'd had a fulfilling sexual relationship, she reflected as her clitoris swelled. Thinking back, she realized that her relationship with Charles could hardly be described even as sexual, let alone fulfilling. In fact, Christina had *never* had a fulfilling sexual relationship, and she put that down as the reason for her unusual feelings about Bryony.

Massaging the solid nub of her clitoris, Christina closed her eyes and sank into a warm pool of satisfaction. She'd never masturbated regularly. Apart from rubbing her clitoris during her younger years, her only self-induced orgasms had been when Charles had swiftly pumped his sperm into her vagina, withdrawn from her unsatisfied quim and left her in desperate need of sexual relief. Had *Bryony* left her craving sexual relief? she pondered, picturing again the fleshy swell of the girl's hairless vulval lips. Christina knew instinctively that Bryony wouldn't give up. The girl obviously had a powerful crush on her teacher, and would pursue her quest for love until . . . *Love?* Christina mused, her clitoris ripening beneath her caressing fingertip. She'd not found love with Charles. Would she ever find love? she wondered. Then the doorbell rang.

Leaping to her feet and adjusting her skirt, she had a nagging feeling that it was Bryony. She'd been wondering whether the girl would turn up. Wondering or hoping? If it *was* Bryony, then she'd talk to her, she decided, walking to the door. Talk over her problems, try to get the girl to see sense. Opening the door, she gazed at Bryony, her long blonde hair, her tight T-shirt and red miniskirt. She looked older out of her college uniform – mature, sensual, alluring . . .

'I thought you might come round,' she said softly. 'You'd better come in.'

'I wasn't going to,' Bryony said as Christina closed the

door behind her. 'I waited outside for ages. I wasn't going to—'

'Come into the lounge and sit down,' Christina interrupted the girl. 'I need to ask you something.'

'Oh?' the girl murmured, sitting on the sofa as Christina stood with her back to the window.

'Why have you shaved, Bryony?'

'I . . . I don't know.'

'You don't know?' Christina chuckled. 'You mean, it was an accident?'

'No, no, I . . . I prefer it that way.'

'I see. Tell me about yourself, Bryony. You've said that you can't go to your doctor, you can't talk to your mother . . . What about your father?'

'He went off with some young girl,' she sighed. 'My mother's always drunk. The house is a tip, there's never any food . . .'

'Do you have brothers or sisters?'

'No, I don't. It's just me and mum.'

'Mum and me,' Christina corrected her, wishing she hadn't.

'Mum's always on the gin. She never does housework or cooking. No wonder my dad went off.'

'What do you do during the evenings? Have you any interests?'

'I sit in my room. It's the only tidy place in the house. There's no television so . . . We do have a telly, but the aerial blew down and mum can't afford to get it fixed.'

'Bryony, I think it would be an idea if you joined a club. Say, tennis or swimming. Something to give you an interest and get you out of the house.'

'I like swimming, but we haven't got any money. What

money we get from the social, mum spends on drink. It's nice here. I wish I had a flat.'

'It's above a Chinese takeaway, Bryony. It's hardly nice.'

'Compared with my house, this is brilliant.'

'Would you like some tea or coffee?'

'Tea, please. No sugar.'

'Switch the TV on. There might be something you can watch while I make the tea.'

Filling the kettle, Christina felt sorry for Bryony. The girl didn't have a proper home, a loving mother, meals waiting for her . . . She probably did her own washing and ironing, cooked her own meals if there was any food in the house. But that wasn't Christina's problem. In a run-down area of London, this was to be expected. There again, Christina realized that not all mothers drank gin. There was no excuse for wasting money on alcohol, and no need to live in a hovel. Pouring the tea, Christina knew that she could only help Bryony by giving her advice. She couldn't help financially, but she could befriend the girl and help her as best she could by advising her.

'No, Bryony,' she gasped as she took the teas into the lounge. 'Please, put your clothes on.'

'But I thought . . .' the girl began, standing naked by the sofa.

'For God's sake. What the hell do you think you're doing?'

'But, Miss . . .'

'You come round here when I specifically told you not to, you string me a load of lies about your mother and your home . . . And now you're naked in my lounge. Get dressed and get out of my flat.'

Watching as the girl picked up her panties from the sofa, Christina scrutinized the violin curves of her naked body. She was young and attractive, her beautiful body not yet fully developed. Her breasts were pointed, not fully rounded, her nipples elongated out of proportion to her firm mounds. Eyeing the hairless crack of Bryony's pussy, Christina felt her clitoris swell as her juices of desire seeped into her tight panties. Unable to finish masturbating, she was already in a high state of arousal. Gazing at Bryony's delicious body was too much for her to bear. If she just touched her, caressed her, stroked her . . . But this was wrong, she decided as the girl tugged her panties up her long, shapely legs.

Placing the teas on the small table by the TV, Christina focused on the girl's young breasts, the sensitive buds of her ripening milk teats. Bryony was innocent, she concluded. Although the girl had stripped naked, she probably didn't know right from wrong. Perhaps she was trying to find love, and thought that this was the best way to do it. She might have seen her father chasing after a young girl, and thought as a result that sex was the way to get what she wanted. Her upbringing was at fault. Bryony was innocent.

'I'm sorry, Miss,' she sighed, picking up her bra from the sofa. 'I thought . . .'

'I know what you thought, Bryony.' Christina smiled. 'You want to be loved, don't you?'

'I've never been loved.'

'I can't love you, Bryony. You do understand that, don't you?'

'No, I don't. You said in class that you haven't got a boyfriend. I thought that you might be lonely, like I am.'

'I do get lonely at times. Tell me, why do you believe

that sex is a means to forming a relationship? We could have become friends without having . . . It's lesbian sex, Bryony. That's what you're offering me. Lesbian sex.'

'I've never liked boys. When you smiled at me in class, I thought—'

'Smiled at you? Bryony, my smiling at a girl isn't a signal. It doesn't mean to say that I want lesbian sex just because I smile at you.'

'OK, so I got the wrong message. I'm sorry.'

'No, no, don't be sorry. It's not your fault.'

'I just want to be held.'

'Put your bra down,' Christina said softly. 'Move your clothes and sit on the sofa.'

Joining the girl as she did what she'd been told, Christina felt her stomach somersault, her clitoris swelling as she reached out and stroked Bryony's thigh. This was very wrong, she knew, but . . . but what? she wondered. The girl wanted to be held, loved. Was that so very wrong? Christina needed love and physical contact. After Charles, she needed to find . . . she needed to find a man to share her life with, not to embark on a lesbian relationship with one of her students. But if she only saw Bryony once a week, perhaps invited her round once a week for . . . She was trying to convince herself that having sex with the girl was acceptable.

'I can't have a relationship with you,' she said softly, her fingers dangerously near to the girl's hairless vulva.

'It's just nice to have someone sit with me and touch me,' Bryony murmured, parting her young thighs and reclining on the sofa.

'I'll sit with you and touch you. But you must understand that we can't go further than that.'

'Yes, I understand. That's nice. I like you stroking me.

My mother has never held me, loved me. It's nice, being loved.'

This wasn't love, Christina thought, her fingers caressing the smooth flesh just above the girl's sex crack. This was fulfilling a need. Whose need? she wondered. Bryony craved love and physical attention. What did *she* crave? Alone in her bed at night, alone with her naked body, her clitoris . . . What did she crave? Her fingertip hovering at the top of Bryony's vaginal slit, only half an inch from her clitoris, Christina knew that she was weakening in her soaring arousal. She dared not masturbate the girl, she knew as she gazed longingly at her erect nipples rising alluringly from the darkening discs of her areolae. If she massaged her clitoris, took her to orgasm, the girl would want to reciprocate and . . .

'That's nice,' Bryony murmured dreamily as Christina's fingertip brushed the sensitive tip of her solid clitoris. 'No one's ever touched me there.'

'Do you masturbate?' Christina asked.

'Yes, most nights. It's all I have. It's the only way I have of escaping my horrible life.'

'Life needn't be horrible.'

'It needn't be, but it is.'

Deciding to bring the girl her much-needed pleasure, Christina massaged the nub of her ripe clitoris. *Just this once*, she thought, vowing never to touch Bryony again. With Alison usually around in the evenings, she knew that she'd not have much opportunity to masturbate the naked girl. Temptation wouldn't raise its ugly head, she wouldn't have to fight her inner desires. And if Alison happened to be out . . . Christina wouldn't answer the door. The stockroom would remain locked, out of bounds to all students, particularly Doogan and Brown. And Bryony.

Massaging the girl's clitoris faster, Christina leaned forward, her mouth dangerously close to the young beauty's nipple. Fighting temptation, she expertly masturbated the girl, desperately trying not to suck the teat of her barely developed breast into her wet mouth. Bryony was close to her climax, Christina knew as she began her gasping and writhing. Sucking on her ripe nipple would add to her pleasure, take her to her goal and . . .

'God,' Christina breathed, taking the elongated protrusion into her hot mouth and sucking hard. She'd fought her inner battle and lost. Now she'd set out on an unknown road, begun an uncertain journey to . . . She dreaded to think where her journey was taking her. This wasn't love, she tried to convince herself as she mouthed and suckled at the girl's breast. This was cold comfort, a means to an end, giving physical pleasure for the sake of pleasure. A hundred questions battered Christina's mind as Bryony teetered on the verge of her orgasm. Why had she been so weak? Why couldn't she have fought her inner desires? Why did she *have* such desires?

'Oh, oh,' Bryony gasped as she arched her back and flung her legs wide apart. She was there, Christina knew as she felt the girl's rock-hard clitoris pulsating beneath her vibrating fingertip. Her naked body shaking violently, Bryony squirmed and writhed, crying out as her obvious pleasure gripped her very soul. Christina had never touched another girl sexually, let alone witnessed one in the grip of a massive orgasm. Sucking and biting Bryony's nipple, she slowed her masturbating rhythm as the girl shuddered and fell limp. Twitching, her naked body glowing, she finally let out a long sigh of pleasure as she relaxed in the aftermath of her orgasm.

Slipping the girl's nipple out of her mouth, Christina looked down at Bryony's inflamed vulval flesh, the pouting wet lips of her hairless pussy. She was tempted to lick her there, taste her teenage juices of arousal and suck another orgasm out of her detumescing clitoris. Bryony lay still, her eyes closed, her legs parted as she recovered from her lesbian pleasure. Gazing at the girl, the smooth flesh of her youthful body, Christina tried desperately to drag her gaze away from the beautiful sight of her yawning sex crack, the opaque liquid clinging to the pink wings of her inner labia.

'Rest your head on the arm of the sofa,' she said, stroking the girl's long blonde hair. Leaving one foot on the floor, Bryony lifted her leg and placed her other foot behind Christina, resting her head on the sofa arm. Her thighs parted wide, her vulval crack gaping, she closed her eyes again and relaxed. Christina leaned forward, her mouth close to the girl's hairless pussy. This was wrong, she kept telling herself. To lick a young girl's pussy, to lap up her vaginal cream and . . .

Rising to her feet, Christina paced the lounge floor. Glancing at her naked student every now and then, she clenched her fists as she tried to fight temptation. More than temptation, she felt that she was fighting for her femininity, her womanhood. She wasn't a lesbian, and vowed not to succumb to the young girl's naked body, the wet slit of her teenage pussy. To lick the girl there would be . . . It would be wonderful, she knew. To run her tongue up and down her sex crack, tasting her, teasing out her clitoris, sucking her . . .

'Shit,' Christina whispered, gazing at the sleeping beauty's swollen pussy lips. This was a fight she knew she was going to lose unless . . . *Why doesn't Alison come home?* she thought, hoping for something or someone to take temptation away from her. *Why did Bryony have to come round? Why did she strip? Why can't I control myself?* 'Shit.' *Am I a lesbian?* Dashing into the kitchen as the phone rang, she was relieved to hear Alison's voice.

'Are you coming home yet?' she asked hopefully.

'No, that's why I'm calling. I knew I was going to be late, but it looks as though I might stay overnight.'

'Overnight?' Christina breathed, disappointedly. 'Alison, you don't have to stay . . .'

'I haven't seen my parents for a while. You know what it's like.'

'I suppose so.'

'You'll be all right on your own, won't you?'

'I'm not— yes, yes I'll be fine.'

'OK, I'll see you tomorrow.'

'Yes, tomorrow.'

That was all she needed, Christina thought, standing in the lounge doorway and staring longingly at Bryony's naked body. She felt that she was climbing the walls, craving a drug. She'd never smoked, but now she had some idea of what it must be like to crave for a cigarette. How long should she allow the girl to sleep on the sofa? Bryony's mother would wonder where . . . No. Her mother was probably drunk, sprawled across a sofa in a state of semi-consciousness. Christina decided to talk to Bryony. She'd wake her and get her to dress. Bryony needed to talk. They both needed to talk.

'Bryony,' she said, kneeling on the floor by the sofa. 'Bryony, wake up.' The girl stirred, breathing deeply as Christina focused on her naked body. Her long blonde hair cascading over her fresh face like a curtain of gold silk, the teenager looked like an angel. The wet crack of her exquisite vagina glistening in the light, she was a temptress, impossible to refuse. Moving her head forward, Christina kissed the girl's naked mons, breathing in her female scent, trying again to fight her inner desires.

'Just this once,' she whispered, pushing her tongue out and tasting the creamy valley of her girl-sex. Trembling, Christina repeatedly swept her tongue up the young beauty's vaginal crack, lapping up her teenage juices of arousal, savouring the aphrodisiacal taste of her young pussy. Parting the fleshy pads of Bryony's outer sex lips, Christina slipped her tongue into her vaginal hole, licking and tasting her there as her own juices of arousal seeped between the inner wings of her labia. *Just this once*, she thought, parting the girl's love lips further, exposing the pinken nubble of her ripe clitoris. Licking her there, teasing her solid pleasure bud, she locked her lips to the girl's wet flesh and sucked hard on her inflated clitoris.

Bryony stirred again, her breathing fast and shallow as she responded to the lesbian licking. This was the girl's own fault, Christina mused. Had she not persisted, had she not stripped and offered her young body for lesbian sex . . . Schoolteachers were supposed to be in control, Christina knew. They were supposed to teach their students right from wrong, to help them grow up and develop into decent people. What had she done to help the girl? she wondered. Masturbated her, sucked and bitten her nipple, tongued her vagina, licked her sweet clitoris . . .

'That's nice,' Bryony murmured dreamily. 'I like feeling your tongue there.' Reaching down, Bryony pulled her sex lips wide apart, stretching the fleshy cushions and exposing the intimate folds of her wet valley. Her clitoris fully emerging from beneath its pink bonnet, she trembled as Christina sucked and licked her sensitive pleasure spot. The girl suddenly shuddered, her naked body shaking violently as she cried out and gripped Christina's head. Grinding her open cunt flesh hard against her teacher's mouth, she let out her orgasmic juices as her clitoris exploded.

Drowning in the young girl's cuntal juices, barely able to breathe, Christina sucked and mouthed on her pulsating clitoris, lost in her sexual delirium as Bryony screamed out in the grip of her illicit lesbian pleasure. The smooth flesh of the girl's wet vulva pressed hard against her face, she sustained her student's orgasm, licking and mouthing, sucking and slurping. Never had Christina known that such pleasure was obtainable from lesbian oral sex. Drinking from the teenager's cunt, swallowing her fresh orgasmic juices, she swept her tongue up and down her valley, repeatedly caressing her pulsating clitoris, taking the girl ever higher to her sexual heaven.

'No more,' Bryony finally gasped, her inner thighs crushing Christina's head as she convulsed wildly. Sucking out the girl's creamy offering, Christina drank from her hot cunt, swallowing her flowing juices until she'd drained her sex sheath and the girl pushed her away. Licking her lips, she sat back on her heels and gazed at the rubicund cushions of Bryony's inflamed outer labia, the engorged petals of her inner lips.

Guilt consuming her, she watched the girl shuddering as she recovered from her lesbian-induced orgasm. Christina should never have succumbed to her vulgar desires, she knew. She'd behaved immorally, taught the young girl things she was far too young to know. Christina should have known nothing about lesbian oral sex. *What have I done?* she thought guiltily, watching the smooth plateau of the girl's stomach rising and falling as she recovered from her orgasm. *What the hell have I done?*

'You'd better get dressed and go home,' she said as Bryony hauled her naked body up from the sofa.

'What about you?' the girl asked, her pretty face framed by her sex-matted blonde hair, her succulent lips furling into a smile.

'Me?' Christina said. 'What do you mean?'

'What about . . . You know what I mean.'

'I . . . Oh, I see.'

'Aren't you going to let me love you?'

Her mind racing with a thousand thoughts, Christina bit her lip. Alison would be out all night. This was an opportunity to experience another girl's intimate attention. Did she want to feel another girl's tongue lapping between the full lips of her vagina? Charles had never licked her there – his lovemaking consisted of his penis thrusting into her vagina, sperming over her cervix. Just that. Christina was torn so many ways, riddled with guilt. How could she ever face Bryony in class, knowing that she'd licked and sucked the girl's clitoris to orgasm? If she were now to allow the girl to reciprocate . . .

'Well?' Bryony smiled. 'Don't you want to be loved?'

'It's not that I don't want to,' Christina sighed, pacing the floor in her confusion. 'It's wrong, Bryony. What I did to you was wrong, and if I allow you to—'

'Haven't you ever done anything that was wrong?' the girl asked. 'Anyway, who says it's wrong to love each other?'

'Loving each other is . . . Love should be between a man and a woman, Bryony.'

'Why?'

'Well, because . . . That's just the way it is. Yes, I would like physical attention. I don't have a boyfriend and I do get lonely.'

'If you want me to stop, then I will,' the girl said, her full lips curving in a lascivious grin.

Slipping off the sofa, Bryony stood in front of Christina and unbuttoned her blouse. Christina raised her hands to stop the girl, but hesitated. Looking down, she watched Bryony part the silk material, revealing her full bra. Her heart racing, she thought again that this was wrong as Bryony lifted the cups of Christina's bra away from her firm breasts. Given their freedom, her nipples elongated, standing proud from the chocolate-brown discs of her areolae. Was this what she wanted? she wondered again as Bryony leaned forward and sucked her nipple into her wet mouth. The heavenly sensations transmitting deep into her breast as the girl sucked and tongued her ripening milk teat, she let out a rush of breath.

'Bryony,' she murmured as the girl moved her attention to her other breast, sucking and nibbling her brown teat. She could feel the girl's hands sliding down her hips, her fingers slipping between the top of her skirt and her naked flesh. Her breathing unsteady, Christina stood motionless as her skirt slipped down her thighs, the material tumbling around her ankles and settling on the carpet. Kneeling, Bryony pressed her face into the warm swell of Christina's panties, breathing in her girl-scent, kissing and loving her there.

'Bryony, no,' Christina gasped as she felt her panties

being pulled down to reveal the sparse blonde down covering the gentle rise of her mons, the fleshy cushions of her outer labia. Quivering, Christina looked down at her naked student, the sheen of her blonde hair as she moved forward, her eager mouth close to her teacher's pussy lips. Christina held her breath, waiting in anticipation as she felt the girl's hot breath on the most intimate part of her trembling body. Did she want another girl's tongue there, licking her sex valley, stiffening the pink bud of her clitoris?

Naked apart from her bra rucked above her full breasts, Christina looked around the room. This was her home, she reflected. The photographs of her parents on the mantelpiece, the flowers in the vase that Alison had bought to brighten up the room. Standing naked in front of her naked student, waiting for the feel of the girl's wet tongue licking her sex slit . . . This was wrong, so very wrong. She should never have answered the door to Bryony. She should never have comforted her, stroked the naked flesh of her thigh, massaged her clitoris to orgasm, sucked and licked her pussy . . . No one would know, Christina consoled herself as Bryony parted the fleshy lips of her vulva with her slender fingers. No one, not even Alison, would discover the sordid truth. Christina had had sex with a young female student, Christina had abused her position of trust and tongued a young girl's pussy, Christina had . . . In her weakness, her yearning to be comforted, Christina had fallen prey to her inner desires. Was that a crime?

'Please,' Christina whispered, looking down at Bryony's full lips as the young student examined the intimate folds nestling within her teacher's girl crack. 'Bryony, I don't think . . .' Closing her eyes and breathing heavily,

Christina shuddered as the girl's tongue ran up the full length of her wet vaginal valley. 'God,' she murmured, her clitoris emerging from its hide as if it was actively seeking the caress of the girl's tongue. The sensations driving her wild, Christina felt her trembling legs sagging beneath her as Bryony parted her teacher's pussy lips further and drove her tongue deep into Christina's drenched sex sheath.

Tossing her head back, Christina clutched Bryony's head as her tongue snaked inside the wet sheath of her tightening pussy. Bryony's hot breath, her wet tongue, her nose pressing hard against Christina's solid clitoris . . . Christina had never known such immense pleasure. If only her nagging conscience would free her, she knew that she'd sink into the warm pool of lesbian love and give herself completely to her young student. But the nagging persisted. Where would this intimate relationship lead her? What would Bryony's mother say if she discovered that her daughter's teacher was having a lesbian affair with her darling girl? What if Alison walked into the room?

'Sit on the sofa,' Bryony said, her pussy-wet face looking up at her teacher.

'Bryony,' Christina began as she moved to the sofa and perched her buttocks on the edge of the cushion. 'Bryony, I don't—'

'Shush. Lie back and open your legs,' Bryony said huskily, settling between Christina's feet. 'Let me love you properly.'

Her head back, her eyes closed, her thighs wide, Christina shuddered as Bryony locked her succulent lips to the bared flesh of her teacher's gaping vaginal valley. The girl's mouth hard against Christina's pubic bone, she sucked hard on her erect clitoris, the pressure bringing out the full length of her pleasure bud. Gasping, Christina tossed her head from side to side as the beautiful sensations built. No man could have done this, she reflected. Only a girl knew how to pleasure another girl.

Christina's orgasm came quickly, her pulsating clitoris erupting with pleasure, her womb rhythmically contracting, her juices of lesbian desire gushing from the spasming sheath of her vagina. Riding the crest of her climax, her naked body shaking violently, she clutched Bryony's head, grinding the flesh of her open pussy hard against the girl's face as she drifted through clouds of sexual pleasure, floating on a sea of lesbian sex. Again and again her clitoris erupted, her orgasm peaking, rocking her very soul until she thought she'd pass out with the intense pleasure her naked body was bringing her.

'Enough,' she finally managed to gasp. Bryony knew exactly what to do as her teacher's orgasm began to wane. Licking gently, sucking, mouthing, tonguing, she brought Christina slowly down from her sexual heaven. Her limbs twitching, her trembling body convulsing, Christina lay gasping for breath as her young student brought out the last ripples of pure sexual bliss from her subsiding clitoris. Her eyes rolling, she was unable to focus on the girl as she sat back on her heels and licked her cunny-creamed lips. Christina tried to speak, but the words wouldn't come. She tried to sit upright, but her naked body wouldn't respond.

'Are you all right?' Bryony asked.

'Yes, yes,' Christina finally breathed. 'God, yes.'

'Would you like me to shave you?'

'What? No, no, I . . . Bryony, you'd better go home now.'

'Home?' the girl echoed, her angelic face reflecting an inner sadness.

'Your mother will wonder where you are.'

'My mother never wonders where I am. She doesn't care where I am. She'll be drunk, anyway.'

'Yes, but . . . Bryony, I need time to think, time alone.'

'Think about what?'

'Us . . . me . . . I don't know.'

'What's the matter?'

'Everything's the matter.'

'Haven't I pleased you? I thought I'd loved you properly.'

'Yes, yes, you have. For God's sake. Can't you see that this is wrong? I'm your teacher, you're a girl and . . . You should be loving boys, Bryony. And so should I. Men, I mean. God, I don't know what I'm trying to say. You're what, eighteen?'

'No, no. I'm only—'

'I don't want to know. You're the student and I'm the teacher. This shouldn't be happening between us. Apart from that, we're both females. And then there's your age. Everything about us is wrong, Bryony.'

'I don't see what's wrong,' the girl sighed.

'No, I don't think you do. You're like a flower, Bryony. Fresh, beautiful . . . but not fully bloomed. You need to develop and—'

'You're talking about my breasts, aren't you?'

'No, no, of course not. I'm trying to say that you're too young.'

'You want someone older?'

'God, Bryony. Why don't you understand? Yes, someone older. But a man.'

'Oh.'

'I'm sorry, but we can't take this any further. Please don't come here again.'

'All right, if that's what you want.'

'It is. I'm sorry, Bryony.'

Watching the girl dress, Christina felt her stomach churning. This wasn't what she'd wanted at all. But she knew that she had to end the affair before it became a full-blown lesbian relationship. *Another grave mistake,* she reflected, folding her arms to conceal the erect nipples of her full breasts. Now she had not only Brown and Doogan to face in class, but Bryony as well. *Authority and respect?* she mused as Bryony finished dressing. Again believing that her only option was to leave Spadger Heath College, she smiled as Bryony walked to the lounge door.

'You do understand, don't you?' she said.

'No, I don't,' Bryony sighed, her head hung low, her golden locks falling over her pretty face. 'I'll never understand why two people can't love each other when they both know that they want to. If you were hungry and there was a plate of food in front of you, you'd eat it. Why deny yourself what you know you want and need? Goodbye, Miss.'

Hearing the front door slam shut, Christina sighed. Bryony was right, she reflected. But society wouldn't allow it. The rules and conventions of society had to be observed. Thinking again that, if no one knew of her illicit relationship with the girl, there'd be no harm in carrying on, she left the sofa and went to the front door to call her back. Hesitating, she mooched into the kitchen and filled the kettle. Never before had she known such a battle to rage in her mind. Right, wrong, society . . . Her head aching, she poured herself a cup of coffee and wandered into her room.

   Lying on her bed, Christina stared at the cracks in the ceiling. Wondering what Bryony was thinking, she recalled the young girl's tongue lapping between her pussy lips, her hot mouth sucking an orgasm out of her pulsating clitoris. 'No,' she breathed, wondering about seeing the girl again. She closed her eyes as sleep engulfed her and her coffee went cold while she dreamed her lesbian dreams.

4

Walking to the college, Christina knew that she was going to have to be strong. Avoiding Bryony's longing gaze wasn't going to be easy, but she had to compose herself and try to put the beautiful lesbian experience behind her. She would have loved to invite Bryony to her flat, strip her exquisitely young beauty and love her again, but . . . Love? Christina knew that there was a world of difference between love and lust. Or was there? Love, lust, hate. Such emotions were so complex that it was difficult to understand them, let alone differentiate between them. All Christina could do was try to forget about Bryony and return to normality.

Deciding to keep the stockroom locked, she was pleased that she'd worn a long skirt and high-necked blouse. Concealing her curves and mounds with drab clothes, she might not attract attention from certain randy students. Wandering into the classroom, she dumped her bag on the desk and sighed. This wasn't going to be a good day. She'd not planned her lesson, not slept well, and had missed breakfast. To make matters worse, images of Bryony's hairless pussy lips continually loomed in her racked mind. At least she had the afternoon free, giving her a chance to catch up on some sleep.

'Good morning, Brian,' Christina said cheerily, looking up as the would-be pimp walked into the classroom. 'You're bright and early.'

'Yeah,' he murmured, brushing his long hair away from his face. 'I've been hearing things about you.'

'Hearing things?' she echoed fearfully, her stomach churning. If this was about her escapades in the stock-room . . . She really didn't need this. 'You've heard nothing bad, I hope?'

'That depends, doesn't it?'

'Depends on what?'

'What you reckon is bad.'

'Why don't you just say what you want to say, Brian? It's rather early in the day to play games with words.'

'I thought we'd go into the stockroom and discuss my proposition,' he said, grinning.

'Proposition? Brian, you're not making any sense. What do you want to go into the stockroom for? Is there some thing you need? Some paper or . . .'

'There's something I need, all right,' he sniggered. 'I need you to give me a wank.'

'I *beg* your pardon?' Christina gasped, feigning shock. 'How dare you—'

'You can cut out the acting. Why don't you go to the old man and tell him that I've been a naughty boy?'

'I will, don't you worry. I'll go and see Mr Wright and—'

'And tell him that you wanked Baz Doogan?'

'Brian, I suggest you go and sit down. I think it best that I forget what you just said.'

'*You* might forget it, but other people won't when I tell them that you wanked Baz in the stockroom.'

'Are you threatening me?'

'Yes, I am. All I want is a quick wank. The others will be here soon. You've got about five minutes to decide.'

Biting her lip, Christina leaned on her desk and hung her head. The situation was crazy, she reflected, her breathing unsteady. Her third day at Spadger Heath was going to be the third day of a continuing nightmare. Doogan had obviously opened his mouth, probably boasting to half the school about Miss Shaw wanking him off in the stockroom. There was a choice, Christina decided. She could confine her stockroom masturbation sessions to the three lads on the condition that they tell no one. Or she could end it there and then and take the inevitable flak. The second option wasn't really viable, she concluded. The flak would become a full-scale blitz, not least from the headmaster. She'd already told the first two lads not to open their mouths. *Boys will be boys*, she reflected uneasily. If she complied with Brian's wish, he'd only go boasting to his friends.

'How many people has Doogan lied to?' she asked. 'He's told you some cock and bull story about me, obviously to make himself look big. How many other people has he told?'

'I don't think he's told anyone else. When he told me last night, he said that I was to keep my mouth shut. So what's it to be?'

'Barry and I have what I thought was a secret. Seeing as he's told you . . . If I let you in on our game, you must promise me that you'll tell no one.'

'Yeah, of course,' he said, leering.

'I mean it, Brian. One word to anyone, and that's it.'

'Yeah, yeah, OK.'

'Come into the stockroom, Brian.'

Taking the key from her bag and unlocking the door, Christina glanced at her watch. She had fifteen minutes or so before the others arrived. *Time enough to make another fatal mistake*, she mused, leading the boy into the room and closing the door. Having a supply of fresh teenager cock to play with pleased her, but the attendant dangers worried her. It didn't matter what the boys thought of her. A tart, a slag, a whore . . . But it was imperative that word of her indecent behaviour didn't get out. Too many students knew of her stockroom exploits as it was and, if the other teachers got wind of her sexual activities, she'd not only be out of a job but disgraced.

Scrutinizing Brian as he waited patiently for her intimate attention, she had a feeling of power over him. The students had thought that they'd had power over their new teacher, but the tables were turning. Their taunts and jibes were becoming less and there'd been little or no swearing. Perhaps this was the answer, she concluded. Come to an agreement with the ringleaders, wank their eager cocks regularly to keep their hormones under control . . .

'Well?' she said, looking down at Brian's crotch. 'Aren't you going to get it out?'

'Yes,' he murmured – almost sheepishly – as he tugged his zip down.

'You're not shy, are you?'

'No, no,' he replied, hauling his stiffening penis out of his trousers.

'Remember, one word of this to anyone and you'll get no more.'

'I know that.'

Taking the fleshy shaft of Brian's cock in her hand, Christina rolled his foreskin back and forth over his swollen knob with her thumb. A pang of arousal jolting her contracting womb, she realized that she enjoyed appeasing the boys' cocks as much as they enjoyed her intimate attention. What was Charles doing for sexual relief? she wondered. She thought once more about her life at home with her parents. Living in comparative luxury with no money worries had been fine, but she now realized how sheltered her life had been. She was hardly living a sheltered life now, she reflected. This was the third boy she'd wanked either by hand or mouth since starting at Spadger Heath College, not to mention her lesbian encounter with Bryony.

Watching Brian's purple knob appear and disappear as she rolled his foreskin back and forth, Christina thought about kneeling and taking his ripe plum into her thirsty mouth. Brown had enjoyed her mouthing and sucking, and Doogan had that pleasure to look forward to. Or did he? It was one thing being known for her illicit wanking, but quite another to be named a cock-sucker. Eyeing again Brian's swollen knob, his sperm-slit, she felt her knees bending. She was weakening in her arousal, she knew as she licked her full lips. Weakening in her arousal, and plunging ever deeper into her stupidity.

Again, she tried to justify her actions to herself. Wanking the three boys obviously wasn't the way most teachers behaved, but was it really that bad? They enjoyed it, she was beginning to love it, and she could get on with her lessons uninterrupted. Although she'd planned to talk to Alison about her problems, she now thought it best not to mention anything. Her thinking was changing. What she'd initially looked upon as a problem was now becoming most pleasurable. Wanking the teenagers to orgasm, bringing out their fresh spunk . . . Was that a problem? Only if word got round, she mused again. Keep this secret, and she'd not only enjoy the lads' solid cocks but she'd keep her job.

As Brian gasped, his young body trembling, Christina watched his spunk jetting from his twitching knob-head. Splattering over the floor, the white liquid flowed in torrents from his orgasming cock, and she began to wish that she'd engulfed his purple glans in her mouth and swallowed his sex juices. *Maybe next time*, she reflected, her clitoris rousing, emerging from beneath its pinken hood. Sperm running over her hand, she brought out the last of the lad's pleasure and released his young cock. His face flushed, his legs sagging, he shuddered as he leaned against the wall to steady himself.

Number three, Christina reflected, lapping up the sperm from her hand as Brian watched in amazement. Cleaning her fingers, the taste of sperm lingering on her tongue, she opened the door and ordered him out of the room. Obediently following her instructions, he sat at his desk as she closed the stockroom door and turned the key. *Stockroom?* she mused. *Sex room, more like.* Pleased to think that she only had to get through the morning, she sorted through her papers as the students filed into the classroom. An afternoon off, relaxing at home, was just what she needed.

'Is it all right if I come round this evening?' Bryony asked as she approached Christina's desk.

'No,' Christina said firmly, gazing into the girl's sparkling eyes. 'Go to your desk and sit down, please.'

'How can you be like this after—'

'Do as you're told, Bryony.'

'You'll be sorry,' the girl snapped, mooching across the room to her desk.

Sighing, Christina hoped that this particular student

wasn't going to cause problems. She knew only too well that, at Bryony's tender age, the girl's hormones would be running wild and she might do something stupid Bryony obviously believed that she was in love. Hormones, love, lust . . . They were lethal ingredients that could easily explode into a very dangerous situation. Christina did her best to get through the morning, despite one or two disruptions from a couple of boys who weren't under her control – yet.

Checking Bryony's address before she left the college, Christina decided to visit the girl's mother. She wasn't sure what she was going to say, but she wanted to get an idea of Bryony's home life, perhaps get a chance to look around. The girl might well have been lying, making out that she lived in a hell-hole to gain some sympathy. Perhaps her mother was really a loving woman who kept the home nice and cooked decent meals for her daughter. Knocking on the front door, Christina's first impression wasn't favourable. The small front garden was a mass of weeds and rubbish and the front window had been broken and boarded up.

'Yes?' a scruffy middle-aged woman asked as she opened the door.

'Hello,' Christina smiled. 'I'm Bryony's teacher and—'

'You'd better come in,' the woman snapped, walking down the hall. 'What's the little slut done now?'

'Oh, she hasn't done anything,' Christina said, closing the door and following the woman into the front room. 'I just thought that . . .'

Her words tailing off as she looked around the room and breathed in the unmistakable smell of alcohol fumes, Christina shook her head. The place really was a tip.

Clothes and newspapers strewn everywhere, empty gin bottles littering every available shelf – she realized that Bryony had been telling the truth. Although Christina felt sorry for the girl, she knew that she couldn't invite her to her flat and befriend her. Befriend her? Bryony didn't want friendship, she wanted lesbian sex. Declining the offer of a seat as the girl's mother pushed a pile of clothes off the armchair, Christina asked her whether she was managing to cope with her daughter.

'Cope with her?' she scoffed. 'There's no *coping* with the little slut. She does nothing around the house, nothing to help me. All she does is sit in her room.'

'May I see her room?' Christina asked.

'See what you like. It's top of the stairs, on the right.'

Climbing the stairs, Christina didn't know why she'd gone to the house. She'd gain nothing by speaking to her mother, or by looking at Bryony's room. Opening the door, she gazed at the neatly made bed, a row of books lined up on a shelf above a small desk. Bryony was obviously doing her best to lead a normal life, Christina mused. Albeit under extremely difficult circumstances. Opening the bedside table drawer, she knew that she shouldn't be rummaging through the girl's things. It was just that she wanted to know more about Bryony, what sort of person she was.

Christina frowned as she pulled out a small vibrator. The pink shaft was encrusted with dried vaginal juice, and she imagined the girl lying in her bed taking herself to massive orgasms. Switching the device on, she smiled as it buzzed softly in her hand. Bryony shaved her pussy, used a vibrator . . . *Hormones running amok*, Christina told herself, slipping the vibrator back into the drawer. Leaving the room, she closed the door and went downstairs to the lounge.

'She keeps her bedroom nice,' she said, gazing at the woman sprawled across the sofa. 'Does she have a boy-friend?'

'God knows what she gets up to. I never know whether she's in or out, let alone screwing boys. Knowing that little slut, she's probably—'

'Why do you call her a slut?'

'Her father went off with a girl not much older than Bryony. All teenage girls are sluts.'

'Well, I'll be going,' Christina said, forcing a smile.

'I'll tell her you called.'

'Yes, please do that. Goodbye.'

Leaving the house, Christina realized that Bryony needed some help. Her mother's attitude towards young girls was understandable, but why had her father walked out? There were two sides to every story, Christina reflected, wondering what Charles was doing. Walking the short distance to her flat, she knew that it would be a mistake to invite Bryony there. But she felt that she had to do something. Perhaps, the next time Alison was out for the evening, she'd ask the girl to call round for a chat. *Only a chat*, she vowed, dumping her bag on the hall table.

Filling the kettle, she didn't realize that Alison was in until the girl appeared in the kitchen doorway dressed only in her bra and panties. Scrutinizing the mounds of her breasts, her nipples pushing against the thin silk cups, Christina felt her womb contract. She had to drag her gaze away from her flatmate's curvaceous young body, she knew as she offered her a cup of coffee. Lesbian sex with Bryony was one thing, but to . . .

'How long have you been back?' Christina asked, spooning coffee into two cups.

'About an hour,' Alison replied. 'I didn't expect you home.'

'I have the afternoon off.'

'The afternoon off? I thought teachers worked long hours.'

'They do. Although I'm not at the college right now, I'm still supposed to be preparing lessons. How are your parents?'

'They're OK. We . . . we had a long chat. My mother and I don't agree on certain issues.'

'Oh?'

'She can't accept me, the way I am. Anyway, what did you get up to last night?'

'Oh, er . . . Nothing, really. I stayed in and relaxed.'

'Who was your visitor?'

'Visitor?' Christina echoed, wondering whether Alison knew about Bryony. 'I didn't have a visitor.'

'I found a pair of panties in the lounge. They were tucked beneath the sofa.'

'Oh, they're mine,' Christina said, averting her gaze as Alison stared hard at her.

'Your name's B. Johnson, is it?'

'Er . . . I don't understand.'

'It's all right, you don't have to tell me what you get up to.'

'I haven't been up to anything, Alison. OK, so one of my students came to see me. I wasn't going to mention it since it's not allowed. The college don't like—'

'Not allowed? You think I'd tell them?'

'No, no. It's just that . . . Bryony is a mixed-up girl.'

'And a lesbian?'

'Yes. No . . . I mean . . .'

'Christina, my mother can't accept me because I'm a lesbian.'

'Oh, er . . . Right.'

'Are you?'

'No, no, I . . . Look, we need to talk. Let's take our coffee into the lounge.'

Walking through the hall, Christina wondered why she wasn't shocked by the girl's revelation. *Alison, a lesbian? I'm living with a lesbian*, she thought, wondering whether that would change things. She knew that she was going to have to put her cards on the table. Alison had admitted that she was a lesbian, and Christina felt that she owed it to the other girl to be honest. How was it possible to be honest, though? she mused. She didn't know whether she was a lesbian or not, so honesty didn't come into it. Sitting in the armchair as Alison reclined on the sofa, she recalled her flatmate's words. *I haven't even laid eyes on a dick, let alone my hands*. Wondering why the girl had said that, she assumed that she was trying to conceal her lesbianism by making out that she fancied men.

'So you don't want to lay your hands on a dick, then?' Christina asked.

'My hands . . . Oh, you mean what I said in the pub the other night. I didn't know your thoughts or feelings on the matter. We were getting on very well. Sharing the flat was working out well and I didn't want to ruin everything.'

'Have you got a girlfriend?'

'No, no. I did have but . . . That finished months ago. So, tell me about this Bryony girl.'

'There's nothing to tell, really,' Christina sighed.

'Nothing to tell?' Alison giggled. 'I find her panties

beneath the sofa, and you say there's nothing to tell? How long has this been going on?'

'It hasn't. God, this is only my third day at the college. She came here once, and that was last night. I left her in here and, when I got back, she'd stripped off.'

'And?'

'And . . . and we . . . you know?'

'Yes, I think I do. How old is she?'

'Eighteen, I think. Look, Alison, it was a one-off. I'm not a lesbian. At least, I don't think I am.'

'I remember going through that stage. I was fourteen when I got friendly with a girl in my class at school. We went for a walk in the park and ended up in the woods. At first, we were only mucking about, experimenting sexually. We talked about masturbation and one thing led to another. We were together, as a couple, for about a year. I learned a lot about myself during that time. I discovered that I wasn't interested in the boys and . . . I finally let myself go, found my own path. I'd been fighting my feelings, my desires. Once I stopped fighting, I began to enjoy my sexuality. So, you're not interested in the teenage hulks in your class?'

'That's just it,' Christina sighed. 'I've . . . I've been with three boys since I started at the college.'

'Been with . . . ?'

'No, no. I mean . . . I masturbated them. In fact, I sucked one of them off. God, you must think me awful.'

'Not at all. My only concern would be the scandal if it came to light.'

'I've thought about that. In fact, that's *all* I've thought about. I'm in a mess, aren't I?'

'No, I don't think so. What did you feel after you'd been with Bryony?'

'I don't know. That's the problem, I don't know.'

'I'll tell you what I did. I was only fourteen, of course. But I met this girl again, and we masturbated each other again. I still wasn't sure what I was or what I wanted so I saw her again. That time, we went further. You know, licking and sucking each other to orgasm. I think it must have been after that third time that I made my mind up. We'd been naked in the woods, kissing, licking, mouthing . . . Once I'd let myself go and got into it, I realized that I'd never known anything like it. As I said, we were together for a year or so. If I were you, I'd see this Bryony again and—'

'There are complications, Alison. Her mother, her home life . . . There are far too many complications. Apart from that, she's too young.'

'In that case, discover your true sexual identity by going with an older girl.'

Averting her gaze, Christina wondered whether Alison was suggesting that she have a sexual relationship with *her*. The girl was quite attractive, Christina thought. But to have sex with her . . . Everything would change, she reflected. They'd be in each other's beds, they'd no longer enjoy the privacy of their own rooms . . . Christina had made enough mistakes for one week. To embark on a sexual relationship with Alison would only add to the mess.

'Tell me what you think,' Alison said, rising to her feet and unhooking her bra. Her full breasts tumbling from the silk cups, her nipples stiffening pertly in the relatively cool air of the lounge, she tossed the garment over the back of the chair as Christina gazed open-mouthed at her. Slipping her thumbs between the tight elastic of her panties and her shapely hips, Alison began to pull the garment down. The top of her sex crack came into view and she lowered her panties further, revealing the full length of her creamy pinken slit to Christina's wide-eyed stare.

' 'Well?' Alison smiled.

'I've seen you naked before,' Christina replied, focusing on the girl's ruby inner lips peeping from her sex crack.

'You've *seen* but you haven't *touched*,' Alison said huskily, walking across the room and standing in front of Christina. 'Go on, touch me.'

Reaching out, Christina stroked the soft swell of her flatmate's vaginal lips, her fingertip tentatively brushing the sensitive petals of her inner labia. She tried to fight her inner desire, the overwhelming feeling to move forward and lick the creamy valley of the other girl's pussy. Taking Alison's fleshy outer lips between her fingers and thumbs, she peeled the soft sex pads apart, exposing the wet inner flesh of her sex valley. Examining the girl there, she focused on her ripening clitoris. The pink budling emerging from beneath its fleshy hood, swelling as her arousal heightened, Alison let out a rush of breath as Christina stretched her outer labia further apart, opening her vulval cleft as wide as she could without causing pain.

'Feel inside me,' Alison breathed, looking down at her open vaginal valley. Stroking the pink funnel of flesh surrounding the entrance to her friend's sex sheath, Christina slipped her finger deep into the fiery heat of her wet duct. Massaging the fleshy walls of her vagina, caressing her urethral opening, she twisted and bent her finger, sending the girl into raptures of sexual pleasure. Alison's legs sagged beneath her trembling body as she clung to Christina's head to support herself while the girl drove a second finger into the tightening duct of her sex-drenched pussy.

Having wanked Brian and brought out his sperm that morning, Christina couldn't believe that she now had two fingers embedded deep within the wet sheath of her flatmate's tight pussy. There was going to be no end to her sexual encounters, she knew as she turned her thoughts to Bryony. The girl was so young, fresh, curvaceous, alluring . . . Imagining her lying in her bed with her legs wide apart, the buzzing tip of her vibrator pressed against the solid nub of her clitoris, Christina felt a quiver run through her young womb.

Was it possible to fall in love with another girl? she wondered, easing a third finger into Alison's tightening vaginal duct. Christina had never known love, and was now beginning to believe that love, lust and sex were one and the same. Licking and masturbating a girl to orgasm wasn't love, she reflected. And yet it hadn't been purely cold sex with Bryony. There had been something else in their caressing, their licking – but what? Love was indefinable, she concluded, slipping her creamy-wet fingers out of Alison's hot vaginal duct.

Moving forward, Christina parted the other girl's fleshy love lips and pressed her mouth hard against the glistening pink flesh surrounding her erect clitoris. Alison gasped and shuddered as Christina's tongue repeatedly swept over the sensitive tip of her pleasure nodule. Placing one foot on the sofa, she thrust her hips forward, grinding her cunt flesh hard against Christina's hot mouth, sighing in her ecstasy as her immensely responsive clitoris transmitted ripples of pure sexual pleasure deep into her trembling womb.

'Enjoying yourself?' Alison asked, looking down at Christina. Nodding her head, Christina sucked on the girl's solid clitoris and slipped three fingers deep into the spasming sheath of her tight vagina. More than merely enjoying herself, she was loving with a passion every instant of sucking and fingering her friend's pussy. Managing to force all four fingers deep into the stretched sheath of Alison's vagina, she kneaded her inner flesh. Sucking and licking her swollen clitoris, she knew that her lesbian flatmate was nearing her orgasm as she let out whimpers of satisfaction.

'Oh, God,' Alison murmured, clutching Christina's head as her clitoris exploded in orgasm. Her ejaculatory juices streaming down Christina's hand, she shuddered violently as her lesbian-induced pleasure peaked. 'God, my beautiful cunt,' she whimpered, the crude word surprising Christina and, at the same time, sending her own arousal through the roof. Sustaining the girl's orgasm, Christina repeatedly thrust her fingers deep into the wet heat of her vagina and mouthed and sucked on her pulsating clitoris. Breathing in her girl-scent, savouring the taste of her clitoris, Christina knew that this was only the beginning of the lesbian affair. They'd be having sex at every opportunity now, enjoying each other's naked bodies, loving and licking, sucking and mouthing . . .

'That's enough,' Alison finally gasped, her curvaceous young body crumpling to the floor as Christina's wet fingers left the tight sheath of the girl's inflamed pussy. Lying on the carpet with her limbs spread, Alison's naked body convulsed and twitched as she recovered from her girl-induced climax. Christina watched her flatmate's juices of arousal trickling from her rubicund sex crack, the creamy fluid running down between her rounded buttocks and pooling on the floor.

Would Alison reciprocate? she wondered, recalling Bryony's tongue lapping between her vaginal lips. Gazing at Alison's pretty mouth, her full red lips, Christina wasn't sure whether she wanted to experience lesbian sex with two girls in two days. *Three lads and two girls in three days*? she reflected, her clitoris swelling in expectation. She recalled her flatmate's words. *I'd been fighting my feelings, my desires. Once I stopped fighting, I began to enjoy my sexuality*. Realizing that she had to give herself a chance to discover her true sexual identity, she decided to offer her young body to Alison for lesbian sex.

'I enjoyed that,' she said, looking down at Alison as her naked body stopped writhing. Alison stretched languorously before adopting a cross-legged sitting position on the floor.

'And so did I,' Alison giggled, her sparkling eyes gazing longingly up at Christina. 'There are things I could teach you,' she murmured. 'Things that . . . I think it would be best to take you slowly along the path to true lesbian sex.'

'And how do you intend to do that?' Christina asked, her stomach somersaulting.

'Slip your panties off, lie back on the sofa with your legs open – and I'll show you.'

Lifting her superbly rounded buttocks clear of the sofa, Christina pulled her panties off and reclined, her thighs parted. As Alison settled at her feet and pulled her skirt up over her stomach, she imagined Charles walking in and discovering the shocking truth. Charles would be horrified – he'd call her a filthy slut, a whore. Wondering whether to tell him that she'd found true love with another girl, Christina let out a rush of breath as Alison parted the swollen lips of her vagina and teased the nub of her erect clitoris with the tip of her wet tongue.

Alison knew exactly what to do, Christina thought as the girl's tongue lightly brushed the tip of her sensitive clitoris again. She could feel her juices of lesbian arousal seeping between the engorged wings of her inner vaginal lips, trickling down to the sensitive brown tissue surrounding her bottom-hole. Gasping as her flatmate ran her fingertip over the funnel of pink flesh surrounding the gaping entrance to her contracting vaginal canal, expertly teasing her there, Christina closed her eyes and let herself go.

'That's it,' Alison murmured, her wet tongue caressing the tip of Christina's solid clitoris. 'Relax completely. Close your eyes and let me take you to your sexual heaven.' Her firm young breasts and stomach quivering with nervous desire, Christina parted her thighs as widely as she could, offering the most intimate sexual centre of her beautiful body to her lesbian friend. She could hear the slurping sounds of sex as Alison's tongue worked around the wet portal to her drenched pussy. Lapping up her cunt milk, the girl slipped her tongue into Christina's hot sex shaft, teasing her inner flesh, working on her sensitive urethral opening. To Christina's surprise, Alison moved down, her wet tongue delving between the firm orbs of Christina's buttocks, as if trying to gain access to the tightly closed ring of her anus.

'It's all right,' Alison reassured her student of lesbian sex. 'Move forward on the sofa so your bum is over the edge of the cushion.' Complying, Christina slid down the sofa, the small of her back resting on the edge of the cushion, her thighs still parted wide. She could feel

Alison's wet tongue delving into her anal valley, the girl's saliva mingling with her own juices of sex as she parted the warm globes of her bottom. Gasping, Christina reached beneath her young body and yanked her buttocks wide apart as her flatmate's tongue teased her brown ring, tasting and wetting her there.

'God,' she breathed as the tip of Alison's tongue slipped into her anal hole. 'Alison, I . . . Oh, God. This isn't right.' Ignoring her, Alison continued her anal French kissing, pushing her wet tongue deeper into Christina's tight rectum. Writhing and squirming on the sofa as the new and exciting sensations permeated her very being, Christina yanked the rounded cheeks of her buttocks further apart, offering the open hole of her anus to her lesbian friend.

If Charles could see me now, she thought, imagining the young man's face as he witnessed the crude lesbian anilingus. Had Charles paid Christina's young body this kind of attention, had he taken her to these amazing sexual heights . . . But he hadn't. Charles had only driven his solid cock into Christina's vagina and spunked her cervix, never giving a thought to her feminine needs, to her true pleasure. Charles had lost, Christina reflected, her young body quivering as Alison licked the creamy-wet walls of her tightening vagina. His pompous attitude, his seeming obliviousness to Christina's feminine desires . . . No doubt he'd find a girl who would be willing to lie back and allow him to satisfy his cock once a week. But he'd never experience the crudities of sex, the blissful sensations of anilingus. Charles had lost.

Her body jolting as Alison thrust a finger deep into the hot tube of her rectum, Christina could hardly believe the wondrous sensations produced by the crude act. She could feel the delicate tissue of her anus gripping the girl's pistoning finger, the secret nerve endings tingling as her young womb rhythmically contracted and her juices of desire gushed from the gaping entrance of her tight pussy. Alison was good, she mused as the girl thrust at least two fingers into the wet heat of Christina's vaginal sheath, massaging the thin membrane dividing her sex ducts with her double pistoning.

Christina let out whimpers of sexual bliss as her young friend sucked her ripe clitoris into her hot mouth and swept her tongue over its sensitive tip. Her body glowing, alive with the thrill of crude sex, Christina threw her head back, her eyes rolling, her nostrils flaring as Alison held her on the verge of orgasm. Teetering of the brink of ecstasy, the walls of convention crumbling, she finally accepted that she was bisexual if not a full-blown lesbian. Imagining a boy's cock sperming in her mouth, the creamy liquid overflowing and dribbling down her chin as she drank from the throbbing knob, she cried out as her orgasm erupted within the pulsating nubble of her solid clitoris.

'More, more,' she gasped, her young body shaking violently, her juices of Sapphic arousal streaming from her contracting vagina and flooding over Alison's hand as she repeatedly thrust her fingers in and out of Christina's inflamed sex holes. Convulsing wildly, Christina screamed out as her pleasure ripped through her nervous system, gripping her very soul. If this was taking her slowly along the path to true lesbian sex, then what other sexual delights would she encounter during her journey, she wondered. If this was just the beginning of the road to lesbian fulfilment, then what unimaginable ecstasy lay in wait at the end?

'All right?' Alison asked as Christina's orgasm began to wane.

'Yes, yes,' she breathed, her naked thighs twitching uncontrollably. 'God, I've never—'

'Just relax,' Alison murmured, slowing her double finger-thrusting. 'Come down slowly. This evening, I'll take you higher. This evening, I'll love you like you've never been loved before.'

'Yes, yes,' Christina breathed again, her mind spinning in her sexual delirium.

Her flatmate's fingers finally sliding out of her inflamed sex sheaths, Christina lay quivering on the sofa in the aftermath of her girl-induced pleasure. Her thoughts drifting, she pictured Bryony's hairless vulval lips, the young girl's clitoris pulsating in orgasm. Images of teenage boys' swollen knobs spunking in her mouth loomed in her racked mind, heavy balls, solid penile shafts, fleshy cunt labia, the unfurling petals of inner lips dripping with girl-cum . . .

Sleep creeping up on her as Alison took the quilt from her bed and covered her sated body, Christina felt warm, satisfied, fulfilled, loved. Everything was working out well, she reflected. Her first three days at the college, her flatmate . . . Nothing would go wrong. The boys were happy, Alison was happy, Bryony . . . Bryony would be all right. Christina would take the girl slowly along the path to true lesbian sex. Everything was going to be all right. Wasn't it?

5

Christina woke to find herself alone in the flat. She felt hot and sticky around her vulval area. Her sex juices partially dried on her smooth thighs, her sparse pubic curls matted on her Venus mound, she took a shower before making herself a cup of coffee. As she sat at the kitchen table, wondering where Alison had got to, she pondered on the forthcoming evening. Alcohol would loosen her up, she mused, deciding to get in some vodka for the hours of lesbian lust ahead. Did she need to loosen up? She'd done pretty well with Alison. Letting go, relaxing, offering her young body to the girl for crude sex . . . Vodka would wipe out any remaining inhibitions, she decided, wondering whether she should tongue Alison's bottom-hole.

Anilingus would be interesting. Licking and sucking a girl's anus, tasting her there, tonguing inside the tight tube of her rectum . . . There was nothing more intimate, she concluded. From straight sex with Charles to lesbian sex *and* crude anal tonguing . . . there was nothing more perverse. Or was there? Christina had never given a second thought to her bottom-hole. Charles had probably thought that it hadn't existed, using only her vagina to satisfy his cock. What would Alison's anus taste like?

The notion sending quivers through her young womb, Christina began to wonder whether she was in some way abnormal. Her overwhelming desire to commit anilingus on another girl wasn't normal, surely? She knew nothing about other girls' sex lives, but she couldn't imagine any of her friends licking each other's anuses. But as long as the crude act was committed in the privacy of her flat, no one would think badly of her, she decided, her pink tongue licking her succulent lips as she imagined tasting Alison's anal portal. Would Bryony enjoy anilingus?

As the evening drew near, Christina slipped out to the local off-licence and bought two bottles of vodka and some orange juice. The scene was set, she mused, slipping a CD into the hi-fi and placing the drinks and glasses on the lounge table. All set for an evening of crude lesbian lust. Wearing a short red skirt and white blouse, with no panties or bra underneath these revealing outer garments, she felt her clitoris swell as she waited for Alison to return. Again wondering where the girl had got to, she poured herself a vodka and orange and sat on the sofa. Sipping her drink, the alcohol quickly taking effect, the soft music drifting lazily around the room, her juices of desire flowing between her engorged love lips . . . All she needed now was her lesbian lover.

'She's probably in the lounge,' Alison said, closing the front door. Wondering who the girl had brought back to the flat, Christina felt her stomach churning. This was supposed to be *their* evening, an evening of love, lust, crude sex. Alison must have bumped into a friend. Perhaps it was a fleeting visit, a quick cup of coffee and a look around the flat before leaving. Perhaps the evening was about to be ruined. As the lounge door opened and Alison appeared, Christina looked up.

'Guess who I found hovering outside?' Alison said, her pretty face beaming.

'Found outside?' Christina murmured, frowning. 'I don't know.'

'Hello,' Bryony said softly, following Alison into the room.

'Bryony, I . . .'

'I said that she could join us,' Alison announced, licking her succulent lips provocatively.

'Is that all right?' Bryony asked. 'I mean, you don't mind?'

'No, I . . . I suppose it's all right.'

Bryony sat on the sofa next to Christina, her short skirt revealing her naked thighs as she leaned back. Was she wearing panties? Had she used her vibrator? Christina wondered whether Alison had a threesome in mind, three-way lesbian sex. Not sure whether she wanted to be part of any such games, Christina wondered what to do. This wasn't how it was meant to be. Sex with her flatmate and one of her students? This wasn't what she'd envisaged. Besides, Bryony was too young for such things. Watching Alison pour a glass of vodka and orange and pass it to the younger girl, Christina knew that this could easily get out of hand. Bryony was naive, gullible, and probably easily led. If the girl drank too much and Alison suggested three-way sex . . .

'This is cosy,' Alison said, smiling at Christina. 'Bryony, why don't you go into the bathroom and get ready?'

'Get ready?' the girl echoed questioningly.

'Aren't you going to slip out of your clothes?'

'Oh, er . . . yes, all right,' she replied, leaving the sofa. Knocking back her drink, she placed her glass on the table and moved to the door. 'I won't be a minute.'

'Alison,' Christina whispered as the door closed. 'I don't think this is a good idea.'

'I think it's a *great* idea,' the other girl retorted. 'She wants sex. And who better than us to—'

'I was trying to break off my relationship with her – such as it is,' Christina added hastily. 'She's too young, for starters. She's a student of mine, she believes that she's in love with me . . .'

'Too young, my tongue-hungry arse. Let yourself go, Christina. Just relax and enjoy the evening. I have an idea. Bryony can be our sex slave.'

'*What*?'

'We'll tell her what to do, instruct her in the ways of—'

'Alison . . .'

'Shush, I think she's coming back.'

As the younger girl walked into the room, Christina gazed longingly at the violin curves of her teenage body, the petite mounds of her breasts, the hairless lips of her vulva. She was beautiful, eager, willing . . . But surely it wouldn't be a good idea to use her as a sex slave. Christina realized that she didn't know Alison at all. Although the girl had seemed fairly quiet and reserved at first, she obviously had hidden erotic fantasies. How deep did her sexual desires run? Christina wondered. Suggesting that they should use Bryony as a sex slave wasn't what Christina had expected of her flatmate. There again, she'd not thought that Alison was a lesbian before they'd licked and . . . But then, wasn't Christina herself a lesbian?

'You have a lovely body,' Alison said, refilling the younger girl's glass. 'There, drink that.'

'Thanks,' Bryony murmured, taking her drink. 'I didn't know that you lived with another girl,' she said, looking at Christina.

'Yes, er, er . . . we share the flat.'

Sitting in the armchair and scrutinizing Bryony's curves and crevices, Alison licked her full red lips. 'Why don't you come and stand over here?' she asked. 'I'd like to take a closer look at you.'

Following Alison's instructions, Bryony stood in front of her and allowed her to stroke the petite mounds of her mammary spheres, the fleshy swell of her hairless vaginal lips. Christina watched Alison's hands wandering over the girl's naked body, running over her hips, cupping the firm moons of her buttocks. Christina had to admit that the sight aroused her, but she was still in two minds about allowing her young student to be used like this.

'Turn round and bend over,' Alison ordered the girl. Christina gazed in awe as Bryony leaned over and touched the floor, her naked buttocks projected, the gully of her bottom unashamedly displayed. Parting the full moons of her firm young arse, Alison moved forward on the chair and swept her tongue up and down the girl's anal valley, obviously delighting in the crude act, the bitter-sweet taste of her anus, as she fervently slurped and mouthed between Bryony's bum cheeks.

Her stomach somersaulting, Christina wondered whether she was jealous as she heard the young student's gasps of lesbian pleasure and watched her naked body trembling. Then, recalling Alison's words, she decided to let go and enjoy herself as she settled on the floor beside Bryony. Parting the fleshy swell of the girl's naked vaginal lips, she thrust three fingers deep into her tightening pussy and massaged her creamy inner flesh as Alison licked her sensitive anal ring with her wet tongue. Bryony shuddered, letting out whimpers of pleasure as both holes were expertly stimulated. Perhaps the evening wasn't going to be so bad after all, Christina mused, her fingers squelching the girl's pussy juices.

'You've been a naughty little girl,' Alison hissed, slapping Bryony's rounded buttocks with her palm.

'Ouch,' Bryony cried as the next slap resounded around the room and her naked body jolted.

'A *very* naughty little girl.'

Christina watched as Alison spanked the girl's firm anal orbs, wondering whether her flatmate was in control of her senses as she giggled wickedly. Bryony let out a yelp with every slap on her naked bottom, her young body trembling uncontrollably as Christina slipped her fingers out of her vaginal sheath. This wasn't right, Christina thought, watching Alison stand up. Holding the girl still with one hand and spanking her bum cheeks as hard as she could with the other, she seemed to be delighting in her dominant role. Was this what she'd had in mind for Christina? Had she gazed at Christina's bottom billowing her short skirt and imagined spanking her there?

'Alison,' Christina murmured. 'I don't think—'

'She's our sex slave,' the girl interrupted, grinning. 'Sex slaves should be taught their place.'

'Please, that's enough,' Bryony whimpered, struggling to stand up.

'I've barely started,' Alison chuckled, repeatedly spanking the girl's reddening bottom orbs. 'You *do* want to be our friend, don't you, Bryony?'

'Yes, but . . .'

'In that case, you'll do as you're told.'

Sitting on her heels, Christina watched the gruelling spanking, sure that Bryony could escape Alison's grip if she really wanted to. This wasn't lesbian sex, she reflected. Where was the pleasure, the loving caress of female fingertips, the gentle massaging? Confused, Christina imagined having her own buttocks spanked by Alison. Would she derive pleasure or pain from the cruel act? she pondered. Or both? Although whimpering and putting up what in any case looked like a perfunctory struggle, Bryony seemed to be enjoying the experience. But Alison shouldn't have exploited the fact that Bryony was young and lonely and needed friends.

'Are you going to behave yourself now?' Alison asked the trembling girl.

'Yes, yes, I will,' Bryony whimpered.

'You may stand up now and undress me.'

'All right.'

'All right, *mistress*.'

'All right, mistress.'

Christina was learning, she knew as she watched Bryony unbuttoning Alison's blouse. The girl's buttocks glowing a fire-red, her juices of lesbian desire running in rivers down her inner thighs, she slipped the blouse over her mistress's shoulders and unhooked her bra. Bryony was obviously enjoying playing the role of a slave. Perhaps she'd done this before? Christina reflected. She was into vibrators, and might well have a girlfriend she shared her young body with. Perhaps they regularly spanked each other. Gazing at Alison's stiffening nipples, the darkening discs of her areolae as their slave removed her clothing, Christina wondered whether spanking was something she wanted to learn about. Spanking, pain, pleasure . . . Alison would probably be into bondage next, Christina mused as she climbed to her feet. If she wasn't already.

Pouring herself a large vodka and orange as Bryony

tugged Alison's skirt down to her ankles, Christina settled on the sofa to watch the lesbian show. She wasn't sure whether she wanted to join in, deciding to let the girls get on with it and perhaps make up a threesome later in the evening. Feeling left out, she watched Bryony tug Alison's panties down to her ankles. Bryony was supposed to have been Christina's friend, her secret lesbian lover, but now . . .

'I need a tongue bath,' Alison said, kneeling on the floor and resting her head on the armchair cushion. 'Lick my bottom, slave.'

'Yes, mistress,' Bryony replied, settling obediently on the floor behind Alison.

Kneeling between Alison's spread legs Bryony parted the girl's naked anal orbs and exposed the brown ring of her tightly closed anus. Watching with bated breath, Christina felt her clitoris inflate as Bryony moved forward, her pink tongue emerging between her full lips. Tentatively licking Alison's brown anal tissue, she began slurping fervently at the girl's bottom-hole. Obviously savouring the taste of her mistress's most private orifice, she yanked her anal cheeks wider apart and moaned softly through her nose.

Christina felt a pang of jealousy as she recalled Bryony's first visit to the flat and pictured her naked body, her petite breasts. Her breasts were barely formed, the small mounds cone-shaped, the areolae appearing to be pulled out by the elongated nipples. Christina pondered on the situation once more as Bryony followed Alison's orders and pushed her tongue deep into her rectal duct. This wasn't how it was supposed to be. Bryony was very young – she needed nurturing, loving. Again, Christina felt left out. But there was nothing she could do other than join the girls in their illicit lesbian pleasure.

'Finger my arsehole,' Alison murmured, her naked body trembling as she projected her buttocks further. Her crude words sending Christina's own arousal sky-high, Alison moaned softly as Bryony pushed the tip of her fingers past her yielding anal sphincter muscles. 'Come and join us,' Alison said, turning her head and gazing at Christina. Leaving the sofa, Christina settled on the floor and held Alison's rounded buttocks wide apart as Bryony drove her finger deep into the girl's tight rectal tube.

Christina had never seen the crude act of anal fingering. Gazing at Alison's delicate brown tissue stretched tautly around Bryony's finger, she pulled her flatmate's firm buttocks wider apart, allowing the girl better access to her mistress's anal canal. Following Alison's instructions, Bryony managed to force a second finger into her dilating anus. To her horror, Christina was overwhelmed by a compelling need to commit vulgar sexual acts on her flatmate. She imagined forcing a candle deep into the girl's rectal sheath, pushing a plastic deodorant bottle into her anal canal and abusing her. *Is this normal?* she wondered, grinning as Bryony managed to drive a third finger into Alison's anal tight duct.

Far removed from her life with her parents in a beautiful country house, Christina was discovering a new world. A world of impoverishment in a run-down part of London, a world of crude lesbian sex. More than a culture shock, this was something that Christina had never envisaged. She'd thought that she'd be teaching her students English, not the fine art of masturbation, blow jobs and lesbian sex. She'd imagined meeting a nice young man, perhaps embarking on a relationship leading to . . . It didn't matter what she'd expected, she realized that she was now part of that new world.

Leaning over, Christina licked Alison's naked buttocks, keeping her eye on the girl's painfully stretched
anal ring as Bryony fingered her bottom-hole. Did she
want to lick Alison there? Did she want to taste her anus,
savour the bitter-sweet flavour of her most private hole?
As Bryony withdrew her fingers in readiness to thrust
into her mistress again, Christina licked Alison's taut
anal tissue. Lapping fervently too at Bryony's fingers,
her taste buds alive, she closed her eyes and lost herself in
her sexual delirium.

It was the sheer crudity of the act that drove her on,
sent her arousal soaring – she knew that as she tongued
Alison's dark anal eye. As Bryony slipped her fingers out
of the girl's anal duct, Christina pushed her tongue into
Alison's bottom-hole and locked her lips to her brown
tissue. Sucking hard, licking deep inside her rectal
sheath, she thought that she could plunge no deeper
into the mire of lewdness. Her nose pressed hard against
her flatmate's bared anal gully, she breathed in her rectal
scent. There was nothing more decadent, more debased,
she reflected, forcing her wet tongue deeper into Alison's
delicious rectum.

'Bryony, go to my room and look in the dressing-table
drawer,' Alison breathed, her firm buttocks twitching.
'You'll find my vibrator there. I want it up my arse.'

Licking her lips, Christina sat up and watched Bryony
leave the room. Both girls had vibrators, she mused,
wondering why she'd never owned one. She'd missed
out, she knew as her thoughts turned to Charles. Oral
sex, anal fingering, clitoral vibrating . . . She'd led the
life of a nun. As Bryony returned, clutching a huge
vibrator, Christina was sure that Alison's rectum would
never accommodate the massive pink shaft. Passing the

device to Christina, Bryony yanked Alison's rounded bum cheeks wide apart, exposing the salivated brown ring of her tight anus.

'Do it,' Alison murmured, wiggling her hips as she made herself comfortable. Pressing the rounded tip of the vibrator hard against the girl's anal tissue, Christina pushed and twisted the shaft. Amazed as the plastic phallus drove into the girl, her delicate anal tissue dilating as the tapered shaft sank deep into her rectal canal, Christina switched the device on. Shaking violently, Alison let out cries of sheer sexual bliss as the pink shaft drove deeper into her hot bowels, transmitting its electrifying vibrations into her contracting womb.

Withdrawing the buzzing vibrator until only the tip remained in Alison's rectum, Christina licked the pink shaft. Salivating the hot phallus, lubricating the vibrating rod, she drove the device deep into the girl's trembling body. Alison's bottom bucked as Christina pistoned her arsehole, repeatedly thrusting the vibrator into her hot bowels. Lying on her back, Bryony positioned her head between Alison's splayed thighs and lapped at her dripping vaginal crack. The young student knew exactly what to do, Christina observed, realizing that her pupil might not be as naive as she'd at first thought.

Watching the girl's tongue driving deep into Alison's vaginal sheath, Christina continued to pump her flatmate's rectal tube with the buzzing vibrator. The thrusting phallus taking the girl closer to her orgasm as Bryony tongued and sucked her vaginal opening, Alison cried out again in the grip of her lesbian pleasure. She was about to come, Christina knew as she watched the girl's creamy juices of desire gushing from her gaping vaginal entrance and flooding Bryony's face.

'Yes,' Alison cried, her orgasm exploding, her naked body shaking fiercely. The sound of Bryony's tongue lapping and slurping at the girl's cream-drenched vaginal entrance sent Christina into a sexual near-frenzy as she pistoned Alison's inflamed anal duct with the vibrator. This wasn't love, she thought. This was hard, raw, cold sex. The kind of sex she was rapidly becoming used to. *Who needs love?* she reflected, slapping Alison's twitching buttocks as hard as she could.

Sinking her teeth into one of her flatmate's naked buttocks, Christina continued to piston Alison's anal canal with the vibrator as Bryony sustained her multiple orgasm with her tonguing and mouthing. The idea of using Bryony as a sex slave was beginning to appeal to Christina. She imagined moving the girl into the flat, having her cook and clean and satisfy the needs of her mistresses' clitorises. There'd be no need for the slave to go to college, either. With somewhere to live and work to do, she could put the college and her drunken mother behind her. Realizing that she was fantasizing, Christina slowed her rectal pistoning as Alison's orgasm began to wane. Watching Bryony mouthing and sucking between Alison's inflamed vaginal lips, she leaped to her feet and dashed into the kitchen as the phone rang.

'Hello,' she said, pressing the receiver to her ear.

'Hello, Miss Shaw,' a male voice murmured. 'You have something I want.'

'I'm sorry? Who is this?'

'A work colleague. I've discovered your little secret, Miss Shaw.'

'My secret? I don't know what you're talking about.'

'The things you get up to in the stockroom. I have a proposition.'

'I have no idea what you're talking about,' Christina said softly, her heart racing, her mind spinning. 'Who are you?'

'A fellow teacher. Unless you want me to go to the head, or the newspapers, I suggest you do as I ask.'

'Newspapers? Look, I . . .'

'Don't play games with me, Miss Shaw. Meet me at the college in fifteen minutes. I'll be waiting in your classroom.'

'The college is closed. Besides, I—'

'The caretaker will be there, and *you*'d better be there.'

As the man hung up, Christina bit her lip. This was serious, she knew as she grabbed her bag from the hall table. She'd not recognized the man's voice, but she hadn't met all the teachers yet. Deciding to say nothing to Alison and Bryony as she left the flat, she knew that she had to put a stop to this before it properly started. One of the boys had obviously been blabbing, she mused. She'd taken a huge risk in trusting stupid teenage boys. And now it looked as though she had a serious problem on her hands. Walking down the street, the cool evening air wafting up her short skirt, she realized that she wasn't wearing a bra or panties.

'Shit,' she cursed, walking through the college gates to the main building. Alison had taken over with Bryony, and now some teacher or other was trying to get in on the act. This wasn't at all what she'd expected, and she began to wonder again whether she should leave the college. At least Charles hadn't turned up uninvited, she thought. Her parents would be coming up to see the flat at some stage. If they brought Charles along . . . well, she'd deal with that if and when it happened.

Waiting in her classroom, her hands trembling, Christina tried to devise a plan. Whoever her would-be black-mailer was obviously knew what she did in the stockroom, so there was no point in denying it. And it was pretty obvious what he wanted in return for his silence. But she wasn't going to engage in a sexual relationship with one of the teachers, particularly an enforced sexual relationship. The three lads and Bryony were more than enough, let alone a member of staff demanding that she wank his cock and bring out his sperm. And then there was Alison, she reflected. This wasn't how it was supposed to have been.

'I'm pleased that you decided to meet me,' a balding man said, grinning as he wandered into the classroom. 'Ponting,' he said, holding his hand out. 'Don Ponting, physical education.'

'What's all this about?' Christina asked, declining to shake his hand.

'You wouldn't be here if you didn't know what it was about,' he chuckled. 'You've proved your guilt by turning up. Shall we go into the stockroom?'

'Look, you've obviously discovered that I'm having a relationship with one of my students. I know it's wrong, but he is eighteen and—'

'Only one student, Miss Shaw?'

'What are you implying?'

'I'm not implying anything, I'm stating facts. You're having sex with at least three male students.'

'I am *not*,' she retorted angrily, wondering which of the teenagers had blabbed.

'Let's be sensible about this,' Ponting said softly. 'When you arrived on Monday, I looked at you and thought, now there's a nice piece of fresh meat.'

'Fresh meat?' Christina gasped indignantly. 'How dare you . . .'

'Nice breasts, shapely hips . . . and then I discover that you're rather generous with your young body. All I want is what you gave the students. If not, then I'll just have to—'

'You think you can blackmail me?'

'Blackmail is an ugly word, Miss Shaw. Let's just say that I want to join your gang of lads. I want to be part of the games, that's all. Shall we go into the stockroom now?'

Ponting was a nasty little man, Christina concluded, gazing at his crisp white shirt and tie. Whatever he was, he was deadly serious, and she didn't want any trouble. *This could be a real turn for the worse*, she reflected. Embarking on this particular road to inevitable disaster was like cutting her own throat. But what choice did she have? She either risked Ponting running to the head and shouting his mouth off, or she . . . wanked him in the stockroom? Reckoning him to be in his mid-forties, she looked him up and down. He was clean enough, smartly dressed, but he was also a bastard.

'Come on, Miss Shaw,' he said irritably. 'We haven't got all day.'

'Are you married?' she asked him.

'Married? Oh, I see. You're thinking of telling my wife. No, no, I'm not married. Sorry to disappoint you.'

'It doesn't disappoint me. And it doesn't surprise me.'

'Shall we get on with it?' he sighed, walking towards the stockroom.

'I've left the key at home,' she said triumphantly. 'Sorry to disappoint *you*.'

'In that case, we'll do it here,' he grinned, returning to her desk and unzipping his trousers.

Christina watched as he pulled out his erect penis and

fully retracted his foreskin. He was no better than the teenagers, she thought, wondering how they were supposed to learn anything from an idiot like Ponting. Thanking God that he knew nothing about her relationship with Bryony, she couldn't believe his audacity as he eased his heavy balls out of his trousers and thrust his hips forward. The purple head of his cock pressed against her miniskirt and he squeezed the mounds of her firm breasts.

'Take a good look at my cock,' he sniggered. 'You should think yourself lucky, Miss Shaw. Many a woman would give her right arm to have my cock up her. Look at the size of it, the sheer length.'

'I can't believe what I'm hearing,' she sighed. 'Many a woman would give her right arm for that? You live in a dream world, Ponting.'

'Just get on with it,' he hissed.

Grabbing the fleshy shaft of his cock, Christina rolled Ponting's foreskin back and forth over his swollen knob. He wasn't badly endowed, she observed, imagining him wanking as he thought about the teenage girls at the college. *Fresh meat?* she thought, again unable to believe the man's audacity. Deciding to annoy him, she held his penis by the root, neglecting the bulbous knob of his solid shaft as she wanked him slowly.

'Do it properly,' he breathed.

'It's not that easy,' she said crossly.

'What do you mean?'

'Well, you haven't got much to get hold of, have you?' She laughed sarcastically. 'The boys are far bigger.'

'Shut up and suck it,' he hissed.

'Suck *that*? You must be joking.'

'You'd better . . .'

'Listen to me, Pointing. You're a nasty little man with a small cock. I'll wank you, and that's all.'

Obviously deciding to take what was on offer, Pointing let out a rush of breath as Christina wanked the solid shaft of his cock. His eyes rolling, his breathing fast and shallow as she rolled his foreskin back and forth over his purple glans, Christina realized that he'd soon shoot his spunk over the stockroom floor. Slowing her masturbating rhythm, she decided to rile him again. But, grabbing her hand, he wanked his cock faster with it, his body shaking as he let out a long low moan of pleasure. His sperm jetting from his cock-slit, splattering Christina's skirt as he pressed himself against her, he grabbed her beautifully rounded buttocks and held her crotch tight against his erect penis as his full balls drained. Christina gave a helpless cry of disgust as she felt his stiff prick pulsing against her skirt-covered pubic mound, discharging its slippery load in spurt after spurt.

'You're a sad bastard,' she spat, looking down at her skirt as she finally managed to pull away.

'You can keep your spermed skirt under your pillow and lick it when you think of me,' he grinned, a long strand of spunk hanging from his glistening knob. 'Why don't you suck my knob clean?'

'You could have had *this*,' she said, lifting her skirt and displaying her naked vulval slit to his wide eyes. 'If you hadn't been such a fool, you could have had anything you'd wanted.'

'I will, Miss Shaw. I'll have your cunt – *and* your arse. When I'm ready, that is.'

'You'll have nothing,' she hissed, tugging her skirt down and doing her best to wipe off the spunk.

'I'll meet you after class tomorrow,' he said, zipping

his trousers. 'Make sure you have the key to the stock-room because I'm going to fuck your sweet little cunt.'

'Get out,' she breathed. 'Just get out.'

As Ponting left the room, Christina sat at her desk and hung her head. She should have denied all knowledge of the teenagers and the stockroom, made out that someone had been winding him up. The evil little man would be back for more, she knew. If he started blabbing to the other teachers . . . What was done was done, she re-flected sadly, wondering what Alison and Bryony were up to. Looking at the empty desks, she wondered whether she'd be in class tomorrow. The way things were going, it might be best if she went back to her parents' house and forgot about the college. Her father would laugh, she thought. He'd tell her that she should stay with Charles and take a job with his company.

'I'm not going back,' she sighed, banging her clenched fist on the desk.

'You all right, Miss?' an ageing man asked, standing in the doorway. 'I'm Thompson, the caretaker.'

'Oh, er . . . yes, I'm fine,' Christina said, smiling at the man.

'I'll be locking up soon.'

'I came back for some papers. Sorry if I've kept you.'

'No, not at all. You're new here, aren't you?'

'Yes, I am. Shaw, Christina Shaw.'

'How are you coping with the rabble?'

'Oh, not too bad at all. It'll take me a while to settle in, but I'm enjoying the work.'

'Teachers come and go so fast that I can't keep up with it. Anyway, when you're ready.'

'Yes, of course.'

Leaving the classroom, Christina decided not to go

straight back to the flat. It was a lovely evening. As the sun sank below the chimneys of the engineering works, she walked to the common and sat on a bench to think. Recalling her parents' garden as she looked at the trees around the edge of the common, she wondered whether she'd ever be a city girl. Perhaps a rural school would have been better, she reflected. Younger pupils keen to learn, decent teachers . . . The money would be less, but the rents would be cheaper. She'd be able to afford a flat on her own. Things weren't working out in London. Even Alison hadn't turned out to be . . . Alison couldn't help the way she was, Christina thought, wondering again what she was doing with Bryony. Besides, Christina herself wasn't exactly free of blame.

There was one way to leave the college without her father laughing at her, she concluded. Apply for a job at a school in a village or small town. *It wouldn't be admitting defeat*, she tried to convince herself. Leave the college, London, the flat, Alison, Bryony . . . That had to be the answer.

6

'Christina, you didn't say you were coming,' her mother exclaimed, beaming.

'A surprise visit,' Christina said, dumping her bag on the kitchen table. 'How are you?'

'Fine, fine. Don't you have classes today?'

'I . . . I have the day off,' Christina lied. 'I woke up early and Alison had gone out so I thought I'd come and see you.'

'I'm pleased you did. You've just missed your father. He's gone to the office.'

'Oh, not to worry.'

'You'll see him this evening. If you're staying, of course.'

'I won't be able to stay all day, I'm afraid.'

'That's a shame. He'd have loved to have seen you, dear. Sit yourself down and I'll make some tea. So, how's the job? Tell me all about it.'

Sitting at the table, Christina wasn't sure that she still had a job after lying to the head about being ill. He'd complained that they were short-staffed and that there was no one to take her class. He'd also reminded her that this was her first week and taking a day off wasn't going to look good on her record. Christina had snapped at him, telling him that she hadn't been able to plan her illness to fit in with the college's timetable. He'd said that he wanted a talk with her, which she'd thought had sounded ominous. She was to be in his study at eight-thirty the following morning to discuss her progress at the college.

'Well?' her mother said, pouring the tea. 'How are you getting on? What's your flatmate like? Do you like the other teachers? And have you phoned Charles yet?'

'Alison's OK,' Christina replied, recalling licking and fingering the girl to orgasm. 'She's . . . she's great. The other teachers are all right, not that I've met them all yet.'

'And Charles?' the woman persisted. 'He's been expecting you to call.'

'Mother, Charles and I . . . We're no longer together.'

'Yes, but he's such a nice young man. I'm sure the two of you will be walking down the aisle before long.'

'How can we walk down the aisle and get married if we're not together any more?'

'You have your tea and I'll ring your father. He might be able to get away from the office for a while. I know he'd love to see you.'

Christina left the table and wandered through the back door into the garden as her mother lifted the phone. She didn't really want to see her father. She was in a mess, and he'd realize that something was wrong. And she certainly didn't intend to contact Charles. She began to wish that she'd gone to the college instead of taking the day off to visit her mother. But she'd got to the point where she couldn't face the students, Bryony or Alison. Let alone Ponting. Alison had been in bed by the time she'd got back to the flat last night. She'd been sleeping that morning, and Christina had made her escape to avoid explaining where she'd been all evening. Looking around the garden, the summer sun warming her, she realized that she felt homesick.

'Your father will be here soon,' her mother announced, stepping out onto the patio with Christina's tea. 'He's bringing Charles with him.'

'Oh,' Christina sighed. 'Mother, I . . .'

'You don't seem too pleased, dear.'

'I don't want to see Charles. We're no longer together. Why can't you understand that?'

'It's only because you've moved to London. You and Charles will always be together. Your father says that—'

'With respect, what father thinks can't change my feelings. Charles and I just aren't suited.'

'Yes, but . . .'

'I wouldn't be happy with Charles. You do want me to be happy, don't you?'

'Of course, dear. Now, when Charles gets here . . .'

Christina scrutinized her mother as she rambled on about Charles and her father. It was sad, Christina reflected, gazing at the woman's blonde hair. She was only in her early forties and far from unattractive. But she'd been oppressed by her husband. He ruled the roost, said how things were going to be, laid down the law. She'd wanted to take up painting, but he'd not thought it a good idea. She'd tried to become involved in the local church, but he'd denounced religion and wouldn't allow her to go near the place.

Christina's father meant well, but he tended to bully people. Charles was very much like him, Christina reflected. That was probably why the two men got on so well together. It was a shame that her father hadn't had a son, she mused. Particularly a son like Charles. There again, her father treated Charles like a son. They were always together. In the office, on the golf course . . .

'Don't you agree, dear?' Christina's mother asked.

'What? Oh, er . . . Sorry, I was daydreaming.'

'I was saying that Charles—'

'I really miss this garden,' Christina cut in, trying to change the subject. 'Living in a flat might be all right in the winter, but not in the summer. I remember spending weekends sunbathing out here. The birds singing, no traffic noise or diesel fumes . . .'

'Perhaps you'll find a flat with a garden.'

'Yes, but the rents are very high.'

'Your father was saying that, if you make a go of it at the college . . . You won't tell him that I said anything, will you?'

'No, of course not. What did he say?'

'He was talking about rented accommodation and how much it was costing you. He might buy a flat in London. You could live there and . . .'

'I thought he was totally against my teaching? Especially in London.'

'Yes, but . . . He said that if that's what you really want to do, and you make a go of it, then he'll buy a flat.'

'What if I decided to move to another college?'

'He'd sell the flat. He says that you can't go wrong buying property.'

'That's not strictly true. There again, knowing father, he'll come out of it with a massive profit'

'Ah, that'll be him,' her mother said, leaving Christina on the patio with her tea.

She could hear Charles talking to her mother. Her father's bellowing voice resounding around the house, Christina wrung her hands nervously. She shouldn't feel this way, she knew. But her father was a formidable man. *He should have been a headmaster*, she thought, imagining him wielding a bamboo cane in the study of an independent school for boys. The male voices growing louder, Christina took a deep breath as Charles stepped onto the patio. Her parents had obviously decided to give them some time together. No. Her father had decided.

'Christina,' Charles said, grinning from ear to ear. 'How are you?'

'Hello, Charles,' she murmured, forcing a smile. 'I'm fine. And you?'

'Busy, busy,' he replied, brushing his dark hair away from his forehead. 'How's the teaching game?'

'I'm loving every minute of it,' she said, eyeing his pinstriped suit and imagining him as a teacher.

'Oh, that's a shame. I was rather hoping that you'd give it up.'

'Give up teaching? Why would I do that?'

'Well, because . . . Christina, you have everything you need here. Working for your father, you'd find that—'

'Sitting in a stuffy office, working for my father? That's having everything, is it?'

'And me. You'd be with me, Christina. What is there to do in a flat during the evenings?'

'There's never a dull moment, I can assure you. Alison, she's my flatmate. We go out, meet people and—'

'Meet people? Christina, the sort of people living in that area are hardly the type . . .'

'I'm not looking to meet a certain type of person, Charles,' she broke in, doing her best not to let the man annoy her. 'I'm meeting people, real people with interesting lives.'

'Interesting lives?' he echoed mockingly. 'What, you mean factory workers and . . .'

'You drive a car, don't you?'

'Of course. What's that got to do with it?'

'It was built in a factory, Charles. It was built by people.'

'Yes, but . . . I mean, they're hardly the type of people you'd socialize with.'

'Why's that?'

'Well, because . . . They're just not. They drink pints of beer in seedy pubs and go to football matches . . .'

'I met a chap who works for an engineering firm the other day. He drinks gin and tonic and enjoys cricket.'

'You know what I mean, Christina. So, who is this chap? Where did you meet him?'

Christina thought for a moment and then grinned at Charles. 'I met him in the local bingo hall,' she finally announced.

'The bingo hall?' he laughed. 'You go to bingo?'

'Yes. It's great fun. I won ten pounds the other night.'

'Christina, bingo is for the—'

'The what, Charles? The lower classes?'

'Well, yes.'

'Christina, darling,' her father said, stepping onto the patio and hugging her. 'How are you?'

'Hello, father. I'm fine.'

'It's good to see you, darling. I was saying to your mother that it can't be easy for you, living in a ghetto.'

'A ghetto?' she laughed, realizing how alike her father and Charles were. 'I have a lovely flat. It's not in a ghetto.'

'Yes, but it's amid slums. So, when are you going to forget about this teaching nonsense and come home?'

'Christina was saying that she goes to bingo,' Charles broke in.

'Bingo?' her father chuckled. 'She's pulling your leg, old boy. No daughter of mine would be seen dead playing bingo. Now, Christina. Miss Stapleton is leaving the company. She's been my personal secretary for God only knows how many years. How would you like the job?'

'Father, I already have a job.'

'I'm talking about a real job, darling.'

'Shall we talk about it later?' Christina's mother suggested. 'I expect Charles and Christina have things to discuss.'

As her parents went back into the house, Christina felt her stomach sink. They didn't want to believe that she'd finished with Charles. They were burying their heads in the sand. Talking about walking down the aisle, planning for the future . . . And as for working as her father's personal secretary . . . There was no point in trying to argue. In time, her parents would realize that she wasn't going to be with Charles, let alone marry him.

'I thought you were going to ring me?' Charles said, plunging his hands into his trouser pockets.

'Did I say I would?' she asked, frowning.

'No, but . . . well, I thought you'd give me a call to let me know how you were.'

'Let's walk down the garden, Charles. It's a beautiful day.'

The more Christina listened to Charles and her father, the more determined she became to break free from all they stood for, all they represented. She loved her father very much, but that didn't mean to say that she had to be entwined in his life. Charles was simply trying to be like her father. He agreed with everything the man said, jumped to attention whenever he clicked his fingers . . . Charles wasn't consciously trying to be like him, he just *was* like him. The way he thrust his hands into his pockets, the way he walked . . . Charles could have easily been her father's son. Wondering whether she could get Charles to back off, somehow change his mind about her, Christina decided to shock him. She waited until they were out of sight of the house before turning to face him.

'Ever had a blow job?' she asked him unashamedly.

'Christina,' he gasped. 'I can see that London hasn't done you any good at all.'

'It's a simple enough question. And London has nothing to do with it. Has a girl ever sucked your cock?'

'Good grief. What your father would say, I really don't—'

'I'm asking *you*, Charles. Not my father.'

'Very well, then. To answer your question. No, a girl has never done that. For one thing, I've never known the type of girl who'd even dream of doing such a thing.'

'What's wrong with oral sex?'

'It's just not . . .'

'Would you like *me* to suck your cock?' she giggled.

'Christina,' he whispered through gritted teeth as she tugged his zip down. 'What the hell do you think you're doing?'

'Pulling your cock out,' she chuckled. 'Would you like me to wank you?'

'No, I mean . . . Not here, for God's sake.'

'Let me wank you, Charles. I want to watch your spunk shooting out of your knob.'

'Christina, please . . .'

Dropping to her knees, Christina sucked the man's purple knob-plum into her hot mouth and ran her tongue over its silky-smooth surface. He gasped, looking down at her in disbelief as she took his ripe glans to the back of her throat and sank her teeth gently into the fleshy shaft of his twitching penis. Wondering what he was thinking as she sucked and mouthed on his salty knob, she reckoned that he must have been sucked off before. He must have known some girl or other who'd been into oral sex. There again, knowing Charles . . .

'Christina,' he murmured, clutching her head as his orgasm approached. 'Christina, for God's sake . . .' Ignoring him, she imagined her father witnessing the crude act. The man would go mad and probably sack Charles. Wondering whether her father had ever come in a woman's mouth, she looked up at Charles as she tongued his sperm-slit. He was enjoying her intimate attention, and she reckoned again that a girl had sucked him and swallowed his sperm. Why he seemed to think that oral sex was disgusting, she had no idea. There was something wrong with him, she concluded. All normal men loved having their knobs sucked by pretty girls.

His sperm jetting into her gobbling mouth, bathing her tongue, filling her cheeks, Charles stifled his moans of pleasure as he rocked his hips. Christina gobbled on his throbbing glans, running her tongue around his cock-head's rim, tonguing his slit, sustaining his orgasm as she kneeled in front of him. Drinking from his pulsating knob, she dragged his heavy balls out of his trousers and cupped them in the palm of her hand. Swallowing hard, maintaining his sperm flow by wanking his solid cock and running her tongue around his swollen knob, she drank from his fountainhead until she'd drained his balls.

Lapping up the spilled spunk from his deflating shaft,

she licked Charles's rolling balls, delighting in his gasped protests as he towered over her. Why he was protesting, she couldn't imagine. Did he wank? she wondered, repeatedly running her spermed tongue up his shaft to his glistening knob. Did he imagine crude sexual acts as he wanked his rock-hard cock and brought out his spunk? The next time he masturbated, he'd imagine his cock in Christina's mouth, his sperm jetting to the back of her throat.

'God,' Charles breathed, moving back and zipping up his trousers. 'Who on earth taught you to . . . What *have* you been up to in London?'

'Up to?' Christina echoed, deliberately allowing his sperm to dribble down her chin as she stood in front of him. 'What do you mean?'

'Wipe your face, for Christ's sake,' he whispered.

'You taste nice,' she giggled, licking her sperm-glossed lips. 'I love the taste of fresh spunk.'

'Christina, I don't know what you've been doing in London. In fact, I dread to think. But you've changed.'

'For the better?'

'Yes . . . No, I mean . . . What on earth possessed you to behave like a . . . a common whore?'

'Your cock possessed me. Didn't you enjoy fucking my mouth?'

'Good grief. You've obviously done that before. You're not the sort of girl I thought you were, Christina.'

'Don't pretend that you didn't enjoy it, Charles,' she retorted angrily. 'I can't abide hypocrisy. There's nothing men like more than fucking girls' mouths and you know it.'

'Why are you talking like this?' he asked her, his dark eyes peering closely at her. 'I've never heard you swear before, let alone . . . let alone behave the way you did just now.'

'Behave the way I did? Oral sex is *fun*, Charles. Most people enjoy oral sex. Had our sex life been a little more exciting, we'd have still been together.'

'We *are* together, aren't we?' he asked pathetically.

'You just called me a whore.'

'No, I meant that you'd behaved—'

'What you did or didn't mean doesn't matter. It's over, Charles.'

'If it's over, then why did you just . . . you know.'

'Because I enjoy doing that.'

'Oh, so it doesn't matter who the man is?'

'Of course it matters.'

'What're your criteria? You have to have some liking for the man? Or perhaps it's just—'

'My flatmate Alison is a lesbian,' Christina announced proudly.

'A lesbian? Well, at least you're safe enough living with the likes of her,' he scoffed.

'Am I?'

'Christina,' her mother called from the house. 'I've made some more tea.'

'All right, mother.' She turned to Charles. 'We'd better go back.'

'What did you mean about your flatmate? You *are* safe with her, aren't you?'

'She plays bingo, so I doubt it.'

Walking back to the house with Charles in tow, Christina felt good. She'd made some sort of stand, at long last. She'd also made several decisions. She wasn't going to work for her father, she wasn't going to move back home, and she wasn't going to spend the rest of her life with Charles. And it wouldn't be a good idea to live in a flat owned by her father. She didn't want to be beholden to the man. This was her life and she was going to live it her way. Sitting on the patio as her mother brought out the tea on a tray, she felt confident for the first time in her life. Even the likes of that little creep Ponting weren't going to get to her now.

'This is like old times,' Christina's mother said. 'I wish you'd come home, dear.'

'She won't listen to me,' Charles sighed. 'She should forget this teaching nonsense and take up her father's offer. London's doing her no good at all.'

'You see?' her father interjected as he stepped onto the patio and plunged his hands into his trouser pockets. 'Charles knows what he's talking about, Christina. He knows what's best for you.'

'Does he, father?' she asked, frowning. 'Does he really?'

'You mark my words, young lady. You won't find a better man than Charles.'

'Actually, I've made a new friend in London.'

'Oh?'

'You'd like him, father. His name's . . . Barry, Barry Doogan.'

'And what does he do?'

'He's . . . he's something in the City.'

'Doogan,' her father murmured pensively. 'I can't say that I know of that name in the City.'

'What do you mean by a new *friend*?' Charles asked, suspicion reflected in his frowning expression.

'Just that. We're becoming good friends.'

'What does he do, exactly?' her father persisted.

'He's a stockbroker,' she lied, watching Charles for a reaction.

'How old is he, dear?' her mother asked.

'Thirty-two. He has a lovely flat in Highgate.'

'Was he the one who taught you?' Charles murmured, glaring at Christina.

'Yes, yes, he was.'

'Taught you what, dear? Don't let your tea go cold.'

'No, I won't. I was telling Charles that I've been learning how to roll my Rs. It's all to do with how you use your tongue. It's silly, really.'

'Ridiculous, if you ask me,' Charles mumbled. 'Er . . . hadn't we better be getting back to the office, Mr Shaw?'

'Yes, we had. So, this Doogan fellow. What's his father do?'

'He's something to do with the Diplomatic Corps. I'm not sure what, exactly. He travels around the world most of the time. You'll have to meet him. He's a lovely man, father.'

'Yes, I will. Right, we'd better be going. It's nice to have seen you, darling.'

'And you, father. Goodbye, Charles.'

'Goodbye, Christina.'

Concealing a grin as the men went into the house, Christina felt smug. She'd been ruled by Charles for too long. Had she stayed with him, married him, she'd have ended up like her mother. *Barry Doogan a stockbroker?* she giggled inwardly, sipping her tea. Wondering what the lad would become, she pictured him in a suit, crisp white shirt and tie. *Given a decent education he might have made it*, she reflected. It was all right for the likes of Charles. Money, a private education, university . . . Charles was a pompous git, she mused. At least Barry Doogan was genuine, down-to-earth. And he enjoyed the baser side of sex.

Wandering down the garden, Christina pondered on the idea of her father buying a flat in London. The rent she was paying now was horrendous, even though she was going halves with Alison. A decent home was important, she mused. After a long day at the college, it would be nice to have a garden to relax in, perhaps have some friends round for a barbecue. But she realized again that she would be indebted for ever to her father. Her thoughts turning to Ponting, she sighed. He was going to become a real problem, she reflected. Ponting had to be dealt with if she was going to stay on at the college. Deciding to return to London, she went back into the house to find her mother.

'I have to go,' she said, watching the woman preparing sandwiches in the kitchen.

'I was just making some lunch,' her mother sighed. 'Can't you stay for a while longer?'

'No, I have to get back. I'll be down to see you again.'

'All right, dear. It's been nice having you here, even thought it wasn't for long. Do you want a lift to the station?'

'It's all right, I'll walk,' Christina replied, taking her bag from the table as she followed her mother through the hall. 'It's not far and it's a lovely day.'

'I'll ring you this evening.'

'All right, mother. You take care of yourself.'

'And you, dear.'

Sitting on the almost empty train, Christina wondered what to do about Ponting. She wouldn't mind masturbating him to orgasm now and then, as long as he didn't demand more of her. Realizing that he'd demand far more than a quick wank in the stockroom, she thought about getting Doogan to help her. If he had a word with

Ponting, told him to back off, threatened him . . . But
that might lead to all sorts of trouble. She'd just have to
deal with Ponting herself. Smiling, she pictured the
man's solid cock in her hand, his spunk jetting from
his throbbing knob. Wanking a cock and bringing out the
sperm wasn't at all unpleasant, she reflected. Quite the
opposite, in fact. Would Ponting enjoy mouth-fucking
her? There was definitely something wrong with
Charles, she concluded.

Watching a young man as he got in at the next station
and sat opposite her, Christina stared at the bulging
crotch of his tight jeans. Since starting at the college,
sex was constantly on her mind, and she found herself
wondering whether all men wanked. Did the young man
run his hand up and down the rock-hard shaft of his cock
and shoot his spunk over the floor? Reckoning him to be
in his mid-teens, she reclined in her seat and parted her
thighs just enough to expose the triangular patch of her
tight panties. After only a few seconds, his gaze was
locked between her legs, his expression a mixture of
surprise and delight as he adjusted the crotch of his
trousers.

The next time he wanked, he'd remember her, picture
the bulging patch of tight material covering her full sex
lips. Would he like to spunk over her breasts? Christina
wondered, imagining his white rain showering her naked
body. She was becoming hooked on wanking men to the
point where it might become an obsession. The feel of a
solid penis in her hand, rolling the foreskin back and
forth over the swollen glans, watching the spunk jetting
from the slit . . . Wondering whether her mother wanked
her father's cock, she couldn't picture the act. *They must
have fucked at least once to have had me*, she thought,

trying to imagine her father spunking over her mother's cervix.

Catching the young man's gaze, she knew what he wanted. She knew what *she* wanted. Was his cock big? she wondered, her young womb contracting, her juices of lust wetting her panties. Would he allow her to give him a quick wank on the train? It occurred to her that she'd wanked several cocks since starting at the college, but had not had one pistoning the tight sheath of her hot pussy. Perhaps the young man would enjoy slipping the length of his penis deep into her tight vagina and sperming her.

Parting her thighs further, her stomach somersaulting, she was gripped by an overwhelming desire to behave like a common slut. *A common whore?* she mused, recalling Charles's cruel words. By opening her legs to a stranger, perhaps she was making a stand against her father and what he stood for. It would be exciting to behave like a common whore, she mused, licking her lips provocatively as she gazed at the young man. Perhaps she was trying to prove something.

She had about ten minutes before the train pulled in at her station. Her heart banging hard against her chest, she knew that she couldn't let this opportunity pass her by. If she didn't act now, she might regret it for ever. Wondering whether she'd feel guilty if she allowed him to fuck her, she realized that no one would ever know of her sordid act. Again recalling the words of the pompous Charles, she wondered what her criteria were. The man wasn't bad-looking, his jeans were bulging with his obvious arousal . . . That was good enough, she concluded.

'Why don't you get your cock out?' she asked him,

pulling the tight material of her panties to one side and exposing the swell of her fleshy vaginal lips to his wide-eyed stare. 'Kneel on the floor and push your cock into my hot cunt.'

Saying nothing, the stunned man slipped off his seat and kneeled on the floor. Unzipping his jeans, he hauled his solid penis out and gripped it by the base as Christina slid her buttocks forward on her seat and opened her legs wide. Keeping her panties pulled to one side, she watched the young man pull his foreskin back and slip his purple knob between the pinken wings of her splayed inner lips. She needed this, she knew as his rock-hard shaft glided deep into her cream-drenched sex duct. The last man she'd allowed to impale her on his penis had been Charles, and that had been some time ago.

'You're amazing,' the young teenager breathed, eyeing the outer lips of Christina's pussy stretched tautly around the wide root of his cock as he fully impaled her. 'I've never met anyone like you.'

'And you're not likely to again,' Christina murmured, pulling her panties still further to one side as he began his fucking motions.

'I don't even know your name.'

'You don't have to know my name,' she giggled. 'All you have to do is fuck me.'

Her own crude words delighting her, Christina imagined Charles witnessing her wanton act of decadence, listening to her vulgar language as a complete stranger fucked her tight cunt. He'd go mad, call her every name under the sun. Her father would be none too pleased, either. This was debauchery at its lowest, she mused, listening to the squelching sounds of her copious vaginal juices as the young man repeatedly drove his solid cock deep into her sex-wet pussy. Meeting a total stranger on a train, opening her legs and allowing him to fuck her . . . This was sexual gratification at its highest.

Watching the young man's pussy-slimed shaft repeatedly thrusting deep into her cunny, Christina felt her clitoris swelling, her young womb contracting. She was going to come, she knew as the train rocked and lurched. The man's swollen knob battering her ripe cervix, her lower stomach rising and falling as he thrust into her pussy, she closed her eyes as he gasped and flooded her vaginal canal with his creamy sperm. Her own climax erupting within the pulsating nub of her clitoris, she threw her head back and let out a moan of pleasure.

Her young body shaking fiercely, her juices of lust gushing from the bloated entrance to her spasming pussy, Christina repeatedly pushed her hips forward to meet the young man's thrusts. Again and again his throbbing knob buffeted her ripe cervix, his copious flow of creamy sperm filling her vaginal cavity as his heavy balls drained. Her vaginal muscles spasming, gripping his cock shaft like a velvet-jawed vice, she thought it strange that she'd never see the young man again. *Ships passing*, she reflected as her orgasm peaked, sending electrifying shock waves of sex through her contracting womb.

'God, you're good,' the young man gasped, repeatedly thrusting the shaft of his penis deep into her convulsing cunt with a vengeance. 'Hot, tight, wet . . .' Grinning, Christina drifted in her sexual delirium, her young body shaking violently, her mind blown away on a cloud on lust. Her pleasure finally beginning to leave her trembling body, her head lolling from side to side, she realized that the train was slowing down as the young man made his last thrusts. She had a couple of minutes before arriving at her station, time enough to cover her sperm-oozing vaginal crack with her panties and adjust her clothing.

Watching the man's deflating penis sliding out of her inflamed vagina, Christina leaned forward as he stood up. Taking his sperm-glistening cock into her mouth, she cleansed him, sucking out the remnants of his orgasmic cream as he towered over her, trembling in the aftermath of his fucking. She could taste her vaginal juices as she rolled her tongue around his purple knob. *The taste of sex*, she mused, sucking hard and running her hand up his shaft to squeeze out the last of his sperm.

'I'd like to see you again,' he said, zipping his trousers as she slipped his cock out of her spunked mouth.

'We'll never meet again,' Christina murmured, licking her spermed lips as she looked up at him.

'Why not? After what we just did . . . I mean . . .'

'Ships passing in the night,' she said, concealing her spunked pussy slit under her tight panties.

'We can pass again, can't we? I'm Rob, by the way.'

'And I'm the Devil's daughter,' Christina giggled, leaving her seat as the train stopped at the station.

'Please . . . Don't go without even—'

Walking along the platform with her bag slung over her shoulder, Christina smiled at the young man peering out of the window as the train pulled away. *The Devil's daughter?* she mused. Perhaps she was right. Her tight panties filling with a cocktail of sperm and girl-juice as she moved, she wondered how many more strangers she'd allow to fuck her. Sucking and wanking the students was nothing in comparison to screwing a stranger on the train, she reflected. Tossing off Ponting was insignificant. *The Devil's daughter?* Feeling more confident, she finally reached the flat and let herself in.

7

'Where have you been?' Alison asked almost accusingly, emerging from her room.

'To see my parents,' Christina replied. She dropped her bag on the kitchen table and filled the kettle. 'How did you get on with Bryony last night?'

'It was great. Do you know, she licked me until . . . Where did you go? I heard the phone ring and then the front door close.'

'I had to go over to the college.'

'What, at night?'

'There was a problem about some exam papers.'

'You had to go there at night? I don't know what the time was but it must have been at least—'

'It was important, Alison. The exams are coming up and . . . Anyway, I was up early this morning and decided to go and see my parents.'

'Why aren't you at work?'

'Why all these questions, Alison? I have the day off. Unofficially, that is.'

'I'm sorry. I was worried, that's all. You disappeared last night, you were up and gone first thing this morning . . . By the way, the college rang.'

'Oh, God. Who was it?'

'It was Mr Wright. I didn't know what to say. As far as

I was aware, you'd gone to work. If you're going to take a day off, you should at least tell me.'

'So, what did you say?'

'I could tell by his tone that he was in a bad mood. I guessed that you were skiving off so I said that you were sleeping because you were ill. Luckily, I got it right.'

'Thanks. How long did Bryony stay?'

'Not long. I think she was hoping that you'd come back. She's got the hots for you, Christina.'

'I know. That's why I was trying to break off with her. When you invited her in, I . . .'

'I guessed who she was when I saw her hanging around outside. She was looking up at the window, obviously hoping to see you.'

'She's going to become a nuisance. In fact, she already *is* a nuisance.'

'I feel sorry for her.'

'So do I. Her mother's a drunk, her home is a slum . . . But that's not my problem.'

'She could move in with us.'

'Alison, I really don't think . . .'

'Why not?'

'To be honest, the thought crossed my mind too. The thing is, we've only got two bedrooms.'

'She could spend a night in your bed and the next in mine. She could swap beds every night.'

'That wouldn't work. She'd have to have her own room.'

'I don't see why. She could clean the flat, do the washing and ironing . . . It might work out extremely well.'

Pondering on the idea as she made the coffee, Christina was sure that Bryony would jump at the chance to move in. And she doubted that the girl's mother would object. But this wasn't how it was supposed to have been, she reflected. Since starting at the college, everything had been turned upside down. Wanking the lads in the stockroom, having sex with young Bryony, Alison turning out to be a lesbian . . . At least Charles had finally got the message. Gazing at Alison's stiff nipples clearly defined by her tight T-shirt, the band of flesh just above her short skirt, Christina was aware of her vaginal muscles tightening. She could feel again that her panties were full of sperm and girl-juice. Would Alison enjoy drinking from her sex-flooded pussy? she wondered. Her clitoris swelling as she imagined the other girl's tongue delving into her sex-drenched vagina, she wondered whether her flatmate would realize that she was lapping up sperm.

This was no time for sex, Christina thought, sipping her coffee as she gazed at the neat indent of Alison's navel. Trying to drag her thoughts away from lesbian sex, she wondered whether to ring the headmaster. It might be an idea to let him know that she was feeling better and would be in tomorrow morning. He was a miserable man, she mused, wondering whether he was married and trying to picture him with his solid cock shafting a wet pussy. Her panties soaked with sperm, the creamy liquid trickling down her inner thighs, she decided to take a shower before doing anything.

'Want me to soap you?' Alison asked, following Christina into the bathroom.

'No, thanks,' Christina murmured, knowing full well that she'd succumb to her lesbian desires if Alison ran her hands all over her naked body. 'I'm just having a quick shower since I have things to do.'

'At least allow me to undress you,' the girl breathed,

dropping to her knees and tugging Christina's skirt down.

'Alison, I . . .'

'What's the matter?'

'Nothing.'

Stepping out of her skirt, Christina watched as Alison pulled the fuck-wet panties down and gazed longingly at the sex-sticky crack of Christina's vagina. Would the girl lap up her juices? Christina wondered. Would she realize, Christina asked herself again, that she was drinking sperm as she pressed her full lips to her vaginal entrance and sucked and tongued her there? Christina shuddered as Alison's tongue ran up and down her spunk-dripping sex slit. Peeling her fleshy outer lips apart, Alison lapped at the pink flesh surrounding her vaginal entrance, drinking the heady blend of girl-juice and sperm from the hot sheath of her tightening pussy. She obviously didn't realize what the creamy liquid was, probably thinking that Christina was simply extremely wet in her lesbian arousal.

'I love your cunt,' Alison murmured, her wet tongue snaking inside Christina's hot pussy, licking the cream-coated walls of her vaginal canal. 'You have a beautiful cunt.' The crude word excited Christina and she parted her feet wide and projected her hips, allowing her lesbian lover deeper access to her hot sex duct. The thought of Alison lapping up the young man's sperm from her hot vagina sent an electrifying quiver through Christina's womb. She could hear the slurping sounds of oral sex, feel the girl's saliva running down her inner thighs. The girl's wet tongue sweeping over the sensitive nub of her clitoris, Christina shuddered as she realized that her young cunt was fast beginning to rule her head.

'Say "cunt" again,' she breathed, her ripening clitoris pulsating.

'Cunt,' Alison murmured. 'I love your hot cunt. Do you want me to tongue your arse?'

'Yes, yes – tongue my arse,' Christina replied eagerly.

'Turn round and bend over the bath and I'll tongue-fuck your sweet arsehole.'

Taking her position as she pondered on the crude words, Christina let out a low moan of sexual satisfaction as her flatmate parted the firm orbs of her buttocks and ran her wet tongue over the delicate brown tissue surrounding her private hole. Shuddering, Christina felt the girl's tongue delving into her anus, wetting her there, teasing her secret nerve endings of illicit pleasure. Her feet wide apart, she leaned further over the bath and projected her pert buttocks as Alison slipped a wet finger past the tight ring of her anus.

'Is that nice?' Alison asked, massaging the hot walls of Christina's rectal duct.

'God, yes,' Christina murmured, gyrating her hips as the incredibly arousing sensations rippled through her young womb.

'Has anyone ever finger-fucked your beautiful arse?'

'No, never.'

'You like me talking dirty, don't you?'

'Yes, yes,' Christina breathed shakily. 'I love your dirty words.'

'You have a tight cunt and a beautiful arse. Do you want my tongue up your arse again?'

'Yes, yes.'

'Licking deep inside your hot arse?'

'God, yes.'

'Reach behind your back and open your arsehole for me and I'll tongue-fuck your rectum.'

Parting her buttocks to the extreme, fully opening the brown entrance to her hot rectal tube, Christina felt a quiver run through her pelvis as Alison's tongue drove deep into her anal canal. She could feel her flatmate's tongue inside her, wetting her, licking and teasing the sensitive walls of her rectum. The girl's full lips pressed hard against her anal opening as she tongued deep inside her anal duct, never had Christina known that such incredible pleasure could be had from such a decadent act. Christina knew now that she had two sex holes, two lust sheaths. She had more than just her vaginal canal. Had Charles pleasured her like this, tongue-fucked her tight arsehole . . . But Charles was no longer a feature of her life. Her neglected clitoris painfully' solid, she moaned softly as her lesbian lover massaged her rectal sheath, sending electrifying tremors of crude sex through her naked body. She'd never really needed Charles, she realized.

'Are you ready for two fingers?' Alison asked unashamedly.

'Yes, two fingers,' Christina replied eagerly, holding her rounded buttocks wide apart.

'First one, then two . . . We'll see how many fingers you can take.'

Shuddering as Alison forced a second finger deep into the hot duct of her rectum, Christina let out a gasp of pleasure. The brown ring of her anal eye dilating, the tight tube of her arse stretching as Alison flexed her fingers, Christina felt dizzy in the grip of her new-found decadence. She'd never dreamed of opening her vagina to another girl, let alone her bottom-hole. To hold her anus wide open and offer her rectal sheath to a lesbian's tongue and fingers was debased in the extreme, so obscene that the very notion of the act sent her arousal sky-high.

'Three fingers,' Alison announced gleefully.

'Yes, yes,' Christina breathed.

'OK, are you ready?'

'Just do it.'

'Anything you say.'

Grimacing as Alison pushed the tip of her third finger past her already stretched anal ring, Christina held her breath. The mixture of pain and pleasure driving her wild as the girl's finger began to slide into her inflamed anal sheath, she finally let out a rush of breath. Alison's three fingers completely impaling her, massaging deep inside her trembling body, she was sure that she could take no more as the girl pushed and twisted her hand, trying to force all four fingers into her arse.

'No,' she breathed, the delicate tissue of her anus dilating to capacity. 'Alison, I . . .'

'Relax,' the girl said, licking the rounded cheeks of Christina's buttocks. 'You're all tensed up. Just relax and I'll fist your beautiful arse.'

'Fist?' Christina gasped surprisedly. 'For God's sake—'

'It's OK, I've done this before. Just relax.'

Doing her best to relax her muscles as her lesbian lover managed to drive four fingers into her inflamed anal canal, Christina knew that she'd never be able to accommodate the girl's whole fist. There *were* limits, she reflected, trying to picture the brown tissue of her anus stretched painfully around Alison's wrist. It just wasn't possible to take a complete fist up her arse, she was sure.

Squeezing her eyes shut as her flatmate again pushed and twisted her hand, Christina sensed that the girl was obviously determined to sink her fist deep into Christina's anal passage.

'Lubrication,' Alison murmured, grabbing a shampoo bottle from the shelf. Christina could feel the cooling liquid running down the splayed gully of her buttocks, oiling her painfully stretched anal tissue. Alison continued to twist and push her hand, her fingers slipping slowly into Christina's bottom-hole as the girl's brown ring yielded. Christina couldn't believe that her lesbian lover had succeeded in her illicit mission when she announced that her entire fist was embedded in Christina's rectal canal. Twisting her fist, Alison massaged the inner core of Christina's naked body. The shampoo lubricating the crude coupling, lather emerging from her bloated rectal duct and running down her thighs, Christina rocked back and forth with the anal pistoning. To her surprise, the sensation wasn't one of pain, but a pleasurable bloating feeling deep within her pelvis.

'I told you that I'd do it,' Alison trilled victoriously, the sucking sound of the shampoo resounding around the bathroom.

'God,' Christina breathed shakily. 'I can't believe it.'

'You should see your bum. Your arsehole is tight around my wrist. Does it feel nice?'

'Yes, yes, it does. It's incredible to think that—'

'Don't think about the physiology,' the other girl laughed. 'You just concentrate on your clitty. I'm going to bring you off.'

Reaching between Christina's thighs with her free hand, Alison parted the trembling girl's fleshy love lips and began to massage the swollen nubble of her sensitive

clitoris. Christina shuddered, her naked body alive with
sensations of crude sex as her rectal muscles tightened
around her lover's clenched fist. Her juices of desire
streaming from the gaping entrance to her neglected
vagina, she leaned on the side of the bath to steady
herself as the incredible sensations permeated her very
being. Her clitoris painfully solid, her flatmate's fist
driving deep into the dank heat of her bowels, she shook
uncontrollably in her debauched act.

Wishing that Bryony was helping Alison to pleasure
her naked body, Christina wondered whether the young
student would call round that evening. Perhaps she'd
enjoy an anal fisting, she thought as her vaginal muscles
spasmed, squeezing out her copious juices of lesbian lust.
Would the girl enjoy a double sex-fisting? Her teenage
cunt bloated by Alison's clenched fist, her rectal cavern
stretched to accommodate Christina's fist . . . Young
Bryony was in for the time of her life the next time
she called at the flat.

Shuddering with her building pleasure, Christina
whimpered in her lesbian desire as her partner in lust
continued to massage the swollen nodule of her painfully
hard cumbud and fist-fuck the hot duct of her rectum.
Her whimpers growing louder, her womb rhythmically
contracting, she leaned further over the side of the bath
as her vagina tightened, spewing out its creamy sex
juices. Her clitoris close to orgasm, her inflamed rectal
sheath gripping Alison's pistoning fist, Christina
breathed heavily as she teetered on the brink of her
climax.

'I'm going to shave you,' Alison announced, her fist
twisting deep within Christina's inflamed rectal tube.
Saying nothing, Christina pictured Bryony's hairless

vulval flesh, the smooth love lips of her naked pussy. Wondering whether to allow Alison to strip her pubic hair from her cunt lips and Venus mound, she realized that she'd travelled so far down the path of crude sex that whatever she did now wouldn't really make any difference. Wanking the students in the stockroom, sucking off Charles in the garden, licking and fingering Bryony's teenage pussy, fucking a stranger on a train, and now allowing Alison to fist-fuck her tight arse . . . Shaving would be the least of the decadent sexual acts that she'd committed.

'Yes,' Christina cried, her orgasm exploding within the solid tip of her palpitating clitoris. Increasing her anal-fisting rhythm, Alison fervently massaged Christina's orgasming clitoris, taking her to heights of sexual ecstasy she'd never known before. Her pelvic cavity bloated to the extreme, she felt that her entire body was inflating as her flatmate repeatedly thrust her clenched fist deep into the hot depths of her bowels. Her orgasmic juices streaming from the dilated opening of her vagina, running in rivers of cum-milk down her inner thighs, she realized that her bladder was about to drain as her orgasm peaked.

As the sound of liquid splashing onto the floor between her feet rang loudly in her ears, Christina felt no shame. In her mind, this was just part of her ever-deepening decadence. The profane act added to her sense of debauchery, heightening her illicit pleasure. She could feel Alison's head between her legs, her tongue running up her inner thighs, lapping up the stream of golden liquid coursing down her smooth flesh. Slurping at her drenched pubic hair, lapping up the golden offering, Alison continued her rectal fisting, her clitoral massaging, sustaining her lesbian lover's multiple orgasm until the girl could barely stand on her sagging legs.

'You dirty little cow,' Alison giggled, her tongue running over Christina's wet vulval lips as the flow of golden liquid began to slow. 'I'll thrash you before I shave your sweet cunt.'

'God,' Christina breathed shakily, her pleasure beginning to recede. 'That's enough. I can't take any more.'

'Of course you can,' the insistent lesbian returned, twisting her fist and pistoning the girl's rectum. 'You're going to have to take a lot more than this.'

Finally crumpling over the side of the bath, Christina's naked body convulsed wildly as Alison withdrew her fist from the burning sheath of her abused rectum. Christina felt as though her bottom-hole was gaping, sagging open at least three inches, as she quivered and breathed heavily in the aftermath of her incredibly decadent experience. Wondering whether the inflamed ring of her anus would ever recover, she clung to the basin and finally managed to climb to her feet.

'No more,' she breathed, her glazed eyes staring at the razor and shaving foam in Alison's hand. 'I need to rest. I'm going to lie down.'

'Yes, you lie on your bed and rest. I'll shave you while you relax.'

'Alison, I . . .'

'Come on, go to your room. I'll look after you.'

Staggering to her room with Alison in tow, Christina collapsed onto her bed and lay on her back. She was in no fit state to protest as she heard a hissing sound and then felt cooling foam smothering the sex-wet flesh of her crimsoned vulva. Almost delirious in the aftermath of her massive orgasm, her naked body exhausted, she closed her eyes and drifted in a sleeplike state as her flatmate massaged the white foam into her mons, the fleshy swell of her love lips. She felt the razor running over her vulval flesh as Alison worked between her thighs, stripping away her pubic curls, taking her back to prepubescence. Was this what she wanted?

Christina recalled her younger days of sexual discovery, the dreamy nights of toying with her naked love lips, tentatively running her fingertip up and down the wet valley of her pink pussy. She'd discovered the delights her clitoris had to offer quite by accident when playing in the garden one afternoon. She'd been straddling a low wall, her legs open wide, her panties pressing against the rough brickwork. Rocking to and fro, she'd felt unfamiliar sensations emanating from within the moist valley between her firm pussy lips. The feeling was pleasant, nothing more. Until she decided to experiment.

Out of sight of the house, she'd slipped her panties off and sat on the wall again. The rough bricks scraping and grazing her hairless sex cushions as she'd writhed and squirmed, she'd been surprised by the new pleasures her young body was bringing her. Looking down, she'd investigated between her legs, her fingers probing within her pink crack, rubbing the hard spot there. She'd often examined herself after that day, but had never achieved an orgasm until she'd been lying in the bath one evening.

Rubbing between the rise of her firm sex lips, massaging the hard nodule nestling within the top of her girl-slit, she'd found that her pleasure had built. The more she'd massaged her solid sex spot, the greater her pleasure had become until she'd achieved her pioneering orgasm. Shuddering in the bath, the water lapping at her swollen pussy lips, she'd continued to rub her clitoris, sustaining her orgasm as she'd whimpered and cried out in the grips of her self-loving.

Her mother had opened the door and walked in when she'd heard the whimpers. Christina had said that she'd been singing, but her mother had noticed the girl's flushed face, the sparkle in her blue eyes. The woman must have known that Christina had discovered her clitoris, but had said nothing. Perhaps she had masturbated in the bath when she'd been young. Christina had thought it unlikely, but she often wondered whether her mother massaged between her sex lips. Had she sucked the sperm from an orgasming knob and swallowed the male cream of orgasm? Probably not.

'Almost done,' Alison said, taking a tissue from the dressing table and wiping away the foam and pubic curls from Christina's vaginal lips. 'Oh, yes,' she trilled excitedly. 'You look just like a little schoolgirl. I'll get a flannel from the bathroom and clean you up before giving your beautiful cunt a good licking-out.'

As the girl left the room, Christina managed to lift her head and gaze at Alison's handiwork. Her pubic curls had gone and her pussy lips were smooth, the gentle rise of her mons pale in its blatant nakedness. Christina recalled again her younger years before her pubic hair had sprouted. The firm lips of her vulva had been soft to the touch, smooth in her tender years. Stroking the outer lips of her pussy as she recalled her early days of masturbation, she decided that she was pleased with the result of Alison's work. What would Charles think?

'Like it?' the girl asked as she breezed back into the room, holding a wet flannel.

'Yes, I think I do,' Christina replied, resting her head on the bed again. 'It's taken years off me.'

'Years off your pussy, at least,' Alison chuckled, sitting on the edge of the bed and cleansing Christina's vaginal hillocks with the warm flannel. 'What do you want first? A good cunt-licking or a thrashing?'

'I don't want a thrashing,' Christina murmured, her head lolling from side to side. 'God, I feel knackered.'

'You'll soon recover. How does your bum-hole feel?'

'Damned sore. It feels as if it's hanging wide open.'

'Good – that's what I like to hear. Right, I'll go and get my leather belt and bring a warm glow to your buttocks.'

'Alison, I . . .'

Sighing as the girl left, Christina told herself that she wasn't going to allow her to thrash her with a leather belt. A mild spanking was one thing, but a severe whipping . . . Were there no limits to her flatmate's debauchery? She lifted her head again and gazed at her hairless pussy lips. Fisting, shaving . . . There *were* no limits, she concluded, deciding to take a shower and wash away the girl-cum and urine from her naked body. Propping herself up on her elbows, she was about to swing her feet off the bed when Alison appeared in the doorway, wielding a leather belt.

'I don't want a thrashing,' Christina said firmly as the girl crossed the room and rolled her onto her stomach. 'Alison, if you—'

'Of course you want a thrashing,' she giggled, bringing the belt down across Christina's rounded buttocks with a loud crack.

'Alison! For God's sake, I—'

'And another one,' Alison shrieked gleefully, the belt landing squarely across the tensed orbs of Christina's naked bottom.

Squeezing her eyes shut, Christina buried her face in

the pillow as the girl repeatedly lashed the burning globes of her stinging buttocks with the leather belt. She could have easily clambered off the bed and put a stop to the gruelling punishment, but the notion of a thrashing intrigued her. As her buttocks grew numb, the pain turning to pleasure, she recalled reading about spanking and bondage in a women's magazine. She'd been surprised by the number of women who'd admitted to having their naked bodies bound with rope and their bottoms spanked until they'd glowed a fire-red. They'd enjoyed the degradation, the enforced spanking of their naked bottoms, and the crude act had become part of their sex lives. Now Christina was beginning to understand why.

Listening to the crack of the belt each time it swished through the air and lashed her fiery bottom cheeks, she heard Alison chuckling softly. The girl was obviously in her element, Christina concluded as her naked bottom bucked beneath the leather belt. There certainly was far more to Alison than met the eye, she mused, her juices of arousal seeping between the hairless lips of her vulva. When she'd first met the girl in the letting agency, she'd had no idea that she was a lesbian, let alone a sex-crazed nymphomaniac. Had Alison guessed that Christina would offer her naked body in the name of lesbian lust?

'Turn over,' Alison told Christina.

'I was enjoying that,' Christina said, rolling onto her back. 'Why do you want me to . . . Argh!' she cried as the leather belt swished through the air and bit into the firm flesh of her young breasts. 'Alison! Please—'

'Relax,' the girl laughed, bringing the belt down across the elongated teats of her erect nipples. 'I'll thrash your little pink pussy next.'

'You won't,' Christina protested, grabbing the belt. 'I didn't mind you thrashing my bum, but you're not going to—'

'At least try it,' Alison cut in. 'I love having my tits whipped, and my cunt. I'll be gentle, OK?'

'No, it's *not* OK,' Christina retorted. 'What the hell do you think I am?'

'A girl who enjoys lesbian sex. A girl who enjoyed an arse-fisting, a bum-thrashing, a . . .'

'All right,' Christina finally conceded, releasing the belt as she realized that she'd probably enjoy the illicit act. 'But you must do it gently.'

'Gently it is.'

Her arms by her sides, Christina allowed her flatmate to whip the firm mounds of her young breasts softly. The leather belt repeatedly slapping the brown teats of her sensitive nipples, darkening the discs of her areolae, she decided that she quite liked the unfamiliar sensations. Never had she dreamed that she'd allow anyone to whip her young breasts, let alone another girl. She was learning, she reflected, her nipples becoming puffy as her breasts warmed beneath the lashing belt. Learning about her young body, other girls' bodies, their teenage breasts and juicy pussies. Becoming keener to learn more, to experience the baser side of sex, she spread her limbs, offering her nakedness to her lesbian lover.

As the leather belt struck her swollen vaginal lips, she let out a yelp and jumped. But, knowing that she could halt the moderate lashing at any time, she was able to relax and enjoy the new pleasures her lesbian lover was bringing her. As she listened to the soft sound of the belt slapping her swollen sex cushions, the wings of her inner lips emerging as if to meet the rough leather strap, she parted her thighs wider. The sensations were strange, she mused as her inner lips protruded fully from her opening sex crack and swelled beneath the lashing of the belt. Slightly painful but most pleasurable, she found that the whipping of her hairless vulval flesh was sending her libido sky-high. She wanted Alison to lash her pussy harder but, to her surprise, she was somewhat embarrassed and decided not to ask the girl.

'All right?' Alison asked, smiling, her lust-sparkling eyes peering at Christina.

'Yes, very much so,' Christina replied, returning her smile.

'A little harder?'

'Well, I . . . OK, but not too hard.'

The leather belt biting harder into the soft pads of her vaginal lips as Alison added a little severity to the lashing, Christina tensed her naked body and dug her fingernails into the quilt. Again, she found that she was enjoying the combination of sexual pain and pleasure. She already knew the feeling of a wet tongue running up and down her vaginal slit, her clitoris pulsating in orgasm, a penis shafting the tight sheath of her pussy. But the leather belt was bringing her new and strangely stimulating sensations.

Her pussy lips reddening, her clitoris solid, she could feel her milky juices of desire trickling from her vaginal opening and running down between her thrashed buttocks to soothe the sensitive tissue of her inflamed anus. Again and again the leather belt whipped her burning vulval flesh, each lash becoming progressively harder as Alison chuckled wickedly in the grips of her debauchery. Christina didn't want to halt the punishment until she was sure that she could take no more. Her naked body rigid, she endured the beautiful vulval whipping until her puffy vaginal lips became painfully swollen. Lifting her head and gazing at her abused vulva, her pretty face grimacing, she finally ordered Alison to stop the thrashing.

'Oh, I was just getting into it,' the girl murmured despondently, lowering the belt to her side.

'God, that was . . .'

'Amazing?'

'Yes, yes, it was. I've never known anything like it. You've obviously been into this sort of thing before.'

'Let's just say that I have a little experience in bondage and spanking. Talking of which, how about bondage? Would you like to try it?'

'Er . . . no, I don't think so,' Christina replied softly. 'I'm absolutely knackered. I think I'll sleep for a while.'

'Go on, you'll love it. I'll tell you what I'll do. I'll tie you to the bed with headscarves. Just loosely knotted around your wrists and ankles and tied to the legs of the bed. I have some long scarfs that I used to use for—'

'Not now, Alison,' Christina sighed. 'Maybe another time.'

'You are an old stick-in-the-mud, Christina. Why don't you let yourself go and have some fun?'

'Haven't I already done that? I've let you shave me, I've—'

'I'll go and get the scarfs.'

Sighing again as Alison went to her room, Christina really didn't want to be tied down. Exhausted, she'd had more than enough sex for one day. Besides, she had to phone the headmaster and let him know that she'd be in the following morning. The thought of returning to the college worrying her, she wondered how far Ponting would demand that she go in return for his silence. Had he mentioned his blackmail threats to his friends, she wondered. If he was in with some of the other male teachers and had told them about Christina's illicit exploits, they might demand that she should wank or suck their cocks, too.

Wondering where it would all end as Alison returned and secured her ankles to the bed legs with the headscarves, Christina thought again about the incredible changes she'd been through since starting at the college. Her whole life turned upside down, her sexual identity in turmoil . . . She stretched her arms out and allowed the other girl to run the headscarves from her wrists to the bed legs. Her limps spread, she watched her friend settle on the bed between her thighs. The girl's tongue running up and down her opening sex slit, Christina let out a sigh of pleasure as her clitoris immediately responded to the lesbian attention. Did she want this to end?

'You taste nice,' Alison murmured, pressing her succulent lips hard against the pink funnel of wet flesh around Christina's vaginal entrance. 'I love drinking from your cunt. Make some more milk for me.' Relaxing as the girl's tongue slipped deep into the hot shaft of her tight cunt, Christina closed her eyes and revelled in the delicious sensations of lesbian oral sex. This was sheer sexual bliss, she thought, her clitoris swelling, her milky juices of desire flowing from her inner nectaries. Listening to Alison slurping and drinking from her sex-drenched cunt, she felt her womb contract, her nipples stiffen as her arousal lifted her higher, closer to her sexual heaven.

'Shit,' Alison breathed as someone hammered on the door. The bell rang too as she leaped off the bed and released Christina. 'I think I know who it is,' she said, wiping the girl-cum from her mouth with the back of her hand.

'Who?' Christina asked, grabbing some clothes from the wardrobe and hurriedly dressing. 'What's the panic?'

'Look, you stay in your room and I'll get rid of them. Or I'll try to. Just stay in here, OK?'

'If you say so.'

'I do say so. This could be trouble,' she murmured, walking to the door. 'Big trouble.'

8

'Settle down, please,' Christina said, watching a paper dart fly across the classroom. 'I'd like you to take out your books and begin your essays on . . .' Christina's words tailing off as the door opened, she gazed at the headmaster. 'I was just . . .' she began, realizing too late that she should have been in his office at eight-thirty that morning.

'My study, Miss Shaw. Now, please,' he snapped.

'Yes, yes, of course. Er . . . While I'm gone,' she said, turning to her sniggering class. 'While I'm gone, you can begin your essays.'

Leaving the room, Christina was fuming as she followed the head to his study. To snap at her like that in front of her class was outrageous. The man obviously had no idea of etiquette. Her hands trembling as she closed the study door behind her, she was about to yell at the man but managed to restrain herself. After all, she had taken a day off and then not turned up at his study that morning. Deciding that they were both in the wrong, she calmed herself as she sat in front of the head at his desk.

'I'm not at all happy, Miss Shaw,' he began, his beady eyes peering intently at her.

'I'm sorry about this morning. I was—'

'I'm not talking about this morning,' he cut in rudely. 'You were ill yesterday?'

'Yes, yes, I was. I think it must have been a stomach bug.'

'Then why were you seen entering the railway station?'

'The railway . . . I went to see my doctor. I've only recently moved here and my doctor's surgery is in—'

'You were seen entering the station at the very time I rang you. Your flatmate, or whoever she is, said that you were ill in bed.'

'Yes, yes, that's right. I decided to go and see my doctor and left the flat without telling her. She was in the bathroom and I . . .'

'I'm not interested in the movements of your flatmate, Miss Shaw. But I *am* interested in your sexual activities.'

'My sexual activities?' Christina gasped. 'If you're talking about my private life, then that's my business.'

'I'm talking about your sexual activities during the working day, Miss Shaw. Your sexual activities *here* – in the college.'

'*What*? Look, I don't know what this is all about, but I can assure you that . . .'

'It's about your sexual activities in your stockroom. Mr Ponting has informed me that—'

'Mr Ponting?' she echoed.

'Our physical education master.'

'I haven't met him.'

'Haven't you?'

'I've never heard of him, Mr Wright. Bear in mind that I only started here on Monday. I've not had a chance to meet the other teachers yet. I did get chatting to Mr Carter the other day. But he's the only other teacher I've met.'

'This is all rather odd, Miss Shaw,' the head murmured, rubbing his lined forehead as he stared at her.

'Mr Ponting told me that he'd met you in your classroom and you revealed to him your sexual activities with your students in the stockroom.'

'What?'

'He also told me that you suggested that he join you in the stockroom for . . . He said that you offered to have sex with him, Miss Shaw.'

'*I* offered to have sex with *him*? Good God. This is unbelievable. I've never met the man, let alone offered to have sex with him.'

'This really is most confusing. Don Ponting has been with us for eight years. I know him well and I can't believe that he's . . .'

'Lying?'

'Don Ponting isn't a liar, Miss Shaw.'

'I'm not suggesting that he's lying, Mr Wright. All I can think is that he's mistaken.'

'He'd hardly be mistaken about something of this nature.'

'In that case, he *is* lying. Although I can't for the life of me think why. If you recall, there was an accusation made the other day by one of the students.'

'Yes, but this is . . .'

'This is the same thing. There seems to be a conspiracy against me, Mr Wright.'

'I wouldn't go as far as to say that.'

'Wouldn't you? Mr Ponting doesn't even know me. He might have seen me around the college, but we've never spoken, let alone . . . My God. To say that I offered to have sex with him is . . .'

'I think I'd better get him in here and we'll thrash this out.'

'Yes, I think you better had.'

Wringing her hands as the headmaster lifted the phone and asked someone to send Don Ponting to his study, Christina reckoned that she wouldn't have too much trouble in dealing with this. If she stuck to her story, said that she'd never met Ponting, there'd be no proving otherwise. Whatever happened, she thought Ponting was a first-rate bastard. She'd wanked his cock and brought out his spunk, and he'd dropped her in the shit in return. Ponting was going to have to be dealt with, and Christina reckoned that she knew exactly how to do it.

'Ah, Don,' the head said, smiling at the man as he knocked and entered the study. 'There seems to be some confusion over—'

'There's no confusion,' Christina broke in, standing up and facing Ponting. 'I've never met this man.'

'We met in your classroom,' Ponting returned. 'You said that . . .'

'I'm sorry, Mr Ponting. I've not met any of the teachers yet. I only started at the college on Monday and—'

'She's lying,' the man said. 'I went to her classroom to introduce myself and she . . . I've already told you what she suggested.'

'This is most confusing,' the head sighed.

'I agree,' Christina said. 'I can't think why Mr Ponting believes that he's met me. Are you sure you're not muddling me up with . . .'

'You know damn well that we met,' the man cut in angrily. 'You've been molesting the students in your stockroom. You've had sex with—'

'That's quite an accusation,' Christina gasped. 'I hope, for your sake, that you can substantiate your outrageous statement.'

'Can you?' the head asked.

'I can't prove it,' Ponting replied.

'You'll be hearing from my solicitor,' Christina warned him.

'Er . . . Miss Shaw,' the head said, offering her a smile. 'There's obviously been a mistake. I really don't think we need go to solicitors.' Turning to Ponting, he raised his eyebrows and pursed his lips. 'We don't want to get involved with solicitors, do we?' he asked.

'Well, I . . .' Ponting murmured, obviously realizing that his plan had failed miserably. 'No, I suppose not.'

'Good, good. Let's put this behind us and move on. Is that all right with you, Miss Shaw?'

'It is this time. But if there's one more allegation from Mr Ponting, I shall go straight to my solicitor. And the local paper.'

'The local . . .' the head stammered. 'Yes, well . . . That's the end of the matter.'

Leaving the study, Christina felt triumphant as she walked down the corridor. But she also felt anger welling from the pit of her stomach. Why had Ponting tried to cause trouble, she wondered. He'd got what he'd wanted by threatening her and she'd have wanked him again had he not . . . Hearing him mumbling something behind her, she stopped and turned. He was a nasty piece of work, she mused, eyeing him up and down. But she'd beaten him. This time, at least.

'Think you're clever, don't you?' he sniggered.

'Why did you do it?' she asked. 'Why did you go running to Wright after I'd—'

'To make sure that you do exactly what I tell you when I tell you.'

'What are you talking about?'

'Sex, Miss Shaw. I want full-blown sex with you.'

'You might have got it if you hadn't thrown the shit at the fan.'

'I *will* get it. Of that, I can assure you.'

'You thrive on trouble, don't you? I know your type, Ponting. You're sexually inadequate. You're a weak little man who can't have a proper relationship with a woman so you have to get off on some power thing to—'

'I saw you yesterday,' he interrupted her, his face grinning. 'I had the day off and happened to see you walking to the station.'

'And?'

'I followed you.'

'You really are a sad little man, aren't you?'

'Call me what you like, it doesn't bother me. I want sex with you, and I'm going to get it. If I don't, then you'll find yourself out of a job.'

'And you'll find yourself—'

'Don't threaten me, Miss Shaw. I have far more on you than you realize.'

'Such as?'

'Your relationship with Bryony.'

Watching him walk off down the corridor, Christina felt her stomach churn. Her hands were trembling. He couldn't have known about Bryony, she was sure. There again, he must have known something, otherwise he wouldn't have mentioned her name. Wondering whether the girl had said anything to anyone, she returned to her class and sat at her desk. The students were unusually quiet, which she found odd. Did they know something, she wondered as they got on with their work. Trying not to catch Bryony's gaze, she managed to get through the lesson until the bell rang.

'Don't run,' she yelled as the students left the room. Bryony hung back, obviously wanting to talk to Christina. To be seen alone with the girl would lead to trouble, Christina knew as the others left. If Ponting happened to walk past . . . This was ridiculous, she decided. If she couldn't talk to one of her students without having to worry about Ponting causing trouble . . .

'What is it, Bryony?' she asked as the girl hovered by her desk.

'About the other night,' the girl began sheepishly.

'What about it?'

'You went out and I—'

'Bryony, I'm very busy. Please, get to the point.'

'I need to see you regularly,' the girl confessed. 'I think about you all the time. I've been dreaming about you and . . .'

'Bryony, this has got to stop,' Christina sighed, gazing longingly at the girl's teenage breasts beneath her tight blouse. 'There's already been a lot of trouble because . . . Have you told anyone about . . . about us?'

'No, I haven't.'

'Are you sure? I mean, have you mentioned it to anyone in the college?'

'Honestly, I've not said anything. May I come and see you this evening?'

'Bryony . . . Look, someone's been causing trouble. Word has got out that we . . . I don't know what's been said but people are beginning to talk about us.'

'Don't you want me?'

'It's not a question of whether or not I want you. Don't you understand? I'm your teacher, for God's sake. This sort of thing is not only frowned upon but . . . Christ,

Bryony. We're the same sex. Having an affair with a male student would be bad enough, but to . . .'

'I love licking you, tasting you. All I want is to be with you, have sex with you.'

Biting her lip, Christina gazed into the girl's wide eyes. The situation was extremely dangerous, but Christina couldn't help her feelings, her inner desires. She wanted the girl, she knew as she gazed again at the tight material of her blouse following the contours of her developing young breasts. Wondering whether Ponting had seen Bryony outside the flat and was putting two and two together, Christina knew that she had to see the girl again.

'I have a free period,' she said, glancing at the wall clock.

'So have I,' Bryony murmured.

'We need to talk, but not here.'

'What about the common?' the girl asked eagerly, expectation reflected in her sparkling eyes. 'I could meet you on the common. It's behind the—'

'I know where it is. All right, I'll meet you there. But only to talk, Bryony. You *do* understand that, don't you?'

'Yes, yes, I do. I'll go now.'

'I'll leave in about ten minutes.'

'I'll see you by the pond.'

Christina instinctively knew that this was going to be her biggest mistake yet. She also knew that she was going to do far more than simply talk to Bryony. It was impossible to deny her feelings for the girl, her lust for her curvaceous body. Leaving the college, she felt her clitoris swell in expectation of lesbian sex. She was weak, she knew as she approached the common. Weak in her lust for lesbian sex, weak in her craving for a teenage girl's naked body.

The common was deserted, but Christina repeatedly
turned her head to make sure that she wasn't being
followed. As she walked across the grass towards the
pond, she imagined Ponting following her, spying on
her. The man knew nothing of her relationship with
Bryony, she was sure as she saw the girl hovering by the
pond. He might have seen them talking, or seen the girl
entering the flat, but that proved nothing. Ponting was
shooting in the dark, grabbing at straws in an effort to
force Christina to commit crude sexual acts with him.
Ponting was a bastard, and he'd pay dearly for his
threats.

'So,' Christina said, smiling as she stood in front of
Bryony. 'I think we need to talk.'

'Yes, we do,' the girl agreed, unbuttoning the top of
her blouse. 'It's very hot today.'

'We're here to *talk*, Bryony,' Christina said, trying to
convince herself rather than the girl as she gazed at the
shallow ravine of her student's cleavage between her
barely developed breasts. 'If we're to see each other,
we're going to have to be very careful.'

'Let's go into the woods,' Bryony suggested. 'People
might notice us, here in the open.'

'All right,' Christina replied, walking towards the
trees. 'Bryony, what happened at my flat the other night
was . . . Well, it wasn't right. Alison should never
have—'

'You enjoyed it, didn't you?'

'Yes, yes, I did. Mind you, most of the action was
between you and Alison.'

'That's because you went out. I was waiting for you to
come back. If you had, we could have loved.'

'Yes, we could have. Look, if we're going to see each

other, then we must keep Alison out of it. She's . . . she's a strange girl, to say the least. Her idea of sex involves bondage and whipping.'

'I like that sort of thing,' Bryony confessed as they walked into the woods. 'I love being spanked.'

'Bryony, we're not here to . . . Christ, it's no good.'

'What isn't?'

'It's no good trying to deny my feelings. I want you, Bryony. It's wrong, it's unethical, it's . . . God, how I want you.'

'You can have me,' the girl said, her pretty face beaming as she slipped her blouse over her shoulders. 'Will you spank me?' she asked, wandering along a narrow path into a clearing.

'Yes, yes, I'll spank you,' Christina murmured, eyeing the girl's small bra. 'Take your clothes off and I'll spank you.'

Sitting on the grass as the younger girl slipped her skirt down her slender legs, Christina wondered why she was unable to control her sexual desires. She even found herself thinking about Ponting's cock, remembering wanking him off and watching his spunk shoot from his throbbing knob. Ponting was a bastard, but he had a cock. Imagining the man driving his solid penis deep into the wet heat of her pussy, she felt her womb contract, her juices of lust seeping between the engorged lips of her hairless vulva.

'I shaved again this morning,' Bryony announced, displaying the firm lips of her vagina as she stepped out of her panties and stood naked in front of Christina.

'You have a beautiful cunt,' Christina murmured, recalling Alison's arousing words.

'I like you talking like that,' Bryony giggled. 'Say

something else. Tell me about my cunt, what you'd like to do to my cunt.'

'Bryony, you're too young for this sort of thing.'

'Too young? But isn't that how you like me? You like young girls, don't you?'

'No, no, I . . .'

'I know what you like. You like the thought of young girls' cunts. You like cunts without hair, young cunts with—'

'Stop it, Bryony,' Christina broke in, guilt swamping her as she realized that the girl was right.

'It's all right, I do understand. Do you think I'm naughty?'

'Yes, very.'

'Then you'd better spank me.'

'Not with that,' Christina gasped as the girl snapped a branch off a nearby bush. 'Bryony, that'll hurt you and . . .'

'That's what I want.'

'If you're sure.'

'Yes, I am.'

Taking the branch as the girl got down on all fours and stuck out the rounded cheeks of her naked buttocks, Christina couldn't believe that this was happening. Reckoning the bush was actually a small bay tree, she looked at the branch and felt the sharp edges of the leaves. She was going to have to be careful, she knew as she gazed longingly at Bryony's firm bottom. The rough branch with its projecting twigs could easily damage the hitherto unblemished flesh of the girl's buttocks. She was going to have to be gentle in her thrashing, gentle in her lesbian loving.

'Do it,' Bryony said impatiently, her pretty face

pressed against the grass, her knees parted wide. Kneeling by the girl's side and raising the branch above her head, Christina felt her stomach somersault as she focused on her young student's hairless pussy lips bulging invitingly between her slender thighs. This was wrong, she knew. She shouldn't be in the woods with one of her young students. She should have fought her inner desires, taken control of her craving for lesbian lust. Was Bryony right, she wondered. Did the thought of young girls excite her? Was she into young teenage girls? If she was, then . . . There was no if about it, Christina knew as she watched the opaque liquid of lust trickling between Bryony's naked love lips. Young schoolgirls were extremely arousing, she reflected. Young, fresh, firm, virginal . . . This was a new and potentially dangerous discovery.

'Do it,' Bryony said again, obviously thirsting for the feel of the branch against her pert buttocks. Bringing the branch down, Christina watched the girl's buttocks tense as the rough leaves bit into her pale flesh. Raising the branch above her head again, she brought it down across the girl's twitching bottom with a loud crack. Bryony's naked body jolted, her juices of lust streaming from the opening entrance to her young vagina and streaming down her inner thighs. Again, Christina lashed her naked buttocks to the accompaniment of the girl's whimpers of debased pleasure.

Recalling Alison thrashing the firm globes of Christina's buttocks with the leather belt, Christina had considerable understanding of the pleasure to be derived from the debauched act. Bryony was obviously revelling in the thrashing as the branch repeatedly bit into her crimsoning flesh. Her sighs and whimpers growing louder, her juices of sex streaming from the entrance to her lust sheath, she began to tremble as Christina thrashed the glowing flesh of her naked bottom harder.

'Talk dirty,' the girl said shakily, her bum cheeks turning a fire-red beneath the rough branch. 'Do it harder and talk dirty to me.'

'You're a naughty girl,' Christina said, wondering whether to let go of her inhibitions and allow her true thoughts and feelings to show. 'You're a very naughty girl and . . . I love your little cunt. I love your hard young tits, your sweet bumhole. Your cunt is beautiful. I'm going to lick your cunt, suck out your sex cream, bite your hairless lips, eat you, tongue-fuck you, lick your bottom and—'

'Yes, yes,' Bryony gasped as Christina thrashed the burning flesh of her fiery buttocks harder. 'Talk really dirty to me.'

'I'm going to fuck your tight cunt with my fist,' Christina said, wondering where her crude words were coming from. 'I'm going to lick your arse out and then bum-fuck you with my fist.'

'Piss on me,' Bryony cried. 'Tell me that you want to piss all over my cunt.'

Continuing the gruelling thrashing, Christina thought about the girl's vulgar words, the decadence of the crude act she'd suggested. Recalling her bladder draining as Alison had fisted her rectal canal, she realized again that she had some understanding of the darker side of sex, the immense pleasure that could be had from such debased sexual acts. But where were her thoughts coming from, she wondered. Obviously from the murky depths of her mind – but how did they get there?

Living a sheltered life with her parents, enduring straight sex with Charles, Christina hadn't even dreamed that one day she'd be involved in a debased lesbian relationship, let alone be thrashing a young girl's naked bottom. To think about urinating . . . Wondering whether all girls harboured such wanton thoughts, she continued the naked-buttock thrashing until Bryony rolled onto her side and lay gasping on the grass. Her legs open, her head tossing from side to side, she was obviously lost in her sexual delirium.

'Are you all right?' Christina asked her, eyeing the elongated teats of her nipples rising alluringly from her pert breasts. 'Bryony, are you OK?'

'Yes, yes,' the girl breathed, opening her eyes and smiling. 'Fist me now. Fist my cunt and make me come.'

'I don't think . . .' Christina began, wondering whether the girl could take it. 'Bryony, I think you need to rest before—'

'No, no. I don't need to rest. I want you to fist my cunt. Use me and abuse me, do anything and everything to me. Please, you must use my body.'

'Why are you like this?' Christina asked, shaking her head. 'You're far too young to . . .'

'I'm the way I am, OK? *Why* I'm like this doesn't matter. Fist my cunt, hurt me, abuse me.'

'I'm not going to hurt you,' Christina returned, her blue eyes clouding as she frowned. 'Thrashing you was bad enough, but . . . I'll fist you, OK?'

'Yes, yes.'

Parting Bryony's swollen vaginal lips, opening the sex-drenched entrance to her teenage cunt, Christina slipped three fingers into her tight pleasure duct. Stirring the cream within her hot cunt, Christina lubricated her fingers, wondering whether the girl's young vagina could accommodate her fist. Bryony was a sex-crazed nymphomaniac, she mused, recalling when she'd been the girl's age. Christina had masturbated, but had never thought of having a fist forced into her vaginal canal. She'd never dreamed of fingering her bottom-hole, having her naked buttocks thrashed or . . .

'Keep going,' Bryony gasped as Christina's fingers slipped deeper into her hot pussy sheath. 'Go on, it's all right. Push your fist right up my cunt.' Watching the girl's hairless outer lips stretching tautly around her knuckles, Christina managed to ease half her hand into her teenage pussy. Her solid clitoris forced out from beneath its pinken hood, her inner lips stretching like pink elastic, Bryony opened her legs to the extreme. To her surprise, Christina watched her fist sink into the girl's pelvic cavity as if it had been sucked in. The girl's swollen and inflamed love lips hugging her slender wrist, Christina felt the inner heat of her young body as Bryony's cunt tightened around her fist.

'OK?' she asked, gazing in awe at the lewd sight.

'Yes, yes,' Bryony replied, her eyes rolling, her breathing fast and shallow. 'Fist me and bite my tits,' she said, her head lolling from side to side. 'Fist me hard and bite my nipples hard.'

Leaning over the girl's trembling body, Christina sank her teeth gently into the brown protrusion of her erect nipple and sucked hard on her darkening areola. Bryony gasped, her naked body shaking violently as Christina began pistoning her young cunt with her clenched fist. She was far too young for this sort of thing, Christina reflected again as she bit harder into the girl's swelling nipple. She should have been going to clubs and discos, meeting boys of her own age. She should have been experimenting sexually with boys, discovering her clitoris, the delights of the penis.

But everyone was different, Christina concluded as she listened to the arousing sound of her fist squelching the girl's lubricious sex juices. Bryony had had a difficult life so far. Her mother was a drunkard, her father had run off with a young tart, she lived in a slum . . . Perhaps she'd found some solace in the perverted use of her young body. Perhaps she'd grown to believe that you only got pleasure from sex if pain was involved. Christina doubted that the girl could understand a loving relationship. Sex, in her mind, seemed to be a punishing and torturous act where her young body was subjected to pain and abuse. Was there anything wrong with that? Christina wondered, sucking harder on Bryony's erect nipple as she twisted her fist deep within her bloated vaginal cavern. As long as Bryony was happy . . . But she wasn't, was she?

Bryony was in desperate need of a relationship, and was obviously looking to Christina to fulfil her desires. Christina was enjoying the crude sex, although the acts Bryony had demanded she commit worried her. Moving to the girl's other nipple, she sank her teeth into her areola and sucked hard on the sensitive protrusion of her milk teat. Bryony squirmed and writhed, letting out gasps and whimpers of exquisite pleasure as she neared her girl-induced climax. Wondering about the young girl's previous sexual experiences, Christina imagined her having sex with other girls from the college. It was unlikely that she'd had a string of girlfriends, but she was certainly experienced in the baser acts of sex.

'I'm coming,' Bryony cried, gyrating her shapely hips as her vaginal muscles tightened around Christina's pistoning fist. 'God, my cunt. I'm . . . I'm coming.' Writhing on the grass as her orgasm erupted within her pulsating clitoris, she screamed out her immense pleasure. 'Bite me harder,' she gasped, clutching Christina's head and forcing her mouth harder against the firm mound of her young breast. 'Fist-fuck my cunt. Bite my tit harder. Fuck my beautiful cunt.'

Doing her best to comply with the girl's perverted demands, Christina wondered whether she'd enjoy a pussy-thrashing. Recalling the leather belt lashing her own naked cunny lips, she eyed the branch lying on the ground and imagined lashing the girl's shaved vulva. Knowing Bryony, she'd delight in the decadent act, Christina was sure as she sustained her massive orgasm with her thrusting fist. If Bryony were to move into the flat, there'd be non-stop crude sex, Christina knew. Would that be such a bad thing, she wondered, sinking her teeth into the shuddering girl's areola. Shaving, fisting, bondage and whipping . . . Having Bryony at the flat could prove to be very rewarding. There again, in view of Ponting's comments, having Bryony move in wouldn't be such a good idea.

The only way Christina would be able to have a relationship with the girl would be to keep it secret. Even telling Alison would be out of the question. The girl might let something slip and . . . It was a great shame that people didn't mind their own business, Christina reflected as Bryony began to come down from her mind-blowing orgasm. Too many people knew too much. Too many people were watching, prying.

'God, that was incredible,' Bryony gasped. 'I want you to piss all over my cunt now.'

'No, Bryony,' Christina returned. 'There are limits and I really don't think—'

'Why not?' the girl asked disappointedly. 'What's wrong with pissing on me?'

'What's *wrong* with it? What's *right* about it? I think we've already gone far enough. Too far, in fact.'

'Gone too far? What do you mean?'

'Sex should be . . . Oh, I don't know,' Christina sighed, wondering which of them was right. Perhaps Bryony's perception of sex was right, she mused, massaging the girl's inner vaginal flesh with her clenched fist. 'Bryony, thrashing you with the branch and fisting you—'

'Was beautiful,' the girl said, her pretty face beaming. 'I don't see why what we do should matter, whatever it is. If we enjoy it, then why not do it?'

Sliding her cunny-wet fist out of the trembling girl's inflamed vagina, Christina reflected on Bryony's words. *If we enjoy it, then why not do it?* Was that the way to look at it, she wondered, her fist leaving the girl's abused body with a loud sucking sound. That might be the way to look at it, but would *Christina* enjoy urinating over the girl's naked vulval crack? There *were* limits, she mused, wondering why. Who laid out the rules? Who set out the way things should be? Society?

'We'd better be getting back,' Christina said, rising to her feet.

'Not yet,' Bryony sighed. 'My next class isn't until after lunch. There's no hurry.'

'Bryony, I have things to do. As it is, I took the day off yesterday. Mr Wright isn't too pleased with me, so—'

'He's never pleased with anyone. Apart from Ponting, of course.'

'Ponting?'

'They're good friends.'

'I thought as much,' Christina murmured, settling down beside Bryony again. 'What's Ponting like?'

'He's a pig,' the girl breathed. 'No one likes him. His wife is—'

'His *wife*?' Christina cut in. 'You mean, he's married?'

'He'd have to be to have a wife, wouldn't he?'

'Yes, no, I mean . . .'

'Yes, he's married. His wife works for the council. I think she's a council planner or something.'

'That's interesting,' Christina murmured pensively. 'Bryony, I have an idea in mind. You say that you don't like Ponting?'

'I hate him.'

'Good, good. How about helping me to get him sacked?'

'Sacked? Yes, I'd be all for it but . . . How?'

'I have a plan. Look, I have to get back now. I'll talk to you this evening, OK?'

'You want me to come to your flat?'

'Well, I . . . I suppose you'll have to. I'll explain why later, but I want you to go in the back way. There's a fire escape leading down to an alley. I'll leave the window open and . . .'

'You want me to climb in through a window?' Bryony asked, grabbing her school clothes and getting dressed.

'Yes. I'll tell you why later. I reckon that, between us, we can be rid of Ponting once and for all.'

'I certainly hope so. Do you know, he tried to look at me in the changing room the other week. And another time I caught him sniffing a pair of knickers in the changing rooms.'

'That's excellent,' Christina giggled.

'What's excellent about it? He's a dirty old man.'

'All will be revealed later, my little angel. Now, I really must be going.'

'OK, I'll see you this evening.'

'Right you are.'

Leaving the clearing, Christina couldn't stop grinning. Ponting was married, a sniffer of schoolgirls' panties, a sad pervert, a blackmailer . . . Her plan was going to work, she knew as she walked back to the college. With Bryony's help, Mr Ponting was going to have to face not only the prospect of being sacked from his job but divorce.

9

'Oh, hello,' Christina said, leaning on the phone-box door as a woman answered at the other end of the line. 'Is Don there, please?'

'Don?' the woman echoed. 'I'm afraid he's out. May I take a message?'

'Yes, thanks. This is Sally. I can't make it for our usual drink but—'

'Your usual drink? I'm sorry, but I think you must have the wrong number.'

'Oh,' Christina breathed. 'I must have misdialled. I wanted to speak to Don Ponting.'

'Er . . . in that case, you do have the right number. Who did you say you were?'

'My name's Sally. We usually meet for a drink and then go out but I can't make it tonight.'

'Did he give you this number?'

'No, he didn't. Actually, I got it from the college. I'm a student there. You must be Don's mother. He's told me quite a lot about you.'

'His mother? Er . . . yes, that's right. So, how long have you known Don?'

'Oh, we've been going out together for about three months now. He obviously wants to keep it quiet, seeing as I'm a student. But we're very serious about each other. Has he not mentioned me to you?'

'Yes, yes, he has. How old are you?'

'Only sixteen. I know about the age difference but we're in love. Don reckons that age doesn't matter.'

'Yes, I'm sure he does.'

'Well, I'm sorry to have troubled you. I hope we meet before long.'

'Oh, we will. I can assure you of that.'

'Sorry again for disturbing you. Goodbye.'

Leaving the phone box, Christina ran back to the flat and raced up the stairs. With stage one of her plan completed, she took a bottle of wine from the fridge and grabbed a glass. Bryony was due in about half an hour, giving Alison plenty of time to finish her make-up before going out for the evening. Christina hadn't mentioned Bryony's visit in case Alison decided to stay in and join the sexy fun. Fortunately, she'd decided to go and see a band playing at the local pub.

'Oh, you're back,' Alison said, appearing in the kitchen doorway. 'Did you make your phone call?'

'Yes, I did. And it worked perfectly.'

'Tell me about it later. I want to get a good seat at the pub. If I turn up late, I'll end up standing for the entire evening.'

'When are you going to tell me about that man who called last night?'

'It's nothing, Christina. Just some man I used to know, that's all.'

'You seemed pretty worried about it.'

'Did I? Oh well, there's nothing to worry about. God, look at the time. I'd better go.'

'OK. Have a good time.'

'Are you sure you won't come with me?'

'I can't, Alison. I have so much work to do that I'm just going to have to stay in.'

'Right. Well, don't work too hard. I should be home about midnight.'

'OK, see you later.'

The scene set, Christina opened the wine and filled her glass. Bryony's visit would be fruitful, she was sure as she imagined Ponting getting home to his questioning wife. He was going to have a hell of a job explaining things to her. And once the woman had heard that her husband had been caught in the woods with young Bryony and with his trousers down, all hell would break loose. That was, of course, if Bryony agreed to take part in the plot. Christina was pretty sure that she could rely on the girl. After all, she hated Ponting and would obviously be only too pleased to see the back of him.

Bryony arrived via the back window at seven and wandered into the lounge to find Christina. The girl was wearing a short red skirt, red shoes and a white blouse. She looked far younger than her years, giving Christina another idea. If it got around that Ponting had been screwing an under-age girl, he'd be hung, drawn and quartered. But, before making any further plans, Christina had to get Bryony's agreement.

'You look lovely,' Christina said, rising to her feet and pouring the girl a glass of wine.

'Thanks. It wasn't easy climbing through the window in this skirt. My mum said that I look like a whore, dressed like this.'

'You look beautiful, Bryony. There's your drink. Now, sit down and I'll tell you about my plan.'

'By the way, I . . . . I don't know how to tell you this.'

'What? What is it?'

'Doogan and Brown followed me. They saw me climb through the window.'

'Ah, right. Er . . . not to worry. I don't think they'll come knocking at my door.'

'They said that they . . . The thing is . . .'

'Come on, tell me.'

'They said that they'll come round later for sex.'

'Did they, now? We'll see about that. Don't worry about the likes of Doogan and Brown. I'll deal with them if I have to. OK, so here's this plan of mine: the idea is that Ponting is caught in the woods with you.'

'Having sex with me?'

'No, you won't have to go that far. All we need is for someone to stumble across you and let the cat out of the bag.'

'I'll say that he raped me,' the girl suggested.

'No, we don't need to go down that road. It'll be enough for Ponting to be caught with a young female student. He'll be suspended from the college, and his wife will leave him. That's a pretty good plan, don't you agree?'

'Yes, but who's going to catch us in the woods? Whoever it is might not want to get involved once things start getting—'

'Our witness will want to get involved, all right. The reason being that our witness will be Ponting's wife.'

'God, That'll cause trouble.'

'Exactly. When Mrs Ponting discovers you naked in the woods and her husband with his cock out . . .'

'Won't I be in trouble?'

'Hardly. You're old enough to have sex, aren't you? Besides, Ponting lured you into the woods. He said that he'd make sure that you'd get bad exam results if you didn't go to the woods and have sex with him. OK, do you want to play your part?'

'Yes, yes, of course. It'll be fun.'

'That's one way to look at it,' Christina giggled. 'However, this isn't a game. We're going to have to get it right first time. There'll be no rehearsals, Bryony. And do bear in mind that if his wife doesn't turn up for any reason . . . Actually, that won't be a problem. I'll be on hand to rescue you if things start to go too far.'

'That'll be Doogan and Brown,' Bryony sighed as the doorbell rang.

'OK, I'll go and talk to them. You wait there. Help yourself to the wine.'

Bounding down the stairs, Christina hoped that Alison hadn't come back for some reason. Realizing that the girl would use her key, she reckoned that Bryony was right and Doogan and Brown had come round to try their luck. Opening the door, she gazed at the lads, eyeing the tight crotches of their jeans as they stood on the step, grinning. Doogan spoke first, suggesting that they join Christina and Bryony for a few beers.

'I don't have any beers,' Christina replied.

'We do,' Brown said, holding up two carrier bags.

'I'm helping Bryony with her college work.'

'Does she normally climb in through the window in a skirt that's not worth wearing?' Doogan asked.

'You're fucking her, aren't you?' Brown chortled.

'For you information, Brown, I do not have a penis.'

'No, but you've got a tongue and fingers.'

'For God's sake. What is it with you two?'

'Sex,' Doogan replied. 'You like a length of cock, don't you?'

Looking down at the lad's crotch again, Christina felt

her young womb contract, the lips of her vulva swell. With Alison out of the way for the evening, it might be worth inviting the young studs in for a few drinks, Christina mused. She was feeling somewhat thirsty, but not for wine or beer. The thought of fresh spunk playing on her mind, rousing her taste buds, she wondered whether to invite the lads in for an hour or so. Bryony would be none too pleased, she knew. But there was time enough to drain the lads' balls and still enjoy an evening of lesbian sex before Alison rolled in at midnight.

'You may come in for a while,' she conceded. 'Only an hour, no more.'

'We don't take *that* long,' Doogan sniggered.

'No, that's the trouble with teenage boys,' Christina riposted.

'No, I meant—'

'I know what you meant. Come on up, and close the door behind you.'

Leading the way, Christina walked into the lounge and smiled at Bryony. The girl had heard Christina's conversation with the boys and was gazing, almost expectantly, at the door. She seemed to conceal a smile as they walked into the room and grinned at her. Had this been Bryony's idea? Christina wondered, sipping her wine as the lads swigged lager from their cans. Perhaps the girl wanted to experience a length of cock, as Doogan had so tastefully put it.

'Well,' Christina said, refilling her glass. 'This is cosy.'

'I can come back later if—' Bryony began.

'No, no,' Christina interrupted her. 'I think you might learn something if you stay.'

'I'll teach her,' Doogan chuckled.

'Doogan, you couldn't teach your grandmother to suck cock,' Christina retorted.

'Hey, you're OK,' Brown laughed. 'You're cool.'

'I'm red-hot, Brown. Now, why don't you lads strip off while I sit next to Bryony and watch?'

'Strip off?' Doogan echoed, his deep-set eyes darkening as he frowned.

'I thought you might want to show off. All you two think about is sex, so let's have a good look at your equipment.'

Nudging Bryony as she sat down next to her, Christina watched the lads pull their T-shirts over their heads and unbuckle their belts. She had them just where she wanted them, she knew as they tugged their jeans down. This might have been unethical, she mused as they pulled their boxer shorts down, their erect cocks catapulting to attention. It might have been immoral, wrong . . . But, whatever it was, she reckoned that she was now in complete control of her class. And, having made a fool of Ponting, the future was looking better than ever.

'Do we get to fuck the tart?' Brown asked, grinning at Bryony.

'If you carry on like that, Brown, you'll end up having to wank,' Christina returned. 'What do you think, Bryony?'

'I . . . I don't know,' the girl replied sheepishly.

'I'm talking about their cocks. What do you think about their cocks?'

'Oh, I see. They're all right, I suppose. I've never—'

'It's all right, you don't have to mention that. Why don't you take a look at one? Grab one and feel it.'

'OK.'

'Choose one. Which one would you like?'

'I'll have . . . er . . . Doogan.'

'You heard the girl, Doogan. Come and stand over here and let her examine your cock.'

Grinning, Doogan stood in front of Bryony with the opening of his foreskin only inches from her fresh face. Taking his weapon by the root, she squeezed it as if testing its rigidity before moving her hand up his erect shaft and fully retracting his foreskin. Christina watched the girl examine Doogan's purple knob, wondering whether she'd take it into her hot mouth and suck it. This wasn't how she'd expected the evening to turn out, she thought as Bryony moved her head forward and pushed her tongue out. Would the girl take the purple knob into her mouth and explore the sperm-slit with her tongue? Christina would have preferred her to use her tongue to caress Christina's clitoris to orgasm, but there would be plenty of time later for lesbian sex.

Brown took the liberty of standing in front of Christina and offering his erect cock to her mouth as she turned and looked up at him. Taking his fleshy shaft in her hand, she pulled his foreskin back. She was aware of Bryony watching her as she parted her full lips. Perhaps the girl was waiting for Christina to take the lead and would suck Doogan's swollen knob once Christina had taken Brown's plum into her wet mouth. Deciding to drain the lads' balls and get them out of the flat, Christina engulfed the young man's glans between her succulent wet lips and tongued his sperm-slit.

'Go on, then,' Doogan said, looking down at Bryony as she hesitated, holding his purple knob an inch or so away from her pretty mouth. 'Do what the teacher lady is doing.' Moving forward, Bryony slipped the lad's swollen glans between her full lips and teased the silky-

smooth surface with her wet tongue. Doogan gasped, his
naked body visibly shaking as Bryony explored his
rounded cock-head with her pink tongue. Tasting the
salty knob, she moved her hand slowly up and down his
twitching shaft, watching Christina from the corner of
her eye as if seeking her approval.

Winking at the girl, Christina cupped Brown's heavy
balls in the palm of her free hand, kneading the lad's
sperm-spheres, adding to his pleasure as he breathed
heavily in his soaring arousal. Copying her mentor,
Bryony took Doogan's ball sac in her hand, feeling the
two eggs through the fleshy bag, learning about male
anatomy as she quickened her wanking motions. Would
the girl swallow Doogan's sperm? Christina wondered.
Or would she move back, spit his knob out of her mouth
at the first taste of his salty spunk and leave him to wank?

Gobbling on Brown's solid plum, Christina kept her
eye on Bryony. What was the girl thinking, she wondered. Taking her first cock into her wet mouth, licking
the swollen glans, running her tongue around the salty
rim . . . Would this change her sexual preference? Would
she now take an interest in boys, decide that sucking
cocks was far more satisfying than licking pussies? Christina realized that she was feeling a little jealous as she
watched the girl's full lips rolling back and forth along
the teenager's solid penile shaft.

'Wait,' Christina said, moving her head back and
slipping Brown's swollen glans out of her mouth. 'Bryony, I want to see you take both knobs into your mouth.'

'But that's not possible,' the girl replied.

'It *is* possible. Just do as I say, all right?'

'All right.'

'Go on, Brown. Go and join Doogan.'

Standing beside his friend, Brown offered his purple plum to Bryony's open mouth alongside Doogan's twitching glans. The girl obediently took both knobs into her mouth, her full lips stretched tautly around the rims of their helmets as she cupped the two pairs of balls in her small hands. The lewd sight sending ripples of sex through Christina's young womb, she looked up at the lads. Noticing the sheer pleasure apparent in their expressions as the girl mouthed and tongued their solid knobs, Christina hoped that they'd pump out their sperm simultaneously.

'Use your tongue, Bryony,' she instructed her young student. Nodding her head, the girl slurped and sucked on the bulbous sex globes, obviously realizing that her mouth would soon flood with fresh sperm. The lads' gasps resounding around the room, Christina knew that they were about to shoot their spunk to the back of the girl's throat and drain their full balls. Clutching Bryony's head, she was determined that the girl wouldn't escape the gush of spunk. The boys' shafts rigid, their balls rolling, they let out low moans of debased pleasure as their sperm pumps activated.

Clutching Bryony's head, forcing her to drink the fresh cream from the twitching cocks, Christina watched the white liquid spill from her bloated mouth and dribble down her chin. The orgasmic fluid pouring from Bryony's mouth and splattering her red skirt as the boys pumped out their sperm, Christina ordered her pupil to swallow. The girl did her best, repeatedly gulping down the gushing spunk as her cheeks filled and her pretty mouth overflowed. Christina could hear her swallowing, drinking from the orgasming fountainheads as the boys shuddered and let out rushes of breath.

'Good girl,' Christina finally praised her student as the spent knobs slipped out of her sperm-flooded mouth. 'Did you enjoy that?'

'Yes, I think . . . I think so,' the girl spluttered, wiping her mouth with the back of her hand.

'I know I did,' Doogan chortled, his snakelike penis hanging down over his hairy ball sac.

'That goes without saying,' Christina said brusquely. 'And now, Bryony, I think you should experience a penis inside your pussy.'

'If you say so,' the girl replied, her pink tongue licking her sperm-glossed lips.

'I do say so. Slip your panties off. That's it. Now lie back on the sofa with your bum over the edge of the cushion and open your legs wide.'

'Like this?' Bryony murmured, kicking her moist panties aside and taking her position.

'Yes, like that. Now, you two, which of you is going to . . .' Shaking her head as she eyed their flaccid cocks, Christina sighed. 'Is that the best you can do?' she asked.

'Give us a minute,' Brown returned. 'We're not bloody supermen.'

'You can say that again. I don't know, I really don't. You have a beautiful young girl offering you her shaved pussy, and your cocks look like dead slugs.'

'We've just done her mouth,' Brown moaned. 'What the hell do you expect?'

'Too much, obviously. You're going to have to do better than this. All this talk about girls, and you can only come once? Real studs, I must say.'

'OK, OK,' Doogan said, wanking his stiffening shaft. 'There, you see?'

'It's a start,' Christina murmured. 'OK, Doogan, it looks as if you're about ready so you go first.'

Christina could hardly believe how much things had changed as Doogan kneeled on the floor between Bryony's parted feet. Again, she recalled her experiences since she'd started at the college. It was incredible to think that she'd had so many sexual partners, male and female, within such a short space of time. It was as if she'd suddenly woken up to her sexuality after years of dormancy and was now making up for lost time. Sperm swallowing, cunny drinking, anal fisting . . . Was there anything she'd not experienced during her first week at the college?

'Ouch,' Bryony moaned as Doogan pushed his solid cock deep into the tight sheath of her vagina.

'You're at the wrong angle, Bryony,' Christina said. 'Swivel your hips so that . . . That's it. Good girl.'

'God, she's fucking tight,' Doogan gasped, gazing at the girl's swollen outer lips hugging the root of his penis as he fully impaled her on his solid rod.

'There's no need to be crude,' Christina snapped.

'Crude?' Brown chortled, gazing at the lewd coupling. 'He's got his cock stuffed up the tart's cunt, and you reckon he's crude because he says she's fucking tight?'

'You know what I mean, Brown,' Christina sighed, lifting her buttocks clear of the sofa and slipping her panties off. 'By the look of your cock, you're finally ready to do something useful with it,' she said, reclining on the sofa.

Her rounded buttocks over the edge of the cushion, she ordered the lad to copy his friend by kneeling between her feet and slipping his solid cock deep into the wet sheath of her cunt. Brown didn't hesitate. Taking his penis by the root, he guided his purple knob between the splayed wings of Christina's inner lips and drove the entire length of his rock-hard rod deep into her trembling body. Christina breathed heavily as she watched him withdraw his pussy-slimed shaft and drive into her again. Her love lips rolling back and forth along his sex-glistening member, she could feel the swollen bulb of his knob repeatedly battering her ripe cervix as he quickened his fucking motions. The sofa rocking as the boys found their rhythm, their cocks fucking the girls' cunts to the accompaniment of gasps of pleasure, Christina grabbed Bryony's hand as if to guide her through her first crude pussy-fucking.

'All right?' she asked, turning her head and smiling at the flushed-faced girl.

'Oh, yes,' she breathed, her eyes rolling, her lips furling into a wicked grin. 'I think I'm going to come.'

'Just relax and let yourself go. Feel the spunk filling you, your pussy tightening, your clitoris—'

'Oh, oh,' Bryony gasped, her young body shaking uncontrollably as she neared her climax. 'Oh, I think . . . I . . . I'm coming.'

'Fuck her, Doogan,' Christina cried, her own orgasm about to explode within her solid clitoris. 'Spunk her, for God's sake.'

'I am, I am,' the lad breathed, his face grimacing as he pumped out his sperm.

Christina could feel Brown's sperm gushing deep into her cunt as he too reached his shuddering climax. Gripping Bryony's hand, Christina watched the lad's sperm-wet shaft gliding in and out of her cunt, the dripping petals of her inner lips rolling back and forth along the sticky sex rod. She was in her element, she knew as

Bryony let out a cry of sexual satisfaction, her orgasm obviously peaking as her young stud fucked her senseless.

The boys were OK, Christina mused, gazing in turn at their grimacing faces. They'd obviously lost their virginity some time ago, but they were still learning. Bryony experiencing her pioneering fuck, the boys furthering their sex education, Christina was also learning more of the baser side of sex. But there was one thing she'd not yet experienced, something that had been playing on her mind since her debased sex session with Alison. One sexual act that she'd thought about trying, but hadn't had the opportunity, let alone the nerve, to attempt.

Her immense pleasure beginning to recede, Christina watched Bryony's flushed face, her gasping mouth, her wide eyes, as the girl was obviously in the grips of a multiple orgasm. Bryony's young body twitched and convulsed, her cunt spewing out a blend of sperm and girl-cum as Doogan, apparently proving that he was a stud by fucking her with a vengeance, repeatedly rammed into her. The squelching sounds of crude fucking resounded around the room and he appeared to have amazing staying power.

To Christina's disappointment, Brown withdrew his deflating cock from the spasming sheath of her pussy and sat back on his heels as his friend continued with his forbidden fucking. Realizing that she'd got the wrong lad, Christina was at least pleased for Bryony. The girl letting out a scream as her orgasm gripped her, she tossed her head from side to side as she drifted in her sexual delirium. She was bound to prefer cock to pussies now, Christina reflected sadly, her own clitoris in dire need of attention.

'Come on, Brown,' she hissed. 'You can't leave me like this. Lick my clit and suck your spunk out of my cunt.' Moving forward, the boy parted Christina's hairless love lips and pressed his mouth hard against the pink flesh surrounding her solid clitoris. Sucking and licking, he slipped two fingers deep into the spermed sheath of her hot cunt and massaged her inner flesh as she writhed and gasped on the sofa in her sexual ecstasy. Again, Bryony cried out in her coming as Doogan amazed everyone by continuing to shaft her tight cunt with his rock-hard cock. Doogan was a lad worth knowing, Christina thought, looking down as Brown slipped his fingers out of her cunt and began sucking out his sperm. Doogan was the fucker, and Brown the sucker, she concluded.

Again pondering on the illicit act she'd been thinking about, Christina reckoned that this might be the opportunity she'd been waiting for. The lads had drained their balls twice but Doogan, at least, should be able to muster up another erection and squeeze out a little more sperm. As Brown concentrated on her solid clitoris, Christina wondered whether his cock was stiffening again. Determined to experience the crudest sex yet, she pushed him away and looked down at his penis.

'That'll do,' she said, eyeing the solid organ. 'Can you manage it again?'

'You bet,' he replied, grinning as he grabbed his sex rod by the base. 'I'll fill your tight cunt again, no worries.'

'I'm not talking about my cunt,' Christina breathed huskily.

'A mouth-fuck?' Brown asked.

'An *arse*-fuck,' Christina replied, her crude words sending an electrifying quiver through her young womb.

'You mean . . .' Bryony gasped as Doogan slipped his deflating cock out of her well-spunked pussy.

'Yes, I mean an arse-fuck,' Christina giggled. 'Why not?'

'Yeah, why not?' Brown said. 'I'll go for it.'

'Fucking hell,' Doogan murmured. 'You're some teacher lady.'

'I don't think *lady* is an appropriate word,' Christina said, kneeling on the floor and resting her head on the sofa cushion. 'OK, Brown, do your stuff.'

As Brown scooped up the girl-cream and sperm from her gaping pussy-hole and lubricated the delicate tissue surrounding the entrance to her rectal duct, Christina reached behind her back and yanked the firm cheeks of her bottom wide apart. Her brown hole gaping, inviting the lad's swollen knob, she waited in anticipation as he smeared a good helping of cream between her splayed bum cheeks again. She'd had no trouble accommodating Alison's fist, and knew very well that the boy's cock would glide with ease deep into her hot rectum. It was the very thought of the illicit act that sent quivers of sex all through her young body.

Gasping as she felt Brown's huge plum pressing against the sensitive tissue of her anus, she recalled Alison's words and did her best to relax her muscles. Doogan and Bryony watched with bated breath as Brown's sex globe slipped past her anal sphincter muscles and drove slowly into the tight sheath of her arse. Christina shuddered, her breathing deep and ragged as she felt the teenager's cock-head sink deeper into the very core of her young body. This was it, her fantasy come true, she mused as she stretched her bum cheeks wider apart to allow the intruding member deeper penetration into the dank heat of her bowels.

The lad's balls pressing hard against the swollen lips of her hairless vulva, Christina released her buttocks and slipped her hands between Bryony's parted thighs. Driving two fingers deep into the heat of the young girl's cunt, she felt dizzy in her sexual frenzy. She craved anything and everything depraved, her thoughts lurching from one obscene act to another as Brown began his anal-fucking motions. Her trembling body rocking, her face buried in the sofa cushion, she revelled in the sensations of the boy's rock-hard cock gliding in and out of her tightening rectal tube. This really was sexual heaven, she reflected, massaging Bryony's inner vaginal flesh as her own lust duct rhythmically contracted and spewed out its contents of sperm and girl-cream. Wondering whether she should have asked Alison to stay and join in the debauchery, she shuddered as Brown grabbed her shapely hips and quickened his anal fucking.

'Here it comes,' the lad breathed, his lower stomach slapping Christina's naked buttocks, his swinging balls repeatedly slapping the hairless cushions of her inflamed love lips. Christina could feel his sperm pumping deep into her fiery arse duct, lubricating his throbbing knob as it glided back and forth along her contracting rectal tube. Imagining sucking the sperm out of Doogan's knob as Brown fucked the tight duct of her arse, Christina slipped her fingers out of Bryony's vaginal sheath and shuddered her last shudder as Brown withdrew his spent cock from the burning depths of her bowels.

'That was amazing,' the lad breathed, watching his sperm oozing from the dilated eye of Christina's anus.

'It certainly was,' Christina replied shakily. 'We must do that again.'

'I'll do it,' Doogan rejoined.

'Give me a minute to rest and then . . .'

'When we needed to rest you said—'

'I know, I know. All right, do it.'

Squeezing her eyes shut as she felt the bulbous knob of Doogan's cock slip past her well-oiled anal sphincter muscles, Christina wondered how much more debased sex she could take. Her bowels already brimming with spunk, she quivered uncontrollably as she thought about taking another load deep into her tight arse. She could certainly take Doogan, she reflected, imagining several more lads queuing up to fuck her arsehole. If Ponting knew of her lewd behaviour, he'd no doubt offer her anything to sink his solid cock deep into her hot arse and fuck her there.

'Christ, your arse feels good,' Doogan breathed, withdrawing his solid cock and ramming his knob-head deep into her bowels. Quivering, Christina felt as if her pelvic cavity was being pumped up as the lad repeatedly drove his swollen glans deep into the heat of her sperm-brimming bowels. Her thoughts turning to the planned downfall of Ponting, she listened to the squelching sound of Brown's sperm as Doogan pistoned her tightening rectal duct. If the man's wife caught him with his cock embedded deep within young Bryony's arsehole, she'd scream blue murder.

Bryony was going to have to experience anal sex, Christina decided as Doogan gasped, his cock shaft swelling as his sperm gushed from his throbbing knob and filled her bowels. Anal sex in the woods with Ponting? Why not? As Doogan satisfied his carnal cravings, Christina wondered how to lure Mrs Ponting to the woods to witness her husband's vulgar act of infidelity.

An anonymous phone call? Ponting would realize that he'd been set up, but what the hell?

'Can I do that tart Bryony's arse?' Brown asked as Doogan slowed his anal-fucking rhythm.

'*May* I do that tart's arse?' Christina corrected him.

'Can, may . . . I just want to fuck her arse.'

'No, you may not,' Christina said, her young body shuddering as Doogan's cock shaft withdrew slowly from the inflamed tube of her rectum. Dragging her trembling body up, she flopped onto the sofa beside Bryony. 'Dress now,' she ordered the teenage lads. 'It's time you were going.'

They didn't complain as they donned their clothes. They'd had a damned good time, Christina reflected, deciding to order Bryony to suck the boys' sperm out of her anal duct once they were alone. They had nothing to complain about. Doogan talked about the weekend as they finished dressing. Asking Christina whether they could call round for a Saturday-morning sex session, he moved to the door.

'Is that OK?' he said, his dark eyes gleaming.

'No,' Christina replied. 'I'm away for the weekend.'

'Where are you going?' Bryony asked.

'I'll tell you later. By the way, Doogan, I need you to do something for me.'

'Anything.'

'And you, Brown. I want to run a tight ship at the college. I want our class to be an example to the entire college. Well behaved, hard-working . . .'

'What's that got to do with us?' Brown asked.

'You're the ringleaders. Get our class into shape, and I'll make it worth your while. Do you understand what I'm saying?'

'Yes,' Doogan murmured. 'We control the class, knock them into shape, and we get sex in return.'

'That sums it up very well, Doogan. I don't want any trouble. I want our class to be a shining example to the college. Homework not only done but handed in on time, no absenteeism, respect for the teachers . . . In return, you two will have more sex than you can cope with. Right, off you go and I'll see you both on Monday morning.'

'OK, teacher lady,' Doogan chortled. 'Thanks for having us.'

'I'm not going to answer that.'

As they left the flat, Christina refilled the glasses with wine and retook her seat next to Bryony. She wondered how Alison was enjoying the live music at the pub. Wishing that she'd rented a flat on her own, she recalled her father's idea of buying a flat in London. Bryony would make an ideal flatmate, she reflected. Into anything and everything, the girl would be a good companion, a housemaid, a sex slave . . . But, at this stage, it was only a dream, Christina knew. The phone rang. Grabbing the receiver, she winked at Bryony and told her that they had an evening of lesbian sex to look forward to.

'Hello,' she said, pressing the receiver to her ear.

'Is that you, Shaw?' a man asked rudely.

'Pardon?'

'This is Don Ponting. What the hell do you think you're playing at by ringing my wife and—'

'I have no idea what you're talking about,' Christina replied, her pretty face beaming. 'I didn't even know you were married.'

'I know your game, you slag. You won't get away with this, I hope you realize that.'

'Get away with what? Look, I don't take kindly to people phoning me with threats. If you have a problem with your wife, then that's your problem.'

Slamming the phone down, Christina knew that she was going to have to put her plan into action. Smiling at Bryony as the girl asked what the trouble was, she ordered the girl to dress. There was time enough for lesbian sex later. For now, the downfall of Ponting took priority. Saturday morning? She recalled Doogan's words. What better time to lure Ponting to the woods with Bryony as bait? One phone call to the man's wife, and she was bound to walk to the common and investigate.

10

Bryony's phone call to Ponting went as planned. Fortunately, the man had not only answered the phone but had fallen for the girl's lies. Bryony had asked him to meet her on the common as she had some information about Miss Shaw. Suspicious at first, Ponting had finally agreed to meet her when she'd said that the woman was not only making her life hell but was sexually abusing a dozen or more students.

'OK,' Christina said as they left the phone box. 'You look great in that short skirt. You'll have no trouble luring Ponting into the woods.'

'Will I have to strip off?' the girl asked as they walked to the common.

'I reckon so. Don't worry, though,' Christina said, flashing the girl a reassuring smile. 'We have half an hour before he's due to arrive. I'll make sure that his wife turns up before things go too far. Besides, I'll be lurking in the bushes so, if Ponting does come on strong, I'll be there to help you.'

Reaching the common, the girls headed for the woods and finalized their plans. Watching Bryony sitting on a log, Christina did her best to drag her gaze away from the triangular patch of red material bulging between her student's inner thighs. Gazing at the girl's long blonde hair framing her fresh face, she knew that she had to keep her mind on the plan. There was time for sex, she mused, checking her watch. Biting her lip as she felt her clitoris swell, her juices of lesbian desire seeping between the swelling lips of her vulva, she turned her thoughts to Ponting.

'OK,' she said. 'Ponting will meet you by the pond. You'll bring him here to this clearing where I'll be hiding in the bushes. I've got my mobile phone so I'll ring his wife the minute I hear you approaching. It'll only take her about ten minutes to get here, giving you time enough to—'

'What if she's not in?' Bryony asked, cocking her head to one side.

'I've done my homework,' Christina replied triumphantly. 'More than my homework, I rang her this morning.'

'You rang her?'

'I said that I was from the Post Office and that we had a special delivery. She said she'd be in all morning.'

'She believed that?' the girl asked, frowning as she looked up at Christina.

'Whether she believed it or not doesn't matter. She said that she'd be in all morning. Don't worry, nothing will go wrong.'

'So I start talking to Ponting about you, tell him that you're making my life at the college hell, and . . .'

'He'll be staring at your breasts and thighs. Make sure that your blouse is open and, if you can, sit on the bench and expose your panties. You're very young and very beautiful, Bryony. There's no way that sad old pervert will be able to resist you.'

'OK, so I suggest we take a walk and I lead him into the woods.'

'That's right. From there, you shouldn't have any problems. Ponting will make the first move, I'm sure of that. When his wife arrives, grab your clothes and run. Right, you'd better go and wait by the pond. Good luck.'

'Thanks,' the girl said, offering Christina a smile. 'You *will* be here, won't you?'

'Yes, hiding in the bushes. Off you go. And don't worry.'

As the girl left the clearing, Christina decided to wait behind the bushes at the edge of the woods. She'd have a good view of the common from there, and have enough time to get back to the clearing once Bryony led Ponting towards the trees. Taking up her position, she watched the girl hanging around by the pond. There was no sign of their victim, but it was a little early. Praying that the man would turn up, she checked her mobile phone. The battery was fully charged, the woman's number in the memory . . . Nothing could go wrong – could it?

Grinning with relief as she noticed Ponting walking across the common towards Bryony, Christina ducked behind the bushes. The man started talking to the girl as she sat on the bench. His thoughts would turn to sex the minute he glimpsed the tight material of her red panties hugging her bulging sex lips. Ponting was walking into a trap, Christina reflected. But the trap was his own weakness. He wouldn't be able to fight his inner desires, she knew. Not that he'd want to fight them. As they headed towards the trees, Christina raced along the path to the clearing and settled down behind the bushes there.

Punching the buttons on her mobile phone, she waited for the woman to answer. 'Come on, come on,' she breathed as she heard Bryony and Ponting approaching. 'Ah, Mrs Ponting?' she asked as the woman answered.

'Yes.'

'Go to the common. I think you'll find your husband in the woods with a young student from the college.'

'What? Who is this?'

'Someone who doesn't like adultery, Mrs Ponting. If I were you, I'd hurry up. You'll find them in the woods just beyond the pond.'

'But . . .'

Switching her phone off, Christina felt her sex juices seeping into her tight panties as she imagined Ponting shafting Bryony's tight pussy. But it wouldn't get that far, she was sure. By the time Bryony was naked and Ponting had his erect cock out, the man's wife would appear. It would be up to Bryony to spread the news of Ponting's despicable behaviour around the college Christina would tell the headmaster that the girl had come to her in a flood of tears and . . .

'Do you often come here?' Ponting asked, following Bryony into the clearing.

'Yes, I like it here,' she replied, sitting on the log with her thighs parted.

'Miss Shaw has been making your life hell, then?'

'She always picks on me,' Bryony sighed, hanging her head. 'She's been having sex with several students and she . . . I just want to see the back of her.'

'So do I,' Ponting admitted. 'She's nothing but trouble. Tell me, why did you ring me about Miss Shaw?'

'Well, because . . .'

'It seems rather odd that you should phone me. You could have gone to—'

'The truth is . . . I . . . I like you,' Bryony murmured.

'You like me? What do you mean by that?'

'I've often seen you around the college and . . . Will you think me awful if I say that I like older men?'

'No, not at all,' Ponting replied, his narrow lips furling into a grin as he eyed the girl's tight panties. 'We should get to know each other a little better, Bryony. I must admit that I've always had my eye on you. You're a very attractive young girl. But I'm not convinced.'

'Not convinced? What do you mean?'

'A girl rang my wife yesterday, saying that she was having an affair with me.'

'Really? Who was she?'

'I don't know, but she was obviously out to cause trouble. When you rang and suggested that I should meet you on the common, I began to wonder. You must agree that it's rather odd. A girl ringing my wife yesterday and then you ringing and asking to meet here on the common? Coincidence, or—'

'I know nothing about a girl ringing your wife. I wanted to talk to you about Miss Shaw.'

Come on, Bryony, Christina urged the girl mentally. Time was running out fast, Christina knew. If Mrs Ponting arrived and Bryony was fully clothed, the plan would have failed miserably. Christina hadn't reckoned that Ponting would become suspicious. She'd thought that, with one glimpse of Bryony's tight panties, he wouldn't hesitate to make a move. Breathing a sigh of relief, Christina smiled as Bryony parted her thighs further and told Ponting that she'd always fancied him.

'Do you normally sit like that?' Ponting asked, his wide eyes focused on the tight material concealing the girl's full love lips.

'No,' she replied sheepishly. 'I just thought that . . .'

'What are you offering me?' he asked, the crotch of his trousers bulging.

'What do you think?' Bryony giggled impishly. 'Don't you want me?'

'I'm still not convinced,' he murmured, much to Christina's annoyance.

'Perhaps this will convince you,' Bryony said, standing and tugging her short skirt down.

Ponting watched as the girl slipped her blouse off and unhooked her bra. Tugging her panties down her slender legs, she stood naked in front of the man and asked him to slip his trousers off. He hesitated, checking his watch and looking around the clearing as she ran her hands over the mounds of her small breasts. Christina reckoned that he might have guessed that this was a set-up. A naked teenage girl with a hairless pussy blatantly offering him sex and he was hesitating? His wife would arrive at any minute, and Christina was sure that her plan had gone terribly wrong. Unless Bryony unzipped his trousers and pulled his cock out . . .

'Would you like me to suck your cock?' Bryony asked, kneeling in front of Ponting.

'Now *that* sounds like a good idea,' he replied, unbuckling his belt and dropping his trousers.

'Mmm, you're big,' she breathed, running her fingers up and down the length of his solid penis. 'Take your trousers off, and your shirt. If we're going to have sex, then we should both be naked.'

'You're quite a girl,' Ponting chortled, removing his shirt and stepping out of his trousers and shoes. 'Let's see you suck my knob, then,' he said, retracting his foreskin fully.

Relaxing as Bryony took his swollen glans into her wet

mouth, Christina checked her watch. Ponting's wife should have arrived by now, she thought, hoping that the second part of her plan wasn't going to fail. Ponting obviously wanting more than a blow job, he slipped his cock out of the girl's mouth and ordered her to get on all fours. Complying, she looked towards the bushes as the man kneeled behind her and parted the firm orbs of her buttocks. She was going to have to endure a fucking, Christina decided, praying again for the man's wife to appear.

'You're a tight-cunted little whore,' Ponting gasped, driving the entire length of his rock-hard penis deep into Bryony's vaginal duct. 'I'm going to fill your dirty little cunt with sperm and then I'll fuck your arsehole.' Remaining silent, Bryony rocked back and forth, meeting the man's penile thrusts as Christina watched the lewd scene with bated breath. Her arousal soaring, Christina wished that she could join in the debauchery. Her clitoris solid between her engorged vaginal lips, she slipped her hand down the front of her wet panties and massaged her pleasure spot.

'No,' Bryony whimpered as Ponting slipped his cunny-wet cock out of her well-juiced cunt and forced his purple knob into her anal hole.

'Shut up, you dirty little whore,' Ponting returned, driving the full length of his cock deep into the girl's arse. 'You lure me here and strip off . . . Don't start complaining.'

Biting her lip as she listened to Bryony's whimpers, Christina wasn't sure what to do. By the look of it, the man's wife wasn't going to turn up. This was all she needed, she thought apprehensively as Ponting began spanking Bryony's naked buttocks with the palm of his hand. Repeatedly ramming his purple knob deep into her bowels, he spanked her harder. Her whimpers obviously driving him on, he thrashed her rounded bottom cheeks until her pale flesh glowed a fire-red. Christina was going to have to put a halt to the abuse, she knew. About to leap out from the bushes, she thought that she heard twigs cracking underfoot.

'My God!' Mrs Ponting cried as she entered the clearing and stared open-mouthed at the lewd scene. 'Don, what on earth—'

'Helen,' Ponting gasped, yanking his cock out of Bryony's inflamed bottom-hole, his spunk shooting over the girl's burning buttocks. 'Helen, come back!'

As the woman hurried back to the common, Ponting sat back on his heels and glared at Bryony as she grabbed her clothes and clambered to her feet. He must have realized that he'd been set up, Christina thought as Bryony tugged her panties up her long legs. What he'd do now, she had no idea. Grabbing his shirt, he stood up with his limp penis snaking over his spunk-dripping balls and took hold of Bryony's arm.

'Clever,' he hissed. 'Very clever. But it won't work.'

'What do you mean?' Bryony asked, feigning innocence.

'That bitch Shaw put you up to this, didn't she?'

'Put me up to what? Who was that woman?'

'My wife. I thought it was odd when you rang me this morning. All this rubbish about Shaw making your life a misery. You get on very well with her, don't you? Intimately, in fact.'

'No, I don't,' Bryony said, pulling away from the man. 'I told you, I can't stand her.'

'So, the plan was to have my wife arrive and witness

my adultery. Which she did, so the plan worked. Miss Shaw is clever,' he breathed. 'Very clever.'

Wondering what Ponting's next move would be, Christina remained in her hiding place. His marriage was over, she was sure of that. His marriage in ruins, his job finished, Ponting was getting all he deserved. Bryony had done well, Christina reflected. The girl had had to endure the bastard's cock up her arse, but the plan couldn't have worked out better. Wondering why Ponting wasn't dressing, Christina cocked her head and listened as she heard twigs cracking underfoot again. Had the man's wife returned to have a go at him? she wondered.

'As I said, Miss Shaw has been very clever,' Ponting hissed, snatching Bryony's skirt away from her as she picked it up.

'But not clever enough,' Mrs Ponting said, grinning as she walked back into the clearing.

'But . . .' Bryony gasped, frowning at the woman. 'I . . . I don't understand!'

'No, you wouldn't,' Ponting chuckled. 'Will you explain?' he asked, turning to his wife.

'I'd be delighted,' she replied, standing in front of the quaking girl. 'You see, Bryony, my husband and I have what some would call an unorthodox marriage. We enjoy sex, but not only with each other. Don brings men home for me and I bring women home for him. We were hoping that something like this would happen because, apart from enjoying other men, I also enjoy young girls.'

Christina could hardly believe what she was hearing as the woman told Bryony of her lesbian exploits with the many young college girls her husband had brought home. Don Ponting and his wife were not going to be easy to deal with. Wondering what to do, Christina thought about emerging from her hiding place and confronting the couple. But what could she say? Her plan in ruins, she watched the woman squeeze Bryony's firm breasts. The girl was about to be subjected to a session of lesbian abuse, and there was nothing Christina could do about it.

'You obviously hoped to break up our marriage,' Ponting said, glaring at Bryony. 'But I reckon that there was more.'

'Your job,' his wife murmured. 'She planned to have you sacked.'

'That's a thought. But how? No one would believe her story . . . Wait a minute. Where's Miss Shaw?'

'I . . . I don't know,' Bryony stammered.

'Someone would have to witness this,' he murmured pensively. 'Shaw may be lurking somewhere close by.'

'I doubt it,' his wife said, pulling and twisting Bryony's erect nipples. 'Let's not worry about her. It's this little beauty I'm interested in.'

Tearing the girl's panties from her young body, Ponting's wife gazed longingly at her hairless sex crack, the engorged wings of her inner lips protruding from her valley of desire. Mrs Ponting was in her forties, not unattractive, and was dressed in a shortish skirt and white blouse. Christina watched as she kneeled on the ground and kissed the gentle rise of Bryony's mons. She didn't look like a lesbian, Christina mused. And she certainly didn't look like the sort of woman who'd force a young girl into crude lesbian sex.

Watching Bryony obediently follow the woman's instructions, turning and bending over to touch her toes, Christina frowned as Ponting lay on the ground with his thighs between her parted feet. Realizing what the lewd couple were up to as the man ordered Bryony to suck his cock, she watched with bated breath as the man's wife parted the young girl's buttocks and licked her exposed anal inlet. Christina's clitoris swelled, her juices of lust seeping into the tight material of her panties as she watched the woman tonguing Bryony's inflamed bottom hole. Sucking on the man's swollen knob, her hands resting on the ground, the girl shuddered as her arousal obviously heightened.

'You taste beautiful,' Mrs Ponting murmured, slipping her hand between Bryony's thighs and sinking several fingers deep into her vaginal sheath. 'You'll enjoy having my husband's cock up your bottom again before we've finished with you.'

Again, Christina wondered whether to emerge from her hiding place and confront the wicked pair. Ponting thrust his hips, his buttocks repeatedly leaving the ground as he mouth-fucked Bryony. Was she enjoying herself? Christina wondered, the slurping sound of the woman's anal tonguing filling her ears. Bryony could have made a run for it, she reflected. Or she could have called Christina for help. Perhaps there was more to the young girl than Christina had realized. She'd certainly enjoyed sucking and fucking the young lads, and she'd not really protested when Ponting had forced his solid penis deep into her rectal duct.

'She's been whipped,' Mrs Ponting said, moving her head back and gazing at the girl's weal-lined anal globes.

'I noticed that,' Ponting gasped, repeatedly driving his purple glans to the back of Bryony's throat.

'She's a slut, that's for sure,' the woman murmured, snapping a branch off a nearby bush. 'And sluts should be severely thrashed.'

Standing by the girl's side, Mrs Ponting brought the branch down across the firm orbs of Bryony's naked bottom with a deafening crack. Bryony's young body jolting, she moaned through her nose as Ponting continued his crude mouth-fucking and the branch repeatedly lashed her anal spheres. Christina again wondered whether to leap out from the bushes and halt the abuse as Bryony let out a shriek but, to her horror, Christina realized that the lewd sight was sending her own libido soaring sky-high. Biting her lip as Ponting drove his cock-head deep into the young girl's mouth again, she knew that she should do something to help her friend, but . . . Something was surfacing from the dark depths of her mind, she sensed as she watched the gruelling thrashing. Something sinister, almost evil.

Hoping that the lashing would continue until Bryony begged for mercy, Christina realized that a darker side of her being was emerging. In just one week, she'd changed from a sexually inexperienced young lady with hopes for a teaching career to a bisexual nymphomaniac. Why? Had wanking the boys to orgasm in the stockroom changed her? Had the sight of Bryony's teenage breasts and shaved pussy transformed her? Reckoning that her inner desires had always been there, lurking in the murky depths of her subconscious, Christina began to wonder about her true character.

Recalling a dream she'd often had during her early teens about a young girl tied down to a table with her legs parted as far as they'd go, the hairless lips of her pussy spread wide, she began to wonder whether she'd always been sexually deviant. Her years with Charles had probably suppressed her inner desires, her true character only emerging now that she was free and living in London.

The thought worrying her, she watched the gruelling buttock-thrashing and listened to the sound of the branch swishing and thwacking as Ponting gasped and filled Bryony's gobbling mouth with his spunk.

Her hand down the front of her soaked panties again, Christina massaged the solid protrusion of her ripe clitoris, stifling her gasps of sexual pleasure as the merciless thrashing continued. Running her finger down her wet valley of desire, following the curvature of her pubic bone, she drove her finger up, across the small spot of her urethral opening and into the wet heat of her tightening vaginal canal. Massaging her hot inner flesh, she parted her knees, opening the very centre of her trembling body as her clitoris swelled and pulsated. She was going to come, she knew as her womb trembled and contracted. Listening to Bryony's screams echoing through the trees, she rubbed her G-spot faster, her pistoning hand massaging the sensitive tip of her solid clitoris.

'God,' she breathed, her head hanging, her long blonde hair falling in a curtain of gold silk over her flushed face as her orgasm erupted and shook the very core of her young body. Shaking uncontrollably, she was thankful for Bryony's screams as her gasps grew louder in her self-loving. Her orgasm peaking as she listened to the sound to the branch cracking across the teenage girl's crimsoned buttocks, she felt her panties filling with her copious juices of lust. On and on her pleasure rolled through her trembling body as Ponting clambered to his feet and grabbed his victim, forcing her to remain in the degrading position and take the unrelenting buttock-whipping.

As her pleasure began to wane, Christina knew that Bryony wasn't going to thank her for leaving her to her fate. What did the future hold now, she wondered, caressing the wet walls of her vagina, sending ripples of sex throughout her quivering body. Would Bryony turn her back on Christina? What would the Pontings do now? They might lure Bryony to their house for regular sessions of debauched sex. At least Alison wasn't involved, Christina thought thankfully, slipping her cunny-wet hand out of her soaked panties.

'That'll do for the time being,' Mrs Ponting said, dropping the branch onto the ground as her husband released the whimpering girl. 'I think the time has come for you to pleasure me,' she chuckled, lifting her skirt and tugging her wet panties down. 'Kneel in front of your mistress,' she ordered Bryony. 'Kneel in front of me and lick me.'

Complying, with some rough urging from Ponting, Bryony pushed her pretty face hard against the woman's hair-covered vulva. The woman reached down and peeled apart the fleshy lips of her pussy, and Bryony was forced to lick the wet flesh within her gaping valley. Clutching her head, Ponting wanked his cock, his swollen knob rubbing against the girl's blonde hair as he gasped in his debauchery. His wife gave out moans of girl-induced pleasure as Bryony's tongue worked around the solid protrusion of her sensitive clitoris and she began to tremble as her climax neared.

Christina watched Ponting's purple globe repeatedly appear and disappear as he ran his hand up and down the length of his granite-hard penis. Gasps of sexual pleasure resounded around the woods as she slipped her hand down the front of her sopping-wet panties and again located the nubble of her erect clitoris. She needed to come again, she knew as she encircled her swollen cumbud with her wet fingertip. Reaching behind her back with her free hand, her finger slipping between her firm buttocks, she teased the eye of her sensitive anus as Mrs Ponting's whimpers of lust grew louder.

Christina couldn't help herself as she drove her finger past her brown ring and deep into the heat of her rectum. Her debauched act sending delightful quivers of crude sex deep into her young pelvis, she caressed her solid clitoris faster, doing her best to stifle her gasps as her debased pleasure built and rocked the very core of her young body. Driving a second finger deep into the tight duct of her rectum, she massaged her stretched inner flesh, the sensations transmitting deep into her bowels as her clitoris swelled painfully beneath her caressing fingertip.

'Yes,' Ponting's wife cried as her orgasm erupted within her palpitating clitoris. Christina watched as Ponting's knob swelled and his sperm shot from his slit, splattering Bryony's golden hair. Her own orgasm peaking, Christina forced a third finger past her defeated anal-sphincter muscles and deep into her inflamed rectal sheath. She needed a cock shafting the tight tube of her vagina, a throbbing knob pumping sperm into her thirsty mouth as a third organ fucked the inflamed canal of her rectum. Again wondering whether to join the debauchery, she trembled as her pleasure finally began to recede.

Stilling her fingers deep within her rectal duct, Christina slowed her clitoral masturbating to a gentle rhythm, bringing out the last tremors of sex from her abused body as the last of Ponting's sperm rained over Bryony's blonde hair. His wife staggering back as her orgasm began to subside, she stood with her panties around her ankles, her skirt rucked up around her stomach, her sex-matted pubic curls blatantly displayed. Gazing at Bryony's pussy-wet face, Christina slipped her fingers out of her rectum and shuddered in the aftermath of her self-induced coming.

This hadn't been what she'd envisaged at all, she reflected, licking her juice-glistening fingers as she waited for the Pontings to make their next move. Watching Ponting tug his trousers up his legs, she was thankful that the debauchery was over. How she was going to face the man at the college on Monday, she had no idea. He knew that she'd set him up, and would no doubt retaliate in some way.

'I'll be seeing you at the college,' Ponting said, gazing into Bryony's blue eyes.

'And I'll be seeing you at our house,' the woman rejoined. 'My husband will tell you when to call. If you don't turn up, you'll find that your life at the college will be as miserable as sin.'

'Bear in mind that I'm well in with the headmaster,' Ponting sniggered. 'One or two lies to him, and you'll find yourself thrown out. Do you understand?'

'Yes,' Bryony murmured, her head hung low, sperm running down strands of her blonde hair.

'We have a special room,' the woman chuckled. 'A room where we entertain young girls. My husband has set up a table with handcuffs and . . . You'll enjoy visiting our sex room, Bryony. In fact, I think I'd like you to visit us this evening. Yes, about seven o'clock. Do you know where we live?'

'Yes, but . . .' Bryony began.

'Seven o'clock,' Ponting snapped, grabbing the girl's arm. 'If you don't turn up, then you'll be very, very sorry.'

As the evil pair left the clearing, Bryony looked to-wards the bushes where Christina was hiding. The plan hadn't only failed, Christina mused as she emerged from the bushes, but Bryony was now in a dire situation. If the girl didn't turn up that evening, there was no doubt that Ponting would be true to his word and have her expelled from the college. Wondering what to say as she stood in front of the naked girl, Christina offered her a slight smile.

'I'm sorry,' she murmured. 'I didn't think it would turn out like this.'

'It's not your fault,' Bryony replied.

'No, but I still feel guilty. What the hell we do now, I really don't know.'

'I'll have to go,' Bryony murmured. 'If I don't, then . . .'

'Before you give in, let's think about this. It's a long time until this evening arrives. We have time to think of something. For starters, if they have a special room, a sex den or whatever, we might be able to expose their activities.'

'Is it illegal?' Bryony asked, wiping the sperm from her hair. 'Surely there's nothing unlawful about having a sex den.'

'It depends what you do in that sex den,' Christina replied. 'You're right, there's nothing illegal about own-ing handcuffs and whips or what-have-you. But if Pont-ing is luring young college girls into the den and . . .'

'They're old enough,' Bryony cut in, picking up her skirt from the ground. 'God, my bum's really sore. It's up to the girls, isn't it?'

'Not if Ponting is threatening them the way he threa-tened you. If he's telling them that they'll fail their exams

or find themselves expelled . . . We're going to have to
look at this from a different angle.'

Watching Bryony dress, Christina thought about the
coming evening. The girl would have to visit the evil
pair, she knew. She could think of no way to deal with the
likes of Ponting and his wife. Wandering through the
woods with the girl in tow, Christina checked her watch
as they emerged from the trees and headed across the
common. Feeling somewhat responsible for Bryony, she
wondered whether she should suggest that the girl move
into the flat. That wouldn't put a stop to Ponting's
threats and abuse, but at least Christina could keep an
eye on her.

'So what shall I do?' Bryony asked as they stopped by
the pond.

'I don't know yet,' Christina replied, sitting on the
bench.

'Can't you do something to Ponting at the college?'

'What do you mean, *do something*?'

'Get him into trouble.'

'He's well in with the head, Bryony.'

'Yes, but what's to stop you ringing the head and
pretending to be an irate parent? You could complain
and—'

'I've got it,' Christina cut in, looking up at the girl's
pretty face lit by the sun. 'If I can get Doogan and Brown
to . . . No, it won't work.'

'What were you going to say?'

'I was wondering whether Doogan and Brown could
get their hands on Ponting's reports. His register, sports
line-up, teams, class reports . . .'

'What good would that do?'

'If he was seen to be shoddy, losing papers, getting

football matches wrong, the teams turning up at the wrong venues . . . The trouble is that it would take too long. It might be weeks before the head started to realize that Ponting was getting into a mess.'

'What if I started spreading rumours about him?'

'What sort of rumours?'

'Well, I could say that he's been seen with boys in the changing rooms. You know, gay stuff.'

'That's a good idea, Bryony. But, again, it would take a long time.'

'OK, how about this? I go to his house this evening and you have the place raided.'

'Raided? No, no, I don't think so. Unless . . . Yes, that's it. Doogan and Brown turn up at his house. They find the front door open and then discover you in the sex den with Ponting and his wife . . .'

'But the front door won't be open.'

'Oh, yes, it will. I'll make sure of that. They could go there in connection with some football match or whatever.'

'I'm not going,' Bryony suddenly announced. 'I'm not going to get mixed up in all this.'

'But you *are* mixed up in it,' Christina retorted. 'He'll make your life hell at the college unless you go to his place.'

'No, he won't. He won't be able to do anything to me.'

'Why? What are you talking about?'

'I'm not going back to college. I hate it and, what with all this, I might as well leave.'

'Well, that's one way around the problem, but . . . Bryony, what will you do?'

'I want to leave home. I've wanted to leave for a long time. I don't like my home, I don't like college . . . I'll get a job and find a flat somewhere.'

'OK, instead of going to Ponting's house at seven, come and see me. I have a proposition for you, Bryony.'

'OK,' the girl said, a smile on her pretty face as if she'd guessed what Christina's idea was. 'I'd better be going. I'll see you this evening.'

'Yes. I'll look forward to it.'

Watching the girl walk off across the common, Christina knew that she'd be doing the right thing by suggesting that she should move into the flat. Alison had been all for it, so there wouldn't be a problem there. Ponting would still have to be dealt with, but at least Bryony would be safe. Closing her eyes as she reclined on the bench and relaxed beneath the sun, Christina was looking forward to the evening. And to Monday morning when Ponting would discover that he could no longer threaten his latest recruit.

11

'I've changed my mind,' Alison said firmly.

'But it was your idea,' Christina retorted, pacing the lounge floor. 'I've invited her round to tell her that she can move in with us. What's changed your mind?'

'Oh, I don't know. She'll get under our feet. As you said, she'd need a room of her own. I know that I said she could bed-hop between us, but it wouldn't work. You said yourself that it wouldn't work.'

'I know I did. It's just that . . . OK, not to worry. So, did you have a good time last night?'

'Yes, the band were really good. What did you get up to? Anything interesting?'

'Er . . . no, I just caught up with my work. Will you be in this evening?'

'Why? Is it that you want the girl to yourself?'

'No, of course not. I need to talk to her, that's all. I think she's guessed that I'm going to ask her to move in.'

'I wasn't going to mention this yet, but . . . I might be moving out.'

'Oh?'

'I was waiting to see how things developed between us. I'm also waiting to hear about a job I've applied for at a hotel. I'd be living in, so . . . well, I'd be a damned sight better off financially. I'd have a room, food, drinks . . . The trouble is, what will you do without my half of the rent?'

'God only knows. Bryony reckons that she's going to leave college and get a job, so I suppose we could manage.'

'I don't even know whether I've got the job yet. I was feeling really bad about letting you down, but if Bryony moves in . . .'

'When will you hear?'

'Monday, I hope. If I pay my share of the rent up to the end of the month, that'll give Bryony time to find a job before the rent's due again. Want some coffee?'

'Mmm, please.'

Flopping onto the sofa, Christina realized again that nothing was turning out as she'd thought it would. This was a bombshell that she didn't need. There was no way she could pay all the rent on her income and, unless Bryony found herself a job, they'd be out of the flat. Even if the girl did find a job, they might not get on, living together. Wondering whether to leave the flat and go back to her parents' house, Christina began to feel despondent. The time had come for a major rethink, she decided, grabbing the ringing phone.

'How are you, dear?' her mother asked.

'Oh, I'm fine. I was going to ring you this evening.'

'We were hoping you'd be down to see us as it's the weekend.'

'Yes, I . . . I'm hoping to make it tomorrow.'

'Only there's something we have to talk about.'

'Oh? What's that?'

'Someone from your college rang your father. He said that—'

'Wait a minute. Who was it? Who rang? And when?'

'About half an hour ago. It was a Mr Ponting.'

'God,' Christina breathed, her stomach sinking. 'What did he want?'

'We're very worried about you, dear.'

'Yes, but what did Ponting say?'

'We can't talk about it on the phone. When you come down tomorrow . . .'

'Mother, at least give me a clue as to what this is about.'

'Mr Ponting was saying that you've been mixing with certain people. He was concerned, Christina. He said that you're sleeping with anyone and everyone and . . .'

'And you believe him?'

'Well, we—'

'Mother, Ponting is a liar and a troublemaker. The reason he's saying these things is because he asked me out and I said no. He has a reputation at the college. He hounds the young girls, he threatens—'

'Have you told the headmaster about him?'

'I'm about to do that. I was hoping that he'd back off, but he's obviously got psychological problems and . . . Look, we'll talk about this tomorrow.'

'All right, dear. As long as you're not getting into trouble and . . .'

'I can assure you, mother, there are no problems here. Ponting's a sick man. Just ignore whatever he's been saying.'

'That should put your father's mind at rest. You know how he worries about you.'

'Yes, I know. Look, I'll be down in the morning.'

'All right. And you'll stay for lunch?'

'Yes, yes, I will.'

'All right. We'll see you tomorrow.'

'OK. Goodbye, mother.'

As she replaced the receiver, Christina was fuming. Her heart racing, she knew that Ponting wasn't going to leave her alone. This had become a personal battle, and one that was going to be very difficult, if not impossible, to win. Was this how things were in London? she mused as Alison brought the coffees in and placed the cups on the low table. Sex, blackmail, lies, deception . . . After living in the country where everyone knew everyone else and things were quiet, Christina didn't think that she'd ever fit in with the city. Recalling the local school, she could have got a job there but there'd have been no future. Spadger Heath College, so she'd believed, would provide a stepping stone to bigger and better things.

'Who was that?' Alison asked.

'My mother. She wants me to visit tomorrow. I might do more than visit. I might go back permanently.'

'God, Christina. This is because of me, isn't it?'

'No, no.'

'Yes, it is. I feel really guilty now. I was already feeling bad, but—'

'Alison, this is *not* because of you. I've been thinking about going home for some time now. You might have swayed my decision, but I'm not giving up everything here simply because you might be moving out. There must be plenty of people looking for flat-shares. Bryony aside, I'm sure I wouldn't have a problem finding someone.'

'Why's she leaving college?'

'It's not just the college. She wants to leave home.'

'From what you've said about her mother, I'm not surprised. Anyway, you were asking whether I'm going out this evening. I was going to stay in but as you—'

'Alison, don't let me push you out. If you want to stay in, then . . .'

'You need to talk to Bryony. I'll go to the pub. There's another band on tonight.'

'If you're sure.'

'Of course I'm sure. Besides, I love the music, the atmosphere. What will you do if you go home? Your parents live in the country, don't they?'

'Yes, they do.'

'What will you do for work?'

'I don't know. I'm not even sure yet that I'm going home. I've completed my first week at the college, apart from the day I took off. It's not been easy, but I managed to get through the week. If I stay in London, I'm sure that things will work out.'

'So what's the problem?'

'It's the way of life here. The people here are different. Bear in mind that I'm a country girl. When I landed myself the job at the college, I had the idea that I'd be teaching English and—'

'You are, aren't you?'

'Yes, but I didn't expect . . . I don't know what I expected. I thought I'd enjoy the lessons, setting work for the students, getting to know them . . .'

'You've got to know them, all right,' Alison giggled. 'Intimately, I'd say.'

'Exactly. That's just the point, Alison. I never dreamed that I'd be having sex with my female flatmate, let alone the students. And as for having sex with a young female student . . .'

'You know what your problem is? You worry too much. Sex is sex, Christina. Why dwell on things? We had sex and it was great. I don't spend all my time going over the implications of lesbian sex, wondering whether it's right or wrong, analysing things, feeling guilty . . .'

'That's because you're different.'

'We're the same, Christina. The only difference is that you think too much. As I've said many times before, relax and let yourself go. Right, I'm going to take a shower before I go to the pub.'

She was right, Christina thought as Alison left the room. There was no point in analysing things, worrying about right or wrong. But Christina couldn't help the way she was. Wanking the students in the stockroom, lesbian sex with Alison and Bryony, wanking Ponting and watching his sperm shoot from his throbbing knob, taking cocks up her arse . . . Every lewd act she'd committed played on her mind, and she couldn't help that. Alison was free of guilt, getting on with her life and enjoying crude sex without worrying.

Pacing the lounge floor, Christina thought about her father. If she gave up teaching and went home, he'd harp on about her working for him. He'd also say, *I told you so*. Charles would . . . There was no way Christina was going to work at the same company as Charles. There was only one thing for it, she decided. She was going to have to stay on at the flat and carry on teaching. Evaluating the situation, she reckoned that, apart from Ponting, she had no insurmountable problems.

'I'll see you later,' Alison said, popping her head round the lounge door. 'I hope your chat with Bryony goes all right.'

'Yes, I'm sure it will,' Christina said, putting a smile on her pretty face. 'I'll probably still be up when you get back.'

'Great. We'll have a coffee and you can tell me how you got on.'

Checking her watch as Alison bounded down the

stairs, Christina sighed. 'Fifteen minutes,' she breathed, pacing the floor again. Ponting would be checking his watch, she mused, imagining the man and his wife preparing their sex den for Bryony's visit. The man would have a shock when he discovered that Bryony had left the college. He'd obviously go all out to get at Christina, but she was beginning to formulate a plan. If Brown and Doogan did their bit in return for crude sex and enabled Christina to run the best class in the college, old man Wright would have nothing but praise for her. Ponting's lies wouldn't sit too well with the head, particularly if Christina spread a few lies and rumours concerning the PE master.

The doorbell rang at seven o'clock and Christina bounded down the stairs. Still not sure what to say to Bryony, she wondered whether to allow the girl to share her room until Alison moved out. *If* the other girl moved out, that was. Opening the door, she frowned. Bryony was standing on the step, holding a large black bag. Had she brought her things round thinking that she was moving in? Christina invited her in anyway. Dumping her bag in the lounge, Bryony smiled at Christina.

'So,' Christina said, eyeing the bag. 'Would you like a drink?'

'Vodka, if you have any.'

'I think there's some left,' Christina said, grabbing two glasses from the kitchen. 'Do you want tonic or orange with it?' she called.

'Anything.'

Returning to the lounge with the drinks, Christina passed the girl a glass. 'Here's to your new life away from the college,' she said, raising her glass.

Sipping her drink, Christina gazed at Bryony's slender

legs, the gentle rise of her teenage breasts beneath her tight T-shirt, her stiff nipples clearly defined by the thin material. Her long blonde hair cascading over her shoulders, she was extremely attractive. And very young, Christina thought, wondering whether to ask what was in the bag. Perhaps the girl was too young to share the flat, she reflected. There again, living with a woman who was drunk most of the time, Bryony was no doubt used to fending for herself. Washing, ironing, cooking . . . Bryony had to do everything not only for herself but also for her drunken mother.

'Is Alison out?' Bryony asked, sitting on the sofa.

'Yes, she's gone to the pub,' Christina replied, glimpsing the triangular patch of the girl's red panties.

'You said that you had a proposition for me.'

'Er . . . yes, that's right. Actually, things have changed since I said that. You see . . .'

'I've told my mother that I'm moving out.'

'Why did you tell her that? I mean, have you found somewhere to live?'

'Well, I thought . . .'

'Bryony, we don't have a spare room here.'

'I know, but I could share with you. Just until I find a flat.'

'Alison might be moving out before long. If she does, then you can have her room. What about money, Bryony? I can't pay the rent on my own, not on my meagre income.'

'I've got a job.'

'Already? That was quick.'

'Having decided to leave college, I spent the afternoon looking for work. I start on Monday.'

'Where?'

'A massage parlour.'

'Bryony . . . A massage parlour? For God's sake. You do know what happens in those places, don't you?'

'Of course, I do. I don't mind wanking off old men. I start on two hundred a week.'

'At least you'll be able to pay your half of the rent. But I don't like it, Bryony. The thought of you working in a place like that . . .'

'It won't be for ever. I'm not going to make a career out of it.'

'No, but you get used to that sort of money and you'll find that you won't be able to do anything else.'

'I thought you'd be pleased.'

'I am pleased that you've found work, but . . . As long as it's only for a while. While you're working there, use the opportunity to look for something better.'

'One girl I was talking to said that she earns around five hundred a week.'

'That doesn't surprise me. It's prostitution, Bryony.'

'I'll only be wanking old men.'

'Yes, to begin with. Then you'll want more money and move on to—'

'Aren't *you* prostituting yourself?'

'How do you mean?'

'Don't you remember your words? *In return, you two will have more sex than you can cope with.* That's what you said to Doogan and Brown. You offered them sex to help you control the class.'

'That's different, Bryony. OK, I suppose it's not different but . . .'

'It's exactly the same. They do something for you and in return you have sex with them. I wank off old men and in return I get paid.'

'All right, all right. So, what's in the bag? Your things?'

'Some of my clothes, yes. I'll have to make several trips to get the rest of my stuff.'

'God knows where you're going to put everything. My room's fairly big but . . . I expect we'll be able to sort something out.'

'I'll leave my bag here and go and get some more.'

'All right. What Alison will say, I really don't know. Anyway, let me worry about that.'

'OK, I'll see you again in about half an hour.'

Tidying her room, Christina made some space in the wardrobe for Bryony's clothes. Fortunately, she had a double bed so sleeping wouldn't be a problem – she hoped. Alison wasn't going to be happy but, if Bryony didn't disturb her by getting in the way too much, things should work out. At least Bryony was well away from Ponting now, Christina reflected, dreading the thought of visiting her parents. What Ponting had said, she dared not even hazard a guess. The man was out to cause trouble, that was for sure.

Dashing into the kitchen as the phone rang, Christina hoped that it wasn't her mother again. This was all getting too much, she thought, lifting the receiver. What with Ponting somehow discovering her parents' phone number and causing trouble, Bryony turning up with her things, Alison changing her mind about the girl moving in and—

'Miss Shaw?' a male voice asked.

'Yes,' Christina replied, not recognizing it.

'Mr Wright here. I'm sorry to have to call you at home but I need to speak to you concerning a matter of some gravity.'

'Oh, er . . . yes, of course.'

'It's in connection with certain allegations.'

'Allegations?' Christina echoed, raising her gaze to the ceiling. 'What allegations?'

'Mr Ponting called me and . . . Look, I'd rather not discuss this over the telephone. Are you busy this evening?'

'Er . . . no, not really.'

'May I call round? If it's convenient, that is.'

'Yes, that's a good idea, Mr Wright. I think we should sort this out once and for all.'

'Good, good. Say, half an hour?'

'Yes, that's fine.'

'As I said, I'm sorry to have to call you like this. It's just that the allegations are . . . This is a somewhat delicate matter.'

'I'm sure it is.'

'I'll see you soon.'

'Yes, Mr Wright. Goodbye.'

Slamming the phone down, Christina knew that Ponting had been trying to cause trouble again. Unless she dealt with the man, she was going to be out of a job, she knew. She poured herself a large vodka. Pacing the lounge floor, her stomach knotted, she was fuming. When Bryony arrived with two bulging plastic bags and announced that she was going to make another trip, Christina told her not to return for at least an hour. The girl frowned, cocking her head to one side as she asked what was wrong. Christina lied to her, saying that the landlord was due to call and she didn't want to have to explain who Bryony was.

As the girl left, Christina wondered what Ponting had said to Wright. Whatever he'd said, it was bound to involve sex, she thought. He must have worked out that Bryony not turning up at his house had something to do with Christina and now he was out to cause her more trouble. As the doorbell rang, Christina bounded down the stairs and brushed her long blonde hair back with her fingers. Taking a deep breath, she opened the door and smiled at the headmaster.

'Come up,' she invited him, closing the door as he stepped into the hall.

'Thank you,' he said, following her up the stairs to the lounge. 'I'm sorry to have to call like this.'

'It's not a problem,' Christina breathed. 'In fact, I'm rather pleased that you're here.'

'Oh?'

'This thing with Mr Ponting is going too far. He's been phoning me, ringing my doorbell, following me . . .'

'Oh, I didn't realize that.'

'So what's the allegation? Oh, please sit down.'

'Thank you.'

'Would you like a drink?'

'Er . . . well . . .'

'Tea, coffee? Or I have some beers in the fridge.'

'A beer would be rather nice, thank you.'

'What's Mr Ponting been saying this time?' Christina called from the kitchen. 'More lies, I suppose,' she said, returning and passing the man a can of lager.

'Thank you. This is rather difficult, Miss Shaw.'

'Just say it.'

'All right. Mr Ponting told me that you were in the woods on the common with a young female student.'

'Yes, that's right.'

'You don't deny it?'

'No, of course not. I bumped into Bryony Philips on

the common and she was telling me about fungi. She's into nature – plants and the like. Anyway, we went into the woods and she pointed out some rather interesting mushrooms.'

'I see. The thing is, Mr Ponting said that he happened to see you . . . He said that you were having sex with the girl.'

'Having sex?' Christina laughed. 'Hardly, Mr Wright. Bryony and I were looking at fungi. I think you'll agree that there's nothing further removed from sex than gazing at fungi.'

'Er . . . yes, yes, of course. The point is that Mr Ponting was out walking with his wife. They both saw you having sex in the woods with Bryony, Miss Shaw. Now, Mrs Ponting is a well-respected woman and I—'

'When was this?' Christina asked.

'Today. This morning, in fact.'

'No, no. I was with Bryony on the common yesterday. I had a free period and decided to get some air . . . I've been nowhere near the common today.'

'May I ask where you were this morning?'

'Of course. I woke at seven, met Bryony at the station at eight, and we took the train to Hertfordshire to visit my parents.'

'Oh, I see. Tell me, why did you take Bryony with you?'

'Because she wanted to meet a friend of mine who's heavily into botany.'

'I'm sorry to have to ask you this, but . . . Would your parents confirm your visit?'

'Of course they would, Mr Wright. Bryony spent an hour or so taking my mother around the garden pointing out various types of fungi. My parents have a country house with a large garden. Ideal for fungi, according to Bryony. What I'd like to know is why Mr Ponting is saying these terrible things about me. And Bryony, for goodness' sake.'

'Yes, that's what I'd like to know,' the man murmured pensively, swigging lager from his can.

'Have there been rumours like this before? I mean, has anyone ever said anything about Mr Ponting?'

'Why do you ask?'

'Because I heard something . . . I shouldn't tell tales out of school, but I heard that there have been rumours about Mr Ponting in the past.'

'I'm not at liberty to go into the details but, yes, there have been one or two allegations made against Mr Ponting. What I intend to do is write to your parents for confirmation of your visit, if that's all right with you?'

'Of course. You'd best write to my mother as my father's away on business most of the time.'

'I'm sorry to have to do this.'

'Not at all, Mr Wright. I can see that you're in a difficult position. To be honest, I'd do the same. Would you like another beer?'

'Oh, well . . . If you're sure.'

'Of course I'm sure.'

Wandering into the kitchen, Christina decided to take Bryony to her parents' house the following day. Her mother would write back to the head saying that the visit was on the Sunday, but that didn't really matter. Christina would tell Wright that her mother had mixed the days up and get around the problem that way. Taking a beer from the fridge, she realized that she should make the most of Wright's visit. If she could get to know him, gain his confidence, she'd be in with a better chance of winning the battle against Ponting. Returning to the lounge, she popped the can of lager and passed it to Wright.

'It's a good job I walked here,' he said, swigging from the can.

'You don't live far, then?'

'About half a mile away. To be honest, it's nice to get out for a change. Stuck at home by myself at weekends isn't much fun.'

'Oh, you're not married?'

'No, no. I was, many years ago. Things didn't work out, I'm afraid.'

'I'm sorry to hear that.'

Eyeing the crotch of his trousers, Christina knew of one way to get well in with Wright. But, if she made a move and it went terribly wrong, she'd have blown everything. This was going to have to be played very carefully, she knew as the head rambled on about his lonely evenings and weekends. Deciding to begin by sitting opposite the man and *inadvertently* allowing him a glimpse of her tight panties, she took her drink from the table and sat with her thighs parted slightly.

Nodding and smiling where appropriate, Christina made out that she was listening to his every word as he talked about the college. Parting her thighs a little further, she was pleased that she'd worn a short skirt – but was Wright going to notice that her wares were on display? He seemed so wrapped up in the college, so concerned with the years he'd spent there as head, that she doubted he'd bat an eyelid even if he were to glimpse the tight material of her panties hugging her full love lips. Beginning to wonder whether he was gay, she knocked back her drink and was about to go to the kitchen to refill her glass when she noticed Wright's wide-eyed gaze transfixed between her shapely thighs.

Asking about the history of the college, Christina allowed her thighs to part further as she lay back in the armchair. Wright fidgeted on the sofa, adjusting the crotch of his trousers as his arousal heightened. Christina knew that if she could get his cock out and bring him some pleasure she'd not only be well in with the man but might even gain some control over him. This was the ultimate in using her femininity to gain power, she reflected. She almost had her class under control by using sex and now . . . But, she wondered, was this right? Recalling Alison's words, she realized that she was worrying again, analysing the situation, when all she needed to do was relax and enjoy herself.

'Are you, er . . .' Wright murmured hesitantly. 'Are you seeing anyone? A boyfriend, I mean.'

'No, no,' Christina replied, smiling at the man and licking her full lips provocatively. 'I did have a boyfriend but, when I moved here, we split up. How about you? Any special lady friend?'

'Oh, no,' he laughed. 'I'm too old. Well, I'm only in my fifties but . . . Not getting out a great deal, I don't have the opportunity to meet anyone. I don't think I'd marry again. Having said that, it would be nice to have a lady friend.'

'That's how I feel. A friend, someone to go out with now and then, but no ties. What about sex? I mean . . . sorry, I shouldn't be asking you about sex.'

'Ah, sex,' he sighed, swigging from his can again. 'To be honest, it's been so long that I can't remember.'

'There must be times when you . . . well, you know?'

'Oh, yes, there are plenty of times when I think about sex. You're young – it must be difficult for you at times?'

'It's very difficult. I tend to throw myself into my work, which helps. That's one reason why I thought Mr Ponting's accusations were so odd. I haven't even got a boyfriend, let alone . . . I'm pretty sure that he was mistaken about me. I reckon he's mixing me up with someone else.'

'Oh no, he was positive that it was you in the woods with Bryony.'

'Well, that's most strange,' Christina sighed, wondering where to take it from here. 'Obviously, I won't mention it to Bryony. If she thinks that Mr Ponting has been suggesting that she's having a lesbian relationship with me . . . The poor girl would fall apart.'

'Well, I certainly won't tell her. And I'll have a word with Mr Ponting. I don't want him saying anything to the girl.'

Watching the man finish his lager, Christina went to the kitchen and took another can from the fridge. Reckoning that he wasn't used to drinking, she knew that the alcohol would soon loosen him up as she passed him the can and refilled her glass with vodka and tonic. The man was in dire need of sex, that was obvious. But Christina didn't want to bolster Ponting's allegations by coming across as a wanton whore. If Wright made the first move, she reflected, sitting in the armchair and sipping her drink . . . There was little chance of that, she concluded, again displaying the tight crotch of her moistening panties to his bug-eyed stare.

As Wright dragged his gaze away from Christina's bulging panties and looked out of the window, she pulled the tight material to one side just enough to expose the hairless lip of her vulva. That was as far as she could go without appearing to be a common slut, she knew as the man turned his head and said something about the nice weather. Replying to his comment, Christina watched his expression as he focused on the swell of her exposed labial cushion. His eyes widening, he again adjusted the crotch of his trousers and fidgeted on the sofa.

This was taking too long, Christina thought, glancing at her watch. Bryony would be back with more of her things before long, destroying any chance of Christina having sex with Wright. Tossing caution to the wind, she decided to make the first move. Her fingers running up and down her inner thigh, dangerously close to her bulging outer lips, she let out a sigh of pleasure. Wright finished his can of lager and averted his gaze as his obvious embarrassment got the better of him. But Christina wasn't going to allow this opportunity to pass her by.

'Why don't you come over here?' she asked. 'Kneel on the floor and touch me.'

'Well, I . . .' Wright stammered, sliding off the sofa and walking towards the girl.

'All this talk about sex has turned me on. You're a very attractive man, Mr Wright. We're both lonely so why don't we enjoy each other's company?'

'Yes, of course,' he murmured, dropping to his knees and gazing longingly at her exposed swollen outer lips. 'Why don't we?'

Closing her eyes as the man kissed the smooth flesh of her inner thighs, Christina pulled her panties to one side and exposed the full length of her drenched sex crack. Wright didn't hesitate, pressing his mouth hard against the firm lips of her vagina and licking the creamy-wet valley of her pussy. Gasping, Christina shuddered as he parted her swollen love lips and repeatedly swept his tongue over the sensitive tip of her solid clitoris. She'd got Wright exactly where she'd wanted him, she reflected as he drove a finger deep into the hugging sheath of her sex-juiced cunt. Never again would he call her to his study and accuse her of having sex with the students. The only time he'd call her to his study would be when he wanted her young body, when he craved the tight duct of her hot cunt.

'Fuck me,' Christina murmured, her clitoris near to orgasm beneath the man's snaking tongue. 'I want you to fuck me really hard.' Remaining silent, Wright hauled out his erect penis and drove his solid knob between the splayed petals of her inner labia. Christina shuddered, moving her buttocks forward on the chair as the man's huge cock glided deep into the tight duct of her vagina until his bulbous glans pressed against the soft firmness of her ripe cervix.

Withdrawing his cunny-slimed sex rod, he drove into her again, the squelching juices of her pussy spraying from her bloated vaginal entrance and splattering her inner thighs with every forceful thrust of his massive cock. He was quite a man, Christina mused, her vaginal muscles spasming, tightening around his pistoning shaft. She'd soon have him eating out of her hand, she knew as his gasps grew louder. He might have been her boss, but now she'd call the shots. Taking time off wouldn't be a problem, Ponting wouldn't pose a threat . . .

'God, I'm there already,' he breathed, his swinging balls draining as his spunk shot from his throbbing knob and filled Christina's rhythmically contracting cunt. Again and again he drove his orgasming cock-head deep into her young body, his low moans of male pleasure reverberating around the room as he fucked her with a vengeance. Wondering how long it had been since he'd last sunk his knob into a tight cunt, Christina knew that this would be the first of many illicit fucking sessions with the sex-starved man. So much for writing to her mother, she mused. That would hardly be necessary now that Wright was her partner in lust. Grunting as he rocked his hips, sperm jetting from his knob-slit and filling the inflamed sheath of her vagina, he finally slowed his fucking rhythm.

'I'm sorry,' he breathed, stilling his deflating cock within her vaginal sheath.

'Why are you sorry?' she asked.

'I was too quick for you. You didn't . . . you didn't have time to come.'

'Don't worry,' Christina chuckled. 'We'll have plenty of opportunities to . . .'

'You mean, we'll do this again?' he asked surprisedly.

'Of course we shall. If you want to, that is?'

'Oh, yes. Yes, we'll definitely do this again. And next time . . .'

'Next time, I'll come,' she giggled as he slipped his flaccid cock shaft out of her sperm-drenched vaginal cavern. 'Next time, we'll spend an hour or more having sex. Will you still be writing to my mother?' she asked as he staggered to his feet and zipped his trousers.

'No, I don't think so. It seems to me that Don Ponting is trying to cause trouble.'

'It looks that way,' Christina said, concealing her spermed sex crack with her wet panties. 'But why would he want to do that?'

'Perhaps he was hoping to get what you just gave me.'

'Maybe. Look, I have a friend calling round this evening, so . . .'

'I have to be going anyway. Oh, there's my home phone number,' he said, passing her a card. 'Right, I'll see you on Monday.'

'Yes, of course.'

'Er . . . feel free to come to my study. If you want to chat or whatever.'

'Thanks, I will. Look, I'm sorry to hurry you.'

'No, no, it's all right. I'll see myself out.'

'OK, Mr . . . I can hardly call you Mr Wright now that we've—'

'Ian, Ian Wright. It's Christina, isn't it?'

'Yes. OK, Ian. Until Monday.'

'OK. And, thanks for . . . for everything.'

'You're more than welcome to everything I have.'

Christina couldn't stop grinning as she listened to the man walking down the stairs. Hearing the front door close, she leaped out of her chair and punched the air with her fist. She felt as though all her problems had been solved – albeit by prostituting herself. Again recalling Alison's words, she tried not to worry about her wanton whoredom or to analyse what she'd done. There was still one problem to be faced, she reflected. Alison hadn't wanted Bryony to move in. But that was a minor worry, she decided, topping up her glass with neat vodka. Ponting could go fuck himself, she thought happily. And Alison would be OK, she was sure. Now Christina could really start living – and fucking.

12

Waking beside Bryony on Sunday morning. Christina leaped out of bed and went into Alison's room. The girl still hadn't come home, and Christina could only assume that she'd met someone in the pub and gone back to their place. Returning to her room, she gazed at Bryony's pretty face as she slept. She looked so young and innocent with her eyes closed, her long lashes fluttering and her blonde hair fanned out across the pillow. Young – but not so innocent.

Hoping that she had made the right decision by allowing the girl to move in, Christina looked around the room. There were several plastic sacks full of Bryony's clothes and bits and pieces that would have to be sorted out. But there was all day to deal with that, she thought, suddenly remembering that she'd promised to visit her mother. While walking into the kitchen and filling the kettle, Christina wondered whether to take Bryony with her or not. It wouldn't be easy explaining Bryony to her parents, but she didn't want to leave the girl alone in the flat all day. Particularly since Alison would return at some stage and wonder why Bryony had moved in. The phone rang. Grabbing it before it woke Bryony, Christina grinned as she heard Ponting's voice.

'I just thought I'd remind you that it's Monday

tomorrow,' he said. 'We all hate Monday mornings, but not as much as you're going to.'

'And why's that, Mr Ponting?' she asked.

'There's still one way open to you, Miss Shaw. If you want to hang on to your job, then you'll meet me later this morning – on the common – and have sex with me.'

'All right,' she sighed. 'You win, Mr Ponting. I'm desperate to keep my job and I'm willing to do whatever you want.'

'Good, good,' he chuckled. 'I thought you'd see sense before it was too late and you lost your job. OK, it's now eight-thirty. I'll meet you on the common by the woods at ten.'

'I'll be there.'

'Excellent, Miss Shaw. I reckon that we're going to get along very well together. See you soon.'

'Yes. Goodbye.'

Replacing the receiver, Christina rubbed her chin thoughtfully. This could prove to be yet another break of the type that she needed, she mused, pouring herself a cup of coffee. A wicked plan coming into her mind as she sat at the table and toyed with her teaspoon, she decided to take a quick shower before dressing in a short skirt and loose-fitting blouse. She'd meet Ponting on the common, and allow him to lead her into the woods. But he wouldn't be leading her along the path to sex. He'd be following a path to his own come-uppance. Eyeing Wright's card on the table, she grabbed the phone and punched the buttons.

'Hello, Ian,' she said as the man answered.

'Oh, Christina. You're up bright and early.'

'Sorry if it's too early.'

'No, no, not at all.'

'I've just had a call from Mr Ponting.'

'Oh?'

'He wants me to meet him on the common at ten . . . ten-fifteen.'

'Why?'

'He didn't say. But, in view of his dreadful allegations, I thought I'd better let you know.'

'Yes, yes, I see. This is most odd. Will you go?'

'Well, I'm not sure. After all he's said, I don't think it would be wise.'

'I'll tell you what we'll do. You go along at ten-fifteen, and I'll be there. Out of sight, of course.'

'That's very good of you, Ian I must say that I'm very worried.'

'You must be. I'll be there, you can rely on me.'

'Thank you, Ian. And thank you for last night. It was truly wonderful.'

'Thank *you*, Christina.'

This was going to be very interesting, Christina thought happily as she downed her coffee and took a shower. If things worked out, the headmaster would arrive to find Ponting completely naked and Christina in a state of shock. Dressed and ready to go, she checked her watch. Nine-thirty, time enough to get there before Ponting. Checking on the sleeping Bryony, she kissed the girl's cheek before leaving the flat.

The common was deserted, and Christina reckoned that everyone was having a Sunday morning lie-in. She headed for the pond. She was going to have to get the timing right, she knew as she sat on the bench and gazed at the rippling water glistening beneath the summer sun. It wouldn't be too difficult to get Ponting to strip naked, but the head was going to have to turn up before

Christina herself was forced to strip. Trying to think positively, Christina repeatedly checked her watch and scanned the common for signs of life.

'It'll be all right,' she breathed, praying that Ponting wouldn't bring his wife along. That would really cock things up, she reflected, imagining the woman demanding lesbian sex. Finally noticing Ponting heading towards her, she left the bench and waited by the entrance to the woods. Doing her best to formulate her plan, she smiled as the man approached. This was the opportunity she'd been waiting for, and she prayed for nothing to go wrong as she felt her stomach churning. Dressed in tight blue jeans and an open-neck shirt, Ponting grinned as he reached Christina and stood in front of her. At least he was alone, she thought, licking her full lips provocatively as she asked him whether his balls were full.

'They certainly are,' Ponting replied surprisedly, his face lighting up as he eyed the deep ravine of her cleavage. 'You're looking forward to this, aren't you?' he asked.

'Oh, yes,' she giggled, keeping an eye out for the head. 'Very much so.'

'Why the change of tune? I didn't think—'

'I need my job. Besides, I love sex. Having sex in return for keeping my job sounds like a pretty good deal to me.'

'Well, this is a turn-up for the books. I must say that I thought you were going to be difficult about this.'

'Oh no, no. You see, I had to be sure about you before doing this sort of thing. I loved wanking you off at the college, and I wanted to go a lot further.'

'Really?'

'I've been thinking about you, wanking your cock. You're big – very big. In fact, I've thought of nothing else recently.'

'Well, I don't know what to say.'

'I had to be sure that you were OK before going any further. I have to admit that I didn't like your threats, but . . . well, I suppose that was the only way you'd thought you'd get your hands inside my panties. You only had to ask, and I'd have opened my legs as wide as I could for you.'

'Right. In that case, shall we go into the woods?'

'Yes, why not?' Christina replied, noticing Wright approaching in the distance. 'Before we do, tell me what you like.'

'What I like? Well, anal sex is one of my little fetishes. Are you into that?'

'God, very much so. You may think this is silly, but I like playing games.'

'What sort of games?'

'I used to play this with my boyfriend. You go into the woods and strip off. I'll follow in a couple of minutes and you leap out of the bushes. I have to pretend that I don't know you and—'

'Yes, I'm with you,' Ponting said, his face beaming.

'I know it sounds silly, but . . .'

'Not at all. I'll have to introduce you to my wife. You'd get on well with her.'

'I'm sure I would. OK, ready when you are.'

'Just give me a couple of minutes.'

Watching the man enter the woods, Christina knew that this was going to work. Ponting allowed his cock to rule his head, that was his problem. Falling for a trick like that, he obviously only had one thing in mind. Crude sex.

As Wright edged his way around the bushes by the pond, Christina waved, beckoning him to follow before she entered the woods. This was perfect, she mused, stealthily making her way along the narrow path into the trees. Unless Ponting had some sort of trick up his sleeve, this was going to be the man's downfall.

Christina had only gone twenty yards or so when Ponting leaped out of the undergrowth and blocked her way. His penis was solidly erect, his foreskin fully retracted, his purple knob pointing to the sky. Eyeing his heavy balls, she thought what a shame it was that she wasn't even going to have time to suck his cock and savour the salty taste of his glans. His glistening weaponhead looked most inviting, she mused, her mouth watering as she licked her succulent lips. As he ran his hand up and down his solid shaft, she reached out and brushed the globe of his knob with her fingertip. She was desperate to take him into her mouth and suck the fresh spunk from his throbbing knob. But she wasn't going to allow her weakness to become her undoing.

'And where are you off to, little girl?' Ponting asked, playing the game admirably.

'I was . . . Please, I have to . . .' Christina stammered, hearing a twig crack somewhere behind her. 'I was just walking home through the woods.'

'You'd like to suck my cock, wouldn't you?'

'No, please . . .'

'I'm sure you'd like to suck my cock and drink my sperm. Would you like me to push my huge cock right up your tight little cunt and fuck you?'

'No, please,' she whimpered, aware of Wright close behind her. 'Keep away from me!' she cried. 'You vile man! Get away from me!'

'What's the matter?' Ponting asked, his beady eyes narrowing still further as Christina backed away.

'You vile man!' Christina cried again. 'You tricked me into coming here and—'

'What the . . .' Wright gasped, appearing on the scene. 'My God, man. What the hell . . .'

'Oh, Mr Wright,' Christina sobbed, throwing her arms around his neck and clinging to him as Ponting dived back into the bushes. 'I'm so glad you're here.'

'What happened?'

'He said that he'd found some fungi for Bryony and . . . he disappeared and then leaped out at me with no clothes on.'

'All right, all right. Calm yourself. Let's get out of here. I'll deal with Ponting on Monday morning.'

'I know you don't want any trouble at the college, but the man should be imprisoned for attempted rape.'

'That would be difficult to prove, Christina. But I will sack him, I promise you. Now, are you sure you're OK?'

'Yes, I think so. I've never been so frightened in my life. I should never have agreed to meet the pervert. I might have guessed that he'd planned something like this. If I'd been alone—'

'Well, you weren't. Thank God you'd had the sense to call me.'

Walking across the common to the pond, Christina did her best to suppress the grin on her face. Ponting sacked? This called for a party, she decided. Reaching the edge of the common and walking along the quiet street with Wright, she turned her thoughts to visiting her parents. She wished that she had the day free to help Bryony sort her things out – and also to do some explaining to Alison. But she'd promised her mother and couldn't let her down. Saying goodbye to Wright as they reached her flat, she arranged to see him that evening for a walk on the common. She hadn't had the pleasure of sucking his purple knob to orgasm yet, but that was soon to change, she decided.

'Let's go,' she said, finding Bryony munching toast in the kitchen.

'Go? Go where?'

'To visit my parents. Is Alison back yet?'

'No, she's not. Where have you been?'

'For a walk on the common. We'll sort your things out later.'

'I've done it,' the girl said, a smile on her pretty face. 'I've hung my clothes up and put everything away. Want some coffee?'

'Yes, please. OK, we'll go to my parents' house for lunch. It'll save us cooking and keep my mother happy, if nothing else.'

Sitting at the table, Christina watched Bryony pour the coffee. The girl's skirt was far too short, almost revealing the swell of her panties. She had a beautiful young body, Christina mused, glimpsing her red panties as she bent over to take the milk from the fridge. Working in a massage parlour, she'd be groped and abused by dirty old men. The thought of ageing men fingering Bryony's teenage pussy as she wanked their cocks and brought out their sperm displeased Christina. Bryony was young and fresh, and shouldn't have to have her beautiful body sullied by perverts. But what choice was there? The girl had to work to pay her share of the rent.

Answering the ringing phone as Bryony placed the coffee cups on the table, Christina wasn't surprised to hear Ponting's voice. Ranting and raving, spitting out his threats, he was understandably unhappy with Christina. She listened for a while, delighting in the man's predicament as Bryony gestured silently that she was going to get her bag from the bedroom. Finally interrupting Ponting, Christina made out that she had had no idea that Wright was going to be walking on the common.

'You lying bitch,' Ponting hissed. 'You planned the whole fucking thing.'

'I was looking forward to having sex with you,' she said softly. 'Why would I arrange for Wright to mess things up?'

'You know what'll happen now, don't you? I'll be chucked out of the college.'

'I doubt that it'll come to that.'

'Of course it'll come to that, for fuck's sake. You set me up good and proper.'

'The head told me that he often walks on the common on Sunday mornings.'

'I heard what you were saying to him, you fucking bitch. Making out that you were terrified and—'

'All right, so I set you up. What the hell did you expect me to do? You and your lesbian wife abusing young Bryony in the woods . . .'

'You can talk. I know exactly what *you* get up to.'

'And you rang my mother with your crap. Yes, you will be chucked out of the college. You deserve it, that's all I can say.'

'I'll tell you this, Miss Shaw. I won't go away. I might not be at the college, but I'll always be around. I'll have you for this, believe you me.'

As Ponting hung up, Christina bit her lip. She didn't want to be looking over her shoulder every time she went out. There again, what could the man do? But he was crazy, and crazy people did crazy things, she knew. Finishing her coffee as Bryony appeared in the doorway, Christina grabbed her bag and left the flat with the girl. Walking to the station, Christina found herself glancing over her shoulder every few minutes, looking at the drivers as cars passed. This was ridiculous, she knew. There was nothing Ponting could do to her.

During the train journey, Christina told Bryony about Charles. The girl laughed when she heard what a pompous git he was and burst into a fit of giggles when Christina said that she'd sucked his cock in the garden. It was a shame that the girl couldn't meet Charles, Christina reflected. There again, he was that well in with her father that he might turn up at the house and join them for Sunday lunch. What with Bryony's short skirt and revealing blouse . . . Christina was having wicked thoughts, imagining Bryony in the garden with Charles, sucking the sperm from his throbbing knob. If Charles did turn up, the day might prove to be very interesting.

Arriving at her parents' house, Christina introduced Bryony as one of her students. Her mother didn't appear to be too pleased, but welcomed the girl and offered her a cup of tea. Christina guessed that it was Bryony's short skirt that her mother disapproved of rather than anything else. She should have made the girl wear something more suitable, but it was too late now. Leaving Bryony on the patio with her tea, Christina followed her mother into the house as the woman frowned and beckoned her.

'What is it?' she asked once they'd reached the kitchen.

'Is that girl your lover?' her mother asked directly.

'What?' Christina giggled. 'My—'

'That man who rang said that you were having an affair with a young girl, a student.'

'Mother, that man who rang is being sacked.'

'Oh?'

'He's been lying about everyone, causing trouble at the college and . . . My lover? How on earth could you believe a thing like that?'

'Well, I . . . He described her, went into great detail.'

'You didn't tell me that.'

'No, not over the phone. He said that you'd been having an affair with the girl and you'd been . . .'

'Been what?'

'Spanking her naked bottom in the stockroom.'

'God, as if I'd do such a thing. He's been telling the headmaster that the science teacher has been abusing young lads.'

'Goodness me,' the older woman gasped.

'None of it's true. He's getting the sack tomorrow, so we can forget about him. Bryony is in my class at the college. Her home life is very difficult so, to give her a break, I suggested that she come here with me. I should have phoned and told you, I suppose. But it was a last-minute decision. You don't mind, do you?'

'No, not now that you've explained things. I'm sorry, dear. I didn't think that you were like that. It's just that . . . Oh, I don't know. What with that man ringing and the things Charles has been saying, I just thought—'

'Charles? What's he been saying?'

'He's not said anything to your father, but . . . He came round the other day and had a long chat with me.'

'About me, presumably?'

'Yes. He seems to think that you're mixing with the wrong type of people. When he told me that you have a man friend – a man in his sixties . . .'

'What? This is crazy. Yes, I do have a male friend. I

told you about him when I was last here. His name's Barry Doogan.'

'Charles has been up to London, dear. He's seen your flat, and the college.'

'When was this?'

'I don't know. The other day, I think. He was going to ring your doorbell and . . . Christina, he saw several middle-aged men leaving your flat.'

'Middle-aged men?'

'He made some enquiries locally and . . . well, it seems that your flat is a brothel.'

'This is bloody stupid,' Christina spat. 'I'm sorry, I know I shouldn't have sworn. Charles obviously went to the wrong place.'

'He saw you, dear. He saw you leaving the flat.'

'Several middle-aged men? No one's been to see us. Apart from Bryony and a couple of the other students. Does Charles know that I'll be here today?'

'No, not unless your father's told him. They're playing golf, so Charles might come back with your father.'

'I hope he does because I want to ask him about this. My flat, a brothel? That's ludicrous.'

Christina was becoming increasingly incensed by the allegations and accusations made against her. Charles was obviously lying to cause trouble. Unless the middle-aged men had been to see Alison. No, she'd have mentioned it. It was jealousy, she concluded, following her mother out to the patio. Ponting was jealous because she was young and attractive and had wanked off a few lads. He'd wanted her, wanted to have sex with her, and she'd turned him down. Charles was jealous because Christina was making a new life for herself in London and meeting interesting people.

'This is a lovely garden,' Bryony said, looking up from her seat at the table. 'May I have a look round?'

'Of course,' Christina's mother replied. 'Bryony, it's . . . it's lovely to meet you.'

'I'll show you round,' Christina said. 'We might find some fungi.'

'Fungi?' Bryony echoed, her blue eyes narrowing in puzzlement as she stood up.

'I'll explain later. Come on.'

Walking to the end of the garden, Christina sat on the bench beneath the willow tree and asked Bryony to join her. It *was* a lovely garden, and Christina missed it very much. But she'd left home now and was forging a new life. *A new life?* she reflected. Sex and more sex, that was her new life. But was it, she wondered. She was doing well at the college, had a nice enough flat . . . There was nothing wrong with being a nymphomaniac, she thought, eyeing Bryony's naked thighs.

'I wish I lived somewhere like this,' Bryony sighed. 'London stinks.'

'No, it doesn't,' Christina laughed. 'There's the common with the pond and the woods, there's the park . . .'

'And diesel fumes and too many people.'

'Why not move away, then? I mean, if you hate it that much, get out into the country.'

'What would I do in the country? Where would I work? On a farm?'

'You might enjoy that. In fact, *I* might even enjoy working on a farm.'

'Mucking out horses and milking cows?' Bryony giggled.

'Why not? Think about it. Your job involves milking old men.'

'That's awful. God, put like that it sounds as if—'

'Seriously, I think things are going to turn out all right. If Alison moves out, you can have her room. Things at the college will be different now. I'll tell you all about that later. So, everything's OK.'

'I suppose I'd better let the college know that I'm not going back.'

'I'll deal with that, don't worry.'

Hearing her father's voice, Christina took a deep breath. Charles would have told him about the middle-aged men and the flat being a brothel, she was sure. Hopefully, her mother would put him right, stopping him from launching an all-out attack on Christina's London lifestyle. Her stomach churning as she heard Charles laughing, she decided to confront him. Ponting's lies were bad enough. To think that Charles was running to her mother with *his* crap was infuriating.

'Ah, Christina,' Charles said as he approached. 'And you must be Bryony.'

'Hello,' Bryony said softly, smiling at the man.

'Good morning. Charles,' Christina murmured coldly. 'I hear that you've been to London.'

'Er . . . yes, that's right.'

'I'm going to look around the garden again,' Bryony said, obviously aware of an atmosphere as she wandered off.

'I hear that you've been telling my mother that I'm a prostitute and that I'm running a brothel,' Christina said once Bryony was out of earshot.

'I didn't say that you were a prostitute,' he retorted indignantly.

'You said that my flat is a brothel, Charles. Prostitutes work in brothels, don't they?'

'Well yes, but . . .'

'Did it not occur to you that the men you saw leaving my flat might have been to see Alison?'

'You were there, Christina. I saw you about half an hour later.'

'I was *not* there, Charles. These men, whoever they are, must have been to see Alison. They might have been members of her family. Why you have to jump to the conclusion that they're clients, I really don't know.'

'I didn't say that they were clients.'

'What you did or didn't say doesn't matter. It's what you implied to my mother that pisses me off. And what's all this about a man friend of mine? You told my mother that I was with a man in his sixties.'

'I saw you walking down the street with a man who must have been in his sixties if he was a day.'

'So you immediately thought that I was sleeping with him, fucking him and sucking spunk out of his knob?'

'Christina . . . For God's sake.'

'I don't even know who this man is, Charles. I might have been walking with one of the other teachers. It could have been anyone. Why go running to my mother with your ridiculous tales?'

'I'm sorry, Christina. I worry about you, you know that. Anyway, why have you brought that young girl with you? God, she must be about fourteen. What's going on there?'

'*What's going on there?* What the hell do you mean by that?'

'I—'

'For God's sake, Charles. Are you now thinking that I'm having an affair with an under-age girl?'

'No, I meant . . . It just seems odd that you should be going around with a girl who's obviously—'

'Too young to fuck?'

'Christina, I do wish you'd stop using foul words. They're not necessary. As a teacher of English, you should know better.'

'I don't know which is worse, Charles. My foul words or your foul mind. First you go around saying that I'm screwing a man in his sixties, and then you say that I'm having lesbian sex with an under-age girl. I'd rather say *fuck* and *cunt* than fill my mind with disgusting thoughts about illegal sexual acts with young girls.'

'We're not getting on too well, are we?' Charles sighed.

'No, we're not. How do you expect us to get on well when you go running to my mother and worrying her with all your crap? What I do in London is my business. Even if I was into prostitution and running a brothel, it would have nothing to do with you.'

'I realize that, Christina. Oh, here comes your friend.'

'Well, Bryony?' Christina asked, smiling at the girl. 'What do you think of the garden?'

'It's lovely,' she replied, sitting next to Christina on the bench. 'I've never seen such a big garden.'

'I must go to the loo,' Christina said, rising to her feet and winking at the girl. 'You stay and talk to Charles.' Looking down at Bryony's thighs, Christina winked again and nodded her head. 'I must also ring Alison. You two can get to know each other while I'm gone.'

Stopping once she was out of sight, Christina peered through a bush and watched Charles. He was standing in front of Bryony, his gaze fixed unblinkingly on the triangular red patch of her panties as she parted her thighs. She was an obedient girl, Christina mused. Parting her thighs further, Bryony had obviously understood Christina's winking and nodding and knew exactly what to do. But what would Charles do, Christina wondered. He thought, wrongly, that the girl was no more than fourteen years old. Would he make a move towards her?

'Christina said that we should get to know each other,' Charles said, grinning at the girl. 'I'd like to get to know you a *lot* better, Bryony.'

'Would you?' Bryony asked, parting her thighs even further, the narrow strip of her panties barely wide enough to conceal the hairless lips of her pussy. 'That sounds interesting.'

'It could be. You're a very attractive young girl. Do you usually sit like that?'

'Only when I'm with older men,' she giggled. 'But when I'm with a really good-looking man like you I sit like *this*.'

Christina stifled a giggle as Bryony tugged the tight material of her red panties to one side and blatantly displayed the shaved lips of her teenage pussy. Charles stared in disbelief as she spread her thighs as wide as she could, her vaginal lips parting to reveal the intricate inner folds of her sex valley to his wide eyes. Bryony was great fun, Christina thought happily as the girl stretched the lips of her vulva wide apart, exposing the creamy-wet entrance to her cunt. The girl was going to make an excellent flatmate, she reflected, wondering what Charles would do.

'Well,' Charles breathed, the crotch of his trousers bulging as he stared at the girl's open sex hole. 'I must say that I've never seen a young girl sitting like that before. How old . . . no, I'd better not ask.'

'I'm fourteen,' Bryony lied, counting the fingers that Christina held up in quick succession as the older girl peered over the top of the bush behind Charles.

'Christ,' Charles gasped. 'Fourteen? I don't think—'

'Aren't you going to touch me?' Bryony asked, licking her succulent lips provocatively as she lay back on the bench with her firm bottom over its edge.

'Yes,' Charles replied unhesitatingly, kneeling in front of her and driving a finger deep into the hot sheath of her young pussy.

'If you're quick, you'll have time to fuck me before Christina gets back.'

'God, I . . .' Charles stammered, slipping a second finger into her contracting vagina. 'I really don't think . . .'

'Don't you want to fuck my little cunt?' Bryony sighed.

'Yes, but . . .'

'I'd love to feel your hard cock sliding deep into my wet cunt. And your sperm filling me.'

Withdrawing his cunny-dripping fingers, Charles unzipped his trousers and pulled his solid cock out. He was a bloody hypocrite, Christina mused, watching him stab at the girl's open lust hole with his purple knob. He'd made out that he was some sort of high and mighty man of great morality – and now he was forcing his cock into the wet cunt of a girl he believed to be only fourteen! Watching his rock-hard shaft sink deeper into her young body, Christina was in two minds as to whether or not to leap out of the bushes and confront him. He wasn't going to get away with his hypocrisy, that was for sure.

'God, you're tight,' Charles breathed, fully impaling the trembling girl on his lust staff.

'So I should be,' Bryony giggled. 'I'm only *just* fourteen.'

'Only just . . . Bloody hell.'

'Fuck me really hard, Charles. Fuck me really hard and fill my tight cunt with spunk.'

Repeatedly ramming his swollen knob deep into the young girl's hot cunt, Charles let out moans and gasps of debased pleasure. Groping at her blouse, he slipped his hand inside and squeezed the firmness of her teenage breasts as he fucked her with a vengeance. Leaning forward, he locked his lips to her full mouth, his tongue meeting hers as he rocked his hips and lost himself in the grip of what he mistakenly imagined to be his illicit sexual act. Christina waited, biding her time as her ex-boyfriend committed the vulgar act. Slipping her hand down the front of her wet panties, she massaged the solid nubble of her erect clitoris, the arousing scene sending ripples of pleasure through her contracting womb as her clitoris responded to her intimate caress.

'Coming,' Charles announced, gasping. The girl's young body flopped back and forth like a rag doll as he repeatedly rammed his throbbing knob deep into her tightening cunt and filled her with his gushing sperm. Again and again he drove his purple glans into the fiery heat of her teenage cunt, his balls draining as the squelching and gasping sounds of furtive sex sounded through the garden. Christina stifled her own gasps of sexual satisfaction as her clitoris erupted in orgasm, her curvaceous body shaking violently as Charles made his last penile thrusts into the sex-dizzy younger girl.

Finally coming down from her sexual heaven, Christina sucked her vaginal cream from her sticky fingers and adjusted her clothing. Charles was breathing heavily, his body collapsed over Bryony, his penis embedded deep within her spunked vaginal cavern as he recovered from his forbidden fucking. The time was right, Christina mused, checking her clothing before emerging from her hiding place and standing behind Charles. Once again, hypocrisy was about to be exposed.

'My God,' Christina gasped, holding her hand to her mouth.

'Oh, er . . .' Charles stammered, moving back and slipping his cunny-wet cock out of Bryony's sperm-flooded cunt. 'Christina, I . . .'

'Don't say anything, Charles. I was thinking that we might get back together but . . . Just don't ever speak to me again.'

'Christina, you don't understand,' he whined, rising to his feet and zipping his trousers. 'That young tart made me—'

'She *made* you fuck her?' Christina laughed bitterly. 'She's thirteen years old, Charles.'

'Thirteen?' he breathed, his face reddening. 'But I thought she was at least—'

'*Nearly* fourteen,' Bryony said, concealing the sperm-wet crack of her pussy with her tight panties.

'You'd better leave,' Christina sobbed, wiping her eyes. 'Just leave.'

'Yes, yes, of course,' Charles murmured, walking towards the house.

'That's that bastard dealt with,' Christina giggled once he was out of earshot. 'And now, young lady, I'd better deal with you most severely.'

Kneeling in front of Bryony, Christina pulled the girl's soaked panties aside and pressed her mouth to her gaping vaginal entrance. Sucking out the sperm and girl-cum, she swallowed the heady blend of sex as Bryony trembled and writhed on the bench. The day couldn't have turned out better, Christina reflected, drinking from the brimming sheath of the young lesbian's hot cunt. They could now look forward to lunch – without Charles – and then spend the afternoon relaxing beneath the sun in the garden.

Monday was going to be another interesting day, Christina knew as she drained the girl's hot cunt. Ponting sacked, giving the headmaster a quick blow job in his study . . . She might even wank off Doogan and Brown, she reflected. If they had the class under control, she might even allow them to fuck her tight bottom-hole. Monday morning was going to be most interesting. But she still had Alison to face. And Ponting's threats to worry about.

13

'This morning, we're going to look at spoken English,' Christina said, standing behind her desk as the headmaster appeared in the doorway.

'Excuse me, Miss,' Brown said, rising to his feet. 'The essay—'

'I'm sorry to interrupt the lesson,' Wright said, obviously stunned by the control Christina seemed to have over her class.

'I'm sorry, sir,' Brown said, retaking his seat.

'No, no, not at all, Brown. Might I have a quick word, Miss Shaw?'

'Yes, of course,' Christina replied, walking to the door. 'I'll be five minutes,' she said to the class. 'Presumably you all managed to complete your essays over the weekend?'

'Yes, Miss,' the students replied in unison.

'All right, read through them and then place them on my desk.'

Following the head to his study, Christina realized that Brown and Doogan had kept their word and had ordered their fellow students to behave. What the lads had threatened the class with, Christina dreaded to think. But whatever it was had worked, which was all that mattered. Closing the door behind her as she followed Wright into the study, she wondered whether he'd spoken to Ponting yet. If the man had dared to show his face at the college, that was.

'Your class are remarkably well behaved,' Wright said, perching himself on the edge of his desk. 'Never in all my years at this college have I know such obedience, such good behaviour. You'll have to tell me how you did it, let me in on your secret.'

'It's just a matter of handling them properly,' Christina said, imagining handling the lads' cocks in return for their efforts. 'One or two of the boys were pretty hard to handle at first, but I soon softened them up.'

'It's truly remarkable, Christina. I congratulate you.'

'Thank you.'

'Now, I want to talk to you about Mr Ponting.'

'Have you spoken to him yet? I haven't seen him around this morning.'

'No, you won't be seeing him at the college again. He rang in first thing with his resignation. Which I immediately accepted, of course. I know that you will think that I'm putting the college first, but . . . I don't believe it's necessary to take any further action, do you?'

'No, I don't. We'd gain nothing by taking this any further. As long as Mr Ponting has gone, that's fine by me.'

'Good, good. So, I now have the job of finding another sports master. Er . . . Christina?'

'Yes?'

'About the weekend. I enjoyed . . . er . . . I enjoyed your company very much. I hope we can see each other again.'

'Of course we will, Ian. There's nothing I'd like more.'

'I was hoping you'd say that. If you're free during break, come and join me for a coffee.'

'Thanks, I'd love to. Well, I'd better be getting back to my class.'

'Right you are.'

Leaving the study, Christina grinned as she walked along the corridor. Ponting had resigned, Christina herself was well in with the headmaster, the students were models of good behaviour, Bryony . . . Wondering how the girl was getting on at the massage parlour, Christina decided to tell the head, when she joined him for coffee later that morning, that the girl had left the college. Everything was going so well, Christina reflected. Too well, perhaps? Returning to her class, she was amazed to find a neat pile of completed essays on her desk. This was far too good to be true, she thought, beginning the lesson on spoken English.

As the class filed out of the room at break time, Christina noticed one student hanging back. It was Simpson, a good-looking lad who had pretty much kept himself to himself during lessons. Reckoning that he was trying to pluck up the courage to talk to her as she went through the motions of sorting out his books, Christina wandered over to his desk and asked whether he was enjoying college.

'Sort of,' he replied. 'But I'm not happy with Doogan's threats.'

'Threats?' Christina echoed, feigning puzzlement.

'We behave in class, or we get it on the way home.'

'I see. Don't you *want* to behave in class?'

'It's not that. It's . . . I know what you're up to.'

'Up to?'

'It's not right, what you're doing.'

'Simpson, I'm not doing anything other than teaching English.'

'I know what you do in the stockroom. It's not right, Miss. It's not moral or ethical.'

'What do I do in the stockroom?' Christina asked, realizing that she could have a problem on her hands.

'You know what you do. I don't like it, Miss. You might think me old-fashioned or whatever, but I'm wondering whether to report it.'

'Report what?' Christina asked, sure now that she was facing a major problem.

'It's not right to—'

'To do *this*?' she whispered huskily, massaging the boy's penis through his trousers.

'Yes, no . . . I mean . . .'

'Don't you like it, Simpson?'

'No, I . . .'

'That's nice, isn't it? I can feel you stiffening. You like me stiffening you like this, don't you?'

'This isn't . . .'

'Isn't right? Tell me what's wrong with it. Now you're really stiff. I can feel you, your hardness. Would you like me to stop?'

'Yes, no . . . Someone might come in.'

'No, they won't,' she breathed, unzipping his trousers and pulling his solid penis out. 'That's what you want, isn't it?' she asked, rolling his foreskin back and forth over the swollen globe of his cock. 'No, don't pull away. Let me massage you, Simpson. Allow me to relax you, take all your worries and tension away.'

Watching the lad's eyes roll as she ran her hand up and down the length of his twitching cock, Christina knew that she'd solved yet another problem. This was easy, she reflected. To control teenage boys, all she needed to do was massage their young cocks and bring out their sperm. Wondering whether to kneel down and take the lad's purple globe into her wet mouth, she glanced at the door. It was too risky, she decided, wanking the lad faster. Beginning to gasp, his knees sagging, Christina knew that he'd soon be shooting his sperm all over the floor.

'You like me wanking your cock, don't you?' she asked.

'Yes, yes,' he breathed.

'You'd like me to wank you every day, wouldn't you?'

'I . . . I'm coming.'

'I want your sperm to run all over my hand. Then I'll lap it up, swallow your spunk. You'd love to feel your knob in my mouth, wouldn't you?'

'God, yes. I—'

Kneeling, Christina couldn't help herself as she retracted his foreskin fully and sucked his salty knob deep into her hot mouth. Simpson gasped, whimpering and trembling as he clung to her head and filled her pretty mouth with his gushing spunk. Hauling his heavy balls out of his trousers, Christina massaged the fleshy bag of his scrotum and kneaded his sperm eggs as he gasped in his mouth-fucking. Gobbling and sucking on his orgasming knob, Christina drank from his teenage fountainhead. Wondering whether he'd ever slipped his cock into a girl's mouth and spunked down her throat, she imagined him wanking. He'd think about fucking her hot mouth every time he wanked from now on. He'd picture his purple knob between her full lips, her tongue teasing his sperm-slit as she swallowed his orgasmic offering.

Finally slipping Simpson's spent penis out of her sperm-flooded mouth, Christina stood in front of him and grinned. White liquid dribbling down her chin, she moved forward, locked her glossed lips to his and pushed her tongue deep into his mouth. To her surprise, his cock stiffened again, his solid shaft pressing hard against her lower stomach as he tasted his spunk on her tongue. This was the beauty of young lads, she reflected, grabbing his hard penile shaft. They could come again and again.

'Are you all right now?' she asked, moving back and smiling at him.

'Yes, yes, I . . .' he stammered as she wanked his solid shaft.

'There's no time to wank you again,' she said, reluctantly releasing his cock. 'Tomorrow, I'll let you mouth-fuck me.'

'What about . . .'

'You want to fuck my tight cunt?'

'God, yes.'

'OK, tomorrow you can fuck me properly. Now, you'd better get going.'

As the boy zipped up his trousers and left the classroom, Christina licked her spermed lips. Her clitoris in dire need of appeasing, she checked her watch before making her way to the head's study. Wishing she'd got the lad to slip his hand down the front of her wet panties and massage the solid nub of her pleasure spot to orgasm, she wondered whether the head would oblige her by masturbating her. He'd enjoyed locking his mouth to her vulval flesh, sucking and licking her swollen clitoris. He might enjoy a quick vaginal slurp during break.

Walking to the head's study, the crotch of her tight panties soaking up her copious vaginal juices, Christina wondered how many more students she'd have to satisfy sexually to keep them under control. Did it really matter? She pondered: even if it reached the stage where she was regularly wanking every lad in her class, she didn't see that there'd be a problem. Far from it, in fact. The feel of a solid teenage cock in her hand and sperm running over her fingers was hardly a *problem*.

'Ah, Christina,' the head said, standing and smiling as she knocked on his door and entered the study. 'I was beginning to think that you weren't going to turn up.'

'I'm sorry, Ian. I had to deal with one of the boys.'

'No problems, I hope?'

'Nothing too big for me to handle. He was becoming a little concerned about something. All I had to do was talk to him, show him how to get a grip on himself.'

'You're doing exceedingly well. Oh, there's your coffee,' he said, pointing to a tray. 'Help yourself to sugar.'

'Thanks.'

'I've been thinking, Christina. The college needs people like you. People who are able to take control. I realize that you're fresh out of training college and have little or no experience, but—'

'I'm gaining experience every day, Ian,' she broke in, the taste of sperm lingering on her full lips.

'Yes, yes, of course. Although this is only your second week at Spadger Heath College, you've made remarkable progress, achieved amazing results with your class. What I was going to suggest is that you help one or two of the other teachers.'

'Help them? How do you mean?' Christina asked, sipping her coffee.

'Let them into your little secret,' he chuckled. 'Only this morning, Mr Carter was saying that he can't understand why you're still here. As he pointed out, the turnover of staff at Spadger Heath is very high. Not only are you still here, but you're in complete control of your class. Mr Carter, for one, would love to know how you do it.'

'It's not a secret, Ian. It's just . . . I don't know what it is. I do my best to come across as authoritative and yet, at the same time, friendly and approachable.'

'But the likes of Doogan and one or two others . . . How on earth have you got *them* under control?'

'I talk to them, try to get to know them and understand their problems. It's not that I take their side against anything they're whingeing about but I do show them that I'm aware that there are two sides to any issue or problem. I'm not a great deal older than the students, Ian. I'm virtually of the same generation, so I'm able to relate.'

'Yes, I see what you mean. So, talking to Mr Carter wouldn't really help. He's in his fifties and is obviously seen by the students as an old fuddy-duddy. That aside, are you busy this evening?'

'This evening?' she echoed, finishing her coffee. 'Er . . . I'm not sure what I'm doing yet.'

'I thought we might go out for a drink.'

'I'll let you know before I leave this afternoon. I don't want to arrange to meet you and then let you down. Oh, there's the bell. I'd better be getting back. Thanks for the coffee.'

'You're more than welcome, Christina. Don't forget to let me know about this evening.'

'I won't.'

Leaving the study, Christina returned to her empty classroom and sat at her desk. The students had a geography lesson, giving her some time to sort through their essays. But she couldn't keep her mind on her work. Things were going very well, but she realized that problems could easily rear up. Particularly if the staff continually questioned her methods of controlling the students. But her explanation to the headmaster had sounded plausible, she reflected, trying not to worry about it.

Turning her thoughts to Alison, she wondered where the girl had got to. Having last seen her flatmate when she had left for the pub, Christina began to wonder whether she was moving out. She might have heard from the hotel, Christina mused, sifting through the pile of essays. Wondering again how Bryony was getting on at the massage parlour, Christina decided to go for a walk. Unable to concentrate on her work and with her next lesson not until after lunch, she grabbed her bag and left the college. There were too many things playing on her mind. Bryony, Alison, Ponting . . . Beginning to wonder how she'd become so deeply involved in other people's lives, she realized that it had been her own doing. She should never have grabbed Ponting's cock and wanked him, she mused, walking down the street towards the common. Had she kept herself to herself . . . But she'd not been allowed to, she reflected. Ponting had approached her – uninvited, to say the least – for sex. And Alison had made the first move, as had Bryony.

'Christina,' Alison called, dashing across the street.

'Hi,' Christina said, smiling at the girl. 'How are you doing? I've not seen you since—'

'God, I've been running around doing this and that. I've got the job at the hotel.'

'Oh, that's great.'

'I've been moving my things out of the flat this morning. I've left a cheque on the kitchen table for half the rent.'

'Are you going to walk with me?' Christina asked. 'I'm going to the common to get some air.'

'Yes, I will. I could do with a break. I didn't realize how much stuff I had. Oh, I've left my key on the table.'

'Right. So, what's your room like at the hotel?'

'Huge. It's right at the top of the building and I can see out over London. I know I'm going to be happy there. Has Bryony . . . I went into your room to get that skirt you borrowed and noticed some things.'

'Yes, she's moved in. I couldn't talk to you about it since you weren't around.'

'Well, it makes no difference now. Do you often come here?' Alison asked as they walked towards the pond. 'I could meet you for a chat during your breaks.'

'Yes, I like it here. When I get a free period, I come and sit by the pond.'

'I don't want to lose contact with you, Christina. We'll still go to the pub now and then. Oh, by the way – a woman called at the flat this morning.'

'Oh?'

'She asked for the name and phone number of our landlord.'

'Did you tell her?'

'No, I didn't. She said that she was from . . . What was it? The rented-accommodation something or other. I was suspicious, so I told her that I was just visiting and knew nothing about the landlord.'

'What did she look like?'

'Forties, darkish hair, shortish skirt, quite well dressed.'

'Perhaps she's genuine,' Christina sighed, picturing Ponting's wife.

'She said that she'd call back.'

'What are they doing here?' Christina murmured,

noticing Doogan and Brown wandering across the common.

'Who?' Alison asked.

'Two of my students. They're supposed to be at a lesson.'

'Skiving off, I suppose. Well, I'll leave you to do your authoritative bit. I have to get back to the hotel and sort a few things out.'

'Right. I'll see you around, then. Either here or in the pub. Call round at the flat whenever you want to.'

'I will. You take care. And take those lads in hand for skipping lessons.'

'OK,' Christina giggled. 'I'll take them both in hand.'

As Alison walked away, Christina watched Doogan and Brown approaching. She realized that there was another lad trailing along behind them. Wondering what the pair were up to as they laughed and joked, she focused on their friend. She didn't recognize him, and wondered whether he was from another class at the college. With his dark hair swept back, he appeared to be clean and tidy, she observed. And pretty good-looking. Trying to turn her thoughts away from sex as the threesome approached, she felt her clitoris stir within the moist valley of her pussy.

'We followed you,' Doogan said unashamedly.

'Why aren't you in class?' Christina asked.

'This is Greg,' the lad said. 'He wanted to meet you.'

'Hi,' the boy murmured. 'I've heard a lot about you.'

'I'll bet you have,' Christina replied, frowning at Doogan. 'So, why did you follow me? What are you up to?'

'It's a nice day, the sun's shining, college is boring . . . We thought you might like a walk in the woods.'

'Doogan, I . . .'

'Come on,' Brown laughed. 'Come into the woods.'

As they walked towards the trees, Christina was about to join them. But she hesitated. It was pretty obvious what they had in mind, and she did her best to fight her inner desires. It wasn't that she didn't want sex. In fact, sex with three teenage lads would no doubt prove most satisfying. Imagining three solid cocks, three pairs of hands groping her naked body, she felt a quiver run through her contracting womb. This was the middle of the working day, she thought, wishing she'd not gone to the common. Sex was ruling her life, she knew as the boys disappeared into the woods. Three solid cocks? Three beautifully swollen knobs? More than enough fresh spunk? Christina sighed and looked around the common before following her young studs.

Her panties filling with her juices of arousal, she walked along the narrow path in the direction of the low voices and chuckles she could hear. Christina found the lads sitting on the short grass in a small clearing surrounded by bushes. They thought that she was a slut, she knew as she they looked up at her with lust reflected in their dark eyes. Maybe she was, she mused, her clitoris now solid in expectation of the ministrations of three wet tongues.

'Well?' she murmured as they gazed longingly at her naked things. 'Now what?'

'Greg wants to get to know you,' Brown said, grinning. 'He'd like to see more of you.'

'You want me to strip, is that it?' Christina asked, her stomach somersaulting, ripples of sex running through her pelvis.

'Yes,' Doogan replied. 'We're doing our bit at college, so . . .'

'You want me to do my bit?'

'That was the deal.'

Kicking her shoes off, Christina unzipped her skirt and allowed the garment to slide down her legs and fall around her ankles. Her audience watching eagerly, she unbuttoned her blouse, opening it and revealing the silk cups of her bra straining to contain her firm breasts. She couldn't fight her inner desires, she knew as she reached behind her back and unhooked her bra. Her young breasts tumbling from the cups, her nipples becoming erect in the relatively cool air of the woods, she knew that her life now revolved around crude sex. The very thought of stripping in front of three teenage lads sent tremors through her young womb. A feeling of great power overwhelming her, she ran her hands over the firm mounds of her mammary globes. Her nipples stiffening, her areolae darkening, she tossed her long blonde hair over her shoulder and flashed a salacious smile at her audience.

'Have I gone far enough?' she asked, running her hands over the gentle swell of her stomach and down to the top of her tight panties.

'Not quite,' Doogan replied, his tongue almost hanging out as he gazed at the triangular patch of material bulging to contain her full sex lips.

'You want me to pull my wet panties down?' she giggled.

'All the way down.'

'That would be naughty,' Christina murmured. 'I don't know whether I should be naughty.'

'Of course you should.'

Slipping her thumbs between the tight elastic of her panties and the firm flesh of her shapely hips, she slipped the garment down just enough at first to reveal the top of her hairless sex crack. Leaning forward, the boys gazed at Christina's full sex lips as she slipped her panties further down her slender thighs, allowing the flimsy garment to fall down her long legs and tumble around her ankles. The boys' eyes bulging as they gazed at her perfectly formed love lips, the opening valley of her young pussy, Christina felt her clitoris stiffen.

Standing naked in front of three teenage boys and exposing the most intimate part of her young body sent electrifying ripples of sex up Christina's spine. This was her forte, she reflected, wondering whether to peel the fleshy lips of her vagina apart and expose her intricate sex folds nestling within her valley of desire. Deciding to make the lads wait, she pushed the flesh of her outer lips inwards, squeezing out the pinken wings of her inner labia. Her opaque juices of arousal seeping from her sex crack, trickling over her hairless flesh, she cupped her right breast in her hand and lowered her head.

Sucking her ripe nipple into her wet mouth, sinking her teeth into her areola, Christina slipped a finger into the top of her sex valley and massaged the solid protrusion of her expectant clitoris. The boys were loving every minute of the show – she knew that as she eyed the bulging crotches of their trousers. Their beautiful cocks would be solid, their rolling balls full and in desperate need of draining. But they were going to have to wait for the feel of her hot mouth sucking their swollen knobs.

Finally slipping her sensitive nipple out of her wet mouth, Christina peeled her fleshy sex cushions wide apart and exposed the wet funnel of pink flesh surround-

ing the entrance to her tight cunt. Slipping a finger into
her hot lust hole, she massaged the creamy walls of her
vagina, gasping as the beautiful sensations permeated
deep into the core of her quivering body. Withdrawing
her sticky finger, she lapped up her vaginal cream,
sucking her finger clean before once more driving it
deep into the tight shaft of her young cunt.

'I think it's time you joined in,' Christina said, twisting
and bending her finger deep within the tight sheath of
her young pussy. 'I've stripped, so you can do the same.'

Hurriedly slipping out of their clothes, the teenagers
stood in front of Christina with the bulbous knobs of
their granite-hard cocks pointing to the sky. Hungry for
the salty taste of their purple glandes, she slipped her
finger out of her sex-drenched vagina and kneeled on the
soft grass. The boys stood close together, their swollen
plums only inches apart, their heavy balls rolling. This
was sheer sexual bliss, Christina mused, pushing her
tongue out and tentatively licking each sperm-slit in
turn.

Taking the first plum into her mouth, her full lips
engulfing its rim, she sucked on the silky-smooth surface. This was a good deal, she reflected. Sucking three
teenage knobs to orgasm in return for a well-behaved
class? Until she'd come to Spadger Heath, she could
never have envisaged doing such a thing to her students.
They hadn't mentioned this at training college, she
reflected, wondering whether other young teachers
sucked their students' cocks in return for good behaviour. And to think that she had the headmaster eating
out of her pussy was incredible.

'Can you suck all three?' Doogan asked.

'I'll certainly try,' Christina giggled, slipping the knob

out of her salty mouth. 'I might be able to get your knob in, but that's about all.'

'You're a dirty bitch,' Greg the newcomer chuckled.

'You think this is dirty?' Christina asked, desperate to shock the lad. 'You wait until I have three cocks fucking my arse.'

'All three?' he gasped. 'All three at once?'

'All three at once.'

Taking the plums into her mouth, her succulent lips stretched tautly around the three helmets, Christina snaked her wet tongue over the swollen globes. She'd choke on their sperm if they filled her mouth simultaneously, she mused, gobbling like a babe at the breast as she tried to imagine three solid cocks shafting the tight duct of her rectum. Wondering whether Bryony was sucking the sperm out of an old man's cock-head, she realized that the girl was getting paid for her sexual efforts. *Prostitution*, she mused: Bryony was taking cash, and Christina was enjoying teaching a well-behaved class.

Wondering whether other women did this sort of thing as she sucked on the gasping lads' purple knobs, she turned her thoughts to her mother. Perhaps the woman had sucked on two or more knobs during her younger years. Knowing her mother, though, Christina thought the notion was ridiculous. But no one would have believed how Christina behaved when she was out of sight of the routine world. A conscientious young teacher, respected, well dressed, attractive . . . No one would ever believe that she enjoyed sucking three knobs to orgasm and swallowing sperm.

Pondering on other women as she kneaded the lad's heaving balls and sucked on their twitching cock-heads,

Christina thought that she might not be alone in her debauchery. She didn't reveal her sexual exploits to all and sundry, and neither did other women. The chances were that many women would grab the opportunity to take more than one knob into their sperm-thirsty mouths. No one knew what went on behind closed doors, she reflected. Or in the wooded countryside of England.

As the lads started trembling, Christina knew that they were about to pump their fresh sperm into her thirsty mouth and drain their brimming balls. Fervently gobbling and licking, she hoped that the beautiful cocks would restiffen quickly after their coming and drive deep into the neglected sheath of her tight cunt. Her hot vagina might be able to accommodate two rock-hard penises, she mused. Possibly three huge cocks, if she could think of a way to physically achieve the crude act. As for her bottom-hole taking three solid sex rods . . .

'Yes,' Doogan breathed, his spunk jetting from his knob-slit and bathing Christina's snaking tongue. The other lads releasing their orgasmic cream, Christina did her best to swallow the salty liquid as her mouth overflowed. This was a first, she thought happily, her clitoris close to orgasm, her juices of desire gushing from the entrance to her cock-hungry cunt. Slipping her hand between her naked thighs, she parted her swollen girl-lips and massaged her solid clitoris as she drank the gushing sperm issuing from the three orgasming knobs.

'Swallow the lot, you dirty bitch,' Greg cried, watching the creamy sperm streaming down Christina's chin and splattering the erect teats of her firm breasts. Repeatedly swallowing hard, Christina drank from the spunking knobs until she'd drained the lads' balls and they began to crumple on their shaking legs. Slipping their spent cocks out of her sperm-flooded mouth, she sucked on each one in turn, swallowing the last remnants of their orgasmic fluid before sitting back on her heels and wiping her mouth on the back of her hand.

Watching the lads sprawled out on the grass, their limp cocks snaking over their hairy scrotums, Christina continued to caress the sensitive tip of her clitoris. Her pleasure building, she massaged her clitoris faster. Eyeing the boys' sperm-glistening penises, their rolling balls, she prayed for them to recover quickly and feed the hungry maw of her cunt with their meaty pleasure shafts. In desperate need of a cock repeatedly ramming into her young cunt, she was about to lie on the grass and take her ripe clitoris to orgasm when she heard voices. Ordering her studs to be quiet, she grabbed her clothes and dressed hurriedly as the voices grew louder.

'This is where she brings her clients,' Ponting said. 'She'll probably bring a couple of her students here for sex after college this afternoon.'

'Right, I'll be waiting for her,' Charles said, to Christina's sheer horror.

'I'm glad that I was able to get in touch with you.'

'So am I. She's a lovely girl, but the way she's going . . . I just can't understand why she's turned to prostitution.'

'It's not that I want to expose her and upset her family, but someone's got to do something to help her,' Ponting sighed. 'This is only her second week at the college and . . . well, she's built up a huge clientele. She even tried to lure *me* here for sex, but I'm happily married.'

'What did she say, exactly?' Charles asked.

'She told me that she was into cocksucking. She said that she wanted to feel my cock spunking up her arse and . . . I'd rather not say any more.'

'I quite understand, Mr Ponting. Since she's at work, I'll go and take a look around her flat.'

'There's something I haven't mentioned,' Ponting said softly. 'Christina . . . because of her I've had to resign.'

'From the college? But why?'

'Christina wouldn't take no for an answer. Foolishly, I agreed to meet her here. I was hoping to talk to her, try to help her. She . . . she'd arranged for the headmaster to come along and . . . she made out that I was trying to force her into having sex with me.'

'My God,' Charles breathed.

'I know it sounds incredible, but it's true. Like an idiot, I'd allowed her to . . . I'd stripped off. She'd unbuttoned my shirt and released my belt and . . . I can't deny that she'd aroused me and I'd stripped off. By the time the headmaster arrived . . . well, you can imagine how the situation must have looked to him.'

'Yes, yes, I can. This is terrible, Mr Ponting. I mean, I don't blame you. Christina is a very attractive young woman. Behaving the way she did, I couldn't blame any man for . . . I'll be here this afternoon. If I can catch her with her students, perhaps threaten to tell her parents unless she gives up her life here and goes home . . .'

'I wish you luck.'

'And you, Mr Ponting. I'm only sorry that Christina has wrecked your life.'

As the two men wandered back to the common, Christina felt her stomach knotting as her anger heightened. Watching the lads dress, she wondered what they were thinking. They'd obviously heard every damning word, she mused, biting her lip as she imagined Charles running to her father with his tales. Wondering what to do, she held her hand to her head. Ponting wasn't going to give up, that was certain. The man was obviously obsessed with bringing about her downfall, and wouldn't stop until . . .

'It's OK,' Doogan said, smiling at Christina. 'You leave this to us. We'll sort it.'

'Sort it?' Christina echoed. 'How on earth can you—'

'You just leaving Ponting and that other bloke to us.'

'What shall I do now?' she sighed. 'I don't feel like going back to the college but . . .'

'You go back and do your job. I'll talk to you this afternoon, tell you about the plan.'

'All right,' Christina conceded, realizing that she had nothing to lose.

'Come on, lads,' Doogan said, bucking his belt. 'We've got plans to make.'

As they left the clearing, Christina sat on the grass and looked up at the sun sparkling through the trees high above. Ponting must have contacted Charles through her mother, she concluded. But what the hell did Charles think he was up to? Why was he going out of his way to cause trouble? There was nothing that Doogan and his gang could do to help, she was sure. Why did people have to interfere? Christina decided to go back to the college. Why couldn't people get on with their lives and leave her alone?

14

Somehow managing to get through the afternoon, Christina left the college to find Doogan and his gang waiting for her outside the gates. They were clutching several textbooks and notepads, and she wondered what on earth they were up to as a couple of teenage girls joined them. This was going to look really bad, she reflected as they led her towards the common. Charles was bound to think that she was going to have sex with three lads and two girls.

'It's OK,' Doogan interrupted Christina as she launched into a hundred reasons why she didn't think it a good idea to go to the woods. 'We're on a botany outing.'

'A botany outing?' she laughed. 'What the hell . . .'

'This is the plan. We've all got books about plants and stuff. This bloke finds us in the woods, and we tell him that we often go there looking for plants.'

'I doubt that he'll believe that,' Christina sighed.

'He will,' Brown rejoined. 'We've already told old man Wright that you take us on botany trips after college.'

'Why botany?' Christina asked.

'We could hardly say that we go to the woods looking for seashells,' Doogan laughed. 'OK, so this bloke—'

'Charles,' Christina said. 'He's my ex-boyfriend.'

'OK, so Charles turns up and hides in the bushes, hoping that he'll see you getting fucked.'

'That's one way to put it.'

'We happen to discover him and ask him what he's doing. You see him, talk to him . . . We're studying botany. Innocent, virginal goody-goody students . . . The thing is, he has no idea that we know about his plan. That's why this is going to work.'

'Yes, that's a thought,' Christina said, a smile dawning on her pretty face as she began to feel a little more confident.

Reaching the woods, the students opened their note-pads and began studying the plants under the trees. Christina discreetly scanned the common for Charles, but there was no sign of him. He'd be lurking somewhere in the woods, she was sure as she led her eager students along the narrow path in the direction of the clearing. Doogan and his crowd were brilliant, Christina thought as they began making notes and looking up wild flowers in their textbooks.

'Is this the one you were describing in class?' Doogan asked Christina, kneeling and pointing to a weed.

'Er . . . yes, that's right,' she replied, aware of someone lurking in the bushes. She winked at Doogan. 'Hopefully, we'll find some fungi a little deeper in the woods.'

'Hopefully,' Doogan echoed, returning her wink and nodding towards the bushes. 'This is such an interesting subject, Miss,' he added, going rather over the top, Christina thought. 'I'll take a look over here for some fungi.'

As Doogan wandered into the bushes where Charles was hiding, Christina realized how stupid the game was. But that was Charles, she reflected. Stupid, childish, hypocritical . . . But she had to play the game, she knew.

She wasn't going to give Charles the opportunity to go running to her parents with his tales of prostitution. Feigning shock as Charles emerged from the bushes with Doogan, Christina held her hand to her mouth and gasped. Charles stammered something incoherent as Doogan said that he'd discovered a peeping Tom in the bushes.

'It's all right, I know him,' Christina said.

'Oh, right,' Doogan murmured. 'I'll go and join the others, then.'

'What are you doing here?' she asked Charles as Doogan wandered off.

'I . . . I was looking for you,' he replied.

'What? You were looking for me in the bushes?'

'I heard that you often came here with . . . with some students.'

'Yes, I do. I've come with my botany class.'

'I thought you taught English?'

'These students are very interested in botany, Charles. To encourage them to write, I'm taking an interest in *their* interest. Is that all right with you?'

'Yes, yes, of course. They don't look the type to be interested in plants.'

'What type *do* they look like? Bingo players?'

'No, no, I just meant . . . So, how are things?'

'After you fucked young Bryony in my parents' garden, I don't think things are too good at all.'

'I . . . The thing is, that girl . . .'

'Don't blame her, Charles. It's bad enough you fucking an under-age girl, let alone blaming her for your actions. You said that you were looking for me?'

'I had some business in town and thought I'd see how you are.'

'Who told you that I'd be here?'

'Oh, er . . . someone at the college. I went there first and—'

'Who was it? What did they look like?'

'Oh, I don't know.'

'I only asked because, apart from the headmaster, no one knows about our botany studies.'

'Yes, it must have been him.'

'He's away for the day, so . . .'

'Christina, it doesn't matter who it was,' Charles sighed agitatedly.

'As long as it wasn't Ponting.'

'Ponting?'

'He's been sacked for running some kind of prostitution ring involving a few of the girls.'

'Really? That's awful.'

'It's dreadful. The way he carried on was . . . anyway, I'm not interested in Ponting and his lies. Look, I have to go and find the students.'

'I thought we might go out for a drink this evening.'

'I can't, Charles. And even if I could, I'm not sure that I'd want to after your disgusting behaviour with Bryony. If my father knew . . .'

'You won't say anything, will you?'

'That depends.'

'On what?'

'You cause trouble for me, and I'll cause trouble for you.'

'I wouldn't do that, Christina.'

'Wouldn't you? Anyway, I'm busy now.'

'Right, well . . .'

Walking away and joining the students, Christina thought how sad it was that she had to continually play mind games. Wondering what the problem was with Charles, why he was obsessed with where she was and what she was doing, she turned and watched him following the path back to the common. Perhaps, in his own weird way, he was doing his best to get her to go home to her parents. He probably thought that he stood a better chance of getting back with her if she lived at home. But he must have realized that, after the episode with Bryony, he'd lost Christina for good.

'OK, it worked,' Christina said, grinning at Doogan. 'Thanks. Thanks to all of you.'

'Any time,' Doogan replied. 'So, what shall we do now?'

'I don't know. Go home, I suppose.'

'We could go to the pub,' Brown suggested.

'Is that all you ever think about?' Doogan laughed.

'All right,' Christina said, eyeing the two young girls. 'Let's go to the pub and celebrate our victory.'

Leaving the woods with her students in tow, Christina walked across the common. Wondering how Bryony was getting on with her new job, she pictured once more the girl wanking off old men. Charles was like an old man, she reflected, wondering whether he'd managed to get into her flat. Even if he had got in, which she very much doubted, there was nothing incriminating there. He'd probably been hoping to find a list of clients, she mused, walking towards the local pub. He'd failed miserably in his mission. And so had Ponting. Charles might now give up, but would Ponting? Christina thought hard as she entered the pub with her teenage gang.

Sitting at a table as Doogan asked her what she wanted to drink, she decided on vodka and tonic. Christina wasn't surprised to see the lad pull a wad of notes from his pocket as he walked up to the bar. What he got up to outside college, she dreaded to think. He was a survivor, that was obvious. He'd never go short of money, no matter where his life took him. Perhaps that was the way to be, she thought as one of the young girls sat beside her. No cares, no worries – just living life from day to day.

'It's not a bad pub, this,' the girl said, smiling at Christina.

'You've been here before?' Christina asked, wondering how old she was.

'Most nights. I'm Josie, by the way.'

'I'm Christina. I've not seen you at the college.'

'No, I left a few months back.'

'Where do you work?'

'I don't. If I worked, I'd get a miserable wage every week. The way things are, I'm pretty well off.'

'So how do you earn money?' Christina asked, dreading the answer.

'I do this and that,' the girl replied, flicking her long auburn hair away from her pretty face. 'Fifty quid here, fifty quid there. It soon adds up.'

'Yes, of course.'

'I do a bit for the massage parlour. Sort of part-time – on and off.'

'The massage par— Have you been there today?'

'Yes, this morning. A new girl started. It was really funny. This old guy comes in, takes one look at her and—'

'What's her name?'

'Bryony. She's a laugh. I reckon she'll do well there.'

'Yes, I expect she will. So, what goes on in this massage parlour? I mean, I've heard things, but . . .'

'Old men, mostly. They want hand relief. Mind you, I don't think they could do anything else. We get a few

young lads in. Virgins who want to become men. Sylvia –
she owns the place – she reckons that Bryony will be
pretty good with the lads.'

'Yes, I'm sure she will.'

'I was telling her – Bryony, I mean – I was saying that
she should come out with me in the evenings. She'll earn
far more with me. The parlour's OK, but Sylvia takes
most of the dosh.'

'So, where do you go in the evenings?'

'I have one or two haunts. I don't walk the streets or
anything like that. There's a small club which is pretty
good. Businessmen go there early in the evening. They
either want a hand job or a quick blow. The owner hasn't
got a clue what goes on. If he had, he'd want a cut. I'm
hoping Bryony, the new girl, will meet me there this
evening. She said she would.'

Watching Doogan place the drinks on the table, Christina thought about Bryony. She was obviously going to
be all right for cash, but the thought of the girl hanging
around bars and seedy clubs at night didn't please
Christina. Bryony might have been sexually experienced,
but she was incredibly naive. She was far too young to be
in with the likes of Josie. But there wasn't much that
Christina could do about it.

'Where is this club?' she asked Josie as Doogan and
Brown chatted about football.

'It's called The Rat's Tail. Just round the corner by—'

'Yes, I've seen the place.'

'Why don't you come along this evening? I mean, it's
quite respectable. I usually work at a table in a secluded
alcove where no one can see what I'm up to. The club's
OK for all types, not just businessmen looking for a blow
job.'

'Yes, I might look in later,' Christina replied, eyeing the girl's naked thighs.

'Bryony said that she'd meet me there at six. I have to get there early for the businessmen.'

Knocking back her vodka, Christina made her excuses and left the pub. Walking home, she wondered whether Bryony was going to tell her the truth about going out that evening. Or would the girl make out that she was just visiting a friend? Life in London was far removed from existence in the country, she reflected. Businessmen going to the club for a quick blow job and then home to their loving wives, young girls sucking cocks and swallowing sperm for money . . . Bryony was a city girl, Christina reminded herself as she entered the flat and went into the kitchen. Filling the kettle, she thought about the evening ahead, wondering whether to go along to the club with Bryony.

'Oh, hi,' the young ex-student trilled as she breezed into the kitchen. 'Well, that's my first day over.'

'How was it?' Christina asked.

'Great. Sylvia, that's my boss, she pays us at the end of each day. I earned sixty pounds.'

'That's not bad for one day. What did you have to do?'

'Wank a few guys, that was all. We spent most of the time sitting around, drinking coffee and chatting.'

'Sounds like easy money. What are the other girls like?'

'They're OK. There's one I really like. Her name's Josie. She only works part-time, sort of comes and goes as she pleases.'

'I'm glad you like the job. Although it's not the sort of work . . . Anyway, as long as you like it, that's OK. What are your plans for this evening?'

'I'm going out for a drink with Josie.'

'Oh? Anywhere nice?'

'Er . . . I don't know yet. Shall I make something to eat?'

'Yes, why not? Mind you, I don't think there is much. I'll have to go shopping and stock up the cupboards.'

'I'll knock something up,' Bryony said, smiling. 'This is far better than living with my mum. OK. I'll cook and you go and relax.'

'I'm going to take a shower. I might wander out somewhere this evening, take a look around.'

Washing her long blonde hair in the shower, Christina felt jealousy eating away at her. It was ridiculous, she reflected. Bryony was young, single, free to do as she wished with her life. But Christina couldn't help the way she felt. Perhaps the girl had the right idea. Earning tax-free cash every day, no problems or worries, enjoying her life . . . Christina wasn't sure whether she was jealous because the girl was having sex with other people, or envious of her lifestyle. Wondering whether to leave the college, give up her teaching career and work with Bryony, she towelled her naked body dry and went into her room.

It might be interesting to pleasure a businessman, she mused, dressing in a loose-fitting white blouse and turquoise miniskirt. A quick wank beneath the table, or a blow job . . . Wondering how much Josie charged for her sexual favours, she dried and brushed her hair and joined Bryony at the kitchen table. The girl had done well with the food. The cheese-and-egg salad was perfectly presented and she'd even opened a bottle of white wine. Living with Bryony was going to work out, Christina felt sure as she sipped her wine. She was pretty good with food, earned more than enough to pay her share of the rent . . . This was going to work out very well.

'What sort of day have *you* had?' Bryony asked.

'Oh, the usual,' Christina replied, deciding not to mention her visit to the woods. 'The headmaster asked me out for a drink this evening . . . Shit.'

'What's the matter?'

'I said that I'd let him know before I left the college. Oh, well. Not to worry. When are you going to move into Alison's room?'

'Has she gone?' the girl asked, her eyes widening.

'Didn't you know?'

'Well, I wasn't sure. In that case, I'll move in later this evening. I'm meeting Josie at six, so I'd better get a move on.'

Finishing her meal, Christina watched Bryony clear the table and wash up. The girl left the kitchen in pristine condition before taking a shower and getting ready to go out. Christina finished the wine, realizing that she'd not only found a perfect flatmate but a brilliant housekeeper. Calling out from the bedroom, Bryony said that she'd do the shopping on her way home from the massage parlour the following day. This was getting even better, Christina decided. The girl would be washing and ironing for her before long.

'Right, I'll see you later,' Bryony said as she appeared in the kitchen doorway.

'Yes, OK. Have a good time.'

'I will. I'll try not to be too late. We'll open another bottle of wine when I get back.'

'That'll be nice. OK, off you go. And behave yourself.'

'Certainly not,' the girl laughed, leaving the flat.

Wondering how Alison was getting on at the hotel,

Christina thought it odd that she'd not earned money from sex. There again, not every girl who enjoyed crude sex was necessarily into prostitution. Sighing as the phone rang, Christina left the kitchen and went into the lounge. Flopping onto the sofa, she grabbed the receiver and bit her lips as the headmaster asked her whether they were going out that evening.

'Sorry, Ian,' she sighed. 'I was going to come and see you before I left but I got tied up.'

'I heard about your botany class.'

'Oh, yes. The students are very interested.'

'I can't for the life of me think why the likes of Doogan and Brown are into botany. Bars and girls, yes, but—'

'Ian, about this evening. To be honest, I'm feeling rather tired.'

'Oh, that's a shame. You're sitting alone in your flat, here I am sitting alone in my house . . . Another time, perhaps. By the way, Bryony Philips. Her mother came to see me this afternoon.'

'Oh? Er . . . what about?'

'The girl's left home. Was she in class today?'

'No, no, she wasn't. Actually, she's left the college. I was going to come and talk to you about it but I was so busy today. Did her mother say where the girl was living?'

'She has no idea where she's gone. Bryony just said that she'd found a flat and was moving out.'

'I'm sure she'll be all right.'

'Well, it's nothing to do with us. I just wondered whether you knew anything about it.'

'No, nothing.'

'Her mother was talking about going to the police.'

'The police?'

'I don't know what good that will do. I mean, the girl is of age, so . . . anyway, I'll see you tomorrow. Coffee during break as usual?'

'Yes, that would be nice.'

'You get an early night, OK?'

'OK.'

'Sleep well, Christina.'

'I will. Goodbye.'

There was nothing the police could do, Christina was sure. Bryony had left home, which wasn't surprising. She'd not broken the law or . . . Not as far as the police were aware, at least. Grabbing her bag, Christina left the flat and headed for the club. If she was lucky, she'd be able to find somewhere to sit where she could observe Bryony and not be seen herself. If the girl did see her, then she'd say that she'd just been passing and had decided to take a look at the place.

Walking into the bar, Christina was thankful that the place was littered with alcoves and secluded tables. Ordering a vodka and tonic, she noticed Bryony and Josie sitting at the far end of the bar. They were laughing and joking, chatting with a couple of besuited men in their thirties. They were far too busy to notice Christina as she sat at the bar and sipped her drink. The club was nice, Christina observed, looking about her. As Josie had said, it was respectable, and Christina decided to use the place rather than the local pub.

'All alone?' a man in his early thirties asked.

'I'm waiting for someone,' Christina replied, looking up and smiling. 'I'm rather early, though.'

'In that case, mind if I join you?'

'No, not at all.'

'I'm John – John Baxter.'

'Christina. This is my first time here. I rather like it.'

'I come here most evenings on my way home from work. I only work around the corner. I'm an accountant.'

'Oh, right. I work at the college, teaching English. What's this place like? I've heard one or two rumours.'

'Rumours?' he echoed, frowning at her.

'I was told that this wasn't the sort of place for a young lady.'

'Oh, right. Yes, there are a few girls who work the club.'

'Work the . . . Oh, I see what you mean.'

'Jim McConnor, the owner, knows nothing about it. Don't get me wrong, it's not a big-time haunt for prostitutes. There are a handful of young girls who make a living from . . . well, you know?'

'Yes, of course. Do *you* know any of the girls? I mean, have you met . . . I don't mean . . .'

'It's all right,' Baxter laughed. 'I do know one or two of them, yes. Why do you ask?'

'I'm curious, that's all.'

'McConnor could make a small fortune if he was clued up. All he seems interested in is boozing. Still, each to their own.'

'Is that what you'd do if you owned this place?'

'No . . . well, possibly. I mean, there's nothing wrong with prostitution. It's as old as the hills, as they say. I reckon, in a place like this where the girls muck about beneath the tables, there's no harm in it. There's no decent work in an area like this and the girls have to make a living somehow. The rents are sky-high, there's food, clothes and other stuff they have to buy . . . I'm surprised you can afford to live here on your salary.'

'It's not easy. I share a flat, which halves the rent, but it's still not easy.'

Wondering again about Bryony's new profession, Christina realized that she was becoming increasingly interested in the work. The money was good, the lifestyle relaxed – meeting people, enjoying a few drinks . . . Her heart had been set on a career in teaching. But now? Gazing at the young man as he ordered her another drink, Christina wondered whether he'd ever used the services of the young girls. Was he married? Reckoning that he was single, she was thankful that she hadn't married Charles. That was one nightmare she'd been lucky to avoid.

'I'm rather fortunate,' John said, leaning on the bar. 'I own my flat. It belonged to my grandfather and he left it to me.'

'That must be nice,' Christina murmured. 'No rent, no mortgage . . .'

'It gets better. I also own the shop below the flat. The rent I pull in from the shop more than doubles my salary. It's a pretty big shop.'

'God, that's brilliant. My father was thinking about buying me a flat, but . . . well, I'd be for ever beholden to him.'

'Go for it, Christina. You yourself would have no rent to pay – and you could charge your flatmate rent. You'd be a damned sight better off.'

'I hadn't thought of that. My parents live in Hertfordshire, so they're far enough away not to hassle me.'

'I'd definitely go for it if I were you. Another drink?'

'Er . . . yes, why not?'

Deciding to take her father up on it if he offered to buy a flat, Christina realized that she'd be far better off financially. Bryony could pay the same rent, which would cover the everyday bills, leaving Christina's salary to build up. But the thought of turning to prostitution still haunted her. The money to be made from sex was unbelievable, far more than she'd ever get from teaching, or any other straight job for that matter. Eyeing Bryony at the end of the bar, Christina smiled as she saw the girl going to a secluded table with Josie and the two men. She'd probably earn her half of the rent in one evening, Christina mused. A few wanks or blow jobs, and she'd be laughing. Not to mention free drinks for the evening.

'Are you married, John?' Christina asked.

'Me? No, no. One day, maybe. I'm too busy enjoying life to get myself tied down. Take this evening, for example. I can stay here chatting to you for as long as I like. My life's my own, Christina. That may sound selfish, and I have to admit that I get lonely at times. But I'm free to do what I want when I want.'

'Marriage doesn't suit everyone,' Christina said. 'Still, neither does living alone. Do you have a girlfriend?'

'No one special. Between you and me, I *have* joined the girls over there on the odd occasion. I think there's a new girl with Josie. I noticed her earlier. The young blonde with—'

'I've not been looking,' Christina cut in, wondering whether to tell John the truth about Bryony.

She was also wondering whether to make this her paid-sex debut by taking John to a secluded table and wanking his cock to orgasm. But, having no idea how much the girls charged, and reckoning that John wasn't in the mood, she decided against the idea. But it certainly was easy money, she reflected. Free drinks, getting to wank a man and bring out his sperm, and getting paid for the pleasure? Deciding to play it by ear, she sipped her drink and crossed her long legs. Her naked thighs showing, she wondered whether John fancied her as he looked down at her shapely legs and smiled.

'You said that you were waiting for someone?' he breathed. 'That's a shame.'

'Is it?' she asked, grinning at him.

'I think so. Especially if it's a man friend.'

'No, no. I'm meeting my . . . my sister later. Not for another hour or so.'

'Oh, right. er . . . Would you like to sit a table? I don't like propping up the bar and there are no stools free.'

'OK.'

Slipping off her stool, Christina followed John to a corner table and sat down. He settled next to her, the crotch of his trousers out of sight from the people standing at the bar. This was her opportunity, she knew. But how to start the proceedings? Hoping that he'd make the first move, she toyed with her glass as he talked about his flat. She'd have to let on that she knew Bryony and Josie if she was going to charge him for wanking his cock and allowing his spunk to run over her hand. There again, she could make out that she'd never met the girls and worked alone.

John talked about Josie, saying that the girl wanted to rent one of his spare rooms. Christina sipped her drink as she listened to his plans. He had three bedrooms and was wondering whether to move a couple of girls in so that they could work from his flat and pay him half their earnings. He hadn't come to a decision yet, but he was tempted by the idea. The notion got Christina thinking. By allowing Bryony to work from the flat . . . Biting her lip, she reminded herself that she'd come to London to pursue a career in teaching.

'The only problem would be the law,' John said, downing his pint. 'The girls would only bring back decent clients, of course. But the law . . . I wouldn't want to end up in court for running a brothel. Anyway, we'll see.'

'It's certainly an idea,' Christina thought aloud, wishing immediately that she hadn't.

'You reckon?'

'Well . . . the girls would have somewhere decent to live, and they wouldn't have to hang around bars looking for clients.'

'And I'd earn a small fortune,' he laughed. 'Of course, there'd be an added bonus.'

'Oh? What's that?'

'Well, you know? I'd be OK with a couple of young girls living in my flat.'

'Oh, yes, I see,' Christina giggled. 'I suppose I should be honest with you.'

'Honest? What do you mean?'

'I work at the college, but I also have part-time evening work.'

'God. You mean . . .'

'Yes, I do.'

'Oh, right. Well, why not?'

'Why not, indeed?'

'I'd never have thought that you'd be into that. You don't look the type.'

'Don't I?'

'What do you charge?'

'You want something here, now?'

'That depends on how much. One of the girls charges fifty for a hand job. Needless to say, she gets very little work. The average is twenty.'

'I charge thirty,' Christina said, deciding not to under-price herself. 'Above the average – but then, I am above average.'

'You certainly are,' John murmured, taking thirty pounds from his wallet. 'OK, I'll go for that.'

Unzipping his trousers, Christina looked around the bar as she pulled John's solid penis out and massaged his foreskin over his swollen knob. This was easy, she thought, kneading the warm, fleshy shaft of his huge cock. No one could see what she was up to beneath the table, and she doubted that anyone cared. They were all too busy drinking and laughing to take any notice of her illicit activities. Parting her thighs and exposing the tight material of her panties to John's wide-eyed gaze, she pulled the material to one side and displayed the fleshy swell of her hairless sex lips to add to his pleasure.

'You *are* above average,' he murmured, his eyes rolling as he stared at her wares. 'How much to go down?'

'Not in here,' she said softly. 'People will see. Perhaps another time, if we can find a better table where we won't be seen.'

'I like girls who shave,' he said as she pulled her panties further aside.

'You like my cunt?' she asked impishly as he began gasping in his male pleasure.

'Very much. Show me inside.'

'Like this?' she giggled softly, parting the firm cushions of her love lips and displaying her dripping inner folds. 'You'd like your tongue there, wouldn't you?'

'My tongue, my cock, my fingers . . . God, I'm coming.'

His sperm running over her hand as she wanked his solid cock faster, Christina eyed the money lying on the table. Thirty pounds to wank a man to orgasm? *And* he'd paid for her drinks. This really *was* easy money, she thought as he hung his head, his white liquid streaming over her fingers as she drained his heaving balls. Wanking off two or three men each evening would . . . No wonder her young ex-student was so keen on the work, she mused, wondering whether she should not only allow the girl to work from the flat but also join Bryony in her new-found profession. Deciding to give the idea some serious thought, she continued to wank John's twitching cock until he grabbed her hand and stopped her.

'That was great,' he breathed, obviously dizzy in the aftermath of his coming.

'I'm glad you enjoyed it,' Christina replied, gazing at her spermed hand.

'What are you going to do with that?'

'I'll find a tissue. I should have one in my bag.'

'Lap it up,' he whispered, zipping up his trousers. 'Another tenner if you lap it all up like a good girl.' Placing the money on the table, he gazed into her blue eyes. 'Well?' he whispered.

Licking her creamed fingers, making sure that John could see the sperm hanging in long strands from her pink tongue, Christina swallowed the salty liquid. He was loving every minute of her lewd act, she knew as she finished cleansing her fingers before slipping the money into her handbag. Wondering how much Bryony had earned, she sipped her drink, washing down John's salty spunk. She reckoned that, between them, they could earn a fortune.

'Another drink?' John asked, grabbing his empty glass.

'Thanks,' she replied, wondering whether to find another client before leaving the club.

'I'll get you a large one. After all, you deserve it.'

'Yes, I believe I do.'

Watching him walk up to the bar, Christina smiled. Forty pounds better off, and another free drink? This was turning out to be a most pleasant and profitable evening. One of many evenings she'd spend at The Rat's Tail Club, she decided. London wasn't so bad after all, she thought, wondering again how much Bryony had earned. They'd have to compare notes later, chat about their sexual exploits over a bottle of wine. *And over a vibrator*, she thought in her rising wickedness. After wanking and sucking her clients, Bryony was bound to be in a high state of arousal. And Christina was the very person to bring her relief.

15

Christina had waited up until midnight for Bryony, and had finally gone to bed when she realized that the girl might not be home until the early hours. Her young ex-student had obviously had a good evening, and had probably earned a fortune. Waking to the sun streaming in through her window, Christina put on her dressing gown and went into the kitchen. Filling the kettle, she wondered what the day would bring. Although her class would be on their best behaviour, she didn't relish the thought of spending the day at the college. Again, she thought about the money she could make by visiting The Rat's Tail two or three evenings each week. Trying to drag her thoughts away from prostitution, she took a quick shower and dressed.

'Morning,' Bryony murmured, wandering into the kitchen.

'What time did you get in?' Christina asked, sipping her coffee and glancing at the wall clock.

'About one, I think.'

'I'd better get going, otherwise I'll be late. I did wait up for you, but . . . We'll talk this evening. Unless you're going out again, that is?'

'I'll be out from about sixish.'

'Ah, The Rat's Tail Club.'

'How do you know about that?' the girl breathed, frowning at Christina.

'I was there, Bryony. For most of the evening, as it happens.'

'You were there? I didn't see you.'

'No, you wouldn't have. Not the way you were carrying on, anyway.'

'How did you know about the club?'

'That's my secret. Right, I'm off to work. I'll see you later.'

Leaving the flat, Christina grinned as she walked down the street. Bryony would spend the day wondering how Christina had discovered the club, and why she'd not seen her there. Reaching the college, Christina looked in on the headmaster before going to her classroom. Knocking on his door and entering the study, she found the man sitting behind his desk, fiddling with a piece of paper. Rubbing his lined forehead, he looked worried. Deciding that she wouldn't want to be head of a college and deal with one hassle after another, Christina sat opposite him and asked what the problem was.

'I'm pleased you called in to see me,' he sighed. 'I've just received a letter from the board of governors.'

'Oh?'

'Mr Ponting has been in touch with them. It seems that he's given them a list of complaints against you.'

'Against *me*?' she gasped. 'But he was the one who lured me into the woods and—'

'The complaints are all fictitious, of course. The point is that the board have to look into such matters. I'll be speaking to them later and, obviously, I'll put them in the picture. I would have thought that Mr Ponting would rather the incident in the woods wasn't mentioned. All he's doing by contacting the board is digging his own grave. Once they hear that I witnessed what was tantamount to imminent rape . . . As I said, Mr Ponting is digging his own grave.'

Watching the headmaster leave his chair to gaze out of the window, Christina realized that Ponting wasn't going to go away. He'd try anything and everything to cause trouble, and he'd trample on anyone who got in his way. But there was nothing the man could do to cause any real harm. Once the board of governors were told of the sordid incident in the woods, Ponting would back off. Wouldn't he? Giving up teaching would solve all her problems, Christina thought. No Ponting, no classes . . . She could quite happily fuck anyone and everyone in the woods, and there'd be nothing Ponting or anyone else could do about it.

'I'd better get to my class,' she said, moving to the door. 'I'll see you at break.'

'Yes, yes,' the head murmured abstractedly. 'I'll get onto the governors.'

'You do that. And don't worry.'

'No, no, I'm not worried. It's just that I don't need these problems. I shall tell the board how pleased I am with you, Christina. You've achieved amazing results in the short time you've been at Spadger Heath College. You have a well-behaved class, you—'

'Talking of my class, I really must go.'

'All right, I'll see you at break.'

Walking down the corridor, Christina entered her classroom to find her students sitting quietly. This really was incredible, she mused as Doogan winked at her. The headmaster was right, she *had* achieved amazing results.

But he had no idea how she'd achieved such great success. Ponting had guessed, but had no proof. Ponting could go to hell. Checking her watch, Christina filled in the register and ordered her class to go to their geography lesson. As they left the room in silence, she again wondered what Doogan and Brown had threatened them with. By the way they were behaving, she reckoned that murder might have been mentioned. Whatever the threat, it was working.

'Excuse me, Miss,' a pretty dark-haired girl said softly as she approached the front of the classroom.

'What is it, Becky?' Christina asked, smiling at the girl.

'I know what you get up to in the stockroom. I know what's been going on.'

'Going on?' Christina echoed, realizing that she had yet another potential problem on her hands. 'I'm not with you, Becky. What do you mean?'

'Doogan has been telling us to behave or else. Now I know why.'

'Doogan told you to behave? I can't believe that. And, if he did, then I'm very pleased with him. Perhaps he's decided that it's worth making an effort to learn something, after all.'

'No, it's not that. He wants us to behave because he gets something in return if we do.'

'I'm sorry, Becky, you've lost me. Doogan wants you to behave because he's getting something in return?'

'That's right. He gets sex in return for keeping us under control.'

'Sex?' Christina laughed. 'Now you *have* lost me. Let me try to understand this. You know what I get up to. Doogan has been telling you to behave. He gets sex in return for your good behaviour . . . Are you saying

that he forces you to have sex with him if you mis-
behave?'

'You know what I'm talking about, Miss.'

'I only wish I did, Becky. I'm sorry, but you're going
to have to spell it out for me.'

'In the stockroom . . .'

'Right, let's start in the stockroom.'

Opening the door, Christina led Becky into the stockroom and looked around her as if she was searching for
something. The girl wasn't doing a very good job of
trying to blackmail Christina, if that was her aim. Tidying some books, Christina asked the girl what it was
about the stockroom that was so important. Becky lowered her eyes, obviously wondering how to word her
threat as Christina moved about the small room and
discreetly closed and locked the door. Mumbling about
the mess, Christina asked her again to explain her concern and tell her what was supposed to have happened in
the stockroom.

'You bring the boys in here and play about with them,'
Becky finally replied.

'Play about with them?' Christina chuckled. 'This is a
sixth-form college, not a kindergarten.'

'Play about with them *sexually*.'

'Sexually? This is a pretty serious allegation, Becky.
Are you saying that I bring male students in here and
have sex with them?'

'Yes, I am.'

'What on earth gave you that idea?'

'It's no good pretending that you don't know what I'm
talking about.'

'All right, let's suppose that I *do* bring the lads in
here for sex. The notion is ridiculous, of course. But

let's assume that I have sex with the lads. What about it?'

'I'm going to report you.'

'Where's your evidence? I mean, what proof do you have to substantiate this ludicrous allegation?'

'Well, I . . . Everyone knows what you get up to.'

Eyeing the girl's partially opened blouse, Christina focused on the shallow cleavage of her small breasts. She could just make out her nipples pressing through the thin material of her blouse, and she imagined sucking the girl's petite tits. With long black hair framing her fresh face, Becky was an attractive little thing, Christina mused, her clitoris stirring in anticipation of lesbian sex. Wondering whether the girl was a virgin, she pictured the full lips of her pussy, the creamy-wet wings of her inner lips protruding alluringly from her tightly closed sex crack. The cheeks of the girl's bottom would be firm in their youth – lickable, biteable. Imagining sinking a finger deep into the hot tube of Becky's rectum, Christina felt a quiver run through her young womb.

'You say that everyone knows what I get up to?' she asked the girl. Christina's juices of lesbian desire started to seep into her tight panties.

'Yes, they do. I've heard people talking about it.'

'That's your evidence, is it? Hearsay is all you have, Becky. You won't get very far—'

'Simpson told me what you did to him.'

'Simpson . . . Bend over, Becky.'

'*What?*'

'You heard me. Bend over and touch your toes.'

'No, I . . .'

Forcing the girl to bend over, Christina held her tightly and lifted her short skirt up over her back.

The girl struggled as Christina yanked her panties down, exposing the beautifully firm cheeks of her pert bottom, but she could do nothing to escape. Raising her arm, Christina brought her hand down across the girl's naked buttocks with a loud slap. Again and again, she spanked Becky's twitching bottom globes, delighting in administering the punishment as the girl cried out and struggled to free herself.

'*This* is what I do to naughty little schoolgirls,' Christina hissed, repeatedly spanking her reddening buttocks. 'How *dare* you accuse me of sexually abusing my students.'

'You can't do this,' the girl whimpered. 'You'll end up in trouble if you—'

'I'll show you what trouble is,' Christina retorted, tearing the girl's panties from her trembling body.

'Please – what are you *doing*?'

'What's this, Becky?' Christina giggled, cupping the swell of the girl's vaginal lips in her hand. 'What's this I've found between your thighs?'

'What are you doing?' she cried again. 'Get off me, you, you . . .'

'You have a sweet little cunt, Becky. I like young girls' pretty little cunts.'

'You're insane. Let me go!'

'Unless you stop struggling, I'll tell the headmaster that you lured me in here and pulled your knickers down.'

'He'll never believe you,' Becky gasped as Christina's finger located the moist entrance to her tight vaginal sheath. 'Stop it! For fuck's sake, stop—'

'Swearing, as well? Oh, dear. You *are* a naughty little schoolgirl, aren't you? Keep *still*, Becky,' she snapped, as if possessed by an inner force, a craving to have her wicked way with the girl. 'Stand with your legs apart and allow me to finger your cunt, or you'll find yourself in the head's study.'

Kneeling behind the girl as she finally stopped struggling, Christina drove a second finger into the tight duct of her teenage pussy and massaged her inner flesh. Eyeing the girl's crimsoned buttocks, Christina couldn't help herself as she leaned forward and ran her tongue up and down her anal crease. Breathing in the heady scent of her anal gully, Christina realized that she had no control over her rampant desires. Breathing in the aphrodisiacal perfume of the girl's bottom-hole, she completely lost control of her senses and sank her teeth into the firm flesh of one naked buttock. The girl's young body went completely still as Christina's tongue circled round and round the tight hole of her anus and Christina wondered whether her young student was actually enjoying her crude lesbian experience.

'You taste heavenly,' Christina breathed, lapping at the girl's most private hole.

'Please, this isn't right,' Becky whimpered.

'Right or wrong, it's beautiful. You taste beautiful, Becky. You like me licking you there, don't you?'

'Yes, no, I . . .'

'God, you have a beautiful little hole. I could tongue you all day.'

Christina knew that word of her illicit escapades was getting round fast. Before long, her entire class would be demanding sexual favours in return for not only their obedience but their silence. But that wasn't so bad, Christina thought, pushing her tongue into the girl's bitter-sweet anal entrance as she continued to finger-fuck the tight sheath of her young cunt. If this is what it took to keep her students under control, then she was only too willing to administer sexual abuse on a regular basis. Wanking, knob gobbling, cunny licking, anal fisting . . . Whatever it took, Christina would be only too happy to oblige her young students.

Becky obviously hadn't realized the extent of her teacher's decadence. Thinking that she could put the fear of God into Christina, she might have had the idea of demanding money in return for her silence. Money, falsified exam results, favours . . . The girl wouldn't have expected a severe spanking following by debased lesbian sex. Slipping her pussy-wet fingers out of the girl's well-juiced vaginal duct, Christina forced the globes of her firm buttocks wide apart, completely exposing the brown tissue surrounding the entrance to her rectal canal. There again, perhaps Becky *had* hoped that her teacher would sexually abuse her. Having heard the rumours, she might have blurted out her threat knowing that she'd have her panties ripped off and her young cunt pleasured by her nymphomaniacal teacher.

Becky quivered as Christina pushed her wet tongue deep into the girl's anal canal and licked the dank walls of her rectum. Her cries of protest now whimpers of pleasure, she parted her feet wide and projected her rounded bum cheeks, offering Christina the open portal to the very core of her teenage body. Holding her pert buttocks wider apart, painfully stretching her anal hole open, Christina sucked and slurped, delighting in the bittersweet taste of her inner core. Christina was hooked on young girls' bottom-holes, she knew as she tongued Becky's anal portal. Licking her sensitive brown tissue, sucking the eye of her hot anus, tonguing her rectal duct, she took the girl to dizzy heights of sexual arousal.

Slipping her hand between Becky's firm thighs, Christina kneaded her full sex lips with her fingers, delighting in the feel of the young girl's hot vulva. Slipping a finger into the valley of her wet pussy, she located the solid protrusion of her clitoris and massaged her there. The girl breathed heavily, her young body shaking fiercely as her pleasure built deep within her young womb and her girl-juice streamed from the gaping entrance to her hot cunt.

Becky too was now hooked on lesbian lust, Christina knew as she tongued the tight sheath of her anal tube. This was another conquest, another young girl who'd want more crude sex. Her mouth locked to Becky's brown anal tissue, Christina sucked hard, savouring the arousing taste of the girl's inner core. Her saliva running down the girl's anal valley as she tongued and slurped at her brown hole, Christina couldn't get enough crude sex. All she wanted now was to spank young girls, tongue their tight bottom-holes, finger-fuck their sweet cunts and take them to massive orgasms. She'd earn money from cocksucking in the club, she mused as the girl's vaginal muscles tightened around her thrusting fingers. And derive immense pleasure from young girls' naked bodies. The best of both worlds, she reflected.

'I'm coming,' Becky breathed as Christina slipped her cunny-dripping fingers out of her pussy sheath and massaged the sensitive tip of her clitoris. Caressing the hot walls of her rectal duct with her wet tongue, Christina knew that her student was about to experience the orgasm of her young life. 'I'm coming. Oh, oh. You . . . you shouldn't . . . God, I'm coming.'

Whimpering as her orgasm exploded within the palpitating nub of her solid clitoris, her juices of desire gushing from her yawning cuntal opening, Becky shook uncontrollably in her lesbian-induced pleasure. Her creamy-white cunt milk streaming down her inner thighs in torrents, her legs sagging, she begged Christina not to stop as she rode the crest of her mind-blowing orgasm. Christina had no intention of halting the pleasure she was both giving and receiving. Slipping her tongue out of the girl's hot rectum, she drove two fingers deep into the burning sheath of her tight arse, delighting in the abuse as whimpers of pure sexual bliss resounded around the stockroom.

'You're a naughty little girl,' Christina breathed, sinking a third finger into the inflamed duct of Becky's anal canal. 'A very naughty little girl. You'll be punished like this every day, do you understand?'

'Yes, yes,' the teenager gasped, rocking her hips to meet each forceful thrust of Christina's pistoning fingers. 'God, yes. Every day.'

'You dare to accuse me of sexually abusing my students again and I'll force a candle up your bottom.'

Her fingers embedded deep within Becky's rectal tube, Christina pushed her head between her thighs and tongued the fleshy petals of her dripping inner cunt lips. Sucking the girl's distended inner lips into her hot mouth, tasting her juices of orgasm, Christina continued to massage her pulsating clitoris, sustaining her incredible girl-pleasure. Managing to push her tongue deep into the fiery heat of Becky's spasming cunt, she lapped up her flowing juices of lesbian desire, drinking from the sexual centre of her young body as she cried out in her complete and utter satisfaction.

On and on Becky's orgasm rolled, shock waves of crude sex reaching every nerve ending, tightening every muscle until she crumpled to the floor in a quivering heap. Christina's fingers sliding out of her bottom-hole, her tongue leaving the wet sheath of her cunt, Becky lay trembling in the aftermath of her lesbian abuse as Christina sat back on her heels and grinned in her triumph.

'Let that be a lesson to you,' she said, slapping the girl's rounded buttocks with the palm of her hand.

'Yes, Miss,' Becky murmured, her limbs convulsing wildly, her milky juices seeping between the swollen lips of her vulva.

'To make sure that you've learned your lesson, I want you to lick my cunt,' Christina breathed, lying on her back and slipping her panties off. 'Suck the cream out of my cunt,' she murmured, lost in her wickedness, her lesbian desire. 'Tongue-fuck my hot cunt and make me come.'

'But . . .'

'Do it.'

Opening her thighs wide, Christina peeled the fleshy cushions of her hairless love lips open and ordered her young pupil to lick her clitoris to orgasm. Settling between her teacher's legs, the girl pressed her mouth hard against Christina's fleshy vaginal lips and pushed her tongue into the hot folds of her dripping pussy slit. Becky was obviously experienced at lesbian licking, Christina mused as the girl expertly teased her ripe clitoris with her wet tongue. She'd obviously done this before, and Christina wondered who her latest lesbian lover was and what she had done. Had she enjoyed sixty-nine with Bryony? Had the girls lain side by side and tongue-fucked each other's hot cunts to orgasm?

The students in Christina's class were of the age where they'd be sexually experimenting almost daily. It wasn't unheard of for teenage girls to masturbate each other during their learning, during their early days of sexual discovery. That hadn't been the case at Christina's village school, but in a run-down area of London, where sex shops and prostitutes were rife, it wasn't at all surprising to find girls experimenting with lesbian sex.

Christina was surprised that the girl had not only come to her with her threat but had seemed to have no hesitation when ordered to indulge in lesbian oral sex. But when she thought about it, she realized that word had obviously got round that Christina was heavily into lesbian sex. The girl herself having tendencies in that direction, she'd thought she'd try her luck with her young teacher. And it had paid off. Becky would be another regular, Christina mused as her clitoris pulsated beneath the girl's sweeping tongue and her young womb rhythmically contracted. Becky would be a regular visitor to the flat, that was certain.

London revolved around sex, Christina concluded as Becky slipped at least three fingers deep into the tightening sheath of her hot cunt. But didn't any large city? She should have expected to be confronted with sex at a sixth-form college, she reflected. Teenage girls with hormones running wild, teenage lads with their cocks perpetually erect, their balls always in need of draining . . . Christina should have known that Spadger Heath College, like any other college, would thrive on sex.

Feeling the girl's tongue snaking around the solid nub of her sensitive clitoris, Christina pushed all thoughts of the college to the back of her mind and concentrated solely on the immense pleasure her young girl student was bringing her. Listening to the beautiful sound of her lapping tongue, her sucking mouth, the squelching of vaginal juices, Christina lost herself in her lesbian debauchery as her womb rhythmically contracted and her copious juices of arousal flowed from the bloated opening of her tight cunt. She was close to her orgasm, she knew as she began to tremble uncontrollably. She was fast nearing her lesbian heaven.

This is like a dream, Christina mused in her sex-dizzy thinking. Since starting at Spadger Heath, she had had more debased sex than she'd thought she'd have in a lifetime. Cocksucking, sperm swallowing, cunny tonguing, anal fisting, bondage and whipping . . . Were all colleges really like this? she wondered as her orgasm peaked, taking her ever closer to her lesbian heaven. All teenage boys wanked and most teenage girls masturbated. But the students at Spadger Heath were hooked on crude sex of any and every description. And the staff were no better. Christina had not only wanked Ponting's penis and brought out his orgasmic cream but had allowed the headmaster himself to fuck the tight sheath of her cock-hungry cunt.

Listening to the slurping sounds of Becky's tongue as the girl sustained her incredible pleasure, Christina realized that she'd never be able to leave the college and return to her parents' country home. She couldn't leave behind the crude sex, couldn't live without a continual supply of fresh sperm and hot pussy juice. And she wouldn't be able to survive on the meagre wage of a village schoolteacher. Things were difficult enough on her present salary, but at least she had the opportunity to more than double her income by visiting The Rat's Tail Club. She knew now that she'd never leave London.

'God, no more,' she finally managed to cry out as her pleasure began to fade.

'Did you like that?' Becky asked, her cunny-wet face smiling at Christina.

'Like it?' she gasped, her young body convulsing wildly. 'It was bloody amazing.'

'I like your shaved pussy. It's soft and smooth. It makes you look very young.'

'Yes, it does. You've done this before, haven't you?'

'No, I . . . yes, I have,' the girl confessed.

'Who with?'

'I'd rather not say.'

'Who with, Becky? Who's your lesbian lover?'

'Sally Braithwaite.'

'Sally . . . That pretty little thing who wouldn't say boo to a goose?'

'Yes.'

'I'll have to get to know her a little better,' Christina said, her face grinning as she imagined anal fisting the young girl. 'I'll have to get to know her *intimately*. Where do you meet her?'

'We walk to the back of the old warehouses on Cannon Road. There's a place there, a small room. Come with us, if you like.'

'I think I will. So, what was all this nonsense about? Threatening to me report me and—'

'A couple of the girls put me up to it. Everyone knows that you've been having sex with Doogan and Brown. And with Bryony.'

'Sex with Bryony?' Christina said, lifting her head and frowning at her flushed-faced student.

'You're not going to deny it, are you?'

'What would be the point?' Christina sighed, hauling

her trembling body up from the floor and swaying on her sagging legs. 'You lot seem to know more about my sex life than I do. So, what else do you know?'

'Nothing, really. I'd better go to geography or I'll be in trouble.'

'Just say that you were giving me a hand. After all, you were, weren't you?'

'Yes, but . . .'

'I'll back up your story, don't worry. OK, off you go.'

Unlocking the door, the girl left her torn panties on the stockroom floor and headed off to her next lesson. Grabbing the flimsy garment, Christina pressed the wet crotch to her face and breathed in the heady scent of the girl's teenage cunt. *A souvenir*, she mused, returning to her desk and slipping the garment into her handbag. Wondering whether to start a collection of panties, she grinned as she imagined the girl students donating their wet knickers. Deciding to catch up on some work, Christina sat at her desk and began going through the students' essays.

'Excuse me, Miss,' Sally Braithwaite murmured, walking into the classroom.

'What is it, Sally?' Christina asked, realizing that Becky had spoken to the girl.

'I was wondering whether . . .'

'Yes?' Christina said, wondering how the girl was going to suggest lesbian sex.

'I . . . It doesn't matter.'

'Did you want to show me something in the stockroom?'

'She said you . . . Oh, yes, yes, that's right.'

'Start by slipping your panties off,' Christina told the girl.

'What? Take them off in here?'

'I want to see what you're offering me before I take it, Sally. Take your panties off and give them to me.'

Turning, the girl looked at the open door before slipping her hands up her short skirt and tugging her panties down her slender legs. Slipping the garment off over her feet, she passed it to her teacher. Christina examined the crotch of the red material, smiling as she focused on the white stain. Holding the garment to her face, she breathed in the fresh scent of the young girl's cuntal juices before slipping the panties into her bag.

'Now show me what it is that you're offering me,' she said, her stomach somersaulting as the girl grabbed the hem of her skirt.

'*This* is what I'm offering you,' Sally murmured, lifting the front of her skirt up over her stomach.

'I see,' Christina breathed, gazing wide-eyed at the girl's hairless vulval lips. 'Why do you shave? Do you prefer it that way?'

'Yes, I do. Also . . . Becky prefers me shaved.'

'I must say that I'm rather partial to a hairless pussy. Show me inside, Sally. Part your lips and show me what secrets you have.'

Following Christina's instructions, the girl peeled the firm pads of her outer lips wide apart and exposed the intricate folds of her teenage cunt. Focusing on the globules of white cream clinging to Sally's inner lips, Christina felt her heart racing, her hands trembling. Desperate to lick the girl there, to taste her warm cunt-milk, she left her desk and walked to the stockroom. Sally lowered her skirt and followed, grinning as Christina closed and locked the door behind her.

Unbuttoning the girl's blouse, Christina parted the

white material and gazed longingly at her bra. Lifting the cups up over her mammary spheres, she examined the girl's young breasts. Squeezing each mound in turn, Christina grinned. Topped with chocolate-brown teats, the girl's breasts were small and firm to the touch. Opening her blouse further, Christina gazed at the gentle rise of her stomach and wondered whether one of the lads had spunked her there. Picturing the small indent of her navel flooded with sperm, she kneeled on the floor and tugged the girl's skirt down to her ankles.

'Sit on the table,' Christina ordered the teenager. 'That's it. Now place your feet on the table, either side of your bum.' Taking up her position, Sally looked down at her hairless vulval lips bulging alluringly between her parted thighs. Watching Christina press her mouth hard against her naked vulval flesh, she let out a gasp of lesbian pleasure as her teacher's wet tongue ran up her valley of desire. Tasting the girl's vaginal cream, Christina parted her love lips with her slender fingers and lapped at her open cunt hole.

'You taste wonderful,' she murmured, her tongue snaking over the pink funnel of flesh surrounding Sally's vaginal orifice. 'Tell me what Becky does to you.'

'She licks me,' the girl breathed, her young body trembling. 'She licks my clitoris and pushes a candle into my pussy.'

'A candle?' Christina echoed, looking up at the girl's sex-flushed face. 'I'm afraid I don't have a candle.' Looking around the room, she smiled. 'I could make use of this,' she said, taking a small plastic bottle from a shelf. 'I wonder who left this in here?'

'Someone with the same idea?' Sally proffered.

'Maybe.'

Parting the fleshy lips of the girl's young pussy, Christina eased the flat end of the bottle into the tight duct of her young cunt. Quivering, Sally watched wide-eyed as the bottle slipped deep into the hugging sheath of her wet cunt. Her swollen outer lips stretched tautly around the plastic phallus, the nub of her erect clitoris fully exposed, she let out a rush of breath as Christina slipped a finger into the gully of her bottom and located her anus. The girl whimpered as Christina's finger glided into her rectal duct and massaged the dank walls of her inner core. Her clitoris visibly pulsating, she was about to come, Christina knew.

Licking the sensitive tip of her cumbud, Christina pistoned her student's cuntal sheath with the bottle, delighting in the squelching sounds of her lubricious juices as the girl shook violently in her lesbian pleasure. Slipping a second finger into the girl's tight anal tube, Christina sucked hard on her clitoris and increased the rhythm of her vaginal pistoning. Gasping, Sally leaned back and rested her hands on the table as her pleasure built within her young womb. Double fucking her tight sex holes, Christina fervently licked and sucked on her clitoris as she teetered on the brink of her climax.

'Coming,' Sally finally gasped. Wailing as her orgasm exploded within her pulsating clitoris, she pumped out her cunt-milk. The creamy liquid splattering Christina's face as the girl shook and whimpered in her coming, she screamed in her lesbian ecstasy. Someone would hear her, Christina knew as she mouthed and licked Sally's orgasming clitoris. Praying for her to be quiet, she hoped that her orgasm would soon wane as she repeatedly rammed the bottle deep into the drenched shaft of her tight cunt. Again, Sally screamed out as her orgasm peaked, her wails of pleasure reverberating around the stockroom.

'Who's in there?' a male voice bellowed.

'Only me,' Christina replied, slipping the bottle out of the sex-dizzy girl's inflamed cunt. 'I'm just having a tidy-up.'

'Christina?' the headmaster called. 'Are you all right?'

'Yes, I'm fine. Hang on, I'll open the door.'

'I heard a scream.'

'It was someone outside. I heard it, too.'

Ordering Sally to dress and hide beneath the table, Christina composed herself before unlocking the door. Wiping her sex-wet mouth on the back of her hand, she took a deep breath and opened the door. The head was frowning, his beady eyes trying to peer into the stockroom. Christina wondered if he was suspicious. Smiling at the man as she closed the door behind her, she walked across the classroom and gazed out of the window.

'Just some kids messing around,' she said. 'I heard them shouting and screaming earlier.'

'I came to find you since it's almost break time,' the head said, gazing at the stockroom door. 'Is there someone in the—'

'Coffee,' Christina cut in, taking his hand and leading him out of the classroom. 'Coffee and a chat in your study, OK?'

'Yes, yes, of course.'

Walking along the corridor, Christina realized that she was going to have to be more careful. The stockroom was becoming infamous, she reflected, hoping that Sally had had the sense to get out before anyone else wandered into the classroom. The stockroom, the woods . . . They were fast becoming no-go areas. But the old warehouses Becky had mentioned sounded promising. She'd meet the teen-age girls there after college, she decided. After all, she had unfinished business with Sally.

16

Sitting at the kitchen table, Christina read through the letter again. 'Dear Miss Shaw,' she breathed. 'You are required to vacate the rented accommodation immediately. The property has been deemed unfit for habitation due to structural defects in the rear wall.' Unable to believe the letter from the local council, Christina bit her lip. This was all she needed, she thought, tossing the letter onto the table and sipping her tea. She'd have to contact the letting agency and see whether they had any other flats for rent.

Recalling that Ponting's wife worked for the council, she wondered whether the woman was behind the letter. It would have been easy enough to take a piece of letter-headed paper, she mused. Deciding to ignore it, she took a shower and prepared to go out to The Rat's Tail Club. She was looking forward to the evening, and hoped to meet John again. If she didn't, there'd be plenty of other men to amuse her and buy her drinks. Hearing the front door close as she finished brushing her hair, she left her room and went into the kitchen where Bryony was filling the kettle.

'Good day?' Christina asked.

'Not bad. Twelve old men,' Bryony giggled. 'Twelve wrinkled old cocks to wank. You look nice. Are you going out?'

'I am,' Christina replied. 'I'm going to The Rat's Tail Club for the evening.'

'How do you know about the place?'

'I happened to pass by and thought it looked interesting. And you?'

'Josie took me there. I'll be there at six, so we'll meet up and I'll introduce you.'

'I've already met Josie,' Christina said mysteriously.

'When? Where?'

'You'll find out later. Right, I'll be going.'

'You're rather early, aren't you? It's only just gone five.'

'I want to get a decent table,' Christina giggled. 'If you get my meaning?'

Leaving the flat as Bryony called down the stairs, Christina strutted along the street in her stilettos. It was a lovely evening, she thought. The sun warming her, she swung her bag as she walked. She felt that all her problems were over as she neared the club. Ponting's trick would get him nowhere. She now had Becky and Sally to amuse herself with, and Charles had obviously given up all hope of rekindling their relationship.

Walking into the club, Christina ordered herself a vodka and tonic and sat at the bar. She *was* rather early, she mused, looking around the deserted bar. But she'd be able to grab a secluded table before the place started filling up. A table where she could wank cocks and lap up spunk from her hand without being seen. Sipping her drink as the barman busied himself, she pondered on her decision to stay in London. It was the right thing to do, she was sure. She'd made new friends, her job couldn't have been better, and she was getting more sex than she could handle.

'It'll pick up later,' the barman said.

'I'm sorry?' Christina breathed.

'The bar. It'll get busy later. Are you waiting for someone?'

'Several people, actually.'

'You were in last night, weren't you?'

'Yes, yes, I was. It's nice place. Have you worked here for long?'

'A couple of months. I came up from Kent where I worked for an insurance company. I was made redundant and thought I'd try my luck in London.'

'Any regrets?'

'No, none at all. Oh, sorry. I'm Doug.'

'Christina. I came here from Hertfordshire. It was quite a culture shock after living in the country. Like you, I have no regrets. I'm surprised you earn enough here to pay your rent.'

'I don't,' he chuckled. 'There's no way I'd earn enough doing bar work. I have a sideline.'

'Oh?'

'I'm into photography. Pretty successfully, even though I say it myself.'

'Then why work here?'

'Ah, that would be telling.'

'Oh, go on,' Christina begged him. 'I'm intrigued.'

'Well . . . I get a lot of my work from the club. There are girls who . . . well, let's just say that they make money from being photographed, and I make money by clicking the shutter.'

'Porn?' Christina asked.

'Yes, porn. You might frown upon it, but we all have to make a living.'

'No, no, I don't frown upon it at all. How much do the girls make?'

'That depends.'

'On?'

'On what they do. They get around fifty quid for your basic open-legs shot.'

'Is that all?'

'They get a couple of hundred for oral stuff. It's entirely up to them how much they earn. Why, are you interested?' he laughed.

'I might be,' Christina replied, wiping the grin off his face.

'Oh, right. Well . . . here's my number,' Doug said, taking a card from his pocket. 'Give me a ring some time.'

'I might just do that,' Christina said as a young couple walked into the bar.

'I also work here because it gives me an identity. Income tax, insurance contributions . . . as far as anyone official is concerned, this is my job. Excuse me for a moment.'

As the barman served the couple, Christina realized that she could earn a fortune in London. She also realized that the college was, for her, the same as the club was for the barman. It was her base, as well as a source of teenagers permanently ready for crude sex. She'd definitely made the right decision, she concluded. Thinking about photographic work, she knew that she'd have to be careful. The last thing she needed was incriminating photographs of her being bandied about the college – or anywhere else, for that matter. As the young couple a few feet away from her mentioned the college, she pricked her ears up.

'The caretaker's always gone by eight,' the young man murmured. 'By nine, the place will be deserted. We won't have any problems.'

'I hope not,' the girl replied. 'How long will it take?'

'Twenty minutes, no more. With the alarms out of action, we'll be in and out inside fifteen minutes and no one will be any the wiser. Another five minutes to load the van, and we'll be away.'

'That's not long to lug eighty-odd computers out of the place.'

'Long enough.'

As they moved to a table, Christina wondered what to do. She reckoned that they were planning to take the computers that evening, giving her little time to do anything. She doubted that the police would be interested in bar talk. But she couldn't just sit there and do nothing. Ordering another vodka, she watched the young couple out of the corner of her eye. They were whispering, obviously planning the robbery, and Christina wondered who else was in on the raid. All she could do would be to call the police and tip them off, she decided. If they weren't interested, that was their problem.

'Hi,' Bryony trilled as she entered the club.

'Hi. Where's Josie?' Christina asked.

'She'll be along soon. How do you know her?'

'It's a long story,' Christina replied. 'What are you drinking?'

'Same as you, please. From what you were saying earlier about getting a table, am I to assume that you come here to earn money?'

'I might,' Christina giggled, ordering the girl a drink.

'I thought so. You are awful, keeping secrets from me like that.'

'Bryony, do you happen to know Doogan's phone number?'

'No, I don't. Why?'

'I need to speak to him.'

'He'll be in later. I saw him on my way here.'

'Good.'

'What's it about?'

'I'll tell you later.'

Deciding to get Doogan and his mates to deal with the young couple, Christina smiled as Bryony said that she was going to nab her favourite table before someone else sat there. She sat and thought for a while. What was Doogan up to, coming to the club? He'd never mentioned the place. It might have been his regular haunt, she mused. This particular area of London was very much like a village, she reflected. Everyone seemed to know everyone else, and she wondered whether Doogan knew the young couple. Perhaps he was in on the scam? The man had said that the alarms were out of action, so they must have had someone on the inside.

As the barman refilled her glass without charging her, Christine reckoned that he wanted her to model for him. Again pondering on the idea, she wondered whether he took gynaecological-type shots, leaving her face out of frame. She wouldn't mind that, she thought, imagining the camera lens focusing on the sex-dripping entrance to her cuntal shaft. Her stomach somersaulting as she let out a giggle, she wondered whether to take her own snaps of her open pussy and sell them to lonely old men.

'Hi,' a middle-aged man said as he approached the bar and stood next Christina.

'Oh, er . . . hi,' she replied, watching him pull a note from his pocket and order a pint.

'You OK for a drink?'

'I'm fine, thanks.'

'A friend of mine suggested I come here.'

'Really?'

'He reckons that I'll get what I want.'

'Well, you've got a drink.'

'I was looking for more than a drink.'

'I don't think they do food,' Christina said, knowing full well what he was after.

'I'm hungry, but not for food,' he riposted. 'Anything else on offer?'

'I don't know. You'll have to ask the barman.'

'Shall we stop playing games?' he murmured. 'How much?'

'For what?'

'A blow job.'

'Sixty,' she replied softly.

'That's a bit steep, isn't it?'

'You get what you pay for in this world,' she replied, watching the young couple leave the club. 'I'm good, and I charge sixty. Take it or leave it.'

'I'll take it,' he said, walking over to a secluded table.

Joining him, Christina looked down as he unzipped his trousers and pulled his semi-erect cock out. This was her first real client, she mused, grabbing the fleshy shaft of his penis. No chatting up, no free drinks . . . Straight into cold sex in exchange for hard cash. Taking his wallet out, the man slipped sixty pounds into her handbag as she rolled his foreskin back over the bulbous swell of his glans. Well out of view of the bar, Christina leaned over and examined the man's purple globe. This was what prostitution was all about, she thought, opening her mouth wide. Meeting a stranger in a bar, taking cash, giving a quick blow job and then on to the next client. Christina was now a real prostitute.

Sucking her client's ballooning cock-head into her wet

mouth, she ran her tongue around his sperm-slit to the accompaniment of his stifled gasps of pleasure. Savouring the salty taste of his ripe plum, she took his knob to the back of her throat and sank her teeth into the root of his solid cock. Breathing in the scent of his pubes, she raised her head and went down on his cock again. Bobbing her head up and down, his glans repeatedly meeting the back of her throat, she knew that she shouldn't bring out his spunk too quickly. He obviously wanted his money's worth, and wouldn't take too kindly to her swallowing his spunk before he'd enjoyed the full pleasure of her wet mouth. Stilling her head, the helmet of his purple glans between her wet lips, she rolled her tongue slowly around his sex globe.

'You *are* good,' he murmured, clutching her head as the tip of her tongue prodded his sperm-slit. Sucking hard on his twitching knob, Christina could feel his bulb enlarging as the vacuum built within her hot mouth. Slipping her hand into his trousers and fondling his heaving balls, her clitoris swelling as her arousal heightened, she was desperate for the taste of his sperm. Suspecting that she was becoming addicted to male sex fluid, she recalled licking Becky's bottom-hole, the aphrodisiacal taste of her brown tissue. She loved the various tastes of sex, she mused. Salty knobs, sperm, girl-cum, tight anal inlets . . . The tastes of lust.

Humming softly, the vibrations running through the man's bulbous glans, she continued to tease his sperm-slit as he began to tremble in his rising pleasure. 'That's good,' he breathed. 'Ah, yes, yes. Slowly, slowly. I don't want to come yet.'

Allowing her saliva to run down the man's shaft, Christina kneaded his rolling balls and sucked on his purple plum. He'd feel the cooling liquid coursing down his shaft, adding to his debased pleasure, she knew as she licked and teased the small bridge of skin linking his foreskin to the base of his swollen knob. Unable to hold back, he gasped, gripping her head and thrusting his hips as his penis swelled and his glans throbbed. Sucking, slurping, mouthing, she was thirsty for his cream, desperate now to drink from his huge cock-head. He mumbled words of crude sex as his orgasm welled and his sperm began to course along his penile shaft. Ordering her to suck harder and swallow his come, he let out a long low moan of pleasure.

'Drink it,' he breathed as his spunk jetted from his throbbing knob. Her mouth filling with the salty fluid, Christina repeatedly swallowed hard, desperate not to waste one drop as she drank from his orgasming glans. Once more, he mumbled his words of debased sex. Whore, filthy slut, cum-guzzling slag . . . His words only serving to heighten Christina's arousal as she swallowed his gushing spunk, she knew that she was going to have to find sexual relief of her own that evening. She'd order Bryony to climb into her bed, she decided. The girl would run her tongue up and down Christina's wet sex valley, lick her clitoris to several massive orgasms.

Hearing Doogan's voice as she sucked the last remnants of the man's spunk out of his deflating cock-shaft, Christina sat upright and licked her glossed lips. Standing at the bar with Brown and ordering two pints of lager, he'd not seen her. Brushing her long blonde hair away from her flushed face, she watched her client slip his penis back into his trousers and pull his zip up before downing his drink. By the look on his face, he was happy with her efforts, she thought. And so he should have been.

'I'll be seeing you,' he said, leaving the table. 'You here most nights?'

'Yes, I am,' Christina replied, sipping her vodka.

'Good. I might become a regular, if that suits you?'

'It suits me.'

'Good.'

Placing his glass on the bar, he flashed her a knowing smile as he left the club. Opening her bag, Christina gazed at the cash. She'd done well, she reflected. Sixty pounds in a few minutes? Not many jobs paid that sort of money. Looking up as Doogan and Brown approached, she smiled. She was going to have to tell them about the young couple, she thought, checking her watch. There again, if Doogan was involved . . .

'All alone?' Brown asked, sitting down opposite her.

'I'm with Bryony,' Christina replied. 'She's talking to someone at the other end of the bar. So, what are you two doing here?'

'Drinking,' Doogan chuckled, standing by the table. 'We usually come here because they stay open later than the pub. The botany thing worked out OK, didn't it?'

'Yes, yes, it did,' Christina murmured pensively. 'Have you any plans for this evening? Later this evening, I mean.'

'Yes, we're staying here and getting wrecked,' Brown laughed. 'Why?'

Relating her story about the young couple, Christina hoped that the lads would be able to do something. If they hung around the college gates, they might at least deter the couple, prevent them from stealing the computers. Brown didn't want to get involved, saying that he'd probably end up in trouble if the cops turned up. But Doogan was keen. To Christina's surprise, his attitude was that no bastards were going to nick anything from the college and deprive the students.

'There was a robbery last year,' he said. 'All the computers went and the cops reckoned that it was an inside job. No one was nicked for it.'

'I wonder whether it was the same people?' Christina murmured. 'The young man said that the alarms would be out of action, so there might be someone on the inside.'

'I don't like it,' Brown complained. 'What are we supposed to do? Rough them up, or something?'

'Don't be a prick,' Doogan laughed. 'What we do is hang around and see whether we know these people. If we don't, and they break in, we call the cops.'

'I don't want any involvement with the law,' Brown sighed.

'We don't get involved, do we? We call the cops and then come back here.'

'I suppose so.'

'You'll have to wait until they're inside the building,' Christina said.

'I'm not stupid,' Doogan chuckled. 'I know what to do. OK, let's go.'

'It's rather early,' Christina said, checking her watch.

'I want to check the place out, find somewhere we can hide. We'll see you later, OK?'

'OK. And thanks.'

'Any time.'

As the boys finished their drinks and left the club, Christina realized how much she liked Doogan. He was rather rough, somewhat coarse, but a very likeable young man. He was right, he wasn't stupid. If he kept out of trouble and got down to his college work, he'd probably do well in life. Checking her watch for the umpteenth time, Christina wondered what the evening would bring. Bryony had obviously found herself a client and there'd been no sign of Josie. Unless the girl had arrived while Christina had had her head beneath the table.

'Hi,' Alison said, smiling as she walked into the club. 'What are you doing here on your own?'

'Having a drink and relaxing,' Christina replied, pleased that she had some company. 'How's the hotel?'

'Awful,' the girl sighed. 'The manager's a complete wanker, the chef's a fucking idiot, and there's this waitress who thinks she owns the fucking place.'

'Are you going to leave?'

'Yes, but not just yet. Don't worry, I don't want to come back to the flat.'

'No, no, it wasn't that.'

'I've decided to go down to Devon.'

'Devon? There's not much life there,' Christina giggled.

'There will be when I get there. Seriously, there are some smaller hotels there. I like the hotel business. You get to meet different people, have somewhere to live, free food . . . It suits me. And if I get pissed off with it, I'll come back to London. What am I doing sitting here without a drink? I'll be back in a minute.'

Christina didn't reckon that Alison would last for five minutes in Devon. But the girl was free with no ties, so why not move around? Wondering whether to tell Alison about her new profession, Christina realized that she could work anywhere in the country. Even in Devon

there must be men who'd pay for her services, she
reflected. Alison returned to the table and announced
that she'd seen a friend and would be back later. Christina smiled as the girl walked away. Alison was a free
spirit, she mused. But wasn't Christina?

The time dragged on with no would-be clients hovering. Growing bored, Christina downed yet another vodka as she wondered what Doogan and Brown were doing.
'Nine-fifteen,' she sighed, checking her watch again.
Wishing that she'd arranged to meet Becky and Sally
at the old warehouses, she decided to stay until ten and
then go home for an early night. Perhaps there wasn't
such a demand for call-girls as she'd reckoned, she
thought, looking around the bar.

'Good evening,' the headmaster said, grinning as he
approached Christina's table with a pint of beer in his
hand.

'Oh, er . . . hello, Ian,' she stammered, wondering
what he was doing in the club.

'Mind if I join you?'

'No, of course not.'

'I called round at your flat earlier. Then I went for a
walk and ran into Doogan and Brown.'

'Oh? Did they say anything?'

'Only that you were here when I asked whether they'd
seen you. Oh, you're not with anyone, are you?'

'No, no. I was with my flatmate – my ex-flatmate – but
she's gone off somewhere. Ian, I don't know whether to
stay on at the college or not.'

'What? You're not thinking of leaving, surely?'

'Oh, I don't know,' she sighed. 'What with Ponting
and . . . I feel that I've made rather a mess of things since
I've been in London.'

'How can you possibly say that? Good grief, you've done wonders with your class and . . .'

'I know, but . . . Ponting isn't going to go away. He's going to try to cause trouble for me for as long as I'm in London.'

'Yes, I . . . I spoke with the board of governors. Mr Ponting certainly has it in for you, Christina. It seems that he's been trying to associate you with prostitution. The thing is, the board might have to suspend you while they look into it.'

'What? That bloody man . . . I'm sorry, Ian, but I've just about had enough of Ponting.'

'I quite understand. If they do suspend you, obviously I'll be right behind you. Hopefully, it won't come to that.'

'That's it, Ian. I'm leaving the college.'

'Christina, don't be too hasty.'

'Hasty? As I said, Ponting isn't going to give up. All the time I'm here in London, he'll hound me. I'll have to leave, I'm afraid.'

'Well, I . . . Look, I'll get you another drink and we'll talk about this. I need a refill. Don't go away, OK?'

'OK.'

Christina could hardly believe that she might be suspended because of Ponting's lies. She supposed that the board of governors had to look into the allegation, no matter how ridiculous it was. But to suspend her on the word of an idiot . . . At least she had the headmaster on her side, she reflected. And the students. Recalling the letter she'd received, she was sure now that Ponting's wife was behind it. Between them, the evil pair could go on causing problems for ever.

'Well,' Doogan said, his face beaming as he entered the

club and walked over to Christina. 'You'll never guess what happened.'

'We were undercover,' Brown began. 'There were six of them, armed with automatic rifles and—'

'Shut up, Brown, you prick,' Doogan snapped. 'I'll tell you all about it once I've got a beer. Come on, prick-head. It's your round.'

Christina had lost all interest in the robbery. In fact, she'd lost all interest in the college. Watching the lads walk over to the bar, she wondered what the headmaster would say when he found his students hitting the booze. Still, they were of age and it was up to them how they spent their spare time. He'd no doubt be pleased to hear that the boys had stopped the robber, if that was what they'd done. As he returned and sat beside Christina, he told her that he'd be meeting with the board of governors the following morning.

'I'm not really interested,' she sighed. 'I won't be there for them to suspend me.'

'At least hear what they have to say,' the head murmured. 'Don't make a decision until you've heard.'

'I suppose not. But even if this is cleared up, Ponting will start something else.'

'I told the board about the incident in the woods.'

'And?'

'Well, they said that they'll look into it. We should have called the police, Christina. Basically, it's our word against Ponting's. It doesn't look at all good, I'm afraid.'

Hanging her head, Christina reckoned that Ponting had won. The board of governors must have thought it odd that such a sordid incident hadn't been reported to the police. Obviously Ponting had no proof of his allegations but, whether it was true or not, the board couldn't have one of their teachers linked with prostitution. Wondering whether to go to Devon with Alison, Christina was sure that her teaching career was over. It had been mostly her fault, she reflected. Wanking the lads in the stockroom in return for their good behaviour had been a dreadful mistake. And as for becoming sexually involved with teenage girls . . . Still, what was done was done, she concluded. Ponting would never find her in Devon. Or would he?

'Oh, er . . . sorry, sir,' Doogan muttered as he stood by the table with his beer. 'We'll find another seat.'

'No, no. Please join us,' the headmaster said.

'I think the lads have something to tell you,' Christina said.

'Oh? And what would that be?'

'It was like this,' Brown began. 'There was this armed robbery planned and we—'

'I'll tell him,' Doogan cut in irritably. 'Christina . . . I mean, Miss Shaw told us that she'd overheard a couple talking about robbing the college.'

'Really? Is that right, Christina?'

'Yes, it is. They were planning to steal the computers and Doogan and Brown went to intervene.'

'So what happened? When was this? You should have called the police.'

'We did,' Doogan said triumphantly. 'We were in hiding and this van pulled up, driven by a woman. Two blokes got out and unlocked the gates.'

'They had keys?' the head gasped.

'Yes. Anyway, they opened the gates and the woman backed the van in. They broke into the college through the library window.'

'Didn't the alarm go off?' the head asked, shaking his head in disbelief.

'No, it didn't. Once they were in the building we called the cops.'

'A dozen squad cars came racing round the corner and—'

'Shut up, Brown,' Doogan hissed. 'The cops turned up and nabbed the villains as they were loading the van. We stayed in hiding because we didn't want to get involved.'

'They had a key to the gates and the alarm didn't sound?' the head murmured, rubbing his chin. 'That's exactly what happened before.'

'This is the best bit,' Doogan chuckled, gulping his pint and keeping everyone in suspense. 'Ponting was the inside man.'

'*What?*' Christina gasped, choking on her vodka.

'Ponting was loading the computers into the van with the other two men.'

'Good God,' the head breathed. 'Ponting? *Our* Mr Ponting?'

'That solves my little problem,' Christina giggled.

'I'll get the drinks in,' the head chuckled, rising to his feet. 'You've done very well, lads. Two beers?'

'No, it's OK,' Doogan said. 'We'll leave you two to chat. Come on, Brown. Let's take a look round.'

Unable to believe her luck, Christina downed her vodka in one gulp and laughed out loud. The head sat in stunned silence as he pondered on the incident. Neither of them could believe that Ponting was the inside man, and had obviously taken part in the previous year's robbery. Once this came to light, his wife would probably have to resign from the council, Christina mused happily. The police would obviously search his home for stolen goods and discover his sex den. Not that a sex den was illegal, but it still wouldn't look good.

'Oh,' the head sighed. 'I've just thought of another major problem.'

'What's that?' Christina asked, wondering what else there was to worry about.

'Young Simpson.'

'Oh, er . . . has he said anything?'

'He's coming to see me in the morning. He said that he wants to report something. He wouldn't say what it was, but . . .'

'I think I know,' Christina breathed.

'You know?'

'Simpson has been—'

'Oh, I should explain,' the head broke in. 'Simpson is Ponting's son.'

'What?'

'He uses the name so as not to be treated differently in any way by the other students. Of course, now his father has been . . .'

'Do you have any idea what he wanted to report?'

'No, all he said was that one of the teachers would be sacked. Perhaps he was talking about his father. Simpson is a weird lad at the best of times. He doesn't live with his parents, by the way. He lives with an aunt. I've always thought it an odd arrangement.'

'It certainly sounds odd.'

'Christina, now that . . . You will stay at Spadger Heath, won't you?'

'Yes, yes, I will.'

'And us? I mean . . . we haven't been able to see much of each other, have we?'

This was getting better by the minute, Christina mused, placing her hand on the headmaster's knee. Moving up to the crotch of his trousers, she massaged his stiffening penis. He remained silent as she kneaded his balls and rubbed the swollen knob of his cock. Even when she tugged his zip down, he said nothing. He was obviously in desperate need of relief, she thought as she pulled his solid penis out of his trousers. Rolling his foreskin back and forth over the globe of his swollen knob, she kissed his cheek. Ponting was out of the way, and life was looking good, she thought happily as the head breathed deeply in his soaring arousal.

'I'm really thirsty,' Christina murmured.

'Oh, er . . . I'll get you a drink,' the head offered.

'I'll get my own drink, thanks,' she giggled.

Looking around the bar before leaning over and taking the headmaster's glans into her wet mouth, Christina ran her tongue around the salty-tasting helmet of his cock. The head gasped as she took his ripe plum to the back of her throat and bit gently into the fleshy root of his cock. He needed this as much as she did, she mused, slipping her hand into his trousers and cupping his rolling balls in her palm. Breathing in the scent of his pubes, she could hardly wait for his sperm to gush into her mouth and bathe her snaking tongue. Sperm, girl-juice, the anal ring . . . The tastes of sex.

Young Simpson was in line for a naked-buttock thrashing, Christina decided as the headmaster trembled uncontrollably. A bamboo cane might come in useful, she thought. She'd keep it in the stockroom and correct her students' wicked ways when they stepped out of line. Becky would enjoy the cane, she knew as the head let out a gasp of pleasure, his sperm jetting from his throbbing knob and filling her pretty mouth. Repeatedly swallowing hard, she drank from his fountainhead, delighting in her decadent act.

'God,' the man breathed as Christina bobbed her head up and down, mouth-fucking herself with his granite-hard penis. 'God, that's . . .' Wondering whether the head master had ever fucked a girl's mouth before, she slowed her bobbing motion, tonguing his throbbing glans as his sperm flow lessened to a trickle. Bringing out the final ripples of his orgasm, she sucked out the last remnants of his sperm before sitting upright and grinning at him. Gazing at the white liquid dribbling down her chin, the head zipped up his trousers and let out a chuckle.

'I think we're going to get on extremely well together,' he said, downing his pint. 'This calls for a celebration. Er . . . are you still thirsty?'

'No, but I'll have a large vodka and tonic,' Christina giggled, wiping her mouth on the back of her hand.

'OK. Don't go away.'

'Oh, I won't,' she said as he made his way to the bar.

'I see you're with a client,' John said as he sidled up to the table.

'Oh, er . . . yes, that's right.'

'Will you be in tomorrow evening'

'I can book you in,' she replied. 'Seven o'clock?'

'Seven it is.'

'There we are,' the head chortled, returning to the table as John moved away. 'Let's drink to us,' he said, raising his glass.

'To us,' Christina trilled, winking at John as he leaned on the bar.

'Good God, Christina. To think that Ponting was the inside man. And he tried to make out that you were involved in prostitution. What a dreadful thing to say about such a beautiful young lady.'

'Yes, absolutely dreadful. Cheers, Ian.'